ex display

DEEP WATERS

Also by Lydia Bennett

The Folly
The Golden Stag

DEEP WATERS

Lydia Bennett

Hodder & Stoughton
LONDON SYDNEY AUCKLAND

Copyright © 1994 by Lydia Bennett

The right of Lydia Bennett to be identified as the Author of the Work has been asserted by her in accordance with the Copyright, Designs and Patents Act 1988.

First published in Great Britain in 1994 by Hodder and Stoughton. A division of Hodder Headline PLC.

Reprinted in this edition 1994 by Hodder and Stoughton.

10 9 8 7 6 5 4 3 2 1

All rights reserved. No part of this publication may be reproduced, stored in a retrieval system, or transmitted, in any form or by any means without the prior written permission of the publisher, nor be otherwise circulated in any form of binding or cover other than that in which it is published and without a similar condition being imposed on the subsequent purchaser.

All characters in this publication are fictitious and any resemblance to real persons, living or dead, is purely coincidental.

British Library Cataloguing in Publication Data.
Bennett, Lydia
Deep Waters. - New ed
I. Title
823.914 [F]
ISBN 0-340-60073-X

Typeset by Phoenix Typesetting, Ilkley, West Yorkshire.

Printed and bound in Great Britain by
Mackays of Chatham PLC, Chatham, Kent

Hodder and Stoughton Ltd
A division of Hodder Headline PLC
338 Euston Road
London NW1 3BH

For Irmingard and for Siegfried,
with thanks to them both
for sharing their adoptive city with me
before the Wall came down . . .

'These are much deeper waters than I had thought.'

The Memoirs of Sherlock Holmes

PROLOGUE

He tried to enter my life by stealth, foolish man. No way could someone like him blend into the background. I was deeply submerged in a book I should have been cataloguing rather than reading, but even so I heard his tread: soft yet confident. Not local, I said to myself as I swam up from the depths and swivelled my chair round to inspect the newcomer.

Had I been younger and more amazable, I might have fallen off it. My father had been a London art dealer and had taught me to appreciate beauty wherever it was found. There was an abundance to appreciate in the stranger. He was about fifty, and the high cheekbones and strong planes of his face were unmistakably Slav. His upright posture made me instantly nostalgic for the continent. His size, too, had no hint of apology for his existence on this planet. He was big – a match for me – and carried his weight with grace. Proud. Very proud. His head thrown back, he had an air of arrogance probably unintended. The tilt of that big strong head made me think of a bird of prey confident of success on his next hunting trip. And yes, his nose was like a hawk's beak, joined at the top by two bushy black eyebrows perched like crags over the forbiddingly handsome face. His face was tanned – by genes rather than sun – and a great mane of steely hair, once black but now dusted with grey, sprang away from it to complete a portrait of barely contained vitality.

But what struck me most was his eyes, or rather, my inability to look into them. This should have alerted me. I'd learned early on that other people had a horror of staring and I'd used this knowledge shamelessly. A second or two of eye contact was usually enough to make the other person turn aside, leaving me free to look. Not so today. Two seconds, three, four . . . and I was the one who gave way. Only after I'd taken in the rest of the stranger's appearance did I dare return to his eyes.

He was still staring. This time, and after a deep breath for courage, I stared back. His eyes were deep, deeper than any I'd ever seen. To call them black and hard would be to miss the point. This man used the impenetrability of his eyes as a one-way mirror. Sure that no one could see in, he saw out.

The oak panelling wavered, dissolved, the library reconstituted itself as a St Petersburg ballroom. In front of it stood the stranger, his suit now a uniform glittering with the insignia of high office. A Russian prince, no doubt the host of this occasion, bowing slightly to his guests, a gracious smile on his arrogant face. A chandelier glistened. An orchestra played. A princess floated in front of him.

Maxine, my library assistant and protégée. Every bit a princess despite her farmer father, she wafted across my vision and obscured my view of the stranger. She was taking in his appearance too, with clear approval.

The spell was broken. The ballroom was once again a library and the stranger a stranger, now walking towards one of the window recesses overlooking the courtyard. He browsed through the books in the alcove, then selected one and sat down in a brown leather armchair. The chair suited him, as did the leaded window behind him and the greenly waving trees beyond. But then, it was difficult to imagine a setting which wouldn't. He was one of those people so utterly at home with himself that he couldn't help being at home wherever fate chose to set him down. A real European, I thought, crossing borders as effortlessly as most people cross a street. One of my own.

I looked away, strangely hurt, the nostalgia grown too

strong. For the first time in years I willed myself away from this town I loved, back to the continent where I, too, had crossed borders instead of streets.

I don't know how long I brooded or when it was that I remembered the presence of the stranger, but when I did look up again, something odd happened.

He was no longer a stranger. *I knew him.* Somewhere deep in my mind a half-drowned memory stirred. I could feel it trying to struggle to the surface and failing. Too deep, I supposed. Somewhere even beyond my decade of gypsy wanderings.

But something else was happening now. The stranger was looking up from the book, and I knew with absolute certainty he'd only been pretending to read. He hadn't come here to read. He'd come here for me. There was something in his eyes that told me. Though deep and black as before, they were no longer opaque. They had opened up a fraction – not far, but enough to let me in. *I know you*, I said to him silently, *and I'm going to know you a good deal better still. Am I right?*

He nodded.

ONE

But I forget: none of this makes sense without some background.

Background, then, and to a soundscape of surf-washed sands, for this is a seaside town. Yorkshire, east coast, population 5,000. It's an attractive little town and from a gull's-eye view appears as a rent in the cliffs carved out by the estuary. On either side of the estuary the town rises in a higgledy-piggledy red-roofed mass beloved of artists. From the top of the cliffs the scene moves inland in a mixture of village, farm and moor – if you go far enough, the North York Moors themselves, also beloved of artists.

Sedleigh lives off a mixture of fishing, tourism and a little light import-export via the ships using our harbour. Mostly they carry timber and mostly they come from Scandinavia and the Low Countries, but quite a few are from further afield. Every so often we get one from Russia, though none carrying cargo so exotic as my St Petersburg prince. Usually they're a pretty rough lot and pub brawls still compromise the main crimes committed in this sleepy little town. From time to time I meet some of the crews in the Dolphin. They're always amazed when I speak to them in Russian and more than once I've helped avert a resumption of the Cold War with a sentence or two in their own language. (Also more than once I've been called to the police cells to translate when all else failed.)

Until the 1920s Sedleigh was dominated by Sydney Holroyd, whose large estate began at the southern outskirts of our town. From his delightful little mansion surrounded by woodland, he played the role of local squire. Most of his philanthropy, however, was on a fairly small scale. At least in the beginning.

Sydney lived to a great age, surviving both his wife and his children. Perhaps something of himself died with them. In any case, the older he grew the more suspicious he became of his more peripheral relatives, viewing them as vultures just waiting to get hold of his money. His greatest fear was that however rigidly his will excluded the vultures, their lawyers would find ways of overturning it in their favour.

In the end he thwarted them all in the most devastatingly simple manner possible: he broke up his estate. It must have hurt, parting with the very thing he cherished most, but disposing of the estate himself while still alive was the only way to ensure that none of it fell into his relatives' hands.

It caused a sensation of course. People didn't do that kind of thing. But by then Sydney was acknowledged to be more than a little eccentric, and as the local people were the main beneficiaries, why complain?

First to go was the land, thousands of acres sold to nearby farmers (including Maxine's grandfather) who couldn't believe their luck. Next were the properties in town – some sold, others given into the care of the local authorities. Finally he had to dispose of the money he gained from selling his property without generating more money.

This was Sedleigh's golden age. A new hospital, new sewage works, new water supply – all of it built and paid for by Sydney Holroyd, not a farthing from the rates.

This is where I come into the picture, for Sydney's last great benevolent work, and the one into which he poured the most money and care, was the Sydney Holroyd Library. Designed, built, furnished and stocked on a lavish scale, the library was opened by Sydney himself in 1920. Two years later he died, and the modest (by Sydney's standards) investments on which he'd planned to live out his last years were by prearrangement transferred to the maintenance of the library. In perpetuity.

So it is that the modest little town of Sedleigh has the most stupendously immodest library. Visitors walking along the quay on the north side of town are always amazed. While the rest of the quay consists of little shops crowded up against each other, the library occupies a spacious site with trees to either side and a sumptuous courtyard garden at the back formed by the two wings. On a sunny summer day, readers can stroll into the garden and play the scholar accompanied by bird song and a light breeze filtered through the trees. The rest of the year is equally well catered for, with numerous window alcoves, solid oak tables, comfortable leather chairs and, in the main section, even a coal fire to give the illusion of a stately home. Instead of official notices saying DON'T DON'T DON'T, our walls have paintings. Instead of chrome and plastic machinery linking us to the libraries of the nation, we have a simple issue system unchanged in more than seventy years. Instead of the dour bunned and bespectacled custodian of stereotype, the Sydney Holroyd Library has me: Attila the Librarian.

'Attila,' Maxine whispered.

The whisper told me something was up. This isn't a whispering library. I run it as a cross between a London club and a refuge for the homeless.

'Attila, I think I know who he is.'

'He who?'

'Don't be obtuse.' She glanced furtively in the direction of the stranger. 'I'm almost positive he's the one renting the mansion from Dad.'

I groaned inwardly. The last thing I wanted was yet another complication to the Holroyd mansion saga.

Maxine continued undaunted. 'I'm sure he had a foreign name. He's from London.'

'That's not very foreign.'

'He's taken it for six months – paid quite a lot for it, in advance.'

'I thought it was uninhabitable.'

'A few of the rooms aren't too bad. That's all he wanted – a few rooms.'

'Then why didn't he rent a cottage?'

Maxine shrugged. 'Maybe he likes mouldering old mansions. Maybe he's a vampire.'

I burst out laughing. Several readers gave me a severe look. One hissed a loud 'Ssshhhh!' (Not everyone approves of my radical librarianship.) 'So what's his name?'

'Name?' She turned her gigantic cornflower-blue eyes on me in a look of innocence, real or feigned. No one would guess that behind them lurked a first-class brain.

'Name, Maxine. Most people have them. This one's foreign. So what is it?'

The eyes turned crafty. 'That's for you to find out,' she smirked. Two seconds later she was back at the far end of the issue desk, immersed in her overdue cards as if the brief conversation had never taken place.

I wasn't fooled. Two more seconds and I'd dragged my chair across the floor and ensconced myself beside my furtive protégée. 'You don't *know* his name. You don't know it because you haven't asked. You haven't asked because you're still not speaking to your father. *Still.* How long is this going to go on?'

'None of your business,' she said primly.

'It most certainly is. Listen, sprog: your father thinks I've put you up to this. He's going round telling everyone I'm a bad influence on you.'

'You are.'

'Maxine, this is serious. Your father thinks I'm making trouble for him, so he's making trouble for me.'

This time the innocence in the fabulous eyes was real. 'How?'

'Rumours – how else? How else does anything get done in this town?'

'Like?'

'About my parents. About my past. I've made a certain effort to become a pillar of this community –'

Maxine snorted.

'– and along comes Farmer Vesey throwing the entire contents of his muckspreader at the fan.'

'Attila. Is this true?'

The hushed voice, the worried lines creeping over her forehead – there was no doubting her sincerity this time. I melted. As always.

The truth is, I adore Maxine. Of all the kids who have passed through my library, kids on the run from stuffy parents and unhappy homes, Maxine is by far my favourite. Apart from everything else she's probably the most beautiful girl I've ever seen. Tall, slender, not a cell out of place, she has the grace of an elfin princess who's been turned human by some magus wand. The magus has been wise enough to let the elf retain its own hair, a gossamer cascade of gold reaching to the tiny waist. The eyes, too, are generous – almost too big if her face had been less perfect – and gleam with a brilliant blue light that verges on the uncanny. Every feature of that wonderful face is clear, serene, harmonious. It's enough to make a sculptor throw away his chisels in despair. The summer crowds on the quay always stop dead to stare as Maxine floats past on her way to work. Often the stares are openly envious.

I should be envious, too – a large fortysomething spinster librarian with a heap of red hair that doesn't know how to behave – but I'm not. My father again, with his love of beauty. How can I resent such loveliness when it's here for me to enjoy? I could no more be jealous of Maxine than of Botticelli's Venus.

'But what *kind* of rumours?' she persisted.

'The usual kind,' I said. 'Innuendo, nothing you could put into words.'

Her eyes narrowed and began to flash sparks. Someone with eyes like that shouldn't work in a place full of paper. 'Maxine,' I said, 'I appreciate your loyalty but it's counterproductive, you know. Your dad thinks I'm winkling you away from the family hearth. He's probably hurt. Deep down he loves you.' Very deep, I thought drily. So deep it was out of sight. 'Why not make it up with him?'

The strong jaw – the one thing about her that wasn't elfin – clamped. Maxine can be very stubborn.

'Please? It would help me.'

The jaw was immovable.

'Well, if not make it up, at least try to get to the stage of asking each other to pass the salt?'

'I'll think about it,' the jaw said. And returned to the overdue notices.

I took the hint and went back to my end of the desk. In any case, it was nearly time for me to go home. Already most of the readers had gone but the stranger was still there. I'd given him the occasional glance while talking with Maxine. Sometimes he read, sometimes he watched. Right now he was watching as I cleared away the books I'd been cataloguing. Then he stood up and walked across to the issue desk.

'Anna Atwill,' he said.

There was nothing oracular about that – the name plate on the desk was clear for all to see – but the absence of a question mark surprised me.

'Can I help you?'

'I presume there is a procedure for a temporary resident to become a member of your library?'

The oratorical phrases of a man for whom English is a second language. The voice thrilling, a deep bass that made the thick oak floorboards rumble.

'Of course,' I smiled, and handed him an application form.

As he filled it in I studied him more closely. From this distance his skin was slightly coarse and marked by lines, nice strong lines that spoke of a rich life firmly lived. He was even more handsome than I'd thought. I longed to place my hands on either side of that beautifully carved head and draw it to me. I wanted to run a finger down that splendid nose. I wanted to dissolve the desk between us and press close to that body which was emanating such stupendous masculinity.

Instead, I took the completed form from him and made out the borrower's card. *Dr D. Komarovsky*, I copied. 'Dmitri?' I guessed aloud.

He might have said, 'Don't be so impertinent.' Instead, 'You know me?' he asked.

I know you, and I'm going to know you a good deal better still. Am I right? 'Should I?' I countered.

'Your father might have mentioned my father. They knew each other.'

This time I stared with the best of reasons. I was looking for some resemblance, some picture from my past which I might match to his face. There was none. I have a good memory for faces, and if I'd known either him or his father I would have remembered. The knowing I had sensed was of a completely different sort. I shook my head.

'Your father was Edmund Atwill?' he asked.

Was. So he knew my father was dead. There must have been more than a casual acquaintanceship. But I'd come across no Komarovsky in my father's papers.

'Yes,' I said.

'My father died recently, too. Towards the end he talked a great deal about his past. He mentioned you and wondered if you still lived in Sedleigh.'

Something else died: my delight in the stranger. His father and my father would have been contemporaries. If they'd known each other long ago, as he implied, then it was a knowing I wanted nothing to do with.

'Well,' I said briskly, turning myself into the professional librarian I wasn't, 'as you can see, I do.' I wasn't going to add, *not still but again*. My years abroad were none of his business. I handed him the temporary borrower's card. 'No limit on the number of books you can borrow and they're due back in four weeks. Other than that, the rules are much as in any other library. I hope you'll enjoy your stay in Sedleigh.' I smiled.

It was a smile calculated to put as much distance as possible between us, and it did. I thought I saw a flicker of something – hurt? puzzlement? – before he returned my smile with one as distant as mine.

'I'm sure I will, Miss Atwill.'

Miss. So he knew even that. 'If you have any questions or need any help, do ask my assistant.' I gestured towards Maxine. 'I'm already late home,' I explained, and gathered up my things to go.

'Then I must apologise for having detained you,' he said with a hint of a bow whose continental origins wrenched me yet again.

'Oh, no problem,' I said with a heartiness I didn't feel.

And left.

TWO

As I walked along the quay, across the swing bridge and up the twisty little streets of the south cliff towards my house, the town seemed drained of colour. It was as if a surly cameraman had placed a grey filter over the sun which should have been gleaming gold on its way down into the estuary. Sedleigh was the nearest thing I had to a home, the one place – if any – where I belonged. In a single casual encounter, a stranger had threatened the life I'd built for myself here.

I tried to be reasonable. There was nothing to suggest that Komarovsky knew anything he shouldn't. Very probably his father's remark to him had been as casual as his had been to me.

But as I turned into my high and windswept street, a nasty sea breeze smacked me in the face like a pail of cold water and drowned my feeble optimism. Why on earth would someone like Komarovsky rent a mouldy old mansion in an insignificant little seaside town for six months? Six months, for God's sake! Worse, his name *was* slightly familiar, though I was still sure my parents had never mentioned him. He'd probably lied about his father and mine. He must be a government official sent to sort me out.

Reason made a brave comeback: what makes you think they'd bother that much with someone as unimportant as you? Another sea breeze answered: they just do; officialdom is funny that way. I should have been flattered but wasn't. What *do* governments do with people like me?

By the time I reached my front door and turned the key I was thoroughly depressed, and by the time I'd hung up my coat and gone into the sitting room I was too enervated to do more than fall into a chair by the fireplace. 'What now?' I asked aloud.

It wasn't the first time I'd talked to my dead parents. I'd never really accepted that they were dead, and if they were I knew their spirits wouldn't leave this house, filled as it was with their books and paintings and all the mementos of their long full lives.

'So who is this Komarovsky?' I asked Eleanor.

She was the most likely to know. She'd spent her life translating books from all the little countries bordering Russia. She knew Russian, too, but it was the minority languages that she specialised in. Not many did, and so the authorities of those small countries, eager to advertise their best (eager for western currency, too), had given her unlimited access to their officially approved writers. Some of them were quite good, and Eleanor, so highly sought, could pick and choose. She translated the best of them under her own name. Under a pseudonym, however, she also translated dissidents. She was an expert smuggler, my mum. No one ever harassed her. So mild, so respectable . . . so important to their image abroad. Any border official who dared search her would have been sent to Siberia.

I smiled at the memory of my mother. Then I shot up in the chair. Of course: he was one of her authors! But which sort – official or dissident?

I was in the kitchen dialling the library before I thought it through. Maxine's silken voice answered.

'Is he still there?' I said.

'No. He left right after you did.'

'Good. Be a love and go to the card catalogue. Komarovsky, Dmitri.'

A gentle tap as she set the phone down, then silence. She was gone longer than I expected. Finally, 'Attila, how did you know?'

'There is something?'

'*The Icon in Modern Russian History*. London, Weidenfield, 1988. *The –*'

'Maxine, you're reading. How many times do I have to tell you, don't take the cards out of the catalogue.'

'I know, but there are so many.'

'Oh. All right. Read on.'

She read on. There were eight or nine titles, all concerned in some way with European history. No government official could have dashed off those books in his spare time from snooping.

I returned to the sitting room more puzzled than ever. Clearly not one of Eleanor's. She didn't translate non-fiction, and in any case none of these had been translated. Whoever he was, he wrote in English.

Icons. At least two titles had included icons. Art. Perhaps Edmund after all? It seemed a little improbable. The gallery my father and his brother Gerald had founded off Bond Street had specialised in modern art. I was sure no icon had ever crossed the threshold. Still, art was art and Edmund had had as many contacts on the continent as Eleanor did, though mostly in the western countries. His mission in life had been to introduce young continental artists to Britain and vice versa. While Gerald tended the business side, Edmund had roamed Europe winkling out the yet-undiscovered. Many of them became famous, thanks to Edmund. Others, despite years of nurture, never caught on, at least not in Edmund's lifetime. My house was full of paintings that hadn't sold but were, Edmund insisted, very fine. Their day would come. In a few cases, it was coming now. Sometimes it worried me, thinking about the noughts being added to the invisible price lists of my own private exhibition. I'd thought of getting a burglar alarm or selling some of the more valuable ones. But burglar alarms are so intrusive and would give the game away. As for selling, I hated to do it, not with Edmund's spirit wafting about the house. What would there be for him to look at?

There'd been a few Russians – émigrés Edmund had met in Paris or Berlin. Only one was of much note: Anatoly Leskov. A watercolour of his hung above my fridge. A domestic setting for a domestic picture: us, picnicking on a magical summer day in the 1950s. The artist, spoiled for choice, had greedily put in everything – the woodland at the top of the cliff, the paddock, our little garden, the sea, all superimposed on each other in transparent layers that seem to float in the strange watery light. We're floating too, not the least bit grounded by the act of eating. Edmund, Eleanor and a middle-aged man hover in the leafy crowns of the trees, while a young boy and I drift out to sea, our hands resting lightly on each other's shoulders with no boat in sight. It's a picture full of charm, not at all like the bold canvases that came later, but already the abstraction is there. You would have to know us to recognise us in the few wispy brushstrokes. Only my red hair, already unruly at two, is recognisable. That and the black hair of my companion are the strongest notes in the whole composition.

I peered at the painting. It was probably worth about £5,000 now. I looked warily through the French window at the back garden. Surely not an art thief? Not if he'd written all those books. Too crude. Anyway, writing books is hard work, doesn't leave much time for plotting robberies.

It also doesn't leave much time for lounging around libraries in seaside resorts. We're well stocked, but nothing that couldn't be found in London.

I was back at the beginning: nowhere. There was no good reason for Komarovsky to be here at all.

My stomach rumbled. I'd put a pot of Hungarian *gulyás* on the Rayburn's hob the night before. Now I shoved it on to the hotplate. I love peasant food but today I felt too fragmented to concentrate on hunger. I suddenly realised that I didn't want to be alone. I needed company, someone to bring me back down to earth.

Down to earth. Who better than Bernard?

The phone rang so long that I feared the worst. 'You aren't cooking?' I asked when finally he answered.

He laughed. 'I was on my way out to pick up some fish and chips.'

'How about some *gulyás* instead?'

'Are you asking me to supper?' he said hopefully.

'I'm begging you. I'm lonely.'

Already the cobwebs were clearing as I moved briskly round the kitchen, putting together a salad and some garlic bread and making the *csipetke*. I made a lot – Bernard loves dumplings as much as I do.

Even Bernard's long legs take a certain amount of time to cross from his cliffside eyrie to mine, and by the time he arrived everything was ready. I flung my arms round him with perhaps a little more than the usual affection. Bernard is the most reassuring person I've ever met. He's the only person in the world with whom I'd trust my life. I have a superstitious feeling that as long as all is well with Bernard, all is well with the world.

Bernard is literally down to earth – it's his job. He's an engineer, a hydrologist. He spends his working day drilling deep into the earth in search of water. He's in touch with the elements in a special way: when he strides out across the land, he's not walking on a bit of topsoil covered with grass. He's walking on rocks millions of years old, and he knows them all.

Bernard became entranced by the mysteriousness of that hidden world beneath the earth's crust while studying geology at Durham. Afterwards he teamed up with Tim, an engineering student who had a flair for business and a heap of capital looking for a home. Within a few months the business was launched, thanks largely to Bernard's geology degree. Unlike most borehole engineers, he *knows* what's down there, and though he never guarantees finding water, his record is far better than any other company's.

I disengaged myself and scrutinised my friend. Bernard is exceptionally tall and thin. Occasionally his head forgets where his feet are and he can be a trifle clumsy, though never while working the dangerous machinery. A wispy thatch of sand-coloured hair sits atop a head that seems carved out of the rocks he knows so well: lean and hard and nicely weathered from spending so much time outside. His eyes are as grey as our northern skies. They're long-distance eyes and can appear romantically vague and dreamy. In fact, he knows exactly what he's looking at and for. When he gazes out across the sea, I'm sure he's seeing all the way to Denmark. And when he glances idly at the earth beneath his feet he's seeing a hundred metres down and weighing up the quantity of water he hopes is saturating those rocks.

But that evening his eyes seemed clouded by uncertainty. That shook me. I led him into the kitchen, watched him fold himself into a chair by the French window where his long legs wouldn't trip me up, and poured us both a glass of wine.

'What's up?' I said. 'Is Maxine being obnoxious?' Bernard was in love with Maxine. So were quite a few other men but most hadn't the nous to see beyond her pretty face. Bernard, with his long-distance eyes, did. Maxine, however, regarded him only as a friend and teased him mercilessly for being a 'boring' scientist. There wasn't a single pun on his profession she hadn't thought of – and said. A man less confident than Bernard in the value of his profession would have been annihilated but Bernard took it calmly, hoping, perhaps, that one day she would see the deep romance of his work with the elements.

Bernard shook his head. 'Business.'

'I thought it was booming.'

He smiled wryly. 'It is. Sometimes I wish it wasn't.'

I knew what he meant – we'd talked about it before. All over the country, springs were drying up. Borehole engineers were in demand, everyone hoping to find a deep-down well to replace the springs. But Bernard knew that the amount of underground water was limited and he wasn't keen to release it for frivolous purposes.

'I've been asked to do a job I don't want to do,' he explained.

'So? Refuse. It wouldn't be the first time.'

'I can't, not this time. It's the Slaters.'

Now this was new. The Slaters were a decent young couple living in an isolated cottage about two miles inland. They were hardworking teachers who lived simply, not at all the sort of people Bernard would refuse.

'Their spring's drying up and they want me to drill,' he said. 'The problem is, I don't know where. Most of the rock formations round there are straightforward – the only question is how deep and how much water. I didn't give it a thought until I got out the Geological Survey map and saw a fault running smack through their land. A few feet one side and we could hit an artesian; a few feet the other, nothing. They've only got a tiny piece of land – there's no chance to play safe. All I can do is guess, and if I guess wrong, that's several thousand pounds for a hole full of dust.'

I was beginning to understand Bernard's depression. There was an absolute code of practice among borehole engineers: the customer pays for the drilling, regardless of whether water is found. Everybody knows the risk and accepts it. After all, the engineers have to cover their own costs.

'So if there's no water they have to sell up and leave,' I said.

'Worse. They can't even sell. The house is unsaleable without water.'

'Oh, God.'

'But I can't refuse to drill, because there's virtually no water now.'

I gave him a sideways look as I plonked the *csipetke* into the pot. 'Couldn't you just shove it off on to another engineer? Say you're booked up?'

'Attila!'

'Sorry.'

'I'm thinking of calling in a diviner.'

'Bernard!'

He grinned. 'I thought that would shock you.'

'Are you serious?'

'I am. They're used more often than you'd think. What I'll do is take the maps along and have a good look at the site – there might be some cracks in the house that'll give me a clue. Then I'll make my own decision, and if the diviner comes up with the same spot, at least I'll feel a little less worried.'

We spent the rest of the evening talking about his work. Unlike Maxine, I found it fascinating. I could see beyond the dirty machinery, the technology, the businesslike façade Bernard wore in front of his customers. His job was truly elemental: digging deep. I liked to dig, too. It was in my blood. My mother had spent her life ferreting out good literature from a heap of trash. My father had peered at youthful paintings much as Bernard peered at a piece of land, judging the potential beneath. In my previous work (strictly speaking I'm a musician – I fell into librarianship by accident) I tried to dig out the essence of Europe's ethnic music.

The only thing I didn't want to delve into was my more distant past and so I was startled, towards the end of the evening, when Bernard suddenly said, 'I stopped in at the library on my way here. Maxine says there's an exotic foreigner tailing you.'

I laughed to cover my unease. 'Maxine has an exuberant imagination. That's why I love her.'

But Bernard insisted, and so I told him, at least as much as Maxine already knew. As I talked I could feel my anxiety slowly melt away, dispelled as always by Bernard's presence.

By the time I kissed him goodnight the world had settled comfortably into place again. He would find water for the

Slaters, I was sure of it. As for my exotic foreigner, it was obvious. Dr Komarovsky was exactly who all those catalogue cards said he was: a historian come for some peace and quiet in which to write his next book.

I slept well that night. Not even any dreams.

THREE

He was there again the next morning – not the library this time but the beach.

I like to give my horse an early morning run along the sands whenever the tide permits. When I say 'early' I mean it. It's surprising how many seaside visitors force themselves out of bed at an hour they'd never countenance in their city lives. They're hoping for a solitary walk: just themselves, the sea, the sands. They've seen it in films, now's their chance to act it out. I don't blame them but it does clutter up the beach. When I give Ahab his head he goes off like a rocket and I don't want anything in his way. I'm obliged, therefore, to get up even earlier. I'm used to it now, can't imagine my old life when more often than not I went to bed to the sweet strains of the dawn chorus.

I love those virgin hours. Never is the air so clear as in that brief time between night and day before everyone's started breathing their carbon dioxide into it. Of course we've got more air than most, heaps of it rolling in from the sea. Even so, those minutes before the curtain goes up and we all start acting out our petty roles are too precious to waste in bed.

The air was even better than usual that morning. As well as the transition between night and day, the earth was moving between spring and summer, the two seasons bouncing off each other and freshening the sky with good-natured battle. When I closed the French window behind me and stepped out on to the patio I could almost see the tiny swirling lines of conflict etched on the sky's grey surface.

My house is the last one in the last street on this side of town. A hundred years ago there was another one that claimed that title but it fell into the sea. There was plenty of warning, of course; the cliff crumbles slowly and the house had been long abandoned when it went. I give my own house another hundred years, perhaps more. In any case not my problem.

The street runs along a natural terrace with the land rising gently at the back but dropping down more steeply towards the estuary at the front. It has a precarious feel to it which is heightened when you get to my house. Here the land also drops away to the east in a jagged tumble of rocks until it reaches the beach.

My parents originally bought the place as a holiday cottage when they lived in London. The first thing they did was build a massive wall to the east. It runs right along the edge of the cliff, giving an illusion of security to both garden and paddock until you peep over the top and see the abyss below.

Anyone else would have planted a windbreak in front of it, but my parents refused to shut out the sky. The big sitting room which occupies the entire east side downstairs is pierced by windows which, when you're seated, show nothing but sky. Some people find it unnerving but I love it, all those big blank canvases just waiting for nature's brush. The large kitchen next door is cosier, with a French window opening out on to the back garden and another big window to the west filled with the shrubbery which screens us from the neighbours.

A windswept garden, then, but that didn't worry my mother. She filled it with tough bushes that could hold their own against the elements. Here and there they created pockets of shelter in which she planted the slightly more vulnerable things. On either side of the French window are two beds of herbs which manage reasonably well against the south wall of the house. They're cut out of a small paved area just big enough for sitting outside when the weather allows. After that is the garden proper, and beyond that, separated by a sweet briar hedge which saturates the garden with scent, is the paddock, home of Ahab the Arab.

That morning, most of the trees dotted about the paddock were at their freshest, a bright tender spring green. Only the chestnut was dark, a luxurious deep green parasol, its bottom edge clipped to a uniform height by Ahab's greedy teeth. Beneath it stood the culprit himself.

I still couldn't believe I owned something as beautiful as Ahab. Maxine was on loan, so to speak, as were all the other people who delighted my eyes. But a mundane receipt told me I actually owned Ahab. I'd bought him as a yearling in the year of my mother's illness. I knew my parents had mixed feelings about my being home again. On the one hand they wanted me here; Eleanor was, after all, dying. On the other, they felt guilty about what I'd left behind to come home. There'd been no pressure – far from it – and I'd come home willingly enough. But I needed to convince them that I was happy to be here.

Hence Ahab. I'd never trained a horse; it was an adventure I could throw myself into. It also gave us a sense of a future still going somewhere. My parents were fascinated by the process, it was something new for them, too. They'd never kept animals or taken much interest in such things. But Ahab was a work of art in the making and they enjoyed being a part of it. On good days we brought Eleanor's chair outside so she could watch. With the garden relatively low-growing and the paddock rising beyond, she had a ringside seat from the patio.

We must have made a pretty picture, Ahab and I, so perfectly matched in our colouring. His coat and my hair were exactly the same bright reddish chestnut which only wanted a bit of sun to set it alight. I can see us as Eleanor did: two balls of fire at either end of the lungeline, the one who was Ahab prancing himself silly, just tickled to be alive. I only wish Eleanor had lived to see the climax of the whole magical process, when Ahab and I at last turned ourselves into a centaur.

Ahab is a slightly larger than average (fifteen and a half hands) Arabian. His size, combined with the traditional delicacy of the breed, makes him a horse to turn heads. It's all there: the dished face, the widely spaced dark brown eyes full of intelligence and good nature, the arched neck, small alert ears, the strong well-knit back, the high tail plumed like a banner. That morning, canopied by the deep green tree, his coat glowing now that the last of the coarse winter hair had gone, his small hooves half-hidden by a wisp of sea fret, he looked unreal, someone's picture-book fantasy of the perfect horse.

'Ahab,' I called.

He swung his fine-boned head round to scrutinise me, then lowered it to nibble a bit of grass.

'You really know how to make a girl feel wanted,' I complained.

He pretended not to hear. Though at heart every bit as good-natured as the rest of his breed, he's picked up a bolshy streak from his owner. But I like to play these games, too. I approached. 'Come on, Ahab. It's a glorious morning. Just think of all that lovely sand under your feet.'

He nosed his muzzle into my hand, looking for and finding the bit of apple I always saved him from my breakfast. He crunched it noisily. Apple juice oozed over my hand.

'Come on, my lad.' We walked up the paddock towards the tiny stable I'd built from the stone of a ruined outbuilding. I didn't even have to hold his halter; he just walked beside me like an old friend. We chatted, like old friends. At the doorway I removed his halter and hung it on the peg beside his bridle. I put the bridle on. He took it with no fuss. Ahab has far too much dignity to play that particular game. Also, the bridle is such a light one he hardly knows it's there. I'd been so fanatic about not ruining his mouth that I'd kept him on the gentlest bit I could find and I never reined him in with more strength than a newborn baby's.

I couldn't be bothered with a saddle on these early morning rides. Standing on a large stone placed by his stable for the purpose, I put my hands on his sturdy back and heaved myself aboard. He quivered with anticipation, as eager as I now to escape the confines of the paddock. We went through the garden, clattered across the little patio and on to the path beside the sea wall. A moment later we were on the street, making our way towards the centre of town and the harbour. Ahab's hooves clanged like bells, the sound echoing off the houses and ringing clear in the empty air.

We picked our way carefully down the steep cobbled slipway beside the pier and were on the beach. Ahab raised his head even higher and sniffed the air. Already I could feel his muscles bunching. 'Not yet,' I said as always. We turned right and walked sedately along the sands until we were out of earshot of all the houses. Then, 'Go it, Ahab!' I yelled.

The horse sprang without transition into his delicious canter. I let him choose his own pace – I wanted the ride to be as pleasurable for him as for me. He was feeling sparky that morning and soon the canter stretched out into a gallop. The rock face of the cliff sped by in a jagged jumble to my right, to the left a million tiny mirrors glinted off the sea. Beneath, Ahab's hooves thudded on the hard wet sand. The sun was doing its daily renewal, lifting itself out of the sea and spreading a golden path towards the horse. He gleamed like crazy. His mane was whipping out in every direction like flames fanned by his own impetuous flight. My hair was whipping about too, stinging my face, but I didn't mind. The air whistled past my ears. A white shirt flashed in the sun.

I don't think I saw him at the time. My eyes must have taken in the picture subliminally and cast it on to the screen of my mind some seconds later. He'd been sitting on a rock outcrop near the base of the cliff, one knee cupped in his hands. He was wearing jeans this time, not something I would associate with a man like that. But then, what kind of a man was he? I didn't know. All I knew was that his face and neck, rising darkly out of the dazzling white shirt, had looked stronger than ever. His hair had been silvered by the sun and ruffled by the breeze. He'd been smiling, possibly even laughing. I had an after-image of his teeth looking very white and his eyes very black.

I must have transmitted my shock to Ahab because he faltered just a fraction before resuming his wild gallop. My heart was thudding in time with Ahab's hooves, set in motion by the surprise of seeing him so soon again and in such an unexpected place. Ahab ran, oblivious once more of anything except the sheer pleasure of using his muscles, for another half mile or so until we reached the headland. This juts out well into the sea. Even at low tide you can't get round, and though there's a rough footpath snaking up it, it's too steep and rocky even for Ahab's nimble feet. We had no alternative but to go back the way we came.

I didn't want to. I could hardly pass him at a walking pace and refuse to speak and I didn't want to take it at a run again. Two miles of madness was quite enough for one morning; I always walked Ahab back to make sure he was really cooled down before I led him to his water trough in the paddock. What's more, Dr Komarovsky would think it odd if I raced past a second time.

Dr Komarovsky. I felt foolish calling my future lover (oh yes, I knew even then) 'Dr Komarovsky' even in my mind, but years of English manners made me hesitant to usurp his first name. The real problem was, however, that I didn't want to call him anything yet. I didn't want to speak to him. It was too soon, it would ruin the pleasure of the cat-and-mouse game he'd begun in the library.

'Ahab, what do I say?' I whispered.

Ahab ignored me. He was prancing about, still excited by his run. He wasn't interested in my problems. Don't believe all that stuff about perfect communication between horse and rider. It's limited.

A banal 'Good morning, isn't it a lovely day' would hardly do. As we approached the place where I'd seen him, I rehearsed a couple of openings. Both were lousy. I tried a third. Even worse. The jumble of fallen rocks which hid him was looming fast. I reined in Ahab, who seemed rather surprised. I apologised and loosened the reins again. After a shake of his lovely head, he pranced forward again.

At the last moment, with just a few seconds to go, I decided. I wouldn't say anything. I would smile pleasantly and nod in acknowledgment just as he had done in the library. It wasn't brilliant but it would do. It was reasonable enough. Early birds meeting on the beach often just nodded. There was a tacit agreement that each had come for solitude and it was tactless to break it with words. Even so, as we skirted the fallen rocks my hands were shaking just a little. I hoped he wouldn't notice.

I should have known. He was gone.

FOUR

I didn't see him again for another week. At first I was pleased; he was playing the game well, being just that bit elusive. Then the unease began to creep in. Perhaps he wasn't playing at all; perhaps he'd left. I thought of asking Maxine but didn't want to appear too interested.

Then I had another thought: maybe it was me; he simply wasn't interested in me after all. It was a reasonable enough thing to think. I kept forgetting that the years were trundling along, taking me with them. I was getting older every minute. Everyone knows that women become invisible after forty. Further, I'd never been a great beauty even when young. The thing that had attracted men to me in the past had been my lust for life. From my unruly red hair to my big feet, I'd looked the kind of woman who had a surplus of energy and few inhibitions about using it. But did this still hold true after forty? It didn't help that I surrounded myself with beauty. In juxtaposition with the exquisite Maxine and the equally gorgeous Ahab, I was a pretty raw chunk of material.

Well, so be it. I wasn't going to downgrade my surroundings just to make myself shine, let alone for a man, not even a man as desirable as Dr Komarovsky. I'd had a riotous ten years or so before coming home. Surely I could be content with that. Yes, it was time to hand in my cards, settle into a pleasantly routine life of solitude, give up these foolish games.

I nearly convinced myself. So well was I adjusting to my new self-image (bun, spectacles, frown) that Maxine remarked, 'You're awfully subdued, Attila. Are you ill?'

I looked up from a volume of the *British National Bibliography*. 'Just the tread of old Father Time catching up with me, my dear.'

'Clichés, too – you *must* be ill.'

'It'll come to you as well, my pet. Enjoy your youth while you can.'

'People always say that but they never say how.'

I smiled sadly. 'No freebies in this life, sweet. You have to find your own way.'

'Don't play the Wise Old Woman with me, Attila. I know you too well.'

'Brat. There's a trolley of books needing shelving.'

She glided off. Standing by the shelves with an armload of books, lifting each into its place, she looked like a king's daughter distributing largess. Everyone was watching. It's a wonder anyone gets any work done in this place.

But if Maxine had been just a pretty face my interest would soon have faded. I'd known her just a few days when I realised that she had something special. Heaven knows where she got it from – unless from her mother who, after years of being Robert Vesey's doormat, had upped and left and never been heard of again.

For a long time now I'd offered tuition in German, French and Russian. My pupils were by definition the children of the rich. Not Maxine. Or rather, as she explained, 'Oh yes, Dad's got the money. He just won't pay.' She offered to work in my library in lieu.

The Library Board was deeply suspicious. 'A *schoolgirl?*' said Mrs Johnson. She pronounced the words rather like Edith Evans on the subject of handbags. I couldn't blame them. Until then my assistant had been one of those invaluable middle-aged women whose children had left home, the kind of person without whom the whole country would grind to a halt. But she was due to leave, following her husband to a new job in Middlesbrough.

'Maxine's bright,' I said. 'And hardworking. I'm sure of

it.' Mutters of dissatisfaction. Finally, 'No Maxine, no me,' I said. 'I'm sorry, but I feel strongly about this.'

I felt even more strongly when I discovered that Maxine's father, one of the richest farmers in the area, had made it clear he wouldn't help finance his daughter to university. The bulky farmer who now owned much of Sydney Holroyd's former land was a true blue xenophobe. 'What do you want with learning how the Frogs and Krauts talk?' he said. Would he have been less hostile if Maxine had opted for business studies or law? Who knows.

Maxine's determination took my breath away. She had no doubt that she would earn the money somehow and had filled out the forms, with Cambridge as her first choice. There was a good chance she would be accepted. I pushed her wages up. The Library Board muttered every time. Every time I threatened my own resignation. No qualified librarian would tolerate our stone-age establishment, despite the luxury; they couldn't afford to lose me. And they could afford to pay Maxine, thanks to Sydney Holroyd.

I snapped back to the present and felt the gloom descend again. Perhaps it was just the weather. It had rained for a whole week now, not a lot in quantity but it always felt like a deluge the way it whooshed in from the sea in lumpy armloads. I used to enjoy this wild gusty weather but now I felt irritated as each cloud seemed to zero in on me and dump its contents with the accuracy of a laser-guided missile. Old age again. I sighed.

At that moment the clouds parted and Dr Komarovsky entered the library. I don't know which was more dazzling: the golden fan of rays beaming down or his face. He exuded well-being. No doubt he thought the sun had come out specially for him. Perhaps it had. Quelling an urge to shout for joy, I gave him a non-committal smile and nod of acknowledgment. He returned it. And disappeared promptly into the west wing.

I felt personally affronted. Then a private ray of sunshine

all my own broke through my pique. Of course: the weather. He hadn't been avoiding me. He'd simply holed up in Gormenghast, log fire blazing, to get a spot of writing done.

Of course the other side of that was that I was unimportant, not worth a trudge through the rain.

I was back at square one: a foolish provincial librarian concocting fantasies. Served me right. Suitably chastised, I returned to my work.

By lunchtime enough sun had soaked into the courtyard walls to saturate them. The surplus was radiating out again, spreading a pleasant heat over the little tables dotted among the trees. I took my sandwiches and the *Times Literary Supplement* and settled in for a good read.

A cloud darkened the page. All the bells of St Petersburg rang out in two deep-toned syllables. 'May I?'

He was standing with his hand on the back of the chair opposite.

'Of course,' I said. Dilemma: do I abandon the *TLS* and start a conversation? Or do we read together in our separate solitudes like passengers in a railway compartment? I noted that he had no reading matter with him. Also, there were empty tables in the courtyard. I folded up the *TLS* and looked straight into his face as he sat down.

'I'm surprised to see your assistant here at this time of day,' he said amiably. 'Her father said she was at school.'

'A-levels,' I explained. 'She's studying for exams.' So that was it: Maxine. He ought to be ashamed of himself, I thought primly. He's old enough to be her grandfather. Then I softened. I can't begrudge Maxine her due. 'She's bright as well as beautiful,' I added. 'You'd be surprised how much studying she gets in during slack periods.'

'Her father did mention that she worked for you.'

I took a quick reading of his face and ventured, 'I'll bet he did more than mention. I'll bet he badmouthed me.'

Dr Komarovsky laughed, a nice big open sunny burst of laughter. 'He wasn't too complimentary,' he admitted.

'Come on, give us the dirt,' I said comfortably.

He raised one bushy eyebrow, then seemed to have second thoughts and lowered it again. 'He didn't say anything specific, but he did convey the impression that you weren't his favourite person.'

'Robert Vesey and I were destined to hate each other from birth. Not that I really hate him. In a way I almost admire him. He's so single-minded. What's he like as a landlord?'

'Quite reasonable once I'd paid up – in full and in advance.'

I laughed. 'Good old Robert.' I couldn't believe he'd bothered to join me for a bit of idle chit-chat about Robert Vesey, but his manner was so casual as to be almost distant. I decided to probe as gently as possible. 'Whatever made you rent the old mansion?'

He shrugged. 'Peace and quiet.'

'The whole town's full of it,' I pursued. 'Why a derelict mansion in the middle of nowhere?'

'Solitude, then.'

'Is what you're doing that secretive?' I tried.

He laughed. I could see no guile in it. 'I'm writing a book.'

I decided to play dumb. 'Oh, really? How interesting. And are you famous?'

'I'm afraid not.'

'Come on, admit: every town you go to you sneak into the library and have a look at the catalogue.'

The same comfortable laughter. 'I gave that up years ago.' Then he paused and scrutinised my face. For one sickening moment I wondered if Maxine had told him I'd spied on his catalogue cards. 'But I did have a look in your catalogue,' he said at last.

'Oh?'

Another pause. 'Your parents,' he said. 'It occurred to

me that they might have put in a request to the library to order some of my books.'

A jolt of panic turned me cold but only for a moment. After all, if there was some kind of family connection, why shouldn't he mention it? It would be far odder if he didn't. 'And had they?' I said, trying to sound as casual as him.

'I presume so. At least they're there – all of them.'

I hadn't even thought to check the catalogue against *BNB* to see if we had them all. That we did was very odd indeed. My parents must have been pretty keen, and yet they'd never said a word to me about him. Come to think of it, some of those books were ordered while I was librarian. My parents must have been so casual about it that it never aroused my curiosity. 'Did you know my parents well?' I asked lightly. A week ago he hadn't said he knew them at all, only that his father knew mine. There was something askew.

Very askew. Dr Komarovsky was watching me very closely now. I felt like a walk-on part in a play whose main characters were unsure of my role.

'Not very,' he said slowly. 'At least, not directly.'

The words were evasive in the extreme. The air felt charged with electricity and it wasn't, alas, sexual attraction. I was much too confused now even to think about the cat-and-mouse game. This was a different game and he was the one controlling it. I had two choices now: to change the subject and turn down the voltage, or to make a bold move. I wasn't feeling very bold. I also wasn't feeling very hungry. I eyed the paper bag with my sandwiches. Dr Komarovsky didn't have any sandwiches. He was spending his lunch hour talking with me instead.

Briskly I opened the bag and took out the sandwiches. I offered one to him and forced myself to begin eating the other, playing for time. Finally I made my decision. 'Where did you meet my parents?' I asked.

But the sandwich had given him a chance to think, too. By the time he swallowed the first bite he'd come up with another piece of evasion. 'My father had some icons to sell,' he explained.

'The Atwill Gallery doesn't deal in icons,' I said steadily. 'Never has. Only contemporary art. They've always been very particular about that.'

Dr Komarovsky nodded. 'They had a reputation for being more honest than most galleries. My father knew that and hoped they'd be able to give him the name of an honest icon dealer. Icon dealers are a shifty lot,' he explained.

I laughed. 'The whole art world's shifty as hell. So what's new?'

He smiled. 'Exactly. But there are degrees and degrees.'

'And was my father able to help?'

He nodded. 'Very much so. We managed to live off those icons until my father established himself.'

'As?'

'Pardon?'

'As what?'

'Oh, I see. A doctor. A medical doctor.'

'And you?'

'Pardon?'

'*Doctor* Komarovsky?'

'Oh, yes. No, I'm a historian.'

Whatever the game, I was finally gaining the upper hand. I leaned my arms on the table and smiled up at him. 'You seem to know a lot about my family. Why don't you tell me about yours?'

I was pretty sure I'd confused him, though he barely showed it. 'I'm afraid it's not very interesting,' he said with an apologetic smile which didn't fool me for one minute. 'The usual story: the Revolution. My family did better than most. They managed to leave Russia in good time and with many of their possessions, at least the more portable ones. Including the icons.'

I was doing some quick calculations. Surely his parents couldn't have been that old?

He must have read my mind. 'My parents were children then; they never knew each other in Russia. My mother's family and my father's family both settled in Berlin and met there. As you probably know, the White Russians were somewhat snobbish. They preferred to mix with their own kind.'

'And marry their own kind. So you were born in Berlin?'

He nodded. 'My family stayed there all through the thirties and the war . . . and after.'

Perhaps it was my imagination that there was a hint of hesitation before the last words. I wondered what he was hiding. Not that there was anything unusual about his story or any obvious reason to lie. But lying had been a way of life for his parents' generation, and for the one that came after it, especially if they happened to land up in the east. I had been familiar with it in my eastern bloc friends and come to respect it. 'Lying' was too harsh a word: more a matter of shifting layers of reality.

'And so whose were the icons?'

'My mother's. She was very upset at having to sell them, but at least she got a good price.'

'I'm glad my father was able to help, if only indirectly. They saw a lot of each other after that?' I asked casually.

'Not a lot. And when your parents left London that was more or less the end of it.'

We continued eating our sandwiches and watching each other with the air of not watching each other. I wondered what would happen if I suddenly opted out of both games, his and mine, and simply said, *All right, Dr Komarovsky; what do you know about me?* I had an uncomfortable feeling that he wouldn't be at all surprised. But would he tell me what he knew? I wasn't at all sure. He seemed uncertain himself, sometimes drawing near the subject only to pull away again. I couldn't tell if this was deliberate or the sign of some internal confusion. I was back at the central question: why had he come to Sedleigh? I couldn't believe it was casual curiosity, however casual his manner. The daughter of a man who had helped his father sell some icons was hardly a star attraction.

Well, it was no use probing today. Even as I watched, a veil of privacy seemed to be drawn across those deep black eyes, shutting me out once again. Any minute now he would ask me some trivial question about the library or the town, and in the guise of asking about my life here he would gently push that life away from his, and there was nothing I could do about it. Even now the last bit of the sandwich was making its way down into that lovely body of his. That sensuous mouth was curving into a devastatingly impersonal smile. That glorious voice – as deep as the Russian winter, as vast as the steppe – was resonating in the courtyard and down to the tips of my toes with the words, 'Who exactly *was* Sydney Holroyd, Miss Atwill?'

I sighed.

FIVE

My dear Miss Atwill. Anna. Anushka:
What a dilemma you place before me! I knew it would be difficult; these matters are deep and fraught with uncertainties. But I wasn't to know that you yourself would play the trickster and throw my plans into confusion.

How you've changed, my little charmer! I won't pretend that I gave you much thought through all those years of waiting. After all, I had no idea I was waiting; there was no reason to suspect that we'd ever meet again. But if I had thought about you, what sort of picture would have risen in my mind to fill in the intervening years?

Impossible to tell. Certainly not the one which greeted me when I entered your library. I dare say you'll be offended when you read this, whenever that will be, but you must know the image which your profession conjures up. And yes, I admit I was disappointed when my father told me you'd traded in your fiddle for a librarian's scowl. 'Yes, Father,' I said. 'If you insist, I'll go. But you must know how ill-suited I am to such things.' He agreed – a little sourly, I thought – and added, 'There's no one else left. It has to be you.'

Anushka, my treasure, what *are* you doing here? When I opened the door to the Sydney Holroyd Library, it was with an ungenerous heart and a scowl which I assumed would match your own. I looked round for the gorgon of the books, and what did I see? A gypsy temptress, red hair crackling with indignation at its setting. A sexy bruise of a mouth which you'll never train to look prim. Above it, a sleek nose streamlined for the eastern winds to whistle past and two snappy black eyes made for scanning the horizon in search of your prey. Involuntarily I looked to your fist, half expecting to see the hooded bird.

And saw instead a pencil. If I'd had a violin with me I would have known what to do. I would have walked boldly up to you, flung away the pencil and thrust the violin under that lovely big soft chin of yours. Then I would have stood aside and waited until you swept out from behind the odious desk, planted your feet firmly on the floor and, after a perfunctory tuning-up, launched into a *csárdás* which would have lifted the Sydney Holroyd Library clear off its foundations.

Instead, I stood still with the shock and contemplated my mission. For one moment I thought you knew; when I recovered my senses and sedately sought out a book and a table from which to watch you, you looked across at me with such a steady gaze that I was almost sure. Almost but not quite. And now I'm as confused as ever.

You caused me a sleepless night, my Anna, and for more reasons than the obvious. No doubt you thought me an early rising fanatic when you came across me on the beach. Wrong. I hadn't slept at all. Finally I'd given up the attempt and come out to walk off my turmoil of feelings. I was watching the sea, thinking of what lies beyond it for both you and me, when some lunatic switched on a soundtrack of horse hooves thundering across the sands. Vexed at the cliché, and even more vexed at the interruption to my thoughts, I looked up just in time to see a flash of fire hurtling past to rival the sun.

Rival it you did, my queen of the plains and the forests. Neither the sun nor I was fooled for a minute by your disguise of jeans and tatty shirt. You might as well throw a burlap sack over that Arabian brute of yours in the hope of disguising him as a carthorse. The sun knew it was beaten, knew it couldn't pretend to be star of the show. Defeated, it resigned itself to turning its spotlight on both of you, setting hair and mane and tail aflame. What a feast for the eyes, you wicked little artist of the everyday, you witch, transforming the exercise of a horse into a work of art.

Did you wonder why I disappeared? I wonder, too. Even more so than in the library the day before, you threw my expectations into confusion. Perhaps I feared the banal (Good-morning-what-a-lovely-day) on your return, the beautiful canvas streaked with a vulgar banner headline. Or perhaps (let me be frank) I envied that horse. How can you allow those luscious thighs of yours to enfold so unworthy an object? Invidious nag.

And now I sit in your library once again, watching you over a stack of unread books. Thank you for the sandwich, but don't think that's the end of it. It's you I intend to devour, if you don't ravish me first.

What pompous fantasies. Who are we after all? An academic and a librarian, our lives lived out in catalogue cards. Hardly in the first flush of youth either. Do we dare? Is there still time for us to set the world afire, if only the small world of our own lives? That portrait of you racing along the beach – wild, free, crazy with joy – gives me hope.

Dear Miss Atwill. Be my alchemist, turn my gross metal into gold. For my part, I will be your bulky Ariel and give you the magic island of your dreams.

You look up from your mundane task and meet my eyes. Do you guess what lies behind them? What would you do, dear Miss Atwill, if I rose from my chair, walked to your desk and placed this letter on it? I'm tempted, very tempted indeed. I'm growing too old for patience. Impetuosity is not for the young, whatever the clichés say. It's us, conscious of the years piling up behind us, who look over our shoulders and cry, 'Now!'

But no, the time isn't right. There's a maze laid out before us, and if we hack our way to the centre with billhooks we'll find it empty. We need to make our way along its devious paths if we hope to surprise the treasure within. I can wait a while longer, Miss Atwill. (You I'm not so sure about.) Be patient, little Miss Book. Our time is coming, and soon.

Yours (respectfully),
Dmitri Mikhailovich

SIX

And then he vanished again. Not instantly, of course. After our sandwiches and polite conversation we returned to the library. He sat at the same table as on that first day but this time, instead of reading, he took a sheet of paper from his briefcase and began writing. I was pretty sure he wasn't writing his book; the notecards and other paraphernalia of academia were missing. It seemed to be a letter. It occurred to me with a sudden shock that he was writing to his wife. After all, how could a man like that escape marriage for so long? The notion depressed me deeply. A few seconds later I dismissed it. No married man would leave his wife for six months to come to a dotty place like this.

As soon as he'd finished his letter or whatever, he folded it, picked up his briefcase and came towards my desk. He hesitated for a moment and I thought I saw a manic gleam in his eyes. Then he shrugged good-humouredly, put the paper in his pocket and left.

That was it for another week. Meanwhile, there were other things to occupy my mind, most notably Robert Vesey's planning application and Bernard's borehole.

Bernard had finally decided to drill. He'd studied the maps, the land and the geological reports. Then he'd brought in his diviner. They agreed on the most probable spot. This greatly cheered Bernard. Even so, he was anxious to have it over and done with as soon as possible. So were the Slaters. Things were becoming pretty dire for them (showers at the school's sports centre, stern warnings to house guests to 'have a bath *before* you come, *please!*').

The drilling was scheduled for a weekend. Bernard and Tim were free (no families) and could choose their own days off. This meant I was free from my own job, with Maxine manning the library on Saturdays.

All right, perhaps it's Freudian, this fascination with borehole wells, or perhaps it's something deeper than that. Either way, I couldn't stand to miss out on the action. I phoned Kate.

'Kate,' I said, 'if I'm being insensitive tell me where to go, but I'd love to come and see your well drilled. Could you bear to have me around?'

'More than bear,' she said. 'I could do with someone to hold my hand.'

The weather was warm and sunny again the morning Ahab and I set off. The Slaters lived about two miles inland and the quickest route was through the wood. This time I saddled Ahab and walked him to the upper gate at the top of his paddock. After shutting the gate I swung up into the saddle. Five seconds later I was enfolded in the green luxurious arms of the wood.

It always gives me a thrill entering the wood. It's a very special place. It's been here for ever in some form or other, one of those ancient woodlands so loved by conservationists. Nobody knows how it came to be here, so close to the cliffs and the salty sea air, but it's a part of our lives every bit as pervasive as the sea and a good deal more friendly. Instead of the raucous gulls, the wood swarms with honey-throated songbirds skilled at using the acoustics of their green cathedral. Instead of icy water, the wood gives us sun-baked boulders in fairy clearings. The leaves filter the cold sea winds and give them back to us as playful puffs.

Even its size is reassuring. It's on a human scale, our hundred-acre Eden. Big enough to get lost in (if you really try) but small enough to make us feel intimate. It begins right up against the cliff path and wanders inland with the whimsicality of a child who has nowhere in particular to go but is enjoying the journey. Here and there the land goes up a little hill, taking its trees with it. Little sykes follow the contours. There are thickets and glades, places where the canopy squeezes out the light to make a sombre brown floor, other places where a festival of wildflowers suddenly springs up to cover the turf. When finally it reaches its western edge it wraps its big green arms round the house, much as it caresses any other object straying into its domain. There it stops, just winking a seductive come-hither which few can resist.

There used to be an old manor house near the western edge, and a lot of people are annoyed that there were no planning restrictions in those days to prevent Sydney Holroyd from tearing it down. In its place he built his little mansion. That was in the nineteenth century, at a time when plant-collecting was the national mania. All over the world helmeted Brits swarmed up mountains to fetch down the seeds of exotic trees for the gardens of the rich. Sydney inspected the struggling remnant of the ancient wood and decided it needed a bit of cheering up. He engaged a gardener keen on the latest fashions and between them they designed a wood to incorporate the best of the old and the new.

The result is a United Nations of trees. However much their human counterparts may squabble, the trees seem quite content with each other's company. There are delegates from almost everywhere: Norway maple and Italian alder, Turkish hazel and Algerian oak, horse chestnuts from Greece and sweet chestnuts from Spain. The contingent of firs is pretty impressive: Siberian, Greek, West Himalayan, Japanese, Caucasian, Alpine, Colorado, Spanish and even a Nikko fir from Korea. The pines have sent a weighty group too: as well as the Swiss stone pine and the Scots, there are representatives from Corsica, Austria, Macedonia, Bhutan and Monterey. Sweden sends us whitebeams and junipers, Ireland a juniper too, and a yew. The cedar of Lebanon is finding our climate pretty tough but the Atlas cedar has no regrets about leaving its north African home.

No doubt about it, I feel at home in this woodland of the world. Each time I enter, the international babble of its leaves whizzes me back to Paris, Berlin, Vienna. The soothing resin of all those pines and firs heals the gap between past and present and once again I am whole: *Weltbürger, citoyenne du monde.*

All this in homey little Yorkshire. And now Robert Vesey was threatening its existence.

His planning application, which was dividing the town, was simple enough: an estate of breathtaking exclusiveness, half a dozen houses in the first phase, each set in its own chunk of mature woodland, each with the mandatory Jacuzzi, covered swimming pool, fleet of luxury bathrooms and (here we come to the point) spacious offices designed to take the latest electronic equipment. For the clientèle Robert had in mind was the international businessman who wants it both ways: house in the country, business all over the world. With his computer-linked offices he can have the best of both and at a cost far lower than anywhere on the continent.

There was nothing new in any of this. Already businessmen from Holland and Germany were buying up the best country houses in Yorkshire for this purpose. But the areas they most coveted – by the sea – were conspicuously short on such houses and hedged in by planning restrictions to preserve the coastline. In addition, some were finding it a bit lonely on their country estates. What Robert was offering was irresistible: privacy and the company of their own kind, all in spectacular surroundings with easy links by air and sea to the continent.

And Robert was doubly cunning; he'd put together a package of immense appeal to the town itself. Local traders saw a wealthy market for their goods. Town councillors saw prestige. Even the conservationists got something out of it, since Robert had neglected the wood and threatened to neglect it permanently if his application was turned down.

He'd planned the estate with great care to ensure that not *too* many trees would go. The rest (he argued) would be lovingly cared for by their new owners.

He was probably right. Even I had been almost seduced. However idyllic, Sedleigh was a parochial little town bursting with Yorkshire pride. I was not averse to a few urbane foreigners stirring things up. True, I would have preferred an artists' colony, but I was realistic enough to see there was no money in that. They could be a breath of fresh air, our foreigners, a precious link with the world outside.

Pièce de résistance was to be the mansion itself. This, too, Robert had neglected. Now he proposed to turn it into the showpiece of the estate. I'd seen the plans; they really were quite something. I tried to imagine Dr Komarovsky in the sleek modernised mansion envisaged, and failed. He was a man of the pen, my St Petersburg prince. I doubted if he'd ever used a typewriter, never mind a computer terminal.

I was approaching the mansion now. 'Mansion' is too impressive a word for a mere eight bedrooms plus servants' quarters in the attic. Nor is it built on a grand scale. It's a simple building with nice neo-Georgian proportions. From a distance you don't see the peeling paint, the rotting windows, the sagging gutters, the gaps in the roof. Even from close up there's no hint of the water-stained walls inside, the missing floorboards, the rusting boiler Robert had bought secondhand to save a few quid. If I couldn't imagine Dr Komarovsky in the spruced-up version, I couldn't imagine him putting up with the house in its present state either.

Yet again: why had he come here? And why had he rented this of all places?

The more pressing question, however, was whether I should drop in on my new neighbour. Nothing could be more natural, given my perfect excuse for being in the vicinity. I was sure he would welcome me. But that was part of the problem. I didn't want to be welcomed with the same bland courtesy as at our last meeting. He'd drawn away from me during our chat in the courtyard, and a man like that didn't do anything absent-mindedly. If he meant to put space between us, so be it. I wasn't going to spoil my day with a banal encounter. On the other hand, it would seem odd if I simply rode past.

'Ahab, you decide,' I said as we approached the junction of two paths. One (not a bridleway) led under an arch cut out of the thick yew hedge which encircled the house. Beyond it was a grassy terrace dotted with trees and running right up to the back of the house.

The other path led round past the rose garden on the south side. Well, it wasn't much of a choice. Ahab took one look at the low arch and turned smartly towards the rose garden. I registered a twinge of disappointment but didn't contradict.

The hedge was tall and meant for privacy, but from my perch high up on Ahab I could see over it into the grounds. It was a warm day, windows were open all over the south-east corner of the house. Clearly this was the bit he was occupying. I was nosy as hell but the windows were just a little too far away for my prying eyes. I had to content myself with an imaginary picture instead: Dr Komarovsky bent over a desk littered with notecards, gazing out towards the trees beyond his hedge.

Wrong. He was in the garden. I felt an odd little lurch of fear as my eyes travelled from the imagined desk to the real one set among the roses. They weren't flowering yet but the sharp greenery of their leaves was almost as good. The garden, like everything else, was overgrown, and most of the bushes were big old-fashioned shrub roses run wild. Tentacles of green, neither pruned nor pinioned to a wall, waved in the faintest breeze. In the middle was a centre of stillness: Dr Komarovsky at work.

He had his back to the hedge, no doubt to cut down the sun's glare. The rose garden was beautifully sheltered: the house to one side, the hedge to the other, and elsewhere the ubiquitous waves of encroaching trees to filter the wind. None of the trees was close enough to shade the garden though, and the result was a suntrap.

Dr Komarovsky was wearing light grey trousers and a white short-sleeved shirt. The table he'd set up as a desk was white too, as were the papers spread over it. He'd placed stones on some of them because of the breeze but it still teased the papers, ruffling their edges. Their sound matched the gentle rattling of leaves from a nearby aspen.

It was a picture full of charm, a quiet and serious sort of charm. I didn't want to disturb it. The path beside the hedge was deep in needles from the yews on one side and a grouping of larches on the other. Ahab's hooves were small, his step delicate. It was just possible . . .

But not quite. The air was so quiet, despite the faint breeze, that even Ahab's gentle tread made an audible counterpoint to the tiny sounds issuing from the desk. Dr Komarovsky turned round suddenly and we both burst into spontaneous laughter. In an instant of empathy I saw what he saw: the disembodied head of a statue seeming to glide, serene and detached, along the top of the hedge. A splendidly ludicrous sight and impossible to resist. Our laughter drowned out Ahab's hooves, the papers, the aspens.

A moment later Dr Komarovsky was on his feet and making his way towards another arch cut through the hedge. Then he was beside me, his hand on Ahab's neck, his smiling face turned up to me. He looked like a god. Against the white shirt his skin was golden-dark and his hair a great dusky Pan's wreath. He was wearing dark glasses but through them I could see the dancing amusement of his eyes.

'My dear Miss Atwill! Am I Pygmalion greeting at last my Galatea? Or has the goddess Juno herself become a statue to grace my rose garden? Come in, statue; I have just the place for you, by a pretty little fountain surrounded with thyme.'

If I hadn't been securely mounted I would have been swept off my feet. I was unaccustomed, after so many years away, to the joking gallantry of Continental Man. Dear God, what a charmer! Recovering, I said, 'With respect, sir, you mistake the image. I am Penthesilea, Queen of the Amazons. Separate me from my horse at your peril.'

He took a step or two back and scrutinised us. 'Who would do the violence of separating such a perfectly matched pair? My classics are rusty, but surely there must have been centaurs of the fairer sex?'

Ahab tossed his head, snorted and took a step towards Dr Komarovsky. Ahab is spoiled rotten, used to praise and the usual treat from admirers. 'Ahab's all too mortal,' I laughed. 'He's trying to prise a sugar lump from you.'

'And he shall have it, and you a coffee at least or a glass of white wine if you'll permit me to detain you.'

I shook my head regretfully. 'May I defer? I'm late already – on my way to a borehole drilling.'

Now it was he who turned to stone. He stared, dumbfounded. 'A what?'

The magic was gone and I was the one who'd killed it. I could hear Maxine chiding from her vigil in the library, *Attila, you berk! Here's this gorgeous man wooing you with poetry and you talk about boreholes?* 'My friend Bernard's drilling for water over at the Slaters',' I explained.

There was a stunned pause. 'Am I to understand this is some sort of public occasion?' he asked.

'Not really,' I said, feeling more foolish by the second. 'A private well, actually.'

Another pause. 'Ah. This is like the quilting bees of the old American west? Everybody brings a shovel and digs together to help the young couple?'

I felt exasperated by his ignorance. 'Bernard's a hydrologist, a borehole engineer. That's his profession: drilling borehole wells. I'm only going along to watch.' Too late

I heard the hidden mockery in his previous words. With the next, it was out in the open.

'Fascinating,' said Dr Komarovsky.

My face burned: humiliation, anger, indignation. 'Yes, it is. A good deal more fascinating than icons. Also a good deal more useful. If he doesn't find water the Slaters are ruined.'

Dirty tactics, and ones I never would have used in the past. I don't believe in separating the 'useful' from the 'useless'. To me, studying icons is as important as anything else. But I'd had enough of Maxine belittling Bernard's work. I wasn't going to take another dose from Dr Komarovsky.

'Anna Atwill,' he said softly. 'Is this really you? Have you really put away your fiddle for a horse? The Berlin Philharmonic for a borehole engineer? Is this really how you idle away your spare time now? Watching someone dig a hole in the ground?'

I froze. The warm sun whipped away behind a cloud. The breeze blew a gale-force wind right through my centre. I sat up stiffly and fixed on him a look bristling with icicles. 'It is,' I said shortly. Then I pressed my knees to Ahab and we sprang away.

SEVEN

How on earth did he know about the Berlin Phil? It had been such a small episode, just an anecdote for friends and family. One of the ways I scraped together a living during my years on the continent was to deputise for friends in orchestras, including (once) the Berlin Philharmonic in the days of Herbert von Karajan.

Leni and I had got a little drunk one night and she'd told me a string of horror stories about the old maestro – in particular, about his reputation for missing nothing. 'He hears every note from every instrument,' she'd claimed, 'and heaven help anyone who tries to pull a fast one.'

I scoffed. It was just one of those myths which accumulated around Karajan. 'He wouldn't even notice if a total stranger barged into his orchestra,' I challenged.

Well, it so happened that Leni wanted to spend that weekend with her boyfriend in Frankfurt. It also so happened that I was short of money and dying to play with the Berlin Phil. Karajan disapproved of depping and so I'd never gained an entrée. The Philharmonie was a fabulous hall. I'd been to many of the famous Sunday morning concerts and loved the place as much as the Berliners did. It was the most wonderful modern building, and its acoustics were probably the best in the world. I longed to try them myself.

It was dead easy. The programme that Sunday was a familiar one ending with Beethoven's Fifth, which any fiddler who's been in the trade more than ten minutes can play in her sleep. Leni was the same size as me. The problem of her blonde hair was easily solved by renting a wig from one of those fancy-dress hire places.

Come Sunday, I simply arrived at the last minute (as Leni herself often did) to avoid having to mingle with 'my' colleagues. Seated in the obscurity of the back desk, my face bent over my violin, wearing the drab black dress which was the women's uniform, I was utterly indistinguishable from Leni. So confident was I in the success of the deception that I soon ceased worrying and simply enjoyed the deep sensuality of the famous Berlin Phil sound.

I was still reeling from it in the interval and was startled back to reality by a bony hand clamping down on my shoulder from behind. Before I could turn round I heard Karajan's voice: 'Too much vibrato, "Fräulein Fichtner". And try the little place on Nollendorfplatz. They do a better quality wig.'

Well, the story soon found its way into the Karajan myth. But only at the lower levels, and only among musicians. There was no way Dr Komarovsky could have heard it.

As Ahab and I cantered up the short avenue away from the mansion, my mind was a crazy cauldron of emotions: shock, puzzlement, and above all anger at Komarovsky's snobbery. I loved Bernard. He was one of my very best friends. I wasn't going to sit there and hear him belittled by this urbane foreigner who'd condescended to grace our little town with his presence.

By the time we arrived at Greenbank I was in a fury and Ahab in a lather. He was jumpy too, sensitive to my own confusion. To make matters worse our arrival coincided with a noisy spew from Bernard's drilling rig. Ahab took one look at it, did a furious little dance which almost unseated me and then stood stubbornly still, dream horse turned mule. I dismounted and whispered sweet nothings into his ears. Kate came running up the path. She's a round blonde fluffy little person and if the kids in our town weren't so well repressed she'd have terrible discipline problems at school. Right now her face was a mixture of excitement and anxiety. 'Let's take him round the back,' she suggested.

We walked him round the outside of the dry stone wall which encircled the Slaters' little patch of land. Inside it, Ian (also blond but neither small nor fluffy) was jabbing at some nettles with a big gardening fork and even more vigour than usual. Kate and I walked Ahab some more to cool him down. Finally we tethered him to a tree and left him, still sulking.

Greenbank was on its own near a narrow country road. It had once been a pair of labourers' cottages belonging to the Holroyd estate, but the Slaters had knocked them together to form a single house. Even so it was small: a toy house surrounded by a toy garden. Into this miniature establishment Bernard and Tim had driven their two enormous vehicles, one containing the drilling rig and the other the compressor. They'd had to knock down part of the wall to get them in. The spot Bernard and the diviner had chosen was near the front door, which made the rig look even more gigantic.

Bernard was standing on the footplate of the rig, one hand on the bank of levers which controlled the machine, the other on the rod which was slowly being pushed into the ground by the massive rotary head. Somewhere, deep in the ground, at the end of a succession of such rods, the drill itself was smashing its way through solid rock. The earth was vibrating. The noise was deafening. It sounded like the end of the world.

I loved it. All that power! Great chunks of heavy dirty machinery concentrating their forces on one four-inch hole in the ground. Technology zeroing in on the oldest myth of them all: Mother Earth wrapped around her treasure. The most precious material in the world. Water. Somewhere (I prayed) was the hidden mass of rock whose pores were saturated with the water it had been garnering for millennia. The New Age cults had got it all wrong. The myth was still there all right, but not in a ring of standing stones attended by dubious druids. It was here, at the end of a mucky drill, with Bernard bringing together the forces of man and nature.

I waved a greeting. He glared amiably (a talent unique to Bernard) and moved his hand to another lever. The decibels increased. Bernard does not like interruptions to his work. One misjudgment, one slip of the hand and the whole operation could be messed up. When Bernard works he's as hard as the stone, and that, too, I love. He was wearing a hard hat, big metal-capped boots and a waterproof jacket (in hope). His face was streaked with dirt.

He studied the dials on the panel, moved another lever and then signalled to Tim. With the noise so intense, they had a well-worked-out sign language. Tim moved to his own control panel on the compressor and turned up the pressure. The noise was terrific as the air forced its way down and began to push the pulverised rock back up through the hole. A few seconds later came the spew as, with a mighty roar, the debris shot out of the top of the rig.

Dust. Dark grey dust without a drop of moisture in it. It billowed across the garden, coating the plants, the wall, the front of the house. It fell on Bernard like a dismal rain but his face showed nothing of his thoughts.

The machinery was idling now as Bernard stepped down from his platform and went to the plate surrounding the borehole. On it was a heap of freshly spewed chippings. He had picked one up and was inspecting it. I sidled up to him.

'Shale,' he said non-committally.

'Is that good or bad?'

'Depends on whether it's fissured. If it is, it's a bloody great sponge just waiting to be tapped.'

'Otherwise?'

'Otherwise it's one of the worst materials there is.'

'Can you tell if it's fissured?' I asked.

'Not by the time it comes up – it's all like this.' He handed me the chipping. It was dark grey and smooth with nothing to say. Then Bernard smiled – a rare happening when he's at work and one which made me feel weak with relief even before he spoke. 'But there's a good chance it's fissured here, right by a fault line. The only question is whether we're on the right side of it.'

'How far have you gone?'

'Only twenty metres. I wouldn't expect water this soon.'

By the time I left, there was still no water but Kate was confident there would be. She'd retreated into the house and only occasionally hovered by a window to see what was happening.

As I rode away, Bernard and Tim were just fitting a new rod, clamping it on the pulley and then scrambling on to the rig to ease it into position. A switch of a lever and the rotary head once more started its slow journey down inside the mast, pushing the distant drill. I heard the roar of the motor and above it the sharp tattoo as the drill bit into a fresh piece of rock. Ahab pranced sideways, still unforgiving. Then we sped off home.

'Well, it's not *my* idea of a great day out,' said Maxine, puffing as we pedalled up a hill.

'Broaden your horizon,' I said. I could only manage the odd short phrase between gasps. Times like this I knew my age.

'Heaven knows how I let you persuade me.'

All the replies I could think of would take up too much breath so I just smiled encouragingly.

We were cycling to Greenbank. Cycling because I no longer had a car and Maxine couldn't borrow her dad's because she still wasn't speaking to him. So here we were, straining our guts out on a pair of old bikes to go and see a borehole. Well, yes, put that way it didn't sound too thrilling. Already I was having doubts about my plan.

The point is, Maxine had never seen Bernard at work. They only saw each other in his spare time, when (to my disgust) he played courtier to her princess. I wanted to replace that image in her mind with a new one in which Bernard was magnificently in control. Riding home the day before,

I'd had just such an image in front of my eyes: Bernard standing tall and princely beside his drilling rig, his face hard with concentration, his hand on the levers which made him master of the elements. Even the richest business tycoon couldn't come up with a scenario like that. Boardrooms just don't rate, not compared to all those tons of machinery and the strong hand summoning up the sleeping earth itself.

So I had thought the day before. Today I wasn't so sure. I sneaked a look at Maxine's face. The peaches and cream were rapidly becoming tomato. Her lovely head was crowned by a wreath of flies. So was mine. A rivulet of sweat was making its way towards my left ear. Our shirts were glued to our backs. Above us the sun gloated. Worse still, Bernard didn't exactly welcome an audience. He'd probably freak out when he saw Maxine. His hand would jerk. The drill would lurch off course, shriek to a disastrous halt. Oh God.

Kate was ashen when we arrived. 'Forty metres and still not a drop.'

'Only forty?' I said, trying to sound cheerful.

'They hit some hard stuff yesterday, it took ages to get through it.'

But I knew what she meant. Forty metres was as far as the all-in price went. After that, the customer had to pay extra for each metre. Ian and Kate could barely afford the well at all; every metre from now on was plunging them towards the poverty line. Bernard would know that too. It wouldn't improve his welcome.

We skulked round to the back with our bikes and went in through the kitchen door. The three of us (Ian was upstairs trying to work – probably he was saying incantations over the piggy bank, trying to turn the pennies into pounds) went to the sitting room window. It was filthy with the dark grey dust of all the spewings. We peered cautiously through the mist.

Bernard's face was as impassive as ever but I could imagine what was going through the mind behind it. Forty metres. Most of the wells he did had hit water by then. Was he after all on the wrong side of the fault? I'm not sure who I pitied most at that moment: the Slaters or Bernard. Bernard had never had a dud well yet; it would be a hideous blow to his pride and his reputation. As for the Slaters, I just didn't want to think about it.

I measured the rod with my eye. It was about halfway down. I saw Bernard give the signal, heard the increased decibels of the compressor. A moment later came the spew.

I turned from the window in disappointment. 'How about a cup of tea?' I chirped. I wanted to get Kate in the kitchen, away from the disaster. She went meekly enough, but just as I was about to follow her I glanced back and saw Bernard inspecting the heap of chippings at the base of the hole. There was something different in the way he was running his hand over it, and it seemed to me that the stuff near the top was a different colour. Just a new stratum, I decided gloomily. And went into the kitchen.

When we returned with our tea the rod was nearing the end. This was the time when they turned everything up full blast to clean out the hole. I was dreading it. Kate's knuckles were white; if she clutched her mug any harder it would break. Maxine's face was bored. I could have hit her.

The compressor was shrieking like a banshee, the motor was roaring like a lion with a dirty great thorn in its paw and no Androcles to take it out. The whole lorry was shaking. The earth, outraged at the violation, was taking its revenge. I expected the sky to darken and the heavens to fall, annihilating all us horrid little humans who dared to interfere with nature's secret works.

And then it happened. The sky did darken. With a tremendous resonance welling up from the depths and seeming to tear the earth apart, the spew came: a huge fat glorious juicy fountain!

There was a shriek from Kate. A second later I saw her rush through the front door. A streak of blurred colour which was Kate shot across the window and hurled itself into Bernard's arms. They were hugging each other as if they were the last humans on earth. Kate was sobbing herself silly while over her shoulder Bernard's face was split open in a grin which showed as a wild white crescent in his blackened face. Above them the rig continued to dump its thick grey stew all over them, turning them into statues sculpted out of mud. At their feet the stuff was oozing out, pushing itself slowly down the garden like a heavy grey lava from a volcano. Suppressing a shout of triumph I turned to Maxine.

Her porcelain features were contorted in a grimace, her immaculate eyes fixed on the mud spewing all over Bernard and Kate.

'Yuk,' she said.

EIGHT

'But Maxine,' I said, 'it's *always* like that. The rock gets pulverised and when it hits water it turns into a paste. It's *always* sludgy in the beginning.'

'Disgusting.'

'It's not disgusting. It's natural. It'll clear up in no time. They've just got to wait until the water table settles and then they'll pump the lot out and clean out the hole. If you hadn't gone off in a huff yesterday Bernard would have explained everything.'

'I don't want it explained. I don't want to know. Water comes out of a tap and that's that.'

I stared at Maxine, for the first time ever feeling a twinge of dislike. That pained me as much as the failure of my plan.

'Anyway, I don't know why you're trying to throw us together,' she added.

We were in the library. Already people were staring. I lowered my voice. 'You're right,' I said. 'I should be trying to keep you apart. Bernard deserves better than you.'

'Thanks.'

'You treat him like a puppy dog. All I want is for you to open your eyes and see him for what he is.'

'I saw him yesterday. Covered in mud.'

'That mud saved Ian and Kate from the poorhouse. Bernard's a hero.'

'Rah.'

'You heartless little bitch,' I hissed. I jumped up from the chair, grabbed a load of cards and went over to the catalogue to file them. I'd only managed to get one in, hands shaking with fury, when Maxine was beside me.

'I'm sorry,' she said. 'I didn't mean to be so snotty. Let's not fall out over this. Please?'

And I melted. Yet again I melted. No wonder Bernard was smitten. If a tough old nut like me can't resist Maxine's penitent eyes, what hope for Bernard? I mumbled my own peace offering, adding, 'I shouldn't be so pushy.'

'Well . . .' she said. 'It does rather feel like that. You on one side, Dad on the other.'

'What's he got to do with it?'

'He's pushing, too. "Fine young lad, Bernard," blah blah. "Promising career," blah blah. "Lotamoney in boreholes these days," blah blah.'

I stared. Then I clamped Maxine's elbow. 'Let's go to the courtyard. We've got to talk.'

'What about the desk? What if someone walks off with a bunch of books?'

'Let them. This is serious.'

We sat down at a shady table in the far corner of the courtyard. 'All right,' I said. 'How long has this been going on – your dad playing matchmaker?'

'Just the last few weeks. He's only just realised there could be big money in boreholes.'

'There isn't. Bernard and Tim are only just scraping by.'

'They are now. But Dad says they're bound to expand. Five years from now Bernard's going to be managing director of a big fat firm, says Dad. White collar at last. A bank of phones. That's the kind of son-in-law he'd like.'

'Oh, hell.' Worst of all, it was probably true. And the last thing Bernard would want was a bank of phones. He'd be miserable away from his beloved drilling rig and all the excitement of the moment when the water gushed, mud and all. 'Why didn't you tell me this before? I wouldn't have arranged that stupid trip yesterday.'

Maxine shrugged. 'You were so keen.'

I sighed. 'Believe me, Max, I'm not trying to play matchmaker. It's just that I'm terribly fond of Bernard. He's got me through a few rough patches. You learn to appreciate someone at times like that.'

She made an impatient gesture. 'It's all right for you, you've had your fling – ten years of it. I haven't.'

So that was it. I should have known. 'What exactly *do* you want?' I asked, though already I had a pretty good idea.

An irresistible smile. 'The usual. Excitement. Adventure. Romance – the real thing, not some boring tycoon with loadsamoney. The exotic. The mysterious. Foreign places. I'm terribly fond of Bernard too. But . . .'

But. She let the list go unsaid. But she didn't love him. But her face and the brain behind it were her passport out of Sedleigh and she wasn't ready to jeopardise her escape by forming too strong an attachment here.

That part of me which had first twigged to her potential had to admire her. What Maxine wanted was intangible, no amount of money could buy it. I had wanted it too at her age, and I'd gone out to get it. I was in no position to criticise. In any case, she was only a child, something I kept forgetting. All I'd hoped for was . . .

Well, let's be blunt. I'd hoped Bernard would be her first lover. Maxine was still a virgin, despite strenuous efforts by a string of schoolboys, young sailors from afar, salesmen passing through, hordes of summer visitors. Even the reps who filled her dad's farmyard trying to sell him the latest brand of cow cake were after her. It gave me the creeps. I was no Spanish duenna or Victorian nanny trying to protect my delicate charge, preserve her for the wedding day. But I did hope her first lover would be a good one (mine was), someone to remember with a nostalgic smile in her old age.

Viz Bernard. I couldn't imagine a more marvellous candidate for Maxine. He was handsome and intelligent. He was old enough to know what he was doing but young enough to be on her wavelength. Above all, he was the most decent human being I'd ever met. Whatever happened, whatever the course of their affair, he wouldn't hurt her, of that I was sure. But now I had to face up to the other possibility, something I'd wilfully turned away from until now: Maxine could very well hurt Bernard.

Love. Bah, humbug. I felt like Scrooge faced with a Christmasful of melancholy lovers. Why couldn't people just enjoy themselves? Why all this angst, tying themselves and each other up in knots of torment? There were usually warning signs if the imbalance was becoming too strong: too much love on one side, too little on the other. All you had to do was gently untie the rope before it moved up to your neck and strangled you. No harm done – with a bit of tact. But Maxine was too young to have learned the delicate art.

Briefly I considered whether I should tell her my thoughts. I decided against. My relationship with Maxine was a curious one and needed its own brand of tact to negotiate successfully. I was a variant of that useful figure, the worldly old aunt or friend of the family in cahoots with her against the stuffy old parents. She confided in me a great deal more than in her schoolfriends, but there were limits beyond which I knew I musn't go.

'Next time I barge into your private affairs like a hippopotamus, please will you just tell me to buzz off? Or less polite words if you wish,' I said. 'And next time your dad tries to turn you into a child bride, tell him ditto. Honestly! Eighteen! I could strangle that lousy moneybags!'

I rose to go. I'd seen a shape looming up by the desk. It was time to put on my professional cap.

'Attila?'

Her voice arrested my ascent.

'Bernard's asked me to go to the party with him. I said I would.'

'What party?'

'The well. Didn't Kate tell you? I saw her after the exam today – they're having a party to celebrate the well. I'm sure you're invited, they just haven't decided a date yet. Some time after exams are over.'

'What a lovely idea! A well-christening! I've never been to a well-christening!' I peered into the gloom. The shape at the desk was very large. It was turning round towards the courtyard and me. Already I could recognise the heavy grace in even so small a movement.

'What are you staring at?'

'We have a customer. I'd better go.'

She turned right around and scrutinised the distant desk. 'Ah.' Smirk. 'Yes, you'd better go.'

I clamped her wrist and put on my fiercest face. 'Listen, kid. You're too skinny to play the hippo. You barge into *my* private affairs and I'll tell *you* to buzz off. Dr K's a customer and I'm a librarian. Okay?'

She whistled a flippant little tune while gazing innocently at the sky. 'Okay,' she said with utmost insincerity.

I increased my ferocity. 'What are you doing out of your cell anyway?'

We rose together, Maxine to return to the cubby-hole in one wing which she'd fitted out as a study (a sign on the back of her chair read SORRY, I'M OFF-DUTY. ASK ATTILA) and I to my customer.

I suppose it was the relief I felt on having patched up the tiff with Maxine that made me forget I was angry with Dr Komarovsky. I swept behind my desk with a flourish and smiled at him. 'Sir?'

A low dark chuckle rumbled all the way from St Petersburg. 'Anna Atwill.'

'Sir, you have no book to check out. Have you an enquiry instead?'

'I do, Anna Atwill. I have the opportunity of some tickets to the last opera of the season at Leeds. Would you do me the honour? Of course I realise it's not Covent Garden . . .'

I stiffened. We were back by the yew hedge. His snobbery towards Bernard and all the rest of my life here. I put an edge on my smile. 'Don't mistake me,' I said. 'Some of the best operas I've ever heard have been at humble Leeds. But I'm afraid I have a prior booking.'

He raised a bushy eyebrow. 'I've mentioned no date.'

'Neither have I. I'm going to a party whose date isn't set.'

'A party?'

'Yes. Even here. Even here we raise the occasional roofbeam with a provincial knees-up, Dr Komarovsky. This particular knees-up is in honour of that boring – if you will excuse the pun – well. The one I was riding off to see the last time we met.'

The eyebrow came down. The eyes narrowed. I hadn't realised before how heavy the lids were. Voluptuous eyes, made for seduction. I felt my knees weaken and put my hands on the desk to keep from reeling before the intensity.

'You misunderstand me, Anna Atwill.'

He was terribly near, near enough to hear the thump of my idiotic heart. I wished someone would rustle some papers to drown it out. 'I hope I do,' I said.

I also hoped he would go away, fast. I couldn't hold out much longer. A few more seconds and I would revert to my old ways, do something uncontrollably insane. Like, unclamp my hands, place them on those swarthy cheeks, draw that big head to mine and kiss him with the quiet violence those hooded eyes demanded. Dear God, how could he do this to me?

Then he did something even more outrageous. He, with whom I was only on surname terms, wrapped a large strong hand around my wrist. It was the first time he'd touched me and I prayed that sheer will-power would keep me glued to terra firma. Still unblinking, those indecent eyes of his continued to tunnel right down into the core of my mind. I knew he was reading me loud and clear. I might as well have been naked at my library desk.

'You will tell me when you know the date of this party,' he said quietly. 'And I will take you to the opera on a day to suit your convenience.'

There was the faintest trace of a foreign accent in the workaday words, and that, too, plunged me back into my past, to a time when I did crazy things. Like –

'You will do that?' he said firmly, a question in the imperative.

I nodded dumbly. Me, big strong tough Attila, reduced to a floppy-eared little bunny rabbit nodding acquiescence to the stoat who was preparing to eat me.

He smiled. 'Good.'

Then he vanished from the library. I suppose he walked out like any other human being, but I didn't see him go. I was too preoccupied feeling behind me for my nice old chair. I sat down on it heavily and with a sense of danger postponed.

NINE

The day before the party Kate phoned. 'Anna, I don't know how to thank you! I'm not even sure we should accept. You really are marvellous!'

'It's great to be loved, but would you mind telling me what for?'

She laughed. 'Don't play dumb.'

'I don't have to. I *am* dumb. Kate, what exactly are we talking about?'

'The champagne, of course.'

'The what?'

'Don't pretend this isn't your doing. It was delivered this morning. A whole crate. Anna, I really am overwhelmed!'

'So am I: I didn't send it.'

Silence. 'Are you serious?'

'Never more.'

Another silence. 'Then who did?'

I did a quick flip through the possibilities. Ian and Kate's headmaster? He was a nice guy, but even headmasters (part of the aristocracy of our little town) didn't have that kind of money. The council? Kate was, like me, a councillor, our one-and-only Green. But our fellow councillors were as mean with their own funds as with the public's. Bernard? It was the type of gesture he would love to make but already I could hear him: 'Free champagne with every borehole? Nice idea, but more than our bank manager will bear.'

'Who indeed?' I said to Kate.

She laughed a little uncertainly. 'I suppose I'll just have to start believing in fairy godmothers?'

'Looks like it,' I said.

* * *

The night before the party Dr Komarovsky phoned. 'I believe we will be attending the same party tomorrow. Will you permit me to take you there in my car?'

Again that faint trace of an accent, the slight formality of syntax. A man with a headful of words in several languages, always juggling. And again that resonant voice that knew its place in the world: everywhere. At least this time it was disembodied. My knees held without too much difficulty as I said primly, 'Mother told me never to accept lifts from strangers.'

'We are hardly strangers, Anna Atwill.'

'Almost. We're only on surname terms.'

There was a startled silence. Then a rich warm wonderful ripple of laughter surged along the telephone wires. 'Anna. Will you permit Dmitri Mikhailovich to take you to the party?'

'Depends on his car.'

'This Cinderella is fussy about her pumpkin. Will a BMW do?'

'Nope. You'll never get it up the hill. Seriously. These are crazy little streets with hairpin turns. Minis only.'

'I'll manage.'

He would, too. 'Why don't I just walk to your house, meet you there?'

'You insult my driving ability.'

'No I don't. I just like to walk. I would have walked the whole way, otherwise. One of the joys of being a country bumpkin.'

Something funny happened to the telephone wires. They went all heavy and serious and a stern voice at the other end said, 'Anna. You are not a country bumpkin. No one knows that better than I.'

'Don't believe everything you read in the papers,' I quipped. It was a desperate attempt to avoid the message in his words and it failed, as most desperate things do. I tried again, 'My crazy days are over, Dmitri Mikhailovich. I'm a middle-aged provincial librarian. If you wish to play Prince Charming tomorrow night, I'd love to be your Cinderella. But I will walk to your house.'

I walked. As I did, I mused on the reasons for my stubbornness in this as well. (I had never contacted him about the opera either.) The car-hating terrain of my neighbourhood was only an excuse. Dmitri Mikhailovich was one of those omnicompetent people, he would almost certainly persuade even a BMW to do his will. But it was true that I liked to walk. I'd sold my car after Edmund died and there was no longer the fear of Needing It For An Emergency. It was no sacrifice. I'd quickly discovered that I could get nearly everywhere I wanted by foot or hoof. I'd greeted my long-lost legs like old friends and put them to work again. They liked it and so did I. There's something uniquely free about foot power. You're not dependent on a mechanic or the whims of a prima donna engine. There's no iron curtain between you and the outside world.

Right now the outside world was stunning. June was, as the old song had it, bustin' out all over. Even the ashes, as stubborn as me, had finally added their greenery to the wood's palette. They and all the other trees were competing like mad for their own niche in the colour chart. I wondered if anyone had ever counted the shades of green possible in this world. It seemed likely that most of them were here right now, surrounding me in this magic mini-forest.

I opened my arms to the soft early evening air and whirled a few paces down the path. I stopped, dizzy with the simple pleasure of colour-in-motion. Only then did I notice that I'd added my own speck of green to the festival: a loose-fitting mossy dress.

And suddenly, a memory of another occasion when I'd worn it flooded in with the overwhelming force of something so long forgotten that it builds up behind the dam unnoticed, just waiting for its opportunity to burst. Another forest, another lifetime. Bohemia, a beautiful piece of woodland in the heart of Czechoslovakia, where I'd gone for one of my music research trips.

Past and present fused and for a fraction of a second I felt muddled, unsure of where I was. That's all it was: a fraction of a second. But in it I could feel the beginning of something I wasn't sure I welcomed: a dissolving of boundaries between this little woodland and its grander brother in Bohemia, between the countries themselves, and between my own past and present. I'd told Dmitri Mikhailovich that my crazy days were over, and yet here they were, crowding my memory and disturbing the small peaceful existence I'd established for myself in Sedleigh.

My thoughts and my feet together had brought me to a clearing. It was at the centre of the wood and in it rose the spring which never dried up. A long time ago there'd been a hermit's hut here, no doubt because of the spring, but it had long ago disappeared. Instead, the spring itself had been made into a bit of a feature. The water emerged from a cleft in a tumble of rocks to be channelled into a small stone spout which then directed it into a little pool. The pool was the beginning of a syke meandering its way to the cliff and hence into the sea. The rocks and the sides of the pool were covered in moss, but further away the ground was taken up by an ever-changing display of flowers unplanned by Sydney Holroyd or his gardener. Tonight's invisible gardener had chosen a pink and white and blue scheme in defiance of the greenery surrounding it. Campion and ragged robin glowed a deeper pink in the lowering sunlight while stitchwort and pignut tried bravely to stay whiter than white. Swathes of speedwell played at being blue streams cutting their way through the other flowers. A blackbird sang, his clear beautiful tones amplified by the natural acoustics of the forest. There had been blackbirds in Bohemia, too.

I shook the thought away and looked at my watch. I

was early. I didn't want to appear over-eager. There was a big smooth mossy rock beside the pool. I laid a cautious hand on the moss and felt the bristly dry texture of several rainless weeks. Satisfied, I sat down.

The trickle of the spring made a counterpoint to the blackbird's song. It was too tempting to resist. I leaned forward and, cupping my hands, filled them with the fresh cool water. I should have known better. En route to my lips, some of it splashed on to my dress. Oh hell, what did it matter? I filled my hands over and over and drank deeply, letting the water drip off my chin. I was no debutante keeping her fragile beauty intact to make a grand entrance at the ball. And I didn't give a damn what Dmitri Mikhailovich would think of my splodgy dress.

And then I saw what I'd been evading all evening: the real reason I'd insisted on walking to his house. Nothing to do with twisty streets or even the joys of walking. It was simply a foolish attempt to right the balance between us. Somehow, and so gradually I hadn't noticed, an imbalance had crept in, giving him the upper hand. There was something earnest beneath his amusing manner, and his enigmatic remarks were adding up to a statement I could no longer ignore. He was interfering with my life in a way that could have serious consequences. Just as the memory of Bohemia had invaded the peace of the evening, Dmitri Mikhailovich was invading my peace of mind. The worst of it was that part of me wanted just that. But what would happen when the six months were over and he vanished from my life again? My emotional muscles were showing signs of age. I couldn't be sure they would spring back to life-as-normal this time. I didn't think I should risk it. The tiny crazy acts that had earned me my nickname were one thing. They were limited to spheres under my control: the library, my music group, mad gallops on Ahab. Dmitri Mikhailovich wouldn't be satisfied with anything on that scale.

I rose from my stone feeling distinctly disgruntled.

* * *

From somewhere inside the old mansion a clock was striking eight. I'd gone round to the front of the house as befitted the formality of the occasion. Dmitri was sitting on the stone banister at the bottom of the steps, looking – as always – completely at home.

He smiled. 'I didn't expect such Prussian punctuality from you.'

I smiled back. 'Then you must have been preparing for a long wait outside.'

'On such an evening, where better to wait than here?' His hand described an arc taking in the sweep of parkland in front of the house.

'In that case, why not prolong the pleasure? Let's walk to the party.'

His hand dropped and a very small frown appeared on his forehead. 'Your appetite for walking is voracious.'

'Not at all. We rustics take walking for granted. When one lives in the country, one adapts to country ways. One walks.'

He fixed on me a long shrewd look which exposed both the lie (rustics never walk) and my foolish little plan of battle beneath it. I could see him calculating all the moves and countermoves like an experienced old chess player. Finally he said, 'And if I refuse?'

'Please drive slowly when you pass me. The road is rather dusty after so long without rain.'

I don't know what I expected, but not the big spontaneous roar of laughter that burst from him. 'Very well, Anna Atwill. But on one condition.' He lifted himself gracefully from the banister and crooked his elbow. 'That you take my arm.'

I should have known. It was always like that with Dmitri, right from the start. Even when he lost, he won. He should have been a diplomat.

I took his arm and together we walked down the sycamore

avenue to the road. It was then that I first noticed the paradox that became so much a feature of my relationship with him. On the one hand, the feel of his arm under the thin summer shirt maddened my senses and made me greedy for more. That simple touch contained such a superabundance of eroticism that I needed a matching superabundance of will-power to prevent myself from ravishing him on the spot.

On the other hand . . . nothing could be more natural than walking down a country road arm in arm with Dmitri. He was my father, my brother, my best friend. We had known each other for ever and shared the easy intimacy of an ancient friendship. I never could think straight when I was with him. The thinking always came later, when I would brood and see in every gesture or word some significance that didn't bode well for me.

We walked into the sun most of the way. It turned us into red-gold giants and cast equally immense shadows behind us. On either side the fields had been mown for silage. The cut grass exuded the intoxicating smell of summer, more potent than any perfume. The hedgerows were a tangled mass of flowers and weeds continuing the battle for supremacy they'd begun long before humans arrived on the earth. The land was vibrating with lusty energy and so was I. I wanted nothing more than to drag this magnificent man off into some scented secret corner and resolve at last the delicious tension which was tearing me apart. Instead, we chatted of inconsequential things. Like old friends. Quite a few cars passed us en route to the party. Everyone offered us a lift. No one seemed too surprised when we declined.

We arrived at Greenbank to a Green councillor's nightmare: a row of parked cars seeming to stretch to the horizon, all tilted nervously towards the ditch, pulling their sides in from the traffic. The section of wall Bernard had had to demolish to get his machinery in had been repaired.

Inside, several virtuous bicycles were propped against it. We were, of course, the last to arrive and came just as Kate was explaining, probably for the fiftieth time that evening, how the well worked.

'Well, yes, it *is* artesian, but only just. It goes up and down depending on how much rain there's been. Right now the level is about three metres down.'

The crowd of people stared at the concrete inspection chamber which was all that could be seen of the miraculous well. It was further hidden by a prosaic cast-iron manhole cover. The scene was both comic and touching.

Some distance away Bernard was trying hard not to be the star of the show. It wasn't easy. Even if he hadn't been the magician who'd conjured out of the ground the water we were celebrating, he would have stood out in any crowd. His height was only part of it. He was wearing a cream-coloured shirt which made his weathered skin look even more rugged. The out-of-doors was truly his element, and never more so than this evening.

Even Maxine had noticed. She was on the other side of the crowd, talking with her French teacher, but her glance kept straying towards Bernard and his towards her. She was dressed with the devastating simplicity that only very beautiful women can manage, in a plain white cotton dress without a speck of ornamentation other than the gold cascade of her hair.

Kate caught sight of us. 'Anna! Dmitri!'

I was a little startled at her use of his first name. I hadn't even thought to wonder how he came to be invited to the party. A table had been set up beside the well. On it stood the few glasses that weren't already in the hands of the guests. Several champagne bottles protruded from a bucket filled with ice against the cool north wall of the house.

The first sip was heavenly. The second was pretty good, too. 'Not only champagne but *good* champagne,' I commented. 'You still haven't discovered who sent it?'

'Nope. But who are we to question the gods?'

'Quite.'

All this time Bernard had been making his way towards us. It was slow progress, as he kept being detained by people asking him questions about the well. I could see he was flustered. Bernard's a one-to-one person and not entirely happy with crowds. He's also by nature modest and all this attention was fidgeting him. I was all the more surprised, therefore, when his troubled face cleared on reaching us and, after greeting me, he put out his hand towards Dmitri like a ship seeking anchor.

'Dmitri, it's good to see you!'

My jaw dropped. 'You know each other?'

Kate's head swivelled round in surprise. 'Didn't Dmitri tell you? He was here on the Great Day.'

'What Great Day?'

'The first pumping, of course. When Bernard lowered the pump into the well. It was marvellous, Anna, I do wish you'd been here! Of course we knew the water was there, but it was such a thrill seeing it come up. We pumped for an hour – to clean out the gunge and test for quantity – and all the time it kept coming clearer and clearer. And at the end we all gathered round to have the first tasting.'

I stared at Dmitri. 'You?'

'Sheer good fortune,' he smiled. 'I just happened to be passing by on my walk at the crucial moment.'

'On your *what*?'

'Walk, Anna. When one lives in the country, one adapts to country ways. One walks.'

What was he playing at, my enigmatic Russian prince? Once again the ground shifted beneath my feet and I was thrown into confusion. I'd assumed that Dmitri didn't know anyone in town except me. I'd pictured him secluded in his Gormenghast writing furiously except for occasional forays to the library. I'd taken for granted that I would spend much of the evening introducing him to people.

No way. Turns out that he regularly lunched at the café where Sara, a sculptress, worked part-time. He bought sour cream at Ken Fyfe's tiny deli. He'd early discovered that the best fishmonger in town was Tony Markham and had become quite chummy with him as he worked his way through the repertoire. He took his clothes to the launderette owned by the Lamberts and had a coffee with them while he waited. He'd met Laurel, Maxine's French teacher, walking her dog on the beach. He'd met Gillian, a frustrated writer who worked as a clerk at Barclay's, in the first week he'd been here. He'd even met Josh, my violist, at his music shop and Josh hadn't bothered to tell me. They were all here, and more. I watched Dmitri moving smoothly among the guests, charming the hell out of everyone.

We didn't meet up again until quite late into the party. It was a good party. Everyone felt celebratory, genuinely pleased at the happy ending to the Slaters' water problems. A few years ago it was something that wouldn't have aroused much notice, but we'd had several drought summers in a row. Hosepipe bans now came early in the year and everyone was relieved that so far we'd avoided the dreaded standpipes. So water was on people's minds, and since Kate and Ian were so well liked there was a general feeling of relief that their chronic water crisis was now at an end.

The champagne helped too, as did the wonderful weather. The same weather that was depleting the country's water supplies was at least enjoyable to be in. The earth was soaking up so much heat these days that it gave it out again long into the evening. Kate and Ian had provided a lovely buffet inside, but everyone filled their plates quickly and rushed out again to enjoy the continental pleasures of al fresco. The tiny garden surrounding the cottage was awash with people, their light summer clothes fading into ghostly garments as the last remnants of daylight finally gave up and turned the lighting effects over to the moon.

It was a full moon and the air was so clear that I could see the shadows on its face. I was sitting in an absurdly pretty little bower Ian had concocted against the back garden wall. Ian was a genius of a gardener. He'd crammed his tiny patch full of goodies and now looked covetously over the wall at the fields owned by Robert Vesey. Thwarted, he concentrated his energy on devising ways of fitting still more plants into fewer spaces. The bower was a particular success. He'd covered it with old-fashioned roses chosen to give a rich succession of flowers, all of them the most highly scented varieties he could find. The result was indecently sensuous. I'd come here for a quick dose of quiet after several hours of non-stop party chatter. I'd felt a bit dizzy from too much talk (well all right – too much champagne as well). Now I felt dizzy with the onslaught of so many scents. The warm evening air was coaxing the fragrance from all the flowers and concentrating it in a great swirl around my head. I breathed it in greedily while watching the shadows on the moon.

And then another shadow. 'May I join you?' The deep voice wafted into the bower. A moment later its owner joined it and sat beside me. I'd barely seen him all evening, or rather, had seen him mainly at a distance. I didn't see him now either; I was too hypnotised by the moon and the heady fragrance filling the bower. I could hear him breathing it in too. Then he said, 'Does it make you nostalgic for Bulgaria and the Valley of Roses?'

I was in too much of a trance to query his knowledge. My mind drifted dreamily into the months following my visit to the Valley of Roses. I'd gone on from there to the Rhodope Mountains on another of my research trips. The Rhodopes were famous for their singers, as was the whole of Bulgaria. Orpheus was said to have come from the Rhodopes, and it took little imagination to hear the tremulous echoes of his music on the mountain peaks and in the trees and rocks he sang to. The Bulgarian government had exploited its reputation for music as much as the roses. I was there on a government grant to study (and, they hoped, publicise) the ethnic music of its most remote villages. The peasants couldn't believe that an experienced western musician, a graduate of the Royal College of Music, had anything to learn from them. They couldn't have been more wrong.

A burst of piano music erupted from inside the cottage and snapped the thread of my revery. I suddenly saw that Dmitri was beside me and that my champagne glass was tilting at a dangerous angle. I righted it and took a sip.

And suddenly the bubbles in my head gathered together in one concentrated point and I saw something that should have been blindingly obvious right from the start. I took another sip, this time looking hard at Dmitri over the rim. 'It's wonderful champagne,' I said. 'You have excellent taste. Not to mention a large bank balance.'

He spread his arms in that continental gesture of mock helplessness, then smiled. 'It will be our little secret, Anna.'

I nodded agreement. What's life without a few small mysteries? Like a valentine, so much more thrilling for not knowing the sender. 'But why?' I asked. 'When I saw you before you were utterly scathing about the borehole. Now you're sending a crate of champagne to celebrate it.'

He shrugged, still smiling. 'You think I am too old to learn?'

The words silenced me. That part of me which burned with the memory of his belittling of Bernard's work made me long to give a waspish reply. But there was something new in his voice. The protective barrier was down. Only a heartless monster would attack him now.

Before I could think of a different reply I was being propelled gently towards the house. Both doors were open and the inside of the house was dimly lit so as not to clash too severely with the moonlight outside. Gillian (the frustrated writer) was messing about at the piano in the sitting room. She was clearly very drunk and her efforts were depressing the spirits of the people now drifting indoors from a night suddenly gone chill. She looked up at Dmitri with an inane smile on her face. Then, as if he'd transmitted a message, she slid off the piano bench and vanished into the crowd. Dmitri gestured me towards it. 'Please.'

I stood where I was. 'What makes you think I can play?'

'It would be a very stupid graduate of the Royal College of Music who couldn't improvise at the piano,' he said. 'Please.'

I sat down at the piano bench. Dmitri whispered to me the title of a song. He even stated the key in which he wished it to be played. Even as I protested, my fingers began to search out the key. Then, after a nod from Dmitri, I began an improvised run-in to the song. A moment later the room was filled with his voice.

'*Deep river, my home is over Jordan* . . .'

Deep river, deep well, and deeper than them all, Dmitri's voice, resonating from every crevice of the room. It was a wonderful voice, untrained and yet practised. It suddenly occurred to me that Dmitri had a life of his own away from our town, a life in which this kind of improvisation might well be a normal feature. There were Russian émigré drawing rooms in that life, no doubt a balalaika or two. Dmitri was slipping into his past and drawing me with him.

The room had gone quiet as soon as Dmitri began. Now one or two people twigged to what he was doing and chuckled at his little joke. Dmitri himself was smiling. Next time round he came right out with it:

'*Deep river, my home is under Greenbank* . . .'

The chuckles became widespread now, mingling when he finished with a tumult of applause and cheers. There were cries of 'More! More!' Dmitri's face as he bowed to his audience registered surprise. He didn't fool me. He knew exactly what he was doing. In that one simple gesture he had consolidated his popularity. From now on he would be an accepted feature of our town. Everyone would greet him in the streets, he would be invited everywhere. But why? Why did he want this?

The cries of 'More!' were increasing. He placed his big hand on my shoulder, leaned down and whispered again. I tried to shoot him a knowing look, let him know I knew what he was up to, but it came out rather shaky. Not until that big warm paw left my shoulder again could I think straight and begin fumbling for the tune. Already I felt apprehensive, and even before his voice began the first words of 'The Volga Boatman's Song' I could feel myself weakening. Of all Russian songs, one of the most clichéd. And yet, one of the most evocative. If he'd sung it in English it wouldn't have happened, but the moment the first mournful Russian syllables filled the room I felt my heart tighten and had to concentrate hard simply to keep playing.

What the sound of those syllables did to Dmitri I didn't know, but they transported me back into the rose bower and from there into the Rhodope Mountains again, to the language that was so similar and to those magnificent Slav basses no other countries could rival. As Dmitri's voice rumbled through the small sitting room, I heard superimposed on it the voices of all those Bulgarians who had sung and played their music into my tape recorder and into my heart. Dmitri vanished and I heard instead the bass who had been the acknowledged best singer in the village, smelled the pine resin rolling down off the mountain slopes, saw the broad smiling faces of another audience. I had loved that village. No one had warned me that Bulgaria, so small in world affairs, would be so large in welcoming a stranger. It had been the most terrible wrench when my time was up and I had to leave. I had still been weeping when I arrived at the railway station in Sofia.

It took me a while to realise that something was wrong. The Slav syllables that had evoked my memories were no longer there. Nor could I hear the sound of the piano. There was no sound at all in the sitting room. I looked down at my stilled hands. There were tears on them.

TEN

You have good reason for tears, my Anna. You have given up too much for too long. You have wrenched up your roots and like a feckless plant thought to find sustenance in an alien soil. I don't deny that you have flourished – for a while. But now your roots are growing again, burrowing deeper into a soil that is not by itself enough.

No doubt you think me cruel to urge on you these memories of a time long gone. What is the saying? – I am cruel to be kind. My position, too, is difficult. I came to you with a mission imposed on me by my father. My intention was merely to fulfil that mission with – I hoped – some efficiency and kindness. How was I to know that you would tug at something deep in my own memory? It was not my intention to love you, Anushka. I am far too old for that kind of nonsense. Affairs, yes, but always with the understanding of a time not too long distant when there will be a sad but needful good-bye. I admit that when I first saw you in that ridiculous library, I thought to myself: yes, an affair. Six months. Two for an amusing little cat-and-mouse game, four for the affair itself. I understood within minutes that you were one of my kind. It would be a good affair too, and make my time in Sedleigh pass most pleasantly.

Who ever discerns the moment of change? Not I. It was, after all, quite unexpected, and certainly unwelcome. Perhaps the moment when you urged that horse of yours to spring away from me, angered by my slighting words about your friend? For I knew it was more than anger that spurred you away from me that morning. It was fear. I had touched your past, that mountain of living memory that you have for so long reduced to a heap of anecdotes, catalogued and classified like your wretched books to keep them in place. You sensed then, I'm sure of it, that if only one of those memories escaped and grew again, the placid little life you have built for yourself would be threatened.

Risk it, Anna. It's not too late. But it will be if you wait too long.

You resent my interference. Very well: I resent yours. I came here with one mission and you have given me another. I, too, had a placid existence to protect, filled with books and ageing friends. And now I have on my hands instead a volcano who pretends to be a provincial librarian with a penchant for walking. 'Rustic' indeed.

Do not think to treat me lightly, Anna. I will walk you off your feet and worse. Just as Orpheus sang the rocks to life, I will sing you back to the life you had thought to relinquish. You have wept for me already. I will make you weep much more. If you close your heart to what I offer you, they will be bitter tears indeed.

ELEVEN

After the party I avoided Dmitri. The emotions he stirred in me were too turbulent a brew: lust, anger, sadness ... and fear. He had some kind of power over me that I hadn't experienced before and I wasn't sure I liked it.

It was easy to avoid him in the library. While Maxine waited for her A-level results I was kept busy training up her two replacements. 'I suppose I should be flattered,' she said. 'Am I really twice as good as anyone else?'

Probably. But the main point was that with our long opening hours a staff of two was precarious. It only took a touch of flu to dump the whole load on to the remaining person. Surprisingly, the Library Board agreed. I asked Maxine to scout among the younger sixth formers for 'a deserving case' and for the other chose a sterling middle-aged woman whose children were finally off her hands. It made sense to train them together but it did mean I had little time for chats with Dmitri.

Maxine alternated between gracious co-operation and melodramatic gloom. 'Now I know how Hamlet's dad felt,' she said one day.

'Eh?'

'His corpse barely in the ground before his wife remarries. The funeral meats used for the wedding feast.'

'You do come out with some odd notions, Maxine.'

'Well, I might flunk. I might need this job. And here you are, training my replacements before I'm in the ground.'

'I think you're mixing your metaphors. Anyway, you said you did well.'

'I might be wrong.'

'People never are when they think they did well. It's only when they think they did badly that they're sometimes surprised. What's got into you, Max? It's not like you to mope.'

'Limbo blues.'

'Well, limbo yourself over to the catalogue. Nancy's floundering among the Smiths, I can tell it from here.'

When I wasn't run off my feet at the library I was busy with my group. It was the wedding season and we were increasingly in demand. We'd already done two in June and early July and were now rehearsing for a third.

The music group, like Ahab, entered my life at the time I came home to nurse Eleanor. My parents knew I'd get restless if I didn't keep busy and so they urged me to do something with my music. I thought they were daft. The kind of music I was into could hardly be more incompatible with an English seaside town. Much of my time abroad had been spent studying ethnic music, mainly in east European countries, mainly funded by governments anxious to promote a good image. Sometimes I'd been able to use BBC and record company contacts to get a hearing for the music (and some western currency for the countries involved). Mostly, though, I'd simply learned, absorbing the music into my bones. It was wonderful stuff, much of it rough and wild, beautifully suited to the peasant weddings which were its primary outlet.

'I think Sedleigh is a little staid for that kind of thing,' I told Eleanor.

'Don't be so sure.'

As usual, she was right, though it took some years for Attila and Her Huns to catch on.

Our line-up was a movable feast, depending on the comings and goings typical of seaside towns and depending also on who was available for a particular gig. As we improvised everything we could be pretty flexible. One instrument more or less didn't matter.

At the moment we had a typical Romanian line-up: violin, viola and double bass. Why they lugged a double bass around (they marched with their wedding processions) when they could at least have used a cello was something I'd never understood. But that's the joy of ethnic music: it is what it is, take it or leave it. We also had an accordion when Bert felt inclined to join us. The accordion is not my favourite instrument, but in Bert's hands, and combined with the others, it sounded a completely different thing. As it happened, the accordion was a recent addition to Romanian music too, one disapproved of by purists. But we didn't care for purism. In any case, one of the things I'd learned was that there was no such thing as 'pure' anything in traditional music. People just used what they had to hand and they had different things to hand at different times. Our method, such as it was, was simply to make ourselves at home in all the rhythms and devices of ethnic music regardless of origin, combining them as the mood suited. The result was a glorious muddle, extremely exciting to listen to and irresistible to the feet.

The people of Sedleigh were wary at first. Weddings, they felt, were solemn occasions, however happy, and solemnity was not our strong point. But finally a pair of local painters (they would be, wouldn't they) decided to take the plunge. Their wedding dance was a spectacular success, raved about for months afterwards. It wasn't long before one or two other bold candidates came forward. The rest, as they say, is history.

We rehearsed in a church basement. Lewis, the double bass who had been with us right from the start, was a Charismatic Christian. When he wasn't playing with us he was part of the folk group which played for their church services. The church group was of course more respectable than ours, but Lewis even managed to insinuate a bit of the wildness of our music into his fellow Christians.

The vicar didn't mind at all. In fact, he was delighted. He was a madly energetic young man who'd specialised in smutty madrigals at Cambridge before (as he put it) 'God got me.' He was also, I suspect, secretly hoping we might convert, but he didn't seem too disappointed when none of us did. Sometimes he sat in on our rehearsals. Sometimes he recommended us to parishioners about to be married. Few took us up. Our customers were mainly arty types with registry office weddings.

The church was a nice one, on the same side of town as the library but about halfway up the hill. Behind it rose a pleasant churchyard where we sprawled among the tombstones for our breaks when the weather was good.

It was good now. We'd still had little rain, but the night before there'd been a splendid thunderstorm which had lit up the sky for miles around. It was mostly sound and fury, signifying little in the way of rain, but at least it had cleared some of the mugginess and left the town feeling a bit fresher.

Even so, we were stripped as far as decency would permit as we rehearsed. Music is hot work at the best of times and our kind of music is particularly hard on the sweat glands. We had doors open fore and aft, but the breezes that wafted through made little impact as we galloped through the dance which was to be the *pièce de résistance* at the next wedding.

Through the years we've perfected a sort of programme. We open with a fairly lively piece which gets people in the mood. After that we alternate between fast pieces and slow ones used as breathers for the people who are by now dancing. What they don't realise, however, is that as the evening progresses, both fast and slow pieces accelerate in tempo.

Our final piece is the sneakiest of all. It's roughly (very roughly) based on a Romanian fertility dance called the *călușar* but we've pepped it up out of all recognition. None the less, it still begins in a tempo stately enough to make the dancers feel they can just about manage it. By this point in the evening they are, of course, exhausted and more than a little tipsy, but the *călușar* is just too enticing to resist, and few do. Once they're out there on the floor, I keep an eye on things and at the right moment nod to the other musicians. Instantly we slam the music into another key, a faster tempo and sometimes another rhythm as well. The dancers are startled but too caught up in the music to stop. As soon as they've settled into the new tempo, I nod again, and again the music lurches into something new and faster still. The dancers follow us, over and over, as we jack up the music and accelerate the tempo. By the end of the piece (and it's a long one) the tension is screwed to breaking point and the pace so frenetic that the dance floor is nothing but a whirl of colour. It's Bacchanalian stuff, no doubt about it: frenzied, wild, totally uninhibited.

And then, suddenly, with absolutely no warning, we pull the plug. The music stops abruptly at the height of its madness, leaving behind a shocked silence. After that there is usually pandemonium, with shrieks of 'More! More!' But we never give an encore. Never. That much I learned from years in concert halls. A well-planned programme should build up to leave the audience on a peak gasping for more. Any encore, however good, is inevitably an anticlimax.

We're inordinately proud of our *căluşar* and tinker with it endlessly. It was this that we were rehearsing when the vicar slipped into the church basement and pulled up a chair near the door to catch the breeze. His feet tapped vigorously and I wouldn't have been at all surprised if he'd suddenly shot to his feet and started to whirl about the floor.

We were nearing the end, sweating like pigs and barely in control of our instruments. As we lurched into the next tempo, Lewis gave a yelp of excitement, just as the Romanians often do. I was grinning away, sawing like crazy and hoping the fiddle wouldn't slip away from the sweaty chin that clamped it in place. I could feel trickles meandering down my face, my fingers were damp and groping desperately for the absurd quantity of notes they were having to find. My upper arms were wobbling most unattractively and I didn't care, all I cared about was the manic music.

Suddenly the doorway darkened. I looked up to see the familiar shape of Dmitri Mikhailovich nearly filling the space. He leaned against it with a cool casualness which maddened me. The light was behind him and so I couldn't see the expression on his face, but I imagined him scrutinising us much as a music critic might. I made my face fierce, willing him to leave, but the ferocity was too much in keeping with the music for him to get the message. I didn't want him to be there. Emphatically I did not. He had come too close, the night of the party, seducing my memory with music. If I must see him at all I wished it to be in the calm neutral atmosphere of the library. Above all, I did not want him trespassing on my music.

I nodded furiously, a little earlier than usual, and we screamed into the final phase of the dance. I was taking it out on my fiddle, rasping away at the strings and making them deliberately harsh and frightening. But this too was in keeping with the barbaric nature of the music. In any case, Dmitri took no notice of the message I was trying to convey. He continued to lean against the door post, arms folded neatly across his chest, observing.

The music was whirling in and out of major and minor keys so fast it made me dizzy. In the final few bars it went hysterical. Even within the impossible last tempo I was playing just a little bit faster with every note, pulling my hard-pressed group along with me. And then, at the moment of consummation, on the very last note, I scraped the string so violently that it broke. I'd flung my arm wide on that note and it remained suspended, high in the air, in the shocked silence that followed. A moment later the vicar was applauding wildly. Dmitri condescended to unfold his arms and join in the applause.

We bowed to our audience of two. I smiled at the vicar and nodded curtly at Dmitri. Then I turned to the others. They were looking a little shaky. 'You don't half push it, Attila,' said Lewis, wiping his face with a huge handkerchief that was already soaked. He was as big and burly as his double bass and must have shed gallons during that piece.

'Sorry, Lewis,' I said. 'The heat.'

He raised an eyebrow and I knew that he knew it was not the heat but the ominous form of Dmitri. The whole affair was so monstrously preordained. I knew I had no choice, and that lack of choice was one of the things that maddened me. The time would come when Dmitri and I would be lovers and everyone in Sedleigh seemed to know it. Like our *călușar*, the tension increasing with each passing day.

'We'll have to have our break now,' I said, looking at my dead string.

'Well, thank God for that!' said Josh. He was a small wiry Londoner who'd come straight from the Royal Academy of Music to Sedleigh for a summer gig at the Spa. He'd liked it so much that he'd stayed. In time he'd taken over the town's sole music shop and now spent his days selling pop records to adolescents. His true love was string quartets but there weren't exactly a lot of those in Sedleigh and so he'd drifted into our group instead. Like so many violists he was rather timid by nature, but through the years he'd got used to the pace our music required and rather liked it. Even so, I sometimes forgot that the viola, larger and more cumbersome than my fiddle, had to work harder for the same effects. 'I'm sorry,' I said. 'We'll take it a bit easier on the night.'

'Don't you dare – it was great! Anyway, they'll be so drunk by then they won't notice I'm only playing half the notes.'

'You old fraud!' I laughed.

We filed out of the church. The vicar, deep in conversation with Dmitri, raised a hand in greeting as we passed. I ignored Dmitri.

Outside the air felt wonderfully fresh compared to the fug we'd created inside. We trailed up the slope and flopped down on the grass among the tombstones. I got out the spare string I always carry with me and began to replace the one I'd just broken. We talked, in a desultory way, about the music we'd just played, about the wedding it was destined for, about the perils of busting a string mid-concert. One of Josh's had gone in the middle of a piece last year and he'd managed to transpose the rest of it on to the remaining strings. It was a triumph of professionalism of which he was very proud.

It wasn't long before the vicar and Dmitri appeared outside the door. They shook hands and then the vicar went round to the other side of the church and disappeared. Dmitri made his way up the slope towards us. As I'd known he would. He never seemed to appear anywhere by accident. There always seemed to be purpose behind it.

He greeted us and then lowered himself on to the grass beside me. As I'd known he would. I busied myself with the string.

'Wonderful music,' he said to us all. 'Thank you for letting me listen in. Where does that dance you were playing come from?'

'Nowhere in particular,' I said evasively. 'We pick up bits and pieces from everywhere and cobble them together. Very disreputable.'

'You told us it was Romanian,' said Josh.

'No Romanian would recognise what we've made of it,' I said.

After that I managed to steer the conversation on to other things. Not until we were on our way back to the church did Dmitri find an opportunity to resume his questioning. He did so by stopping and taking in his hand part of the necklace I was wearing. I was obliged to stop too.

'Is this also Romanian?' he asked.

It was. Of course. It was also a sensitive subject which I had no desire to discuss. The necklace was extremely flamboyant and not even all that attractive. It had been given to me not by one of the villagers where I'd worked but by a townswoman for whom I'd been able to do a small favour. Years later she'd been shot during the revolution. I always wore the necklace for rehearsals and performances. I needed it – to remind me not to trivialise or romanticise the music, to make me remember the realities of the cultures I had raided for inspiration.

Dmitri had gone too far this time, using the necklace as a means of prying open my past. I gave him a deadly smile. 'Why ask? I'm sure you know the answer. You seem to know everything about me. What's your source: the KGB?'

If I hoped to offend him I failed. A peal of that lovely deep laughter rang down the hillside and he said, 'Before my time, my dear.'

His laughter irritated me, acting as a goad. 'I don't think it's at all amusing. You come here – a complete stranger – and start making mysterious allusions to my life. You make it quite clear that you know a great deal about me but you refuse to tell me how. I think I have a right to know. I think it's time you told me.'

The laughter was gone but his eyes were still dancing with amusement. 'My dear Anna. I thought you'd never ask.'

I stopped again and stared up at him. 'What?'

'For six weeks now I have been waiting for you to show some interest in the connection between us.'

'What?'

'For six weeks I have been throwing out "mysterious allusions" – as you put it – and wondering just how long it would take before one of them would finally strike home.'

'What?'

'For six weeks I have marvelled at the obtuseness and stubbornness of my old friend –'

'Your what?'

'– and waited for her to stop this foolish cat-and-mouse game which she plays me.'

I stood there, speechless, as rooted to the earth as the tombstones around us. My mind was whirling, searching for 'the connection between us' – yet another of his mysterious allusions and one which floated above my head, unreachable. I felt I must be going slightly mad. Either that or it was Dmitri who was unhinged. What on earth?

'You wish to know the source of my knowledge?' He smiled. 'I will tell you. But first' – he took my elbow and steered me towards the door where my colleagues were waiting – 'I suggest you continue with your rehearsal. You have waited for six weeks. I think you can wait an hour or two longer.'

TWELVE

Typical. To dangle the carrot in front of me and then, a few seconds away from my grasp, to whisk it away again. And *he* accused *me* of playing games?

The rest of the rehearsal was a letdown. Partly it was because we'd worked on the *căluşar* too early; after that, the other music sounded almost tame. The vicar had gone home for his supper. Only Dmitri remained, sitting in the chair by the open door, listening attentively. Josh and Lewis seemed to like his presence. They kept asking his opinion. His responses were surprisingly acute. That irritated me even more.

I left Lewis to return the key to the vicarage. Then Dmitri and I started home. Now that the time was approaching I felt unaccountably nervous. A whole host of crazy possibilities flitted through my mind. Most of them were disagreeable. I wasn't sure I wanted to know after all. Sometimes not knowing is a good thing. When Dmitri began to question me again about Romania, I replied freely this time, quite pleased to delay the moment.

'It was a long time ago,' I said. 'I didn't know then what a shit Ceauşescu was. I don't think many people did. Even the Royal Family was still courting him – you know, the one friendly communist, independent of Moscow.'

We passed by the entrance to the library in which Maxine was doing the evening shift.

'All I knew was that the economy was in a mess. I'd never seen such crushing poverty. It was a little better in the rural areas – always is. At least the people had enough to eat, more or less. They certainly didn't have much else.'

We waited at the traffic lights to cross the quay.

'People always think it must have been marvellous to spend all that time in so many different countries but it had its negative side too. Helplessness. There was so little I could do to help. And hospitality, that was almost the worst. It's always the same: the less they have, the more they offer.'

We crossed the quay and a few moments later were on the bridge. Above us the seagulls soared and cried. A ship was coming in.

'The Romanians had nothing and were the most hospitable people you could imagine, and not just in the rural areas. Towns, too. I suppose that's why I never went back after that first stint. Too painful. Cowardice, I guess.'

We began the climb up the hill on the other side, Dmitri quiet and attentive at my side.

'Romania was the worst, but other eastern bloc countries were difficult, too. I always felt uneasy. Aware of the discrepancies. Between my life and theirs. Between the beauty of the music I was recording and the ugliness of so much of their daily lives.'

We turned into my street.

'It was always such a relief to flit back to Berlin or Paris or London after one of my stints, do something simple and straightforward. Like busking. I loved busking. You meet some fascinating people, busking. Or taking a temporary job in an orchestra. Or teaching. Dmitri, there's not a lot in the fridge but I can just about scrape together a meal if you're not too fussy.'

We had stopped outside my front door. 'The less they have, the more they offer?' he said.

'Don't mock. I've had an easy life. So have you.'

My hand was shaking as I unlocked the door. I hoped Dmitri wouldn't notice. If I was nervous of hearing what he had to tell me, I was equally nervous of letting him into my house. The house was my shell, the one place in the world over which I had some control. It was clear to me that Dmitri wasn't someone who could be controlled. But the damage was done already, had been from the day he'd first entered my library. No wonder I'd been so frightened of him – attracted but at the same time frightened. Not just finding out something he shouldn't but also disrupting the well-ordered life I'd carved out for myself.

Well, here it was: my life, displayed in every single object with which the sitting room was crammed. I watched apprehensively as he walked through it, looking at the paintings, the books, the little piano, the rugs, the mass of mementos scattered about the place. I hurried him through as best I could. Wherever it was that he would tell me what he had to say, I hoped it would be away from all this.

The patio. We would eat on the patio.

In the kitchen, I flung open the French window. Outside was the small table and a solitary chair where I ate many of my summer suppers. I rushed out to the shed and fetched a second chair, placing it enticingly at the table. He appeared not to notice. He was wandering round the kitchen, looking at all the bits and pieces with which it too was crammed. At least they were fractionally less personal than the things in the sitting room. He stopped for some time in front of the old grandmother clock whose tick had accompanied my entire life.

'Danish,' I said. 'Not particularly valuable but very nice, don't you think? After the war my father sometimes accepted goods in lieu of payment. That particular Dane was desperate to buy a painting my father had but he was skint. Edmund kept the clock and paid the painter out of his own pocket.'

I took from the fridge a chunk of leftover roast beef and the remains of a flan reeking of garlic and boobytrapped by bits of chilli lying in wait for the unwary. I reminded myself to warn him. There was also some leftover potato salad jazzed up with herbs and spices from the garden. Garden. I would make a lettuce salad. I would also dig up some horseradish root and make some fresh sauce for the beef. On the threshold I hovered, then turned back and grabbed a bottle of wine. I handed the bottle and corkscrew to Dmitri.

'Would you mind? So much nicer when someone else does it.'

When he poured the wine into the glasses I had fetched, I said, 'Wouldn't you like to sit outside while I get things ready? Such a lovely evening, shame to be inside.'

No, he was quite happy inside. I sighed and went out again, leaving Dmitri to soak up my life. I rammed the spade into the earth and dug up the split-off piece of horseradish. Too late I realised how long it would take to clean and peel and grate the ridiculous thing. I should have left it. You don't *have* to have fresh horseradish sauce with cold beef, millions of people manage quite nicely without. Why do I never think ahead? I glanced inside, wondering if by some miracle he hadn't seen me and I could quietly dump the thing and forget about it.

He paused en route to the fridge and smiled straight at me.

I came inside and began washing the root. Dmitri had parked himself in front of the fridge and was looking at the clutter on top of it. It included a small sculpture and a jar of mock orange. Its scent filled the room. Then his glance rose to the little watercolour above the fridge ... and stopped. He put his hands on the fridge and leaned right over to peer at the picture, nearly knocking over the flowers. He stared so long and so hard I began to feel nervous. Nobody in town knew how valuable some of the stuff in my house was. Their ignorance was my burglar alarm, so to speak. Dmitri might well guess. I would have to ask him to keep quiet.

I was just about to open my mouth when he said, very softly and more to himself than to me, 'I had no idea you had this.'

It seemed an odd remark. 'No reason you should,' I replied.

'I had no idea it existed at all.'

Odder still. 'Well, you wouldn't, would you? Hardly anyone knows it exists. It's just a private piece, it's never been on the market.'

He was looking at me very strangely now, a half-smile on his big gorgeous face. Above it his eyes were dancing with amusement. 'Come here, Anna.'

I lifted my mucky hands. 'Now?'

'Now.'

I rinsed and dried them quickly and went over to the fridge. We were standing side by side, facing the fridge, about two or three feet away from each other. What happened next made the hairs on the back of my neck rise. Dmitri turned me round to face him and placed my hands on his shoulders. Then he put his hands on my shoulders. He nodded towards the painting. We were now standing in the same position as the two children in the picture.

'Look, Anna,' he said quietly, with the softest and gentlest of smiles. 'Even then. Were we not a fetching couple? Even then?'

What on earth was he talking about? I looked at the children, their arms linked like ours, floating effortlessly, dreamily, over the sea, away from the family picnic taking place in the tops of the trees in Eleanor's garden. The whole picture was done in quick light strokes, the faces of the people unidentifiable. One could just about discern a dreamy half-smile on the face of the black-haired little boy, but the features of the girl – so young – were just an impressionistic blur. Only the bright red hair identified her as me, and then only to people who knew –

Red hair. Black hair. My mind did a lightning calculation. The boy in the painting. About twelve years old? And myself two? Dmitri was – And I was – No – It couldn't possibly –

I stared at Dmitri, at the dark hair and the dreamy half-smile. Looked back at the picture. Back at Dmitri. I opened my mouth with effort. 'You're not saying . . .'

'Did you never guess?'

'But –'

'Anatoly Leskov. My uncle.'

'Your –'

'My mother's brother.' He was watching me closely now. 'Did your parents never tell you who the people in the picture were?'

'I don't – Not really. I didn't really ask. No, I did ask once, I think. Eleanor was rather vague. "Some friends passing through," she said. I think she was very busy, cooking, she was rather preoccupied. I never thought to press.'

Dmitri pointed at the adults in the picture. 'Your parents you know. The other man is my father.'

Still linked to Dmitri, I leaned across the fridge. The man's features were just a fraction more definite than those of the children. And yes, now I could see they were Slav.

I heard, as from a great distance, someone laughing quietly. It was me. I closed my eyes and listened to the laughter grow. It was sapping my strength, my legs had gone rubbery. I disengaged myself from Dmitri, turned round and sank to a chair by the kitchen table. My laughter was louder now and I detected a trace of hysteria in it.

'Are you all right, Anna?'

I nodded and noticed that my head felt weak, too. I propped it on my hands, leaning my elbows on the table. And laughed. Dmitri had moved to the chair opposite and was watching me across the table, his face full of concern.

'Are you sure you're all right?'

The concern, on his face and in his voice, touched me. My laughter subsided. I reached across and patted his hand. 'I'm sorry. It's just that –'

What could I say? That at the moment of revelation I'd realised that this – Anatoly Leskov – was the source of Dmitri's uncanny knowledge. That at the same moment I'd felt flooded with relief that this was all there was to it, to the thing that had been gnawing away at me for weeks. That I'd been imagining the most extraordinary possibilities and never once thought to look so near to home.

My voice picked up my thoughts. 'Just that I've been imagining the most extraordinary things . . .'

'What things?' he said quickly. He had changed again and was now watching me very closely indeed. '*What* did you think?' he said.

But I was in control of myself now. Now that I knew his knowledge had so harmless a source, I had nothing to fear. Anatoly Leskov had been one of my father's lifelong clients. What could be more natural than Edmund, through the years, mentioning bits and pieces about his daughter's travels. True, it was a little odd that Leskov should bother to pass such trivia on to his family. And then again, not so odd. I'd known Leskov slightly myself and remembered how gregarious he was, a passer-on of amusing anecdotes from his own life and those of others. Clearly mine had supplied a fairish number. Like the trick I'd tried to play on Karajan. As the pieces fell into place I became calm again.

'Nothing very important,' I said. 'Come on, let's eat.'

THIRTEEN

We were sitting at the little table on the patio. As soon as my panic had subsided I'd felt ravenous. Dmitri was a hearty eater too. We ate our way greedily through the cold beef, the flan, the potato salad, the lettuce, then moved on to cheese and fruit. We drank our way through one bottle of wine and opened a second.

Ahab, posing prettily for us in the paddock, grew redder and redder as the sun set, then slowly moved through the shadowy spectrum that would finally blot him out. The garden was awash with fragrance, the mock orange competing with the sweet briar and a few remaining lilac blooms adding their bit. There was a slight breeze pushing the scents about so that they reached our noses in unexpected puffs.

'Anatoly worshipped your father,' Dmitri was saying. 'They took to each other right from the beginning.'

'I remember him slightly. An open sort of person, good-natured.'

'Yes, but shrewd. And as the years passed and he learned what a rackety business the art world was, he appreciated Edmund all the more. You don't mind, do you, if I call him Edmund?'

'Do. I always did. He didn't like any of the names children usually call their fathers. He preferred to use his own. Eleanor, too.'

'Did they?' he said quickly. 'Did they ever say why?'

'No,' I said, suddenly cautious again. 'Just that they were rather older than usual when they had me. I suppose they found it just that bit harder to adapt to childish terminology.'

'They seemed extremely old to me on the day of the picnic.' Dmitri smiled. 'But then, they would. Anyone over thirteen seems ancient to a twelve-year-old. And anyone under eleven deplorably young.'

'Was I a pest?'

'Awful. A hyperactive little demon. The worst of it was that the adults lumped us together as "children" and expected me to keep you amused while they talked. It was the only time I can remember when I longed for my sister to be there.'

'I didn't know you had one.'

'A bit younger than myself. Even she was too old for you but would have been a better playmate than I was.'

'Why wasn't she there? For that matter, why not your mother?'

'My sister was ill and my mother stayed at home to look after her. In any case, it was something of a male expedition. Anatoly had just acquired a sort of patron, a wealthy businessman with an estate in Scotland. He invited Anatoly up for some shooting. Why my father and I were invited wasn't clear. But Anatoly thought it would be amusing to break the journey at Sedleigh and spend the night here. I think he had some business with Edmund as well.'

'You stayed with us? I don't remember that. In fact, I don't remember the picnic either.'

'It would be odd if you did. You were very young.'

'And yet, when you walked into the library I had such a strong feeling that *I knew you*.' I leaned across the table earnestly. 'It was the most extraordinary sensation, Dmitri. Not exactly *déjà vu* but a more general sense of knowing. And stranger still, I felt sure that *you knew me*.'

He laughed that wonderful bass laugh of his. 'Well, now you know: I did. Though I can't pretend that I recognised you. If it hadn't been for that violent red hair of yours . . .'

'But why didn't you *tell* me?'

'I did, more or less. You didn't show any interest.'

As simple as that. All my convoluted speculations and foolish worries. I need only have asked. 'I did ask how our fathers came to know each other – later, in the courtyard,' I tried.

'And I told you. At least, I told you part of it.' And here his face, darkening in the setting sun, took on an enigmatic look.

Immediately I was cautious again. On some level I was still deeply suspicious of him, wary of probing. It was absurd, and yet it was so strong that I felt powerless to prevent it. 'There's more?'

'Yes, Anna. Do you want to know?'

He was so serious that I suddenly felt frightened. I preferred him to be flippant and amusing. But this time I felt I couldn't back down. My cowardice would diminish me in his eyes and I couldn't bear that. 'Of course I want to know.'

He smiled. 'That day of the picnic, Anna. It wasn't the first time we'd met.'

I was puzzled. 'You mean in London, before that?'

'Think, Anna. When did Anatoly become your father's client?'

Now I felt impatient. 'Well, obviously before the picnic. They'd known each other since –' I broke off. Now I knew why I'd been so cautious. Dmitri was pushing my memory too far back, to places I didn't want to go. There was no retreating. 'Since Berlin,' I said calmly. I smiled disingenuously. 'Of course! But Dmitri, why didn't you just say so? Do you really mean we've known each other since I was a baby?'

He nodded. 'I wasn't sure you wanted to remember.'

'But there's nothing to remember – I was just a baby. You can't expect me to . . .' I trailed off, uncertain just what he did expect.

'I expected you to react that day when I told you I was born in Berlin,' he said, as if reading my mind. 'After all, so were you. Don't you think it rather strange – the two of us sitting in the courtyard of your library, both of us born in Berlin, and you didn't even mention it? I assumed you had some reason.'

'Not at all,' I said lightly. 'It's not something I'm ashamed of. People are born all over the place. My parents just happened to be in Berlin at the time. It makes no difference. I'm as British as they were, for what it's worth.' He was scrutinising my dark face, my dark eyes, my unruly hair, my high cheekbones. He knows something, he knows something, I thought, my panic rising. But the next moment he was smiling and I wasn't so sure.

'Of course,' he said. 'I wasn't questioning that. I simply thought it strange that you didn't mention it.'

'I expect I just forgot. Or the conversation took another turn.'

'Of course. I'm sorry. I read too much in it.'

'I expect you did.' I smiled. 'Well well. So we've known each other a very long time indeed. How extraordinary. And to meet again in Sedleigh of all places! I'm sorry I was such a brat the day of the picnic. Is it too late to apologise?'

His laughter rang out across the patio and startled Ahab. 'My dear Anna, much too late. And more fool me for not recognising you in the library. I should have known a bolshy child like you would become what you've become. I was deceived by hearing that you'd turned yourself into a librarian.'

'So it was Anatoly who told you all about me.'

'It was my father he told. I took very little interest. To me, you never grew up. You were still the horrid little brat I remembered and of no particular concern to me.'

'I'm still a little surprised that Anatoly took such an interest.'

'He worshipped your father,' he said again. 'They spent quite a bit of time together. Naturally your father talked about you. You must admit you've had a colourful life . . . until now.'

I ignored the slur. 'I suppose I have.'

'And your father was terribly proud of you.'

'I suppose he was,' I said quietly. That was another area I didn't want to think about too closely. Edmund had been dead for some years now, but I still missed him.

'Terribly proud,' Dmitri went on. 'He could see that you were exceptionally talented, even as a child. As you grew older it was clear that you could become a serious musician. He was afraid of that, you know. He was afraid you would feed yourself into the virtuoso mill and turn yourself into a violin-playing machine.'

'He never told me that.'

'He didn't want to influence you. He wanted you to choose freely. But he knew enough musicians to know how soul-destroying the life can be and how narrow-minded musicians can become if they're determined to claw their way to the top – there's no time for anything else. He loved your spirit, Anna. As do I.'

'You're very generous – especially as I ruined your picnic.'

He smiled. 'I exaggerate. You weren't *so* terrible. But you can imagine how pleased Edmund was when you turned away from the treadmill and took yourself off to a wanderer's life instead.'

'Yes, I did know that. My parents were always so supportive. Other parents were pushing their kids into a steady future. Mine never seemed worried that I wasn't doing the orthodox thing. I went my own way with their blessing.'

'For a very good reason: your "own way" took you where they hoped you would go. To Europe, to the continent. They had been worried that you would become too English. There was a real danger of it – living here in such idyllic surroundings. They had their reasons for moving to such an out-of-the-way place, but they did wonder sometimes if it was the right decision. Your life was so comfortable here . . . as it is again.'

Again the slur on my present life. And again I ignored it. 'Well, they did their best to counteract it. Eleanor especially – teaching me her languages. She must have known I'd be itching to go somewhere to use them.'

'And you did,' Dmitri smiled. 'And I hope you will again.'

So that was it. Suddenly I saw where he had been leading me all these weeks, digging into my past and bringing with him memories I had taught to be quiescent.

'I see,' I said, looking straight at him now. 'So you're my parents' self-appointed successor. That's why you've come. To push me off my primrose path and back on to the rocky road?'

'That's not why I came. But when I saw how narrow your life had become . . . and compared it with all the stories Edmund used to tell Anatoly . . .'

My anger was rising, an anger born of disappointment. I didn't want a guardian or a father-substitute, however well-meaning. I wanted a lover. Even now, knowing he was too deeply implicated in my past to be safe, I longed for him. He had never looked more desirable, his large powerful shape darkening in the darkening evening. That achingly familiar posture of the confident continental. The wild bushy hair indifferent to fashion. And his dark eyes that seemed to see right through me and made me want to dissolve the boundaries that made of us two separate people.

'Thank you for telling me this,' I said calmly. 'I appreciate it. Now I know where I stand. Now I can be equally frank with you and save you wasting any more of your time. I have no intention whatsoever of going back to my old life. I'm far too old for it.'

'You're in your prime, Anna.'

'Sedleigh was good enough for my parents, and it's good enough for me. Does it occur to you that you're doing exactly what they refrained from doing? Pushing. You said yourself that Edmund didn't want to influence me in any way. I'd be grateful if you'd follow his example.'

'You weren't so stubborn then. He didn't have to push.'

I could feel my hands clenching. 'You're right. You're absolutely right. I *am* stubborn. I have stubbornly chosen the life I have here and I stubbornly intend to stick to it.'

He always did the unexpected, my Dmitri. Now it was a raising of his hands, an easy shrug of the shoulders, a smile. 'As you wish, Anna. The decision is yours.'

And with that, he let me go.

For the rest of the evening we took care to avoid sensitive areas, controversial subjects. We amused each other with anecdotes and laughed a lot. When he left, he kissed me lightly on the forehead. I – equally lightly – loaned him a torch and told him to beware of wolves in the forest.

But as soon as the door shut behind him I crumpled in a heap on the floor. It was an astonishing thing for me to do and the flood of emotions which followed shocked me even more. At the heart of it was an overwhelming sense of loss. His departure, however light-hearted, had suddenly left a terrible vacuum, a monstrous black hole. I wanted him back – that was my first coherent thought. What would happen after that didn't matter; I simply wanted him back to fill the horrible emptiness.

But that didn't explain the emptiness itself. Though I'd lived alone for years, I'd had plenty of visitors. Friends regularly came for meals – Bernard, Maxine, members of the music group, all the odd people of the town whose interests coincided with mine. There were weekend visitors, too, though not so many: the occasional cousin from London, people I'd been at music college with, people I'd worked with in London and elsewhere. None of them had left this gaping emptiness when they went home.

I picked myself off the floor and went to one of the big armchairs in the sitting room. From here I could see the whole of the room, filled with all the mementos from my parents' lives and mine.

And then, very slowly, it began to dawn on me. That kiss on the forehead, just as Edmund used to do. He'd kissed me like that just before he'd died. And this monstrous black emptiness Dmitri had left behind, that wasn't new either. I'd felt it before, when Edmund died.

In all our talk of Edmund that evening, the one thing I hadn't told Dmitri was that I'd killed my father. I didn't regret what I'd done. If I had the same choice again, I would make the same decision. But even now it's not something one can talk about freely, and not a memory I wished to revive.

Edmund had been devastated by Eleanor's death. Though both of us were grateful it had come soon enough to prevent too much suffering, we still felt her absence terribly. It was worse for Edmund, of course, and though I tried to make his last years cheerful I knew that a daughter, however loved, was no replacement for a wife.

My parents had been unusually close. It had been as near-perfect a marriage as one could imagine. They were wonderfully matched in intelligence, enthusiasm and a sense of mission. They even shared each other's interests, both of them immersed in the artistic life of Europe. Had they worked in the same field, conflicts might have risen, but even here they were fortunate, having separate but compatible areas in which they specialised. They had married young and had a long life together before I came on to the scene. That they loved me was never in doubt but it was inevitable that I, the late-comer, could never be as fully a part of their lives as they had been to each other.

I knew all this. We talked freely about Eleanor, keeping her alive in our minds. But she was still, inevitably, not there in our lives, and I think Edmund was almost pleased when he discovered he was terminally ill.

'It's time,' he said, and though I didn't want to believe it, on some other level I knew he was right.

We lived through the first months of his illness in relatively good spirits. Edmund was grateful to have been given notice, so to speak. He was a methodical man, however much he loved the seemingly unmethodical canvases of his artists. He wanted to tidy up his life, say his good-byes, leave nothing left unsaid and everything in order. This much at least I could help him with, and did.

Later, when the pain began, it was Edmund who broached the subject. 'I want to die with dignity,' he said. 'You do know what that means?'

I wasn't sure. I hoped he meant a hospice, assuming we could find one with a vacancy.

'Not a hospice,' he said.

And I knew he was right in that, too. If it had only been a matter of controlling the pain, Edmund might have consented, though I knew he would prefer to die at home. But even if hospice help could be provided at home, that wasn't what he wanted. Because the disease that was eating up his body was moving towards his brain, and that was the one thing he couldn't bear: to become a non-person, to cease being Edmund. And that was the one thing a hospice couldn't prevent.

It wasn't difficult getting the pills. Our doctor was very understanding, even if he didn't understand why I wanted them. My reasons were plausible enough. After all, I was looking after an increasingly helpless father all by myself. Though I was, as the doctor said, 'a big strong girl', my sleep was inevitably broken by Edmund's constant needs. The bags under my eyes when I asked for the pills were real. My only fear was that he wouldn't give me enough. But he did, and when I showed Edmund the bottle, the look of relief in his sunken eyes told me I'd done the right thing.

We planned it very carefully. The first question, and the most difficult, was when. Should he wait until his mind began to go and let me administer the pills during a period when he didn't quite know what they were? It would mean that he would live out his conscious life fully, wouldn't miss anything from it. The alternative was to take them while he was completely *compos mentis*. I wasn't at all sure that was a good idea. I was afraid his mind would sabotage him, remind him of what he was leaving behind, perhaps even inject into him an unexpected fear of the death he was consciously bringing about.

And yet I couldn't help feeling proud of him when he chose the latter. It took courage to do that. I'd always known he was a strong man but it wasn't until he made his choice that I realised just how strong. He was going to leave life knowing exactly what he was doing.

After that it was just a matter of details. He wanted me to be away that night to avoid the possibility of criminal prosecution (in principle I could be charged with murder). I pointed out that my absence would be far more suspicious than my presence. This was true enough and convinced Edmund, but my real reason was that I refused to let him die alone. The image haunted me of Edmund utterly alone in an empty house, taking his pills and thinking his thoughts, with no one to share them, no one to comfort him. It was out of the question. I'd rather go to prison than let that happen.

As the weeks passed without Edmund mentioning a day, it occurred to me that he might have changed his mind. Perhaps after all he wished to let me administer the pills when his mind began to go? It would be reasonable, and I certainly wasn't going to raise the subject if he didn't.

They were, as it happened, weeks of great interest to us both. It was the autumn of 1989, when all the countries of eastern Europe one by one rose to accomplish their astonishing revolutions. No one was more surprised than I, despite my experience of these countries. I longed to be there but didn't want Edmund feeling he was keeping me away from the action.

I had brought a radio and our tiny television into Edmund's room. Day after day we followed the news. I bought all the newspapers, read out the details. They were heady days, even for us, far away in Sedleigh. Our great regret was that Eleanor wasn't here to witness it all. She was in spirit a Central European, and now at last this great divided heart of Europe was coming together again. She would have been so happy. She also would have been cautious, foreseeing the dangers ahead. We imagined her here with us, providing the commentary lacking in the official reports. We imagined her presence so fervently that it was almost as if she were indeed here. Never had we been so close as a family as during those exhilarating days of change.

Changes were taking place in Edmund, too. The painkillers were beginning to be less effective, he had occasional lapses of attention which frightened us both, but he was so eager to see what would happen next in eastern Europe that he couldn't bear to leave. I could understand all too well. Romania was in turmoil. No one knew what was happening, but that anything was happening at all seemed a miracle.

Then came the amazing day when we switched on the lunchtime news and instead of the familiar blips heard music followed by the voice announcing that the Ceauşescu regime had fallen. I had never experienced such unadulterated joy. Edmund, too, was ecstatic. When he recovered sufficiently from his excitement, he smiled. 'Anna, it's time.'

I had a bottle of champagne waiting. Well, why not? Should one not go in style? The pills would be more effective taken with alcohol and it seemed right to have the best.

I stayed with Edmund the whole time. We drank a toast to the new Europe. Then he began to take his pills. We had given much thought to the sounds he wished to die to. He had chosen a Beethoven quartet. We listened peacefully to the music. I had no idea when the moment would occur but hoped it would be during the sublime slow movement, the *Heiliger Dankgesang*. It was the most ethereal music I knew, transporting the listener to realms utterly unknown on earth except to Beethoven, who was, I often thought, not quite of this earth himself. It would be a suitable end.

I held Edmund's hand all the while, releasing it only when I had to get up and start the record again. I asked him if he had any thoughts about what was happening, if he wanted to tell me about them. 'You mustn't go alone,' I said to him. 'I'll be with you as much of the way as possible.' But he had thought about it so much in advance, and we had so often talked it through together, that there was little left to say.

There were no dying words, no attempts at final profundities, for which I was glad. Any summing-up would have been trivial, and my father was not a trivial man. His whole life had been his statement. He had sought the good, the true, the beautiful. Often he had found it, and when he did, he nourished it to the best of his abilities. No one could do more.

It was during the *Heiliger Dankgesang* that he seemed to fall asleep. I didn't know if it was sleep or death, but I didn't want to disturb it. When the music finished I remained seated by Edmund's side, my hand over his. Finally his hand began to grow cold and I knew. Still I didn't move. I stayed with him all through the evening and the long dark night. I stayed with him through much of the morning, too. I wanted to be quite sure that no well-meaning medic would try to wrench him back to a life that was properly finished.

When finally I phoned, the doctor was extremely understanding. I explained that I had taken a sleeping pill and badly overslept. The doctor assured me that Edmund had died peacefully, that I had no reason to reproach myself for not being with him. I will never know if he guessed but I'll always be grateful for his tact.

There were no tears until after I had scattered Edmund's ashes in Eleanor's garden, as he had wished, to mingle with her own. Only then did I come into the empty house and understand it to be empty for ever.

FOURTEEN

Now the house was empty again. It shocked me that I could make such a comparison. It was demeaning to Edmund's memory. Further, Dmitri's departure was only temporary. He was returning to London for a fortnight to look up some references available only at the British Library. 'Even your estimable institution has its limitations,' he had said.

So what's a fortnight? I'd lived without him for over forty years, I could manage another fortnight.

But I didn't fool myself. I knew why, as the days of absence passed, I was becoming increasingly ratty. Panic. Disguised panic. Dmitri was giving me a preview of the future. This was how I would feel when our six months were over and he went back to London for good. Our affair hadn't even begun and already I could see the end. I didn't like it, not one bit. I'd been right after all; I was too old for this kind of thing, my emotions were stiff with disuse, too inflexible to spring back into shape with the ease of the past.

Well, I was warned. The only way to avoid future pain was to forego present pleasure. I would give him up. If he objected, too bad. It was easy for him. It always was for men. Especially an old roué like him. In his absence I painted him black. He was a world-weary old reprobate preying upon gullible women, breaking their hearts and then flitting back to London. Well, I wasn't gullible. I knew his type. Scoundrel, cad, libertine, blackguard, rapscallion – all the rich old words defining his type tumbled through my mind. I ran through the vocabulary and emerged refreshed and determined and strong.

For five minutes. Then I remembered his deep gentle voice, the ponderous grace of his big reassuring body, the sense of being enfolded by his rich warm laughter and sunny smile. I longed for him. Without him I was an empty shell, hollow and reverberating with my own loneliness.

Was I lonely? I hadn't been until then. I'd thought my life a full one: work, music, friendship, beautiful surroundings, the lovely Ahab. What more could anyone want?

Dmitri, that's what. He had exploded into my peaceful existence and gone, leaving behind a huge crater. He had opened up the dam I had built between my present and my past. He'd revealed behind it an oceanful of deep waters and then left me to flounder in them alone.

How could he do this to me? I fumed and spluttered and raged. I wanted him to be here so I could rage at him. Instead, I raged at everyone around me. I knew even as I was doing it how unfair I was being, but behind the dam, lurking in the waters, was a sea monster over which I had no control. I snapped at our accordionist for missing rehearsals: did he have to choose this of all times to have his appendix out? I bit off the heads of my two trainees, one right after the other. 'Ignore her,' Maxine said to them. 'She's just sexually frustrated.' I bit Maxine's head off, hard. The ghost of my namesake took over. Attila the Hun was on the rampage.

The crunch (literally) came one sultry Saturday. I was on my way home from the last rehearsal before our gig that night. The rehearsal hadn't gone well. Our accordionist was still away and we were all sweltering in the heat. Sweaty fingers slipped off strings. We sounded terrible. I couldn't believe we were actually going to play that night. We would be disgraced, the wedding ruined.

I stomped down the steep twisty road from the church. Near the bottom was a small cottage owned by old Mrs Eccles and coveted by several developers who'd been trying to buy it off her for years. It was a prime site where the little road joined the quay but Mrs Eccles refused to budge. She and her cat were determined to live out the rest of their lives there. The cottage was a mess – 'a disgrace to the town' said several of the primmer members of the council. They were right, but I rather liked the old woman, despite the fact that she lived on a diet of light romances of the type I loathed and resisted all my attempts to wean her on to something a little more nourishing. She was a stroppy old bird, and her cat – an equally ancient tom – was one of the more colourful characters on the quay.

Right now the cat was preparing itself for a stroll along the quay to scrounge tidbits from the day-trippers. I watched him rise, arch his back in a luxurious stretch and begin to amble across the road. I could hear a car behind me, going very fast. I stepped aside just in time.

The cat didn't. There was a screech of brakes but not for the cat; the car had gone on unconcerned only to find itself suddenly at the junction with the quay. The car stopped just in time to avoid knocking over a couple of teenagers.

I looked at where the cat had been. All I could see was a crunched mess and a spreading pool of red.

Then the red was behind my eyes. Through it I saw the back of the Mercedes and the back of the driver's head, a salon-blonde concoction which even from here I knew would have every hair in place.

Without thinking, I ran towards the car. It turned (more squealing of tyres) and headed for the car park along the quay which I thought a good deal more unsightly than Mrs Eccles' tatty cottage. Someone yelled – whether at me or at the car I couldn't tell – but I kept on running, my beady eye on the target. I saw nothing but the red film before my eyes and the back of the odious car. People were dodging out of its way only to have to dodge again as I stormed along the quay in pursuit.

I hardly saw them. My mind was filled with images of what I would have to do: go back to the cottage and break the news to Mrs Eccles. It wouldn't be easy – she was crazy about the old tom. I would have to comfort her. To do that meant I would have to prevent her from seeing the mess which was her deceased cat. To do that I would have to remove the cat and bury it myself. To do that I would have to borrow a shovel to scrape the cat off the melting tarmac. Oh damn damn damn.

The car turned into the car park. I turned into the car park. A voice yelled my name. I ignored it, watching the immaculate white Mercedes neatly back into a parking space. I was closing in on my target now and I could see her, equally immaculate in a white summer dress, getting out of her car. I saw the star on the bonnet. I considered wrenching it off but that would be too refined. I needed an act of violence as meaningless as the one that had killed the cat. There was only one thing to do. As I approached the car at high speed, I raised my right hand and channelled all my strength into the fist which would crash down on to the gleaming white bonnet and –

Suddenly there was another fist, much bigger than mine, closing round my hand with steely strength. I wheeled round to see Dmitri's face, so full of anger that I froze. The woman had frozen, too. Before either of us could speak Dmitri's voice sailed over us both.

'Please don't think I do this for you or your car,' he was saying to the woman. His voice was as hard as his grip. 'I do this because my friend is a violinist of international standing' – he nodded towards the violin case I was clutching in my other hand – 'and I don't wish her to disappoint her audiences by injuring her hand. But you had better know that the cat which you have just so thoughtlessly destroyed with your car was an extremely rare Hebridean Longhair. Its value was little short of the price of your car. Its owner, Lord Borrowdale, will think its value a good deal more than that; the cat, although insured, is irreplaceable. If you wish to avoid an extremely unpleasant legal entanglement and some even more unpleasant publicity, you would do well to get back in your car, leave this town and refrain from coming to it ever again.'

His eyes were boring into the woman, his smile was ice. The woman was clearly used to getting her own way, unaccustomed to an opponent of Dmitri's calibre. Indignation and fear did battle over her splendidly made-up face. The fear won. She turned abruptly and opened the car door.

'I would also advise you to drive with extreme care as you leave town,' Dmitri added imperiously to her retreating back.

She slammed the door, started the motor and eased the big car out of the space. She didn't look at either of us.

I watched her creep out of the car park, on to the quay and along it with exaggerated care. Then I turned to Dmitri, who was still gripping my fist.

'Hebridean *what*?'

He shrugged amiably. 'It sounded plausible enough.'

'Lord *who*?'

'A pleasant name. I will consider it should I ever be elevated to the peerage.'

'As for my international fame –' I burst into laughter. 'Dmitri, you impossible old liar!'

'Not at all. That much at least is true. Your name is known in most countries of continental Europe, is it not?'

He's back! He's back! Everything else fell away – the heat, the cat, my anger – with the single sudden sentence that roared through my mind. He's back! I looked up at him with idiotic adoration, forgetting that he was a cad, a blackguard, et cetera.

His own face was far from adoring. He was frowning at me. 'Anna, I'm seriously angry with you.' He shook my fist. 'Have you any idea how thick the metal of a Mercedes bonnet is?'

He's back! He's back!

'Do you expect me to be here every time you embark on some rash and thoughtless act? Please in future save your otherwise admirable impetuosity for more worthwhile occasions. Anna, I wish to see you tonight. Shall I come to your place or will you come to mine?'

He's back, and I –

'Oh, shit!'

'I beg your pardon?'

'The wedding. It's tonight. The wedding we have to play for.'

'Tell them to postpone it.'

'Are you out of your mind?'

'Very well, then I will see you afterwards.'

I shook my head mournfully. 'I know these people. We'll still be at it at two in the morning.'

'Very well then, I will see you tomorrow.'

But it wasn't tomorrow. I couldn't wait that long. I'd waited long enough, a whole awful empty fortnight.

The cat was buried, the owner consoled, the wedding dance over. It had gone better than anticipated. In fact, it had been a wild success. I should have been satisfied with that, but wasn't. It was nearly three o'clock in the morning and I was tossing about in my solitary bed, wide awake.

The heat had diminished not one jot since the afternoon. It hung like a heavy curtain outside my open window. I loved it. Despite the difficulty of playing while drenched with sweat, I revelled in the intense physicality of this kind of weather. All the barriers were down; the heat of the air and the heat of the body merged as if the thin skin separating them didn't exist.

It felt so good to be alive on a night like this. The air, though heavy, was moving, rolling in through the window, big and soft and luxurious and warm and full of a cornucopia of scents. I lay awake trying to disentangle them: the sweet briar hedge going mad in the heat; the next-door neighbour's newly mown grass; a tangle of cooked greenery from Ahab's paddock; and above it all, cutting through with its own familiar seduction, the ever-present tang of the sea, now strangely sweetened.

It should have been enough, but wasn't. One scent was missing: the dark musky fragrance of Dmitri. I imagined my nose burrowing into his chest, breathing in his essence. I wanted, wanted, wanted.

Tomorrow. He might as well have said next year. Huge lumps of time stood between now and then, whole hours and minutes. Even the seconds would plod along with agonising slowness while snails whizzed past. How could he be so thoughtless?

And then, the illumination, just like a lightbulb flashing through the dark: it *was* tomorrow! It had been yesterday when he'd said tomorrow, and now it was here! After all, he hadn't said *when* tomorrow . . .

Another lightbulb lit up the dark: and if he'd been away for a fortnight, and if before that there had been about six weeks, then surely . . . I tried to remember the exact date he'd first entered my library.

Yes! Two months *exactly*! They were over, the two months of cat-and-mouse! It was time! In fact . . . good God, I was late!

I lunged at the bedside light and switched it on. The clothes I'd worn for the gig were lying in a heap on the floor: flimsy red harem trousers and an embroidered top to match. It crossed my mind that there might be more suitable clothes to wear for a flit through the wood to my lover, but by then I was halfway into the ones I'd just discarded. In any case my mind was closing down to reason, shutting up shop for the night. It had narrowed to just one simple goal: how to get there as fast as possible.

I don't know what it was that made me grab my violin case just before I shot through the French window, and I only just remembered to lock up before I ran across the patio, through Eleanor's garden, up the paddock.

'Ahab?' I called softly.

A breathy whickering answered me. The moon was full, just as it had been the night of the well-christening. In its light I saw Ahab coming towards me, a little tentative. As well he might be. It wasn't every night that I called upon his services like this. I took the cheek strap of his halter and walked with him up to the little stable. 'Do you mind terribly?' I asked as I removed the halter and eased the bit of the bridle into his mouth. 'It's urgent, Ahab, it really is.'

I swear he smiled in the moonlight.

The wood was dark at first after the clear light of the paddock but it wasn't long before I could see the wide woodland path. I thanked Sydney Holroyd for making this path the widest one in the wood, the one that led straight to his house, Dmitri's house. In places the canopy was thinner and let in the pale silvery gleam of the moon. It was light enough in those places to urge Ahab into a fast trot. I'd been too impatient to bother with the saddle and so I raised my knees a bit to cushion the impact. I must have looked an idiot, had anyone been there to see me: a dishevelled mess in crumpled red harem gear clutching reins in one hand and a fiddle case in the other. I didn't care. I didn't even care what Dmitri would see. He would understand. He would know that the two months were up, that today was tomorrow, that it was time.

It seemed to take hours despite Ahab's ground-eating pace. Days and weeks were passing and still we were in the wood. How could a hundred acres be so big? Months had passed and still we were only at the spring in the centre of the wood. I could smell the dampness of the water, see the pewter of its surface. Ahab smelled it too. He sniffed longingly towards it. I couldn't refuse him, not after his complicity in my urgent task. I loosened the reins and let him walk to the edge of the pool. The moon floated serenely on its surface. Then Ahab's head reached down and shattered it, scattering splinters of light all over the pool. Only a few sips, just to refresh him; any more would wind him. 'Enough, Ahab,' I said gently. He raised his head and nodded, then turned back on to the path.

Not a cloud in the sky, nothing to dim the moon's soft rays. The wood smelled more acrid than the scents which had tumbled into my bedroom. The earth was giving off a dew. I could see it sparkling faintly in the undergrowth beside the path. Up ahead, a clearing cropped by rabbits made a ghostly pale circle. We crossed it and plunged into the last stretch.

Finally, years later it seemed, I saw a new light ahead, the brighter light of a bigger clearing, the clearing around his house. Then the light disappeared. I groaned, thinking it had been a delusion, like a mirage in the desert, then realised it was simply a bend in the path that had obscured it. The path straightened again, and there, unmistakable now, was the house.

I slipped off Ahab at the yew hedge and led him under the arch. The grass inside, once a lawn, had reverted to a tall tangle of high summer meadow. My legs and Ahab's swished through it. The sound was deafening in the unnaturally still air. I stopped, afraid, not wanting Dmitri to hear us yet. Then indignation replaced my fear. There were no lights on in the house. How *could* he simply go to bed as if this were a night like any other? Surely he, too, knew that the two months were up? He should be waiting, a single soft light on in his room, for his gypsy maid to come and woo him.

There were specimen trees dotted about the former lawn, throwing deep shadows across it. I found a slender birch and tied the reins around it. It left enough room for Ahab to move about. To let him graze in comfort, I unhooked the bit on his bridle. I wouldn't be returning to him for some time.

Behind a bush not far from Ahab but far enough to be safe from his hooves, I put down my violin case. Already I knew I was setting a stage; the case was a mundane prop which would mar the effect. I took the violin from it. The violin had been with me all my life, it was as familiar to me as my own body. Tonight, however, it looked different, its old wood glowing with new purpose. I ran a bit of rosin over the strings and then tuned the instrument as quietly as I could, holding it to my ear and plinking the strings with infinite care. I had played in most of the orchestras of Europe, but never had a performance mattered so much as tonight's.

Then I smoothed my clothes and stepped out from behind the bush. I positioned myself near Ahab. He liked music. More to the point, I knew how striking an appearance we would make together when Dmitri, awakened from his sleep, would come out on to the balcony.

Would it be the balcony? I had no idea which room he slept in but was fairly sure he used only a small part of the south-east corner. I planted my feet firmly in the tall grass facing it. My feet in their flimsy sandals were wet, the grass tickled my legs through the thin harem trousers.

I had given some thought as to what I should play. The choice for the first piece wasn't difficult. It had to be a *csárdás*. My baggy trousers, my swarthy features, Ahab – so evocative of the horsemen of the Hungarian plain – all of it cried out for the wild gypsy dance that embodied the swings between despair and exultation.

My bow was poised, my fingers hovered above the strings. I hesitated. It suddenly occurred to me that rushing through the night-time wood to stand before my lover's window serenading him with my violin at three o'clock in the morning was a slightly odd thing to do.

Too late. My fingers and bow had touched the strings. The first mournful notes were winding their way across the grass, up to his window. It was a wonderful tune, its minor key deep and soulful, the great upward swoops sounding like cries from a heart about to break. It was unspeakably schmalzy and yet was one of the most authentic songs I'd collected. It bared the player's soul with luxurious melancholy, its tempo gaining speed quickly as if the urgency of the message could not be held in check. When it reached a piercing last note, it stopped and then immediately began again at the beginning, with the same slow pleading tempo.

As I played the repeat, pouring my own soul into every note, I kept a beady eye on the house. No light, no sign of life. A ghastly thought: perhaps he wasn't there after all? Perhaps he was out, though I couldn't imagine where. There wasn't exactly a lot of night life in Sedleigh and I couldn't see him driving all the way to Leeds to rave it up in a nightclub. No, he must be at home. Probably just a heavy sleeper. Well, the second part of the *csárdás* would wake him up.

After an emphatic chord which seemed to say, 'That's that; we'll leave all that behind us now,' the music burst into an exuberant *allegro* dance in the major. It swept along in a swirl of whirling notes, faster and faster, with a scattering of sharp chords where the dancer's feet would thud to earth in joy. On one such chord a light went on in an upstairs room and my own joy raced through my violin. The light was soft, a bedside light. I pictured him rising, hastily pulling on his trousers, moving towards the French window that led on to the balcony. Oh, he had to come now, had to! The music was racing along now, spinning madly in the night air that lay between us, faster and faster, *allegro, vivace, presto, prestissimo*, and then he was there, the window open wide behind him, his arms leaning on the parapet, gazing down on me with an enormous smile that made the moon seem dim by comparison.

How could he smile? Didn't he understand? This was no ordinary concert, no ordinary music. It flashed through major and minor keys, its exuberance never far from the desperation which urged it on. It was the ecstasy of imagined release from torment, and still he beamed down at me with simple delight. Dmitri, damn you, I'm trying to tell you something, isn't it obvious? The tempo was frenetic now, my fingers flew across the strings in a blur. If only I could fling myself beyond even *prestissimo*, then perhaps he would understand? At the height of its madness, the first tune returned at an unimaginable speed, wailing through the dance now, a thin and pure heartbreaking shriek. *I need you*, it wailed, and I wailed with it.

Then, at an unbearable pitch of intensity, the music suddenly stopped.

Dmitri was applauding wildly. 'Brava!' he called. 'Brava, my splendid girl!'

I could have hit him. I hadn't ridden all the way over here at three o'clock in the morning to be *applauded*, damn it! And yet – years of habit – I found myself taking a deep bow, smiling up at my audience of one while echoes of the *csárdás* wailed through my mind. Was there no way to get through to this unbearably desirable man who stood there all aloof, condescending to applaud my nocturnal concert? I wouldn't speak. I too could be stubborn. What I had to say was beyond words. Music was my life, it was its own language. All my life I had spoken through my violin – in concert halls, peasant villages, street corners. Surely he understood that?

And then, inspiration. I began to hear, as clearly as if I had spoken them, the words of a Schubert song. It was 'Serenade', one of the best known and best loved of all love songs. The melody was unmistakable, but would he know the words? I could only hope. I raised my violin to my chin and began, silently willing the words to reach him.

> *Softly my songs to you are pleading through the tranquil night;*
> *In the dim and silent woodland, come, my love, and bring delight!*
> *Slender treetops whisper sweetly in the moonlight fair;*
> *No harm shall reach that grove of rapture if only love be there.*

I sneaked a look at him over my violin. Was he getting the message? Impossible to tell. He was leaning his strong arms on the parapet again. I don't think he was smiling. His head was tilted slightly, listening. To the notes alone, or to the words I was breathing to him through the music?

> *Do you hear the nightingales singing, calling, love, to thee;*
> *With their notes so softly ringing, pleading, my love, for me.*
> *Well they know the heart's yearning and the pain of love;*
> *And their silvery tones, I pray, will not fail to move.*

Was he moved? He was standing very still, as silvery in the moonlight as the notes of the song. He might have been a statue. Nothing moved in the sultry air except my violin as I began the final section.

> *Let your heart too be moved – my love, listen to me;*
> *Trembling, I wait for you; come and make me happy!*

I lowered my violin and stood in the grass, my head bowed. I wasn't trembling, just listening for the footsteps. Surely he had understood now. I had risked everything in coming to him. After this there could be no turning back to easy friendship. He would despise me or love me. There was nothing in between.

No footsteps, no applause. The only sound to break the silence was Ahab, whickering softly. I looked up. Ahab gave a toss of his head. I glanced towards the balcony. It was empty.

Then I saw him. He was coming round the corner of the house. His chest was bare. He wore only a pair of trousers very like the loose baggy ones worn by Cossacks. His feet were bare too. They swished through the long damp grass. There was no smile. The expression on his face was grave and tender and filled with love. As he drew nearer, he opened his arms in a gesture also grave and tender. I put down my violin, raised my arms and ran to him.

FIFTEEN

Anna, Anushka, my brave beautiful girl! How I longed for you to come, and how I feared you would hold back to punish me for what must have seemed my monstrous indifference. Could you really believe me indifferent? Or worse: an arrogant male playing games with you and teasing you into making the first move?

This is no game I play. Your life is at the centre, your past and your future and the connection I hope you will be able to make between them. I have things to tell you but no right to make you listen. That must come from you, my Anna, and until you give the signal I must try to remain a little aloof from you. The story is yours, not mine; you must be the one to tell me what you wish to hear of it. I am only an instrument, like your violin. Yours are the hands that must draw the melody from me –

Ah, what rubbish I write! How can I pretend to be nothing but an instrument in your life? That was all my father intended when he sent me to you, but from that first moment when you seemed to stare straight into my soul I must have known I could never play the passive messenger.

What's more, you little minx, I could equally accuse you of being the arrogant female playing games with me! Don't think I didn't see you sizing me up among the books, evaluating me as your dubious ancestors no doubt evaluated a horse they wished to buy. Will he do? Strong enough? Spirited enough? Sufficient stamina for the long hard gallop? Let us have a look at his teeth . . .

Outrageous wench! I could strangle you as you lie there, your sleeping face suffused with satiation by your latest lover. Instead, I watch your face with awe and – yes – a little fear.

Are you beautiful? There must have been a brief moment when I was capable of evaluating your appearance just as you apparently evaluated mine. Very probably in that moment I would have thought: no, not beautiful. I have seen many women more beautiful than Anna Atwill. She is just a trifle too untidy and clearly fond of hearty food. If ever she was young and sleek that time has passed, and in passing it has laid its little lines across her face, just to let us know.

I love every one of those lines, Anna. Each one speaks of a life rich with experience. You have lived well, my impetuous girl. You may not be as polished as some but you have more gusto packed into your ample body than a thousand sleek beauties put together. No young lovely could have staged your astonishing performance tonight. If a lightning bolt from a jealous god chose to strike us dead this instant, my immortal soul (if I have one) would bless you for this night alone.

No doubt you thought me obtuse, a maddening Romeo glued to his balcony while the splendid Juliet sent her unmistakable message. I was not so dense as to imagine that my gypsy queen would urge her horse and her fiddle through the night for mere entertainment. I knew. But I also knew that the moment we came together would destroy my last shreds of objectivity. My arms have long cried out to wrap themselves around you and crush you. In my imagination I have engulfed you over and over again. It was clear from the beginning that ours would be no decorous affair, that the passion we would generate would have seismic implications. My wicked little volcano, I marvel that Mr Holroyd's feeble house still stands after this night!

You can have no idea, Anna, of the self-control I have needed to use in presenting to you a calm façade. And will use again. You rushed into my life and my bed too soon, Anna Atwill, though I also (unwisely) wished it. There is business to attend to, and for that I need to carve out a little distance between us again. I will hate it as much as you will, my dear, but with your vibrant presence filling my vision I lose sight of what I must learn before making my decision.

If only I could speak to you directly, ask the simple question: 'What do you know about your past?' But the question itself would raise questions in your mind which might better be left unthought, if unthought they have been until now. If you had been the prim librarian I expected, my task would have been easier. Or you might have been so hard and matter-of-fact-efficient that I would have been pleased to crash into your life and shatter your complacency. Instead, I find a jewel of a human being, priceless and heartbreakingly cherishable, strong and yet (you think I don't see this?) fragile. A fist through your life would be as monstrous as a blade slashed through a Rembrandt.

Do you know, Anna, that I almost think I would rather die than hurt you? And I like my life too well to make such rash offers to just any chit of a girl.

I am heartily sick of writing these letters to you, Anna, but they are my only outlet. Soon, I hope, the time for writing will be over and we can come together as we were meant to come together. Until then, I must, as the saying goes, be a little bit cruel in order to bring about the greater kindness to us both.

And so, I put my letter away with the others and slip back into bed with my sleeping Vesuvius none the wiser. Sleep well, my little tyrant. And when you awake, try not to dislike me too much.

SIXTEEN

When I awoke, the sun had already moved its searchlight to the south. I opened my eyes a fraction and squinted at it through an unfamiliar window. It had been a long time since there'd been unfamiliar windows in my life. This one was clinging rather desperately to its last few flakes of paint. Where on earth was I?

I blinked and shut my eyes again. In the rosy darkness behind the lids, images began to form. Ahab, tethered to a tree which was also unfamiliar. Beside him, a dishevelled idiot scraping away at a fiddle . . .

I groaned. Had that really been me? Miss Atwill, respectable guardian of the town's books? Councillor Atwill, elected representative of the people?

I turned my head away from the window. As if the light had been obstructing my thoughts, a passageway suddenly cleared in my mind and down it, as through a long delicious tunnel, I remembered the reason for that lunatic serenade.

And its aftermath.

Ahhh . . .

I smiled, humiliation gone, and opened my eyes, slowly, luxuriously, anticipating the gorgeous sight on the pillow next to mine.

It was empty.

'Dmitri!' How dare he deprive me of those first wonderful moments in this affair which (last night had told me) he longed for as fervently as I?

The room echoed my shout but gave no reply. I raised myself on one elbow and looked round. The light streamed in from big windows to the east and south and would have illuminated an impressive master bedroom if the years hadn't whittled away its splendour. The wallpaper, once elegant, was faded, with damp patches inexpertly covered by cheap pictures. The furniture was Junk Shop Modern – all the good stuff had been sold at auction when Sydney Holroyd had died. The less said about the curtains the better.

'Dmitri!' I called again. My voice was less imperious than before; a trace of alarm had crept into it. He couldn't have done a flit. Couldn't. Not after last night. Could he?

No sound, but my nose detected something nearly as good: the faint scent of coffee. A moment later its fragrance joined the sound of footsteps on stairs. I settled back into the battleground of bedclothes which told its own story and smiled, awaiting the first sight of my brand-new lover. The footsteps grew louder, the scent of coffee stronger. Then, with a gentle kick, the door sprang open and there he stood, framed in the splintery doorway like a painting just brought down from its exile in the attic to be viewed for the first time by a hushed art world.

'Dmitri Mikhailovich Komarovsky,' I whispered, making him mine.

'Anna Atwill.' My name was less impressive, but the smile that accompanied it turned it into a little song and I was sure he understood the significance of this small incantation. No marriage vow taken in a dank church could have been stronger.

He walked across the room, set down the tray and then sat himself down on the bed while all the bells of St Petersburg pealed out in celebration. The sun was behind him, casting a golden aureole around him as in an icon. Perhaps it was that that made his eyes seem expressive of so much more than love and lust. He looked at me for a long time, his heavy dark features softened into that strange mixture of judgment and tenderness that shines from the faces of the Byzantine saints; they know us too well, they comfort and discomfort us at the same time.

I was beginning to feel uneasy under this dubious benediction when suddenly he smiled and touched my cheek gently with one fingertip. 'Anna Atwill, how soundly you sleep. The sleep of the just?'

'The sleep of the exhausted. You forget: I had a gig last night before coming to see you.'

'Ah, the dreaded *călușar*! My poor Anna. I should have been more considerate.'

'God forbid!' I heaved myself up into a sitting position, scattering the bedclothes. 'Dmitri Mikhailovich, I've waited two whole agonising months to do this.' I clamped my hands round the beloved face, drew him to me and kissed him. It was the long but light kiss of lovers biding their time safe in the knowledge that time is theirs, a luxurious infinity of it, no need to rush any more. We had earned this kiss, both of us, and in its way it meant more even than the tumultuous night that had preceded it.

'My splendid girl,' he whispered into my hair. 'To find a treasure like you after all these years – I must have done something to please the gods.'

'Not find,' I reminded him with a smile. 'Rediscover. Or have you forgotten? We've met before, Dmitri Mikhailovich.'

Was it my imagination or did a change come over him at that moment? It was so slight as to be almost imperceptible.

'So we have,' he murmured. 'Yes, I had forgotten.' He smiled. 'I had also forgotten the coffee.' He got up and brought the tray over to the bedside. As he poured, the fragrance of the coffee mingled with the scent of aftershave and I realised what I must have seen before but not registered: Dmitri was freshly washed, shaved, and dressed in a clean white shirt. He had awoken before me and, rather than stay in bed and anticipate that first lovely coming-to-consciousness of two new lovers, he had got up and briskly prepared for the day. I couldn't complain. To be brought coffee in bed by my lover was also a gesture of love.

But the wrong one. The night we'd spent together had been the wildest in my life. Dmitri was no Don Giovanni chalking up another conquest, exercising his skills for the pleasure of the game. He had been as committed, exuberant and uncontrollable as myself. Nor had he merely been responding to my own passion. That frenzied demon driving the Russian soul into a maelstrom of excess was deeply embedded in Dmitri. Had we not been big strong people in the prime of life the violence of our love might have killed us. He was not – emphatically not – the kind of person to rise coolly from a night like that to go and put the kettle on.

He handed me my coffee and sipped his. Love had made him more formidable. The wide cheeks supported by the high Slav bones seemed firmer, the strong hawk-like nose sharper, the hooded eyes more sensuous, dangerous. The mane of steely grey-black hair sprang away from his face with increased vigour, despite the efforts of his comb. It was just as well he loved me, I thought, watching him over the rim of my coffee cup. To be hated by Dmitri Mikhailovich would be terrifying. To be regarded by him with indifference would be even worse.

'Do you remember our first meeting? The very first one, in Berlin?' I asked without thinking, more from a craving to hear his voice than from curiosity.

He had been staring at a patch of wallpaper that surely didn't deserve his attention. Now his unfathomable black eyes focused on me. 'Do you?' he countered.

'Of course not. I was just a baby. But you must have been about ten – I just thought . . .' I finished foolishly. Why on earth should he remember something so insignificant as a baby?

'I only meant that your parents might have mentioned it to you. Not our meeting,' he added, 'but that period of their lives. After all, it's a little unusual – an English baby born in Berlin. The sort of thing that enters the family mythology.'

It was more than unusual. It was untrue. But my hand remained steady around my coffee cup as I smiled back at him. 'They were there on business – mainly Edmund's. To evaluate a cache of Expressionist paintings that had just come to light. He also wanted to buy some. The whole thing took much longer than expected – you know how ghastly the bureaucracy was in those days. My mother was pregnant and it turned out that there were complications and ... well, it just seemed better to stay there rather than risk the journey home. Travel was pretty ghastly then, too.'

Dmitri said nothing. The silence stretched on, making me feel the necessity to fill it with words. It was all too familiar, that gentle pressure to talk, as was the expression on his face: kind, intelligent ... patient. I had been 'questioned' a few times in eastern Europe. Luckily, I'd had nothing to give away. Now I did. So did Dmitri, I was sure of it. I wanted to know what he knew, but I didn't want him to know what I knew. Neither of us could give way. Stalemate, and in this of all settings.

The whole morning was going horribly wrong. I'd awoken from the most glorious night of love to find my lover transformed into an interrogator. How this had happened was a mystery, but I didn't even care very much about solving it. All that mattered, as we sat together drinking our coffee, was the future. Last night it had opened up so spectacularly. Now it was closing again, and for no reason I could discern. I felt bewildered and very hurt.

'So what happens this morning?' I asked lightly. This strange atmosphere was of his making; it was up to him to decide the next move.

'Breakfast?' he said, also lightly. Then he laughed. 'Or we could call it lunch.'

The bathroom was as decrepit as the bedroom but, with its dripping taps, stain and rust, even more sordid. Standing under the lukewarm shower I was glad of my sleazy surroundings. It suited my state of mind and made the pain more bearable.

Lunch was a torment. Oh, the food was fine. Dmitri was one of those self-sufficient bachelors practised in putting together a simple but effective meal. He was also a perfect host: considerate, affectionate and full of good conversation. We talked about the wedding dance I'd played for (but not the other celebration for which I'd fiddled my heart out in the moonlight afterwards). We talked about Josh and Lewis and our unreliable accordionist and the difficulties of teaching them to be at home in the strange kind of music we played. We talked about my travels collecting this kind of music. We talked about his book, gossiped about his publishers (Eleanor had known his editor), agreed that the Holroyd mansion left much to be desired in creature comforts. We talked about everything except the night we'd just spent together.

He didn't tell me that it was late, that we'd overslept, that he had work to do. He was far too urbane, too sensitive, even to hint at such a thing. But everything in his manner implied a courteous rounding-off of an episode that had reached its natural end.

After our meal we drifted out on to the grassy terrace, still chatting of inconsequential matters as if this were merely a little post-prandial stroll. But my violin case had been on a chair by the door, inviting me to pick it up. Outside, Ahab was waiting patiently, my four-footed taxi home. Everything seemed to be propelling me towards a leave-taking I didn't want but couldn't avoid.

I untied Ahab's reins from the tree and put the bit into his mouth. His big dark eyes peered at me inquisitively. A circle of munched-off virgin grass and a spritely toss of his head told me he'd enjoyed his little sojourn in these new surroundings. I longed to press my cheek against his and derive a little comfort from my faithful friend but Dmitri was there. Waiting. He formed his hands into a stirrup. For one mad moment I longed to tear those joined hands apart and press my lover to me. But the moment passed and, meekly, I pulled myself up on to Ahab's back.

As Dmitri handed my violin case up, the wonky clasp I'd been meaning to mend sprang open. Dmitri caught the violin just in time. 'A fine fiddle,' he observed, handing it back to me.

I ran a finger down its worn belly. The varnish was smooth, its chestnut colour glowing as richly in the sunlight as Ahab's coat, which it matched. My hair was the same colour, too. In the circle of cropped grass we formed a unity that had been self-sufficient before and would be so again. 'It's nothing special,' I said absent-mindedly. 'Not a Stradivari or anything like that. But I like it. I've had it all my life – my father gave it to me when I was born.'

'You know that?' he said quickly.

I froze. There was something new and urgent in his voice. Slowly I looked up from the violin and into his eyes. They were blacker than ever but with an eager light which I'd never seen before. 'What do you mean?' I said, keeping my voice steady.

He waited just a fraction too long before asking, 'Do you know where it came from?'

'Customers often gave him things instead of money,' I said calmly. 'In lieu of payment. For paintings they wanted to buy. Like the grandmother clock in my kitchen – I think I mentioned it before.'

His eyes held mine for a long time, frighteningly steady and yet with a trace of vulnerability which was also new, almost as if pleading with me. What do you want of me, Dmitri Mikhailovich? What do you *really* want, if my body and soul aren't sufficient? Why have you come into my life in this disturbing and ambiguous way? We were back in the bedroom, in the interrogator's cell, in the deadlock of two minds, each withholding what the other wanted.

It was Ahab who broke it. In a single lovely arc he swung his head round to sniff the violin case, nearly bumping it out of my grasp. I put the violin back in it and snapped shut the lock in a businesslike manner.

Dmitri's gaze wavered. 'Yes, of course,' he murmured. 'You did say – I remember now.' He smiled. 'Well, it's a fine fiddle, whatever its provenance.'

I smiled my own agreement and we set off towards the yew hedge at a leisurely Sunday morning pace. I had to lean down over Ahab's neck as we walked under the arch. Even so, the foliage raked through my hair. When I straightened up again on the other side I was aware of the low-life picture I made. After my shower I'd had no choice but to put on the same crumpled red harem trousers and top. My hair was a burnt haystack and my body a battleground of small bruises from the violence of our love-making. I felt like an Amazon who'd galloped into the fray confident of success only to slink home broken and defeated.

So I wasn't too surprised when Dmitri smiled apologetically and said, 'I'm afraid I have to drive back to London tomorrow.'

'I thought you'd just been there,' I said lightly.

'The writing took a turn I didn't expect yesterday,' he said. 'There's a whole new area I must look into before continuing. You know how it is.'

'Sure.'

'I'll phone you the minute I get back.'

'Sure.'

There was an awkward pause. Then he did something wholly unexpected. As if some spark of the wild Russian from the night before had broken through a fireguard to burst into flame, he suddenly buried his face in my thigh with such violence that Ahab took a step sideways to keep his balance. I could feel Dmitri's lips burning through the thin material, hear his voice whispering. 'Anna.' Just the one word. 'Anna.'

Then he turned abruptly and disappeared under the arch.

SEVENTEEN

The corridor was scarcely less stuffy than the room we'd just left. Kate and I sped down it as fast as our clotted lungs would allow, making for the oasis of an open door. Outside, we gulped the air, refuelling for the second half of the planning committee meeting.

'Next one's the biggie,' said Kate. 'What do you think of our chances?'

'Approximately nil.'

'Anna,' she chided. 'It's not like you to be a defeatist.'

'Realist,' I corrected. 'The schedule's overloaded. Everyone's hot, tired and dying to get home. Things are being whizzed through that wouldn't get a look-in on a normal day. What's more, Robert's stashed a side of beef in every councillor's freezer.'

'Anna! Do you know this?'

I looked at my friend. Her sweet face was suffused with horror, her fluffy halo of curls nearly standing on end with the shock. Greens can be awfully naïve, bless them.

'Well, no,' I admitted. 'But I wouldn't put it past him. In any case, practically everyone on the council is a chum of his.'

'We do try to be impartial.'

'We do. They don't. Kate, I wasn't going to tell you this – trying to be impartial, more fool me – but now I think you should know. I had a nasty little encounter with Robert last week in the course of which he sprang the smelliest bit of blackmail I've heard for years.'

I paused, not knowing where to begin. Certainly not at the beginning, which was my dismal ride home after the night I'd spent with Dmitri. I'd given Ahab his head, too distracted to think of anything so practical as the route home. He'd taken me to the mossy clearing where the spring bubbled into its pool. Yes: a few sips of its ice-cold water, that's what I needed. As if that would change everything.

I'd been about to dismount when a rustling of last year's fallen leaves at the edge of the clearing told me I wasn't alone. I'd looked up to see Robert Vesey pacing out his land – parcelling it up, gloating already over the fortune it would bring him. Our eyes had met. A quick flash of guilt in his (the gloating was premature, the planning committee hadn't met) had quickly given way to satisfaction as he took in my dishevelled appearance and all that it implied. He'd smiled – not a nice smile – and walked over to me.

'I met him in the wood last weekend,' was all I told Kate. 'He was pacing out the land. Very pleased with himself he was. He came over for a chat.'

'Visiting our new neighbour?' he'd said. 'A real gentleman, that one – paid up six months in advance and no haggling. Birth'll out, that's what they always say.' He'd scrutinised my high cheekbones, my broad features, my skin that was tinged with a darkness that had nothing to do with the sun.

Something had snapped in my mind. I no longer cared what he knew or said about me. My world had just whimpered to an end. I was hurt, confused. I wanted nothing more than to get home fast and nurse my wounds in private. I should have pressed my knees to Ahab and let him carry me away from the unwelcome encounter. Instead, my frustration turned to anger and zeroed in on Robert Vesey. Coolly I'd surveyed him in turn, comparing Maxine's appearance with her father's short stubby form, the apple cheeks and cloth cap that turned him into a typical Yorkshire farmer of the sort so beloved of television interviewers. They always made a good showing, his type. Till you got to know them better.

'Oh, really?' I'd said. 'You'd never know it to look at Maxine.' It had been on the tip of my tongue to suggest that perhaps his wife had kept something from him. Just in time I'd stopped myself. Muckraking was his department, not mine.

'Somehow we got on to the subject of Maxine,' I told Kate.

Robert Vesey had frowned. The jolly-farmer face he used in public had slipped off to reveal the man who routinely let a stricken sheep die in agony rather than pay for a vet. 'She was a decent enough lass until you got at her,' he'd said. 'Knew what a daughter's duty was.'

'Like doing the morning milking so you could stay in bed longer,' I'd said. 'Turning up at school with toothpicks holding her eyes open.'

'Good enough for me, good enough for her,' he'd said. 'What does she need with books? She wants to improve herself she can marry Bernard Carr.'

'He's not a cradle-snatcher. Anyway, he's very well educated. He wouldn't want a wife straight out of school. He'd expect any wife of his to have a university education.'

He'd narrowed his eyes. 'So that's your game, is it? You three got it all worked out, eh? Well, if Bernard Carr wants to marry a degree, he can pay for it. Farming's bad these days.'

So bad that Robert Vesey was renewing his Audi and his Land-Rover and all his farm vehicles after three years instead of two. My gaze wandered over the woodland that was quietly providing the backdrop to this scene. If he got his way and sold it for development he'd be able to finance a dozen Maxines through any university in the world.

Was he reading my mind? 'Course it might be different if a little extra cash came my way . . .' he'd said softly.

He was watching me closely. An unmistakable glint of cunning had lit up those pale blue eyes. Surely he couldn't be thinking – No, that would be too crude, even for Robert

Vesey. 'I thought a little extra cash came to farmers every time they opened their mouths,' I'd said.

'Not now. Times have changed. Course, if I manage to sell off that bit of land, well, I guess I might just about squeeze together enough to be thinking more about Maxine's future . . .'

I had groaned inwardly. So obvious. Why hadn't he thought of it before? Why hadn't *I* thought of it before and kept away from him at least until after the planning committee meeting?

I turned to Kate and quickly summed up the rest of that awful conversation. 'He beat about the bush a while and then came out with it,' I told her. 'A straight deal: if I oppose his planning application, Maxine can forget about university. But if I help it along and he sells the land, well, no promises, you understand, but . . .'

Kate gasped. She really did, just like in a bad movie. 'I don't believe I'm hearing this. Not even Robert Vesey could stoop that low.' She paused. 'Could he?'

'He could and he did.'

She was silent. Together we looked out across the estuary. From the steps of the town hall we could just see the tops of the trees that were the beginning of the woodland. Poor trees, I thought; what would they think if they knew it was a straight choice between their lives and Maxine's future? But that was the thing about trees – they didn't think. They just stood there and lived until someone came along and killed them. And the worst thing of all was that Robert's application was cunning: 'only' about a quarter of the trees would be sacrificed. The rest would be preserved to enhance the private-keep-out grounds of the executive development.

'So what do we do?' said Kate.

'Exactly what we intended,' I said briskly.

'You do know that Maxine's the best pupil I've ever had? In the whole of my teaching career. Miles above the rest. She caught me by surprise – I didn't expect anyone with a face like that to have a first-class brain behind it. I can't just abandon her. Surely people matter more? More even than trees?'

'Kate,' I said. 'Maxine's going to university, one way or other. I promise you that. Hang on to your principles – that's why the punters voted for you.'

Just. Like me (standing as an Independent), Kate had squeezed in by just a few votes. In the next election we'd undoubtedly be squeezed out again. We had to do what we could while we could, and as far as I was concerned that meant saving the wood. Not for the tourists, not for the ramblers, not even for the locals but for the trees themselves. Somebody had to speak for the silent victims and who better than Attila the Bigmouth? And Kate.

'Now who's being defeatist?' I smiled. 'Come on, roll up your sleeves. We're off to see Goliath.'

I phoned Bernard when I got home from the meeting. 'I'll swap you a pesto for your Geological Survey map,' I said.

'Done.'

As I waited for him to arrive I bustled about the house preparing the meal. It was essential to keep busy at all times. Best of all was to squash two tasks into the space of one – that way there was no time at all to think or to feel. But my capacity was expanding, leaving little gaps that yawned empty. Into them crept Dmitri. Before I could invent a third task to plug the gap I was plunged into despair again.

Don't think about him, think about the planning application, pick the basil, peel the garlic, grate the parmesan, make the tagliatelle dough. Oops, am I out of wine? No, bad luck; here's a bottle, no excuse to rush off to buy some. Oh, Dmitri, Dmitri, what happened to us? Salad, salad, how's the lettuce doing? Hello, slug, your feast's over; scram. Wash the lettuce, the spring onions, the tomatoes, hack off a chunk of cucumber. Any pumpkin seeds? Good – throw them in. Salad dressing's getting low but not low enough –

no excuse to make up another batch. Dmitri, Dmitri. Feed the dough into the noodle machine, great stuff, just like a kid's toy. Magic. Alchemy. I rammed the pestle into the green goo of basil with a violence verging on hysteria: ten minutes at most till all the tasks would be used up. What then?

Hurrah!

Bernard walked through the doorway. I flew to my knight with a cry of joy and a hug that nearly knocked him over. Comfort me, Bernard, wipe my mind clean of the memory.

My eyes took in the map, the book, the file of papers. 'Use the kitchen table – we'll eat outside,' I said.

'Is this for general information?' he asked as he spread the map on my table. 'Or do you have something specific in mind?'

'Robert's application. The meeting was today.'

'Ah, I'd forgotten.'

'Shame. This is your wood, too. It's riddled with public footpaths for your delectation. Robert *says* he won't try to close them – just "reroute" a few to fit in with his plan...'

'The thin edge.'

'Quite.'

'Well? What's the decision?'

'Passed – but on condition that he provides *his own water supply*.'

'Ah.'

'Ah, indeed. Kate was the smartie who thought of that one. You should have heard her. By the time she finished there was no way anyone would let Vesey have a drop of our dwindling reserves for his swimming pools and Jacuzzis and three-bathrooms-each. If things work out maybe we should commission a little statue of thanks in the wood. You know: Green councillor with fist raised in victory salute towards the trees she saved.'

Bernard wasn't smiling at my little fantasy. He was wearing his Contemplative Look. 'There's a long way to go before we can think of victory salutes,' he cautioned.

A little stab of fear. 'Bernard, I thought you told me coasts were the worst possible places to drill. Especially coasts with cliffs. Didn't you?'

'Yes, but not impossible. There are some coastal boreholes, some quite successful ones. It all depends on local conditions. But usually any water that's there seeps out through the cliff. Or it's contaminated by sea water – the line between land and sea may be obvious on the surface but underneath it often merges.'

The fear began to recede. 'So his chances aren't too good?'

'Depends. Sometimes you get a good borehole near the coast while one ten or twenty miles inland is full of salt.'

'But what about here?'

'That's what I'm trying to find out.'

He leaned across the map and scrutinised it. It was a pretty map, full of graceful curves and swathes of different colours. It looked like some of the abstract paintings Edmund used to sell. It also looked very complicated, as did all the other charts and papers he'd brought with him.

I could see that behind his faraway gaze Bernard was computing all this information. I was dying to get into his mind but this was no time for impatience. Thinker at work, do not disturb.

I moved about the kitchen quietly, getting the meal together.

The tagliatelle and Bernard were ready at the same time. We moved out on to the patio and began to eat.

'Well?' I asked.

'Hmmm,' he replied.

'Is there likely to be water under there?'

'Hmmm.'

I sighed. Clearly he wasn't ready after all.

At last he spoke. 'I would need to look up a few things at home,' he said slowly. 'And phone a few other engineers who've worked in the area.' He manoeuvred a forkful of food into his mouth. He chewed thoughtfully and swallowed. 'But . . .'

I held my breath.

'But if I were Robert I'd give up the whole idea.'

I let my breath out again.

'There could be water, of course. But just off the top of my head –'

I suppressed a smile at this.

'– I'd say his chances are pretty low. Less than ten per cent, I'd guess. Though I could be wrong.'

I held my tongue. The information was coming through at last, no point in jamming his airwaves with questions.

'Chances are that any good water is above sea level, and there might not be enough.' He closed his teeth over a tomato and munched thoughtfully. 'He'd have to go deep – very deep. Which increases the chance of sea water . . . and increases the expense.' He looked at me as if suddenly remembering I was there. 'This "condition" the committee imposed – presumably he has to drill first? They won't let building start without water?'

'Drill first,' I affirmed.

'Not a risk I'd take if I were a businessman.'

'You are a businessman,' I reminded him.

And now I had the joy of seeing that big open smile of his. 'It's other people's money I risk.' Then he took a sip of wine. 'Of course he could drill further inland. Chances are better there, and he does own a lot of that land. But then there's the expense of laying miles of pipeline and cable. Not to mention the electricity involved in pumping across that distance. And who would own and control the borehole? Robert?' He contemplated a lettuce leaf – I hoped I'd got the slugs off it. Bernard shook his head. 'I wouldn't buy a superluxury house with someone else owning and controlling the water supply. Especially a tight-fisted old rat like Robert.'

I laughed. 'Will you tell him that?'

'Among other things. Let some other borehole engineer do the lying. I don't need his business.'

'Yes you do,' I said quickly. 'Or rather, our rescue plan needs you.'

He stared. 'Anna, you're not suggesting that *I* should drill this well?'

'I am.'

His eyes, no longer faraway, were boring into me. 'Are you mad? I despise everything about this development.'

'Exactly. That's why you're the one who should drill. Listen,' I said before he could interrupt, 'Robert's sure to ask you because you undercut the competition.'

'But –'

'Bernard, can you *imagine* what a mess some other firm would make of that wood – getting the equipment in, the drilling itself? At least you'd do your damnedest to limit the damage.'

'The only way to do that is to talk him out of it.'

'By all means, try. Explain the situation exactly as you've explained it to me.'

'He won't believe me. He'll think I'm on your side – and Kate's.'

'So? Tell him that if he doesn't believe you he can get another engineer to do it. He'll probably try someone else who'll say, "Yessir, there's usually water, sir, though no guarantee of course, sir," and give him a quote half again as high as yours. Armed with that, Robert will come back to you and twist your arm. Reluctantly, you'll agree. Don't you see, Bernard? You will have been *seen* to be honest – so when the borehole fails –'

'*If.*'

'All right, *if* the borehole fails, you'll have been proved right, you'll get paid anyway, and the wood will be less damaged than if some of those other thugs had crashed through it. Let's face it, he's going to drill regardless, and there are benefits to us – and to the wood – if you're the one doing it.'

'And to me? I haven't had a failed well yet. I don't like to ruin a perfect record.'

'You won't, not really. You will have successfully predicted its failure – and we'll make sure there are plenty of witnesses to that.' And then, sudden inspiration. 'Look, if you won't listen to me, there's someone else who might convince you. Come with me.' I beckoned mysteriously.

As Bernard and I entered the wood, the temperature dropped and the fragrance of resin from the artful scattering of conifers swam into our nostrils. 'Gorgeous, isn't it?' I murmured. He nodded and breathed deeply. Come on, trees, I begged. Do your thing.

They did. The wood was pure magic. As we strolled along the dusky paths, the trees on either side seemed to nod in greeting – a trick of the light, of course. Underfoot, centuries of leafmould released its musky scent with every step. Overhead, swags of small birds fluttered through the canopy looking for just the right spot to roost overnight – spoiled for choice. And all around us, the trunks of the different trees gleamed their different shades of enchantment as the fading light caught them first this way and then that.

The sky had darkened to a soft royal blue by the time we reached our destination: the clearing which had been the home of the long-dead hermit. There were other clearings, of course, and other places in the wood that would have served my purpose. But this one – more or less in the centre and graced by the delicious little spring – was my favourite. It was the heart of the wood. Most of the main paths converged here, making it a leafy spaghetti junction for humans as well as wildlife.

We stood in silence for a while, just breathing in the sweet sad loveliness around us. The spring was whispering away to itself, a crystal descant above the indefinable scurrying sounds of small mammals in the underbrush. The scent of water – also indefinable – floated over the darker scent of earth bedding down for the night.

An owl hooted. I walked across the clearing to the single tree which, standing a head higher than its fellows, looked like the Wise Old Man of the forest, guardian of the spring. It was a larch, but on this evening of gentle sorcery any tree would have done as well. I put my hand on its thick, grey, deeply furrowed bark. Bernard was beside me. I took his hand and put it next to mine. I looked into his eyes – the same grey as the bark.

'This is your persuasive friend?' he said.

I nodded.

Above us an abundance of branches weighed down by age drooped gracefully. From them a haze of smaller branches hung vertically like soft green café curtains. Most of the lower branches had fallen off naturally with age, but one spread itself over our heads, its lower twigs just within reach. I ran one through my hand. The tufts of soft needles – unexpected in a conifer – tickled my palm. I pushed the twig towards Bernard and watched with satisfaction as he caressed it.

'What would some other borehole engineer do to this tree?' I asked quietly.

'Don't.'

'Life and death, Bernard. Quite a few trees are depending on you. Which is more important: their lives ... or your pride?'

He smiled ruefully. 'Do you ever lose an argument?'

'Most of the time.' I paused. 'Bernard, I hate this choice as much as you do. But it's not in my power to change the terms.'

He nodded.

'Then you'll do it?'

'If Robert asks me.'

We went over to the spring and sat down on the mossy stones. 'Where will you drill?' I asked.

'In terms of water it doesn't matter – one spot is as likely or unlikely as another. I'd choose the easiest access, wherever I could get in with the least amount of felling. Not here, of course.' He smiled. 'I expect your venerable friend would fall on my waggon if I disturbed him.'

'Would that he could. That's the trouble with trees. Utterly defenceless. Dogs can bite. Deer can run. Poor old trees just have to stand there and take it. They depend on us humans to stick up for them. Most of the time we don't. I dithered a bit myself over this development.'

'*You?*'

'Foreigners, you see. I quite fancied the idea of a settlement of foreigners tucked away in the wood. A bit of spice. Broadening of our provincial horizons.'

'I don't think the buyers would be your type. I would have thought Dmitri was more your type.'

My face crumpled with the pain; the blow had been so sudden I was as defenceless as any tree.

'Anna?' He was peering into my face. 'I've hit a nerve, haven't I?' He swore softly at himself. 'I'm sorry, Anna. I just thought – you seemed to get on so well together – in fact, I thought . . .' He trailed off.

'You thought right,' I said, as calmly as I could. 'We did. Past tense.'

We sat in silence for some time. I shouldn't have been surprised that this of all the clearings in the wood was the one witnessing my unhappiness. I had passed through it on my way to the well-christening party and again when Ahab and I flew to Dmitri with our fiddle. And again the following morning, when I'd met Robert here and he'd revealed his own bit of nastiness. It was rapidly taking on a new symbolism in my messy life.

The ruffled circle of sky had deepened to a shade of indigo which made the paler blue of the harebells fade almost to grey. The yarrow and meadowsweet held out a little longer and then they too shrank into the growing darkness. A sliver of moon through the trees failed to give much light. It was time for us to go. I stirred slightly.

'Is it something you'd like to talk about?' Bernard asked quietly.

I sat still again.

'I don't want to intrude,' he continued. 'Only if you think it might make you feel better.'

Would it? Odd that I hadn't run to Bernard after that miserable morning. I'd run to him before in distress. That I hadn't sought him out this time seemed significant. Dmitri had colonised some part of me that was more private than usual, so private that I'd kept out my friends.

I turned to Bernard. 'Yes,' I said, 'I think I would like to talk.'

Fifteen minutes later I was sobbing myself silly inside the refuge of my friend's arms. It all came out in a flood which took even me by surprise. There was no point trying to hold back, save a shred of dignity. I had rushed to Dmitri that night with uncontrollable passion and my grief was now of a matching violence. Dmitri was – had been – the one great love of my life, the one exception to the six-month pattern which had served me so well in the past. *He knew me.* Knew me as no other man had done. And the me whom he knew had somehow failed. If he had known me less, the rejection might have hurt less, but this was the whole of me that had been annihilated that awful morning. There was nothing of me left with which to rise, brush off the debris and proceed with the rest of my life.

I held none of this back from Bernard. If my rejection was total, so was my confession. There was no place for pride in any of this.

I think Bernard understood. Only by slow degrees, as my tears subsided, did he loosen the protection of his arms. Nor did he offer any false consolation. Only, 'Poor Anna. I can't understand it. He just doesn't seem that kind of person.'

'He isn't,' I said, my voice still shaky. 'That's what makes it hurt so much. It's not him, it's me – there's something wrong with me.'

'You don't expect me to believe that?'

'But it's true. He expected something from me that I either didn't have or couldn't give. And the awful thing is that I still don't know what it is.'

'Have you thought of asking him?'

I said nothing.

'Anna,' he chided. 'This is no time for pride.'

'It's more than pride.'

'What then?'

What indeed? The owl hooted again. This time he was answered by the sharp *kee . . . wick* of his mate. 'Fear,' I said finally.

'Of?'

'I don't know. Something cataclysmic. I was totally involved this time. The destruction could be total, too.'

'The way you've talked tonight,' he said slowly, 'it sounds as if it already is. Remember Solzhenitsyn? *The First Circle*? The prisoners who'd lost everything and so had nothing more to lose . . . and were therefore free?'

'I'm not a prisoner.'

'You've been hurt so badly anyway – what do you have to lose?' He paused. 'This thing you feel Dmitri is expecting from you. Could it be that he's expecting you to *ask*? To ask what's wrong?'

I turned to Bernard, trying to make out his features in the near-dark. 'I'm not sure I understand.'

'Me neither. But that last gesture before he left – it doesn't strike me as the sort of thing a man does after a one-night stand.'

I winced at the term, though I'd used it myself.

'We're back at the beginning,' he said. 'He's just not that sort of person. It's obvious that he cares about you. Anna, why not try one last act of courage? Go home, phone him ... and ask.'

'He's not there. He's in London.'

'Maybe he's back by now. Don't you think it's worth a try? I'm sure he'd tell you the truth if you asked. I can't imagine him lying.'

'Of course he lies,' I said irritably. 'He's Russian. All Russians lie. All east Europeans lie. Everyone who's ever lived in eastern Europe lies. I lie.'

Bernard laughed.

'What's so funny?'

'You. Your cranky spirit. You're not defeated yet, Anna, however awful you might feel just now.'

I smiled wanly and stood up. Bernard stood up, too. As we left the clearing we passed by the weary old larch. Bernard patted it. 'You're willing to fight to save this old fellow and his chums. Can't you fight to save yourself?'

Bernard was too tactful to hang around when we got back to make sure I phoned. In any case he must have realised I would have to do it fast, before my nerve failed.

I marched straight to the phone and dialled. My heart was thumping like crazy as the phone rang at the other end ... and rang ... and rang.

I needn't have bothered to get all het up. No one answered.

EIGHTEEN

August was nearly over before drilling began. The complex machinations between Robert, Bernard and a rival firm (Yessir, three bags full, sir) went much as we'd anticipated. It was further delayed by the bureaucracy involved in getting permission to drill. But at last the day arrived for choosing the site.

Bernard held me to my promise that there would be plenty of witnesses – both to his unwillingness to drill at all and to his prediction of failure. It wasn't difficult to round up my motley crew; the library was the centre of information in our town. Sooner or later everyone passed by my desk and it was easy to drop a few hints as to when and where It Would Happen.

That 'It' was merely the choosing of the site was something I kept to myself. The whole town was fascinated by Robert's project and dying to be in on the action. Nothing on this scale had ever been done before – anything large was usually just another public building which would arouse ire for a while and then fade a few months after the building was completed. This project was different. I suppose we all long for a bit of luxury and if we can't have it ourselves we'll make do with it by proxy. These were superluxury establishments Robert was proposing, the sort of thing usually seen only on the telly.

People were intrigued by the borehole well, too. The Slaters had enthused far and wide about the one Bernard had drilled for them and their excitement was contagious. Also, water was rising in local consciousness in direct proportion to its fall in level. The hosepipe ban irritated everyone, and each day without rain brought nearer the much worse possibility of standpipes. There were mutterings of discontent even in people who'd previously supported Robert's development. Word had got round that underground water, like God, moved in mysterious ways. The possibility that it might move away from our taps and into Robert's was remote, but people were feeling edgy about it none the less.

'I'm set to become Public Enemy Number One,' said Bernard gloomily.

'Nonsense. Everyone knows you're against the whole project.' Just to be on the safe side, Bernard had joined the debate in the paper's letters column to make his views known. Robert hadn't been well pleased. 'You're free to hire another firm,' Bernard had replied.

He wasn't, of course. Wonderful, the hold money has over the mean. Robert could no more take his business to a higher quotation than use a hundred pound note to light a cigar.

Or finance Maxine's education. Her A-level results had finally arrived. They were as spectacular as they could be: A in German, A in French, A in English. Even I was a little surprised — to my mind she was a little weak in English. Maxine was ecstatic. Beneath that cool façade which could be so maddening, she was more insecure than people suspected. Living with a father who was a master of bluff had influenced her more than she would like to admit.

'Well done!' I'd cried when she rushed to my house waving the precious piece of paper. I hugged her and thought — not for the first time — that if I'd had a daughter it would have to be Maxine. No one else would do.

When I released her I went straight to the fridge and, with a flourish, produced the bottle of champagne that had been sitting there in hope for the last few days.

'Wow!' she said. 'Champagne for breakfast?'

'Sure thing.' In fact she'd already had breakfast — between milking and the arrival of the post. We took the bottle and glasses out on to the patio. Her eyes were suspiciously bright as I poured out the golden brew, but it wasn't until I raised my glass to hers and said, 'To your future; may it be as bright and golden as this,' that she burst into tears.

A moment later she was laughing through her tears. 'I'm sorry – it's crazy but I'm just . . . so . . . happy!'

I hugged her again and waited for her to settle down. I had to raise the subject some time – it was best to get it out of the way fast. 'How about your dad? He's pleased?'

Maxine shrugged. 'I didn't tell him.'

I sighed. 'You don't make things easy for yourself.'

Another shrug. 'I don't want his money. I'll pay my own way.'

It wasn't that simple, but this wasn't the moment to push more clouds over her horizon. I poured some more champagne instead.

It hardly seems worth recording the weather on the day the site was chosen. Just the usual: warm, sunny, dry. The sort of summer day the English used to long for and now cursed.

The wood was looking a trifle dusty. Without the magic cloak of night the trees were revealed as poor thirsty souls who could do with a shower as well. Even so, it was a relief to enter its parasolled sanctuary and get away from the sun. The leaves, on duty as always, carefully filtered out the full strength of the sun's rays and fed it to us in dappled portions.

'We' included Maxine. She'd insisted on coming with me despite my hints that this wasn't entirely tactful as far as her father was concerned. After a brief argument we'd left the library in the hands of the two new assistants and set out in search of the action. All we knew was that Bernard was driving to Robert's farm and that the two of them would come to the wood together at about three o'clock. We were depending on Robert's loud voice to steer us.

Meanwhile, we enjoyed our stroll. From time to time, as two paths converged, someone joined us in our aimless perambulation. At other times we caught glimpses of colourful clothes through the trees, heard scraps of laughter.

And then the voice I'd been waiting for: Robert's. Decades of bellowing at recalcitrant sheep and ill-trained sheepdogs had strengthened his vocal chords. 'You're the expert; you tell me,' boomed through the wood.

We quickened our step and zeroed in on the sound.

So did everyone else. Within a few minutes the little clearing with the spring was fringed with spectators. In the centre, the main protagonists. Robert, arms folded aggressively across his chest – ominous, that. Bernard, on the surface more relaxed, his long limbs more at home in this setting, the straightforward businessman with nothing to hide, nothing to protect. Both of them looked up in surprise (Robert's real, Bernard's feigned) at each new arrival. I watched Robert's face to see how he was taking the audience. He didn't seem to mind. He'd always been something of a showman and he was proud of this project. The development was oneupmanship on a grand scale, raising his status in the eyes of other farmers who scrabbled about in the foothills of smaller money-spinning schemes.

'I've told you before,' said Bernard. 'It doesn't matter in the least where we drill. There's unlikely to be water anywhere.'

Robert flapped a hand in dismissal of the words he'd heard so many times before. 'That's not what McKenzie says.'

'McKenzie'll drill anywhere,' said Bernard smoothly. 'The customer has to pay if water's found or not. Why should McKenzie care?'

Robert glared at Bernard. 'Thought you had some special

skill. Those maps of yours and all. You're the one supposed to know where the water is.'

'I do – more or less. It isn't here. If you insist on drilling, *you* choose the spot. That's what McKenzie would do, too. To make sure the customer takes full responsibility for the decision. This is your well, Robert. Put it where you want.'

Robert muttered something unintelligible. He was clearly annoyed. He knew there was opposition to his scheme. He wanted the credit if it worked but none of the blame if it didn't. Then his face took on a cunning look that boded no good. 'Here,' he said.

There was a gasp of dismay from the spectators. I thought of a boxing ring. Rob 'Em Robert had just pulled a dirty punch.

'Put it here,' he said, undeterred. He jerked his head towards the spring. 'There's something feeding that thing, right? Tap it.'

'There's not nearly enough for the project you have in mind,' said Bernard.

'How do you know? Go down and find out.'

The gasp of dismay was turning into a rumble of opposition. Mutters of 'You can't let him meddle with the spring' were heard.

'If I drilled here that's all I'd tap: the spring. And it's not enough. What's more, I'd almost certainly destroy the spring,' said Bernard.

A cry of indignation from the crowd.

'So?' said Robert. 'Probably be a road through it anyway.'

'Over my dead body!' shouted one of Kate's more fervid protégés. The anger of the spectators was growing. Robert was either obtuse or bloody-minded. I was feeling nervous for Bernard. How would he extricate himself from this? One false step and the people's anger would spread to him. I was beginning to regret having involved him.

'Not according to the plans I've seen,' said Bernard. 'According to the official plans, this spring is in the grounds of one of the houses.'

'It's also in the middle of the development – cheaper to lay the pipes to each house. Put it here.'

'If you wish,' said Bernard.

I stared at him. How could he give up so easily?

'But,' he continued, 'I'd have a chat with your estate agent first if I were you. He won't be pleased. That spring, if you leave it alone, would slap another twenty thousand on the price of the new house whose land it'll be on – thirty, with the history it's got behind it. Your agent's not going to want to lose that kind of money.'

Nor would Robert. I could see the calculations going on behind his brow as he totted up the loss.

'A lot more than the cost of moving the well somewhere else,' Bernard offered casually. 'A lot more. Still, if you want it here, here it will be.'

'Not so fast,' said Robert.

I stifled a smile.

'Of course,' Bernard continued, 'if you moved the site further south, closer to that farm track at the edge of the wood, you'd have less roadway to prepare for my waggons. That would cut down the cost, too.'

Less roadway, fewer trees cut down. I stole a glance at Maxine, hoping she was noting the cleverness of her friend. Two brains like that, it was a pity they couldn't get together. But the smooth ivory façade gave nothing away. Quite possibly she was thinking about Cambridge. Her own future was beckoning her and it wasn't here. That magic piece of paper with her exam results was only the first thing to begin the long process of her departure.

'Roadway'll have to come all the way through anyway,' said Robert. 'For the cars. To each house. And the builders' waggons.'

'Only if the development goes ahead,' said Bernard.

'Which it won't if you don't find water. You'll have to pay for the temporary roadway and the drilling regardless. You could be cutting a lot of extra roadway for nothing. Still, it's up to you.'

Robert was clearly wavering. Bernard had the sense not to push him. It was best to make Robert think it through himself, calculate the various risks and expenses involved. Especially in front of the audience. He was looking around now, over the heads of the people and into the wood beyond. There was a slightly larger glint of sunlight towards the south. He hesitated, looked back at the spring, still uncertain. Then he turned his stocky body and marched off in the direction of the sun.

There was a sigh of relief from the people as he left the clearing. That much at least was saved. I'd like to think the venerable old larch joined in but I don't suppose it did. It just stood there, as it had stood for a century or more, oblivious of its reprieve.

We followed Robert into the wood. Each time he stopped and considered a site, Bernard was there with a wholly rational cost-cutting reason why it wasn't ideal but, 'It's up to you,' he said every time. And every time, Robert hesitated, then moved on again, moving further south, further towards the farm track which was the end of his ready-made access. Each time he moved on a few dozen more trees were saved. By now Bernard's tactics were crystal clear to me and probably to many of the spectators who moved with him on each stage of this curious pilgrimage.

Not to Robert, though; like most farmers, he simply didn't notice trees.

It was nearly four o'clock when we reached the high stone wall which marked the southern edge of the wood. A rusty gate – once ornamental but now decrepit – hung crookedly on one hinge. Just beyond it was the track skirting the edge of Robert's farm.

'Of course, if you put it over there,' said Bernard, waving vaguely towards the other side of the gate, 'there'd be no need to make any new roadway at all. Cost you nothing if it turns out there's no water. Nothing except the cost of my drilling,' he added.

'Cost a lot more to lay the pipeline,' said Robert.

'Not really. If the development goes ahead and the roadway takes this route anyway, all you need is a single big pipe – you can lay it the same time you make up the road – with smaller ones branching off to each house. And of course there are legal advantages.'

'Eh?'

'If you put the communal well on one person's land, all the other buyers'll be wary. Or their solicitors will be. They usually manage to whittle a few thousand off the asking price for taking the risk.' Bernard turned his faraway gaze across the field towards the sun. Then he looked back at Robert and smiled. 'Still, it's up to you.'

A single curlew flew high overhead, breaking the stillness with its mournful cry. I followed its flight to the southwest, to a slight hill behind which the tops of a few scattered trees marked Robert Vesey's farm. They were just about the only trees left on it to provide a scrap of shelter from the vicious east wind. Today they would be sheltering the sheep from the sun instead. It was beating down with full strength. How long would Robert keep us waiting? The crowd was growing impatient, the novelty of the day long since worn off.

Robert strode towards the rusty gate and with some effort prised it open. He walked through. On the other side he picked up a small branch that had broken off in the wind. There was a strip of tangled grass between the track and the wall. Robert rammed the stick into it.

'Here.'

Bernard glanced indifferently at the spot. 'Are you sure? You don't want to think about it for a while? Perhaps you'd rather have it in the middle of the wood instead? Makes no difference to me.'

Robert glared. 'You said I could have it where I wanted it. I want it here.'

Bernard sighed. 'Very well. Have it your way.'

NINETEEN

Drilling began two days later. With no roadway to cut there was nothing to delay the action. That pleased Robert too.

'Bernard,' I whispered on the morning he and Tim brought the equipment to the site, 'did you work out that ingenious plot beforehand or was it just sheer luck?'

He turned to me and whispered back, 'Thought up the whole lot the night before.'

'Such an honest face,' I murmured, looking at it with new admiration. 'Who would have guessed you were so devious?'

'I've had a good teacher,' he replied with a sly glance towards me.

The reason we were whispering was that most of the spectators were back again to see the drilling begin. Some had brought friends, swelling the numbers further. 'You're not going to like this,' I said. 'Having an audience.'

'It's different this time. It's better there should be people watching. Then everyone can see I'm doing it properly.'

I nodded and moved away. Robert took my place next to Bernard. Clearly he was going to be a major part of the audience – also making sure everything was done properly. Good. I watched him strut about, full of self-importance. I was glad Maxine wasn't here. Seeing her father play the peacock wouldn't endear him to her. At my urging she'd finally told him her A-level results. He'd grunted non-committally.

As the morning wore on, the equipment was set up. Most of the process was pretty dull, but I felt a slight thrill when the tall metal mast slowly rose from its bed on the waggon to be positioned over the future well.

Bernard went around one last time, checking that everything was ready. He looked tremendously in control, the hard hat and metal-tipped boots giving him an even greater air of authority. When he stepped up on to the mesh footplate beneath the control panel I thought of a revolutionary about to deliver a stirring speech. There was a moment of suspense. The morning held its breath. Even the birds at the edge of the wood were quiet. I pictured them in their ringside seats among the leaves, peering out to watch the performance.

Then Bernard's hand closed over a lever and pushed it down. The machinery roared into action. The earth trembled as the drill bit into it. As if a hand grenade had struck its target, chunks of soil and stones and grass flew up.

I shivered with fear and excitement. This was the moment we'd all been moving towards for months. At the end of the drill now eating its way through the topsoil there either was or wasn't water. On that drill a million pounds or more was riding. So was the fate of hundreds of trees. And there, at the control panel, was the single human hand which would decide everything. Bernard, once again transformed into the magician, clever servant of the greatest magician of them all: earth. Over and over, Bernard and the earth had conspired to coax her precious water up to the surface. He had never failed before. Now we had to hope he would. Perhaps he was sending secret messages down into the earth, asking her to rebel, just this once? I hoped so, and I hoped she would listen.

The drilling went on and on. The rock here was particularly hard, reluctant to let the drill through. But the slowness of progress didn't deter the sightseers. Day by day the crowds grew, everyone hoping to be there when water was struck. Even those who hoped it wouldn't be were swept into the excitement of the chase.

I didn't want to be there. Each day I told myself I would stay at home. But each day I trudged through the wood to the site. I had turned over most of my working hours to Maxine and put her in charge of the assistants. The more money she could earn before going to university, the better. In any case, she preferred the library to her home. And given that she might provoke a row which would set her father even more against her, it was safer to keep them apart.

The problem was that, relieved of my duties and the pleasant chit-chat of the borrowers, I was alone with my thoughts far too much. Dmitri was still away – two or three times, emboldened by a double Scotch, I'd steeled myself to dial his number again. Each time I'd heard the endless ringing with a mixture of dismay and relief. I didn't know what to think. Mostly I didn't want to think at all. In the hands of the gods, I told myself when I put the receiver down. Like Robert's well.

At least on the site I could talk with other people during the quiet intervals when another rod was being fitted. And if the action wasn't exactly ripping along at least there was something to watch, something to think about other than my own misery.

And then, at forty-eight meters, it happened. Water. Nothing had prepared us for it, no change of sound in the drill, no change in the chippings and dust thrown up each time the compressor blasted the hole clean. During one clean-out, dust; during the next, mud, the unmistakable ooze I remembered so vividly from the Slaters' well. With an unthinking cry the crowd expressed its solidarity with the driller who'd found what he didn't want.

And Bernard? His face was as impassive as ever. The borehole engineer doing his job. How much effort that bland façade cost him I could only guess.

As for Robert, his gloating face was more than I could bear. I looked away from him, up at the trees at the edge of the wood. Days of dusty coating had been replaced by a heavy layer of grey mud plopping stolidly off the leaves. You poor sods, I thought; you've just received your death sentence.

Everywhere I looked was something I didn't want to see. Excited bystanders, doomed trees, Robert's triumph. Bernard was explaining something to him. Robert's head nodded approvingly. Clearly Bernard could do no wrong, now that he'd found water.

Robert held his arms up for attention. The people quietened down immediately. 'Show's over for the day,' he announced with a grin. 'Tomorrow we do the testing.'

The 'we' grated, but so did everything else. I turned my back on the site and slipped through the gateway before the mass exodus could begin. For once I didn't want to talk to anyone. I wanted to be alone in the wood, to try and remember how it was, before the desecration began, before its familiar paths were ripped up and replaced by raw new tracks to let the builders' waggons in.

It was early September. A few of the beeches were already sporting some golden-yellow leaves among the green. Two small rowans had gone a fiery red. The willows were turning a dull yellow, the leaves dropping off at my touch. The ashes were also shedding but without bothering to turn colour at all. I saw with surprise that the hawthorn berries had nearly all ripened to crimson. The year had slipped into autumn without warning. The monotonous warm dry weather had disguised its advent, made us think we were living in an eternal summer.

When I reached the main clearing I sat down on one of the mossy stones by the spring. Habit. It was that kind of place, it made you want to pause and reflect. To keep myself from reflecting on what mattered, I stared at the harebells instead. They were still bright and fresh: drought flowers, loving the dry ground which this clearing had become. The scabious, though, were on their way out, their blue fading to a dusty pink. The last sneezewort and yarrow were also tatty and the hogweed was starting to go to seed. There was a touch of autumn melancholy about the clearing today which matched my own. I turned, as always, to the spring. It had become a habit, cupping my hands under the ancient spring each time I passed by. The water always seemed to taste better here.

My hands were already shaping themselves into a cup as I turned and reached towards the spring.

The water was gone.

There was a stunned silence when I told Bernard on the phone that evening. It lasted so long I wondered if he'd fainted.

'You're quite sure,' he said. '*Really* gone? Not a drop?'

'Not a drop.'

Another long silence followed by a heavy sigh. 'Sometimes,' he said, 'I really hate this job. Sometimes I wish I'd become a proper geologist and gone off on harmless expeditions to Spitzbergen.'

I felt as sorry for Bernard as for the spring. I'd coerced him into taking this job. Now he had to bear the responsibility for destroying the spring. The fact that any other driller would have done the same was no consolation.

'It's not coincidence,' he said. 'That's what Robert's supply is. I've obviously tapped into the spring's source. God only knows what it's doing over there. But it could have been anywhere – miles away, even.'

'Exactly. It was impossible to know. You mustn't blame yourself, Bernard. You know the score too well for that. If you'd drilled by the spring you still would have hit it. And destroyed the clearing as well.'

'It'll be destroyed anyway. Now that I've found his water the development will go ahead. Sometimes, Anna, I really dislike the human race. Myself included.'

There wasn't much I could say to comfort him. 'I suppose our only hope is that the supply isn't big enough,' I tried.

'Possible. But unlikely. You do sometimes get a little pocket of water cut off from everything else, but it's rare.'

'Still, the rare *does* happen. I mean, otherwise it wouldn't be rare. It would be non-existent, right?'

A tiny scrap of laughter cheered me. 'Dear old Anna. You play the pessimist in your own life and the optimist in everyone else's. Speaking of which . . .'

'Must we?'

'Just one more try?'

'Must I?'

'A deal: I promise not to jump off a cliff tonight if you promise to try phoning him just once more.'

'Blackmail.'

'Deal?'

'Deal.'

As soon as I put the receiver down I phoned Dmitri's number.

No reply.

I turned up at the site a little later than usual the next day. The drill had already been removed and the test pump lowered. As I arrived, Bernard gave the signal to switch on the portable generator. A little later the first dark brown water began to jerk through the temporary pipe. They'd positioned it over a ditch on the other side of the track. The thirsty earth drank up the water as fast as it came.

Bernard was timing the flow. There was little for anyone to do but sit around and wait. With no machinery throbbing, no geysers of dust or mud to witness, people were getting bored, everyone except Robert, who watched greedily as the muddy water gradually began to clear. Then Bernard did a more specific timing. Holding a calibrated bucket beneath the pipe, he measured how long it took to fill. From that he could calculate the rate per hour which – assuming the flow continued – would tell Robert how much water was available for the development. The bucket seemed to be filling awfully fast. Clearly there was a lot of pressure behind it. Robert beamed – Bernard must have told him the significance of this test.

I looked away in disgust. The mud which had yesterday dripped off the trees had dried into caked grey tombs for the leaves. The branches sank heavily under the weight. What did it matter? Those trees would be felled anyway for the road. It was no good getting attached to trees, I thought bitterly, unless they were your own and you could protect them. Even then they would pass out of your control when you sold up or died. Like orphans. Except that there was usually someone to look after human orphans.

An hour later the water was running clear and my optimism was all used up. Bernard handed Robert a beaker – would he like to be the first to try it? Robert – beaming – held the beaker under the pipe. He sipped the water with exaggerated pleasure, a parody of a wine snob. I hoped it would poison him. That would solve Maxine's problems too. Could Mother Earth be that cunning? With revived interest I watched him drain the beaker. My mind did a fast-forward: Robert's legs going rubbery, his face grimacing with astonishment, his hand clutching at his throat. Stumbling, falling. Maxine the heiress going off to Cambridge in style. The wood saved. A statue of Kate *and* Bernard put up in the clearing where the spring, miraculously restored, gave witness to their heroism.

Robert, as sturdy as ever, handed back the beaker, grinning broadly. I switched off my fantasy.

Bernard came over and sat beside me on the dry grass.

'How long do you carry on the test pumping?' I asked.

'Usually just an hour. Usually you know by then if there's any flagging of the rate.'

'Will you measure it again?'

He nodded. 'In a few minutes. I'm putting off the dread moment. It's stupid, but I'm still hoping . . .'

My heart gave a little flutter.

Ten minutes later Bernard did another test. For one mad moment I fancied that the bucket wasn't filling quite as fast, but no: no more fantasies. It was time to grow up, accept that miracles didn't happen.

Bernard glanced across at me and raised an eyebrow.

Or did they?

When he did a third timing, even I could see that the flow had slackened. So could Robert. His face was turning pink and it wasn't the sun.

Half an hour later the flow had diminished to a trickle, about the same trickle that came out of – used to come out of – the spring in the clearing. Bernard and Robert were in consultation. Robert's face had deepened to rose. Bernard's was as inscrutable as ever. '. . . about enough to serve one house . . .' drifted through the clear warm air.

Robert's face vermilion. 'And what bloody use is that?'

Bernard shrugged. 'I can only tell you what's there.'

Scarlet now. 'I need ten times that much at least and you can bloody well find it!'

'Only if I go deeper and even then there's no guarantee. And you'll lose what you've got if I drill further. Frankly, I don't think you'll find more anyway. I always said it was unlikely. This' – he gestured towards the trickle – 'was more than I expected. You know where it's come from, don't you?'

The magenta face scowled.

'From the spring,' said Bernard. 'I've tapped the source of the spring. It's dried up now. That spring will never flow again.'

A cry of dismay went up from the crowd. Clearly this was the first they'd heard about the spring's demise. If we'd been in the wild west Robert might have been lynched.

'To hell with the spring!' he bellowed. 'You go deeper and get more!'

Bernard opened his mouth to speak.

'Just shut up and do it!'

Bernard snapped his mouth shut again. Robert stormed over to his Land-Rover and drove off in a cloud of dust.

The next few days were a jumble of emotions. The crowd increased daily. This was high drama indeed for our town. Nobody wanted to be absent when the *real* water supply was found. That it would be found few people doubted, despite everything Bernard had said. I was pleased to note that the blame for the defunct spring was placed squarely on Robert, not Bernard. There were mutterings of 'compensation' though everyone knew that no money could replace the spring. But crowds are like that; they need heroes and villains. I was no better. It's just that I'd decided which was which some time ago.

If feelings were running high, the action wasn't. The deeper the borehole went, the harder the drill had to work. The time between the dramatic spewings (now dry again) increased, and with it Robert's impatience. If he'd had the slightest sensitivity to local feeling he would have stayed away. But, after the brief period when Bernard could do no wrong, Robert now regarded him with growing suspicion as a conspirator planning to do him down. That the co-conspirator might be the earth herself never crossed his mind.

'Keep up the good work,' I said silently to her each afternoon when I rose from her parched surface to make my way back home. To Bernard I said, 'How long does this go on?'

'Until Robert tells me to stop . . . or we use up the last rod. There's a limit to how deep I can drill. I'm getting near it. I've told Robert this but I don't think he took it in.'

'How near?'

'Probably tomorrow. Some time in the afternoon, I'd guess.'

* * *

Well, yes, perhaps I did intimate to one or two people in the library the next morning that this afternoon should see the climax of the long-drawn-out adventure. Certainly the head count around the site was far higher than on any day before.

One of the heads was Maxine's. Her desire to be present surprised me. She'd taken no more interest in this well than in any of the others Bernard had drilled. 'I want to see that bastard get his comeuppance,' she explained.

'Maxine!'

Her cornflower-blue eyes gazed innocently at me. Then they lit up with recognition and she laughed. 'I meant *Dad*,' she said.

'Oh. Well. Yes. But I don't think it's a good idea. Your dad'll be furious if they don't strike water and that bodes no good at all for you. You'll just make it worse if you're there to witness his humiliation.'

'Too bad.'

'What a hard little madam you can be.'

'Look who my father is.'

And so, despite howls of protest from the two assistants left behind, Maxine and I set off through the wood after lunch. As we approached the dried-up spring she muttered, 'Destructive bastard.'

'Since when are you so keen on nature?'

'That's not the only thing he's destroyed.'

'We all of us do our little share of destruction as we pass through this life,' I said primly. The day was hot. I was irritable and nervous as hell.

'Some more than others. Kate told me what my father did to you.'

'Do say.'

'Blackmail.'

I stopped short next to the ancient larch. I hoped she didn't mean what I thought she meant. 'We all of us indulge in a little blackmail, too, as we –'

'Not that dirty. He made you vote for a project you detested because if you didn't he wouldn't let me go to university.'

Damn Kate. 'That's not why I voted for it. There were complex political reasons. As you grow older, my child, you'll realise –'

She snorted. 'He made you go against your principles. For me. That hurts, Attila, it really does.'

'I'm a hardened old politician, Max. I voted the way I did because (a) I realised it wouldn't make any difference to the outcome, (b) I would be seen to be reasonable by the electorate, (c) I had a pretty good idea there wasn't any water and (d) it might just give me a chance to do a little blackmail of my own.'

She wasn't ready to listen. 'He made you compromise yourself.'

'Sweetheart, I am nothing but one great big fat compromise. My whole life has been a compromise. So is everyone else's. Barring the occasional Hitler. You want I should be a little Hitler? Purity has its price, Max. I'm not willing to pay it.'

She snorted again.

I sighed. It was no use talking reason or explaining my tactics when she was in this mood. To her I was the tarnished heroine who had sacrificed my principles to ensure her education.

We arrived just as they were fitting another rod into the drill. Bernard climbed up the mast. He looked surprisingly agile despite the clumsy boots. I watched him manhandle the ten-foot-long rod into position. Then, with Tim at the controls, the machinery whirred into action and the rod was screwed on to the end of the previous one. Bernard climbed down from the mast and joined Tim at the control panel. They were looking pretty earnest.

Another pull of a lever and the drilling resumed. Fumes rose from the huge engine on the back of the waggon. Over the roar of the motor came the steady tattoo of the drill itself, somewhere unimaginably deep now, still probing, still chewing up the rock in search of the elusive layer which might – still – yield up its ancient store of water. As soon as the machinery was safely settled into its work, Bernard went over to where Robert was standing. There was a conversation inaudible to anyone else, after which Robert scowled.

Then Bernard came over to us. 'The last rod,' he said. He had to shout the words to compete with the motor and even then it was difficult to hear him. 'Machinery straining,' he added. 'Never gone this deep before.'

I contented myself with nodding. Maxine said nothing either. I was grateful she didn't shrink away from Bernard. He was completely covered in grey dust, from his wispy hair to his boots. His eyes shone out as simply a glossier grey against the matt. Beside him Maxine provided the utmost contrast. Her hair had never looked more golden, her eyes never bluer. Her limbs were tanned to a lovely tawny shade that set off the apple green of her shorts and teeshirt. She was squeaky clean, a breath of freshness on this site which had gone as grey and dusty as Bernard. He gave her a brief smile and I was pleased to see there was not a trace of subservience in it. When he was working Bernard was the master. Even Maxine took second place.

'How long will it take?' I shouted.

'The rest of the afternoon,' he shouted back. Another brief smile, this time to me. 'Test the patience of the crowd.'

It did. As the afternoon wore on with no action whatsoever the spectators grew restive. This wasn't at all the grand climax they'd come to witness. Had an ice-cream vendor come along he would have made a killing. There was nothing to do except wait.

'Should have brought a book,' Maxine grumbled.

'You insisted on coming,' I reminded her.

Slowly the sun crept across the sky and wiped another afternoon off its slate. It was early evening. Quite a few of the spectators had had to go home to make dinner for their families. The ones who remained were clearly wondering why. I couldn't blame them. My mind was numbed with heat, noise and boredom. Maxine's patience was incomprehensible. Her hatred of her father must be intense for her to submit to an afternoon like this just to witness his hoped-for humiliation.

I hardly noticed when Bernard gave the signal for Tim to turn on the compressor, barely gave a glance to the air hose jumping wildly on the ground. The decibels increased to a pitch which would surely split open the heavens if not the earth, and the spew began.

Dust. Grey dust. A whole desert storm of dust shot up from the well head and threw its load into the air. Slowly it began to settle, as all the preceding spews had settled, over the waggons and Bernard. The crowd as always edged away at this stage, to a distance beyond the grey cloud.

And then silence. Pure, blessed silence. A silence far more startling than any of the noise we had foolishly subjected ourselves to day after day. Through the silence and through the faint grey haze which still hung over the site came just two words from Bernard.

'That's it.'

It took Robert some time to awake from his own noise-induced torpor. He looked around with glazed eyes, only gradually understanding that this pause in the action had a different quality from all the others. 'What do you mean, "That's it"?' he said.

'The last rod,' said Bernard. 'I've gone as deep as I can.'

'Well, fetch another rod,' said Robert crossly.

'Robert, I've gone as far as I can. It's not a question of another rod. The machinery can't go any further.'

'Then get a machine that can.'

'There are limits, Robert. For any drilling rig. We've reached it. I've done what you told me. I've drilled deeper than I've ever drilled before and there's still no water.'

Robert was gathering himself together, his sturdy body gaining substance as the message sank in. He walked across the ashen circle of ground towards the man at its centre. Beside me, Maxine tensed. I glanced at her. Her eyes were shining with expectation.

'Of course there's water!' Robert shouted. 'There's always water! You told me you'd never drilled without hitting water!'

'I also told you I didn't think there was water anywhere near this wood,' said Bernard, his voice as steady as ever. 'Well, there isn't.'

'Think you're a clever lad, do you?' Robert spat. 'You'll think you're clever when I get McKenzie to come and finish the job.'

'McKenzie won't because he can't. We've reached the limits, Robert. There's nothing anyone can do about it.'

'We'll see about that!' Robert shouted. He pushed Bernard aside, jumped on to the footplate and reached for the levers.

Bernard sprang after him. 'Don't touch that!' He grabbed Robert's arm just as the hand closed over the crucial lever. Robert swung round, his face beet red, and with his thwarted hand lashed out at Bernard.

It was just bad luck that Bernard's face was directly in the path of Robert's fist, and bad luck too that all of Robert's rage had gathered itself into a single powerful motion at the end of his arm. The violence of the impact sent Bernard reeling. A moment later he was flat out on the ground.

A gasp rose from the crowd and no doubt from me, too, but we were all too stunned to move. Nothing like this had ever happened in Sedleigh. We're a sleepy town, the only violence an occasional pub brawl fuelled by drink and carried out with adolescent clumsiness. This was real life and we were unprepared for it. But when my shock began to wear off a rage began to rise as strong as Robert's. I lunged forward blindly – whether meaning to help Bernard or hit Robert I don't know – but someone in the crowd behind me clamped a strong hand on my arm.

Bernard was picking himself up off the ground, and for the first time I could see his face. It was barely there, barely a face at all, the features obliterated by the bright red blood which covered them. Even his eyes were invisible. I groaned and felt my stomach churn. With a massive effort he finally stood up.

The impact which had felled Bernard had toppled Robert from the footplate. He was standing directly in front of Bernard. I couldn't see his face, only Bernard's. The grey circle with the two men at the centre of it was silent. The crowd was silent.

My mind was clearing, reason returning. Don't hit him, Bernard. This is your moment of triumph, whatever your pain. Don't let him unleash the monster in you as well.

Bernard raised his hand and I caught my breath.

I should have had more faith. With a world of contempt in a single gesture, he jerked his hand dismissively towards his opponent. 'Go home, Robert,' he said quietly. 'It's all over.'

Robert was rooted to the ground. For one awful moment I feared he would hit Bernard again. I tried to lurch forward but the hand on my arm clamped down so tightly I winced.

And then another movement, this time beside me. Maxine. I'd forgotten her presence, given no thought to the impact of this drama on her. Suddenly she was walking across the dusty circle, a clean cool vision of beauty in the midst of all the squalor. The fresh green of the leaves now hidden beneath their grime seemed to have transferred itself to her foolish little shorts and teeshirt, the gold of the sun to her hair, and for the brief time it took her to cross the distance I had a crazy vision of a dryad freed from her tree to extract her own inexorable form of justice.

She was standing before the two men now. A spurt of fear: if you touch her, Robert, I'll kill you. But there was no need. Her father seemed as stunned by his daughter's entrance as everyone else was. No one moved, no one spoke. Maxine ignored her father. She was gazing into the ruins of Bernard's face. The blood was still flowing but some of it had already begun drying, mixing with the grey of the dust. Bernard gazed back steadily. If he was aware of Robert's presence he didn't show it. It was as if a fastidious artist had airbrushed the farmer out of the picture. And still no one spoke, no one moved.

And then the miracle happened, one of those amazing moments when the pretty little farmer's daughter transcended time and place and herself. She raised her arms and in each hand grasped a mass of her beautiful golden hair. Raised it further . . . and with movements infinitely gentle, and with the sun gleaming from her improvised handkerchief, began to wipe the filth and blood from Bernard's face.

TWENTY

That evening Maxine moved into Bernard's flat. She refused even to go home and pack a few things to bring with her. I supplied what I could from the remains of my mother's wardrobe. Luckily, Eleanor had been tall and thin like Maxine. The clothes, though a trifle odd by modern teenage standards, fit.

'Are you sure you don't mind?' she asked anxiously.

'Of course not. Eleanor would be delighted for you to have them.' I hesitated. 'Maxine, don't be annoyed with me but I have to say this: if you'd rather stay here, you'd be more than welcome. As you can see there's a perfectly good spare room just standing empty.'

She looked round the room, approvingly but without interest.

'What I mean is,' I tried again, 'that I understand why you don't want to go home. But I wouldn't want to think, well, that you were going to Bernard's place because there's nowhere else to go.'

She nodded. 'I appreciate the offer but there's no need.' She'd washed her hands but her hair was still smeared with blood and grime. Some of it had clotted and formed ugly tangles. I supposed she would wash it at Bernard's.

I took a deep breath. 'I mean, I wouldn't want to think you were, well, rushing into Bernard's arms to spite your father.' There, it was out. 'Not that I would blame you,' I added hastily.

She smiled. There was no spite in her smile. 'What you *really* mean is that you're afraid I'll hurt Bernard.'

'Well . . .'

The smile faded. The face that looked into mine seemed older and wiser than the one I'd known so long. An odd phrase shot into my mind: she's become a woman. In those brief moments it took to walk across to her lover, she had grown up. That suddenly? Surely not. And yet –

'I hope not,' she said softly. 'I couldn't bear to hurt him. Not after today.'

We were moving on to tricky ground. I wasn't sure how to begin. 'Maxine, there are . . . well . . . there are a lot of ways people can be hurt . . . even if . . . you know . . . there's no intention. What I mean is, I can understand how you felt, seeing Bernard all messed up like that.'

'Can you?'

'What I mean is, compassion is a lovely thing, but . . . well . . . there are occasions when compassion can hurt. When it's not what the object of that compassion wants.'

'This isn't compassion, Attila. Something happened. When Bernard got up from the ground. When he stood in front of my father and didn't do anything or say anything. I don't know what. I don't know what I felt when I walked across to him. Just that everything had changed. Do you know what I mean?'

I did.

I eyed the suitcase – also Eleanor's. 'How are you going to get that stuff over there?'

'Bernard's coming to pick me up.' She looked at her watch. 'In a few minutes, actually.'

We lugged the suitcase – it was one of those heavy old-fashioned ones – downstairs and put it by the front door. The door was open. We could have gone to the sitting room and had a drink but Maxine insisted on watching for Bernard. I thought of Isolde impatiently awaiting her Tristan. Some Tristan. Some Isolde. I still hadn't taken in all that had happened on that drilling site. An air of unreality hung over us both.

At last the sound of Bernard's ancient van. I watched him

turn it round and point its battered bonnet homeward. This was it. The time for portentous words of advice. Which was why they absolutely must remain unsaid. I thought Bernard would come in for a coffee, a little ritual of leave-taking, but Maxine was already gripping the case and hastening down the path to the van. He opened the door for her – old-fashioned gentleman still, despite his appearance. He'd washed his face clean of the blood and muck but not of the bruises. He didn't exactly look the standard lover but you'd never know it to see Maxine's adoring gaze.

As Bernard started up the motor she rolled the window down and stuck her head out. The grin was ominous. 'Thanks for the offer to stay at your place,' she called out. 'But' – the grin broadened – 'I'd hate to be in the way. Three's a crowd.' She waved gaily. The van sped away.

I shook a fist after her retreating head. 'I'll get you for this!' I yelled.

Then I went into the house to prepare for my next visitor.

Dmitri.

At the drilling site, while Maxine played Mary Magdalen with Bernard's face, the steely hand had continued to grip my arm. I'd turned round to have a few curt words with its owner. I should have known what I would see.

The coal-black eyes with their sensuous hooded lids. The powerful nose swooping down like a hawk on unsuspecting prey. The unbearably kissable mouth. The forest of hair, as steely as the grip of his hand, springing away from the maddeningly intelligent forehead. The high cheekbones and spacious planes of that not-quite-western face, full of mystery and just a touch of cruelty.

I said nothing. There was nothing to say. For once in my life I was speechless.

'I will speak to you later,' said Dmitri. Then he released my arm and strode into the circle.

Bernard and Maxine had retreated to the edge. Only Robert remained, rooted to the spot, unsure how to make a dignified retreat. Dmitri went up to him. From where I stood the two men were in profile a few feet away from each other.

'Mr Vesey, I have returned to the house you have kindly rented to me, to find it entirely bereft of water. Could you explain to me what has happened to it, please?' Dmitri's voice was strong but not unfriendly.

Robert scowled at his tenant. 'How the hell should I know? Always been water there.'

'That's as may be,' said Dmitri, 'but it is not there now. I have tried every tap. I can assure you that there is not a drop of water in that house now.'

'Must be an air lock,' said Robert. 'Go back and try again.'

'Mr Vesey, I have tried. Repeatedly. There is no water. I must ask you what you intend to do about it and when.'

Robert shrugged. He looked at the silenced drilling rig, no doubt counting the money its stubbornness had cost him.

'Mr Vesey, I have – as you know – been willing to pay a higher than normal rental for your house, given its rather primitive state. But one facility I am not prepared to do without is water.'

Automatically I looked at Bernard. He was detaching himself with great reluctance from Maxine's ministrations. He walked into the circle and faced Robert. I didn't like seeing them that close to each other again.

'Where does the water for the house come from?' Bernard asked.

Robert glared at him.

'You must know,' Bernard insisted.

Robert shrugged again. 'An old well. In the garden.'

'Has it ever dried up before?'

'Of course not.'

Bernard straightened himself. It must have been an effort,

given his bruises. 'The spring,' he said. 'That must have been the source for the old well. They both tapped the same small pocket of water we hit last week.'

'*Have* been?' said Dmitri. 'Do you mean, no longer?'

Bernard shook his head. 'I'm afraid not. We hit that source last week. It dried up the spring and clearly your house, too. It all went into that,' he finished, gesturing towards the failed wellhead. 'I'm sorry, Dmitri. I had no idea the house used the spring's supply – it's not marked on any of the maps.'

Dmitri nodded. 'I see. And this is final? The water is gone from the house for ever?'

'It's final,' said Bernard.

The two men turned to Robert.

Or rather, to where Robert had been. He was quietly making his way towards his Land-Rover.

Dmitri followed him. 'Mr Vesey, I must insist.' The voice not quite so friendly now. 'The responsibility for this is yours and I expect you to take whatever steps are necessary to put some other water supply into that house.'

Robert slammed the door and roared off.

The crowd was dispersing. Clearly they had no interest in this new domestic crisis. The action was over.

Dmitri returned to Bernard. To my surprise he shrugged off the problem with a rueful smile. Then he turned his attention to Bernard himself. 'Borehole drilling is a dangerous job?'

Bernard raised a hand to his face. 'Robert. I didn't find water for him. He's not amused.'

Maxine came up to Bernard and put her hand in his. After a little hesitation I joined the group. Maxine was looking earnestly at Dmitri. 'You can't live there with no water.'

'Quite so,' Dmitri smiled. 'I will take my custom to one of the town's hotels.'

'They're full up,' said Maxine. 'It's still the holiday season. You'll never find a place tonight.' She smiled shyly.

'I'm moving into Bernard's flat tonight. It's not a big flat but I'm sure we could find room...'

Bernard's face was inscrutable as he nodded.

'On the other hand,' Maxine continued, 'Attila's got a spare room – two, in fact. Isn't that right?'

Sly. But ancient laws of hospitality were at work here, this was no time to upbraid my sneaky little friend. 'Yes, of course,' I said heartily. 'Plenty of room. More than welcome to stay with me.'

'Thank you,' said Dmitri.

The deed was done.

So here I sat, on my second whisky already, awaiting Dmitri's arrival. 'I'll kill Maxine,' I muttered at the glass. 'Finds true love and has to dig some up for everyone else as well.'

The glass said nothing.

I'd readied the spare room – the biggest and best, of course. No way was I sharing a bed with him again. His long absence had cured me of the madness. Bernard was wrong. Dmitri *was* that kind of person. Trifling with my affections, wasn't that the phrase? Never again. I would be hospitable but nothing more. 'Nothing more,' I told the glass.

The glass smirked. I resisted an urge to fling it into the fireplace.

The hum of a motor. The glass trembled. I steadied it. There had been other humming motors. My ears were on stalks tonight. I was hearing every motor-operated toy in town. It would take him a while to get here. He'd have to pack. No he wouldn't. He was packed already. He'd arrived from London and gone to make a cup of tea and no water. Went straight to the drilling site. Just has to pick up his suitcase, hop in the car and –

The hum was louder. Oh God. No toy. Real car. Coming this way. Closer. Calm down. Plan of action. Have it out with him. Straight talk. Just who the hell are you and why did you come?

Closer, louder ... stopped. Slam of a door. No, not slam. BMW. Quality thud. Footsteps. Not next door. Here. Door open. Dmitri framed in it. This is it. No more time to think. Act.

'Hello, Dmitri. Nice to see you again. Good trip to London?'

'I wasn't in London.'

'Oh? Where were you?'

'Berlin.'

The glass slipped from my hand and shattered on the floor. I gazed mournfully at its remains. It had betrayed me. There was no possibility now of presenting the smooth façade, of leading up – step by careful step – to the inevitable confrontation in which I, not he, would take control. A single stupid slip of my fingers had destroyed everything. A glass. A stupid bloody glass. What a laugh. Should I laugh or cry? I looked up from the floor into Dmitri's eyes and did neither. He had searched my eyes intensely before but never like this. He was moving across the room now, coming closer, his eyes never leaving mine. I wanted to look away – God, how I wanted! – but that wasn't possible either. I was trapped. There was no escape whatsoever.

'And what did you find?' I asked at last.

'What did you expect me to find?'

His eyes still fixed on mine. Hard, black, utterly without mercy. And then, a mad spurt of mindless hope. Could I be absolutely sure? Was it still possible that he was bluffing? I tried to review all the enigmatic scraps of conversation we'd had before, searching them for clues, stitching them together. Did they add up to absolute knowledge? Think, think, *think*. If only he would look away, leave my mind free for thought. But no, that was part of the technique, wasn't it? Trap them, hold them, give them no escape.

'What did you expect me to find, Anna?'

My heart was crashing about so wildly it would surely break through my ribcage. My head was growing light, my stomach churning. I wouldn't be able to remain upright much longer. No escape.

Then my shoulders slumped. 'That I don't exist.'

TWENTY-ONE

It was all over. Everything. Not only my relationship with Dmitri but the deception maintained for more than forty years. My first instinct had been right after all. From the moment he had walked into my library I'd sensed that he was the instrument that would bring it to its end. All the rest had been a diversion.

Now that it had happened I felt almost free – enough at least to look away from those relentless eyes. I noticed again the shattered glass. 'I hope we can be civilised about this,' I said calmly.

'I'm sure we can.'

'I'll just clear up the mess and then we'll begin.' I went into the kitchen and brought back the dustpan and brush. Odd how soothing these mechanical jobs are in a crisis. I enjoyed each sweep of the little brush, the tinkle of glass as it went into the pan. The glass had been empty. At least there was no sticky booze to wipe up. All neat and tidy. I hoped the other mess about to be cleared up would be as simple.

'The glass wasn't valuable?' Dmitri asked.

'Bohemian. A present from a lover. There was only the one.'

'I'm sorry. I should have been less abrupt.'

A wave of sadness came over me. Not for the glass or even the lover but for my past. I had enjoyed being Anna Atwill.

'Would it be tactless of me to suggest that you bring two more glasses and the whisky?' said Dmitri.

'Not at all.' I fetched the glasses and whisky and then stood there uncertainly. What was the best setting for one's official extinction? Normally I would have gone for the patio – the fresh air, the openness. But tonight more than ever I needed Edmund and Eleanor to be with me. The sitting room was crammed with the objects they'd loved, souvenirs of their wonderfully rich lives. I brought over a little marquetry table – another present in lieu of money for a painting – and put it in front of the fireplace. I set the glasses and whisky on it, sat down in one of the comfortable armchairs which flanked the fireplace and gestured Dmitri into the other. I poured the whisky. 'Water?' I asked.

'Neat.'

I handed his glass over, taking care that our fingers didn't touch – I needed to be calm tonight. It occurred to me that he was being rather kind, letting me play the hostess, letting me take my time. Whoever and whatever he was, he was no conventional villain. He even let me open the conversation. Only after I'd taken the first sip did I begin. 'What exactly did you find in the files?'

'Which files?'

'The Stasi files, of course. I presume that's why you went to Berlin.'

'I'm afraid I lied to you, Anna. I haven't been to Berlin. I've been in the Reading Room of the British Library. As I told you before I left.'

At least this time I had a firm grip on the glass. How could I have been so stupid? After years of questioning by east European officials I had just fallen into the most elementary trap of them all. Well, what did it matter? It was clear that he knew everything anyway. 'So how did you know?' I asked.

'I've known for some time.'

'Perhaps you could tell me what exactly it is that you do know?'

'I would rather you told me what you know first.'

'I'm sure you would,' I said drily. 'They always do.'

'They?'

'The secret police. Under whatever name. In whichever country. I presume it's the British government you work for, not German.'

The look of astonishment that came over him startled me. Could he really fake something like that? He suddenly seemed lost for words. That startled me too. He'd been so self-assured until now.

'Anna,' he said, 'you don't seriously think –' He set his glass down and leaned forward, searching my face. 'Is *that* what you think I am? The secret police?'

'Well?'

He leaned back in his chair and covered his face with his hands. 'Dear God, what have I done?' There was a long pause. Then he lowered his hands and looked mournfully at me over the little table. 'My poor Anna. Is that really what you thought? And for how long have you thought this terrible thing?'

This wasn't going at all as I expected. 'From the day you first came to the library,' I said uncertainly. 'You knew so much about me.'

'But I *explained*. My uncle Anatoly was your father's client. It was a perfectly straightforward family connection. Or did you think that was just a lie?'

'Well, no, but –' I smiled weakly. 'They got everywhere – the secret police.'

His own smile was rueful. 'Anatoly an informer? Dear old Anatoly was the biggest talker in the world. No one in their right mind would ever have told him a thing unless they wanted it broadcast as widely as possible.'

'Somebody must have told him something,' I tried. 'That you knew so much about me.'

'Edmund,' he said simply. 'As I explained before. Edmund was proud of you. He talked a great deal about you, to Anatoly and no doubt to many of his other clients.'

'I didn't mean that,' I said quietly. 'I meant about my past. The distant past. Anatoly must have known about that, too.'

Dmitri shook his head. 'Not a thing, thank God.'

'But – then how did *you* know?'

'My father.'

'I don't understand.'

'You will in a minute. But first I must ask you something else. You shocked me very much, Anna, telling me you thought I belonged to the secret police. I need to know . . . if you continued to think that. Throughout these months we've known each other.' He paused, then continued, his voice soft and uncertain. 'The night when a glorious gypsy fiddler appeared beneath my window . . .'

I clamped my teeth tightly to push back the tears. I didn't want to think about that night, the pain was still too intense.

'Anna, surely not that night . . .'

I shook my head. 'Most of the time I didn't. I thought I must be mistaken. But other times –' I looked at him, pleading to be understood. 'You seemed to be waiting for me to say something, to be leading me again and again back into my past, expecting something from me, some . . . confession. And then I thought yes, my first instinct was right. But so often I felt unsure – I didn't know what to think.'

He sank back into the chair again. He seemed older, no longer the deliciously dangerous St Petersburg prince but a middle-aged man, weary and sad. 'My poor dear Anna, what an appalling mess I have made of this. If only you had told me.'

'You could have told me,' I countered.

He nodded. 'Anatoly talked too much and I too little. What a useless family we are. Anna, will you believe me when I say I never meant any harm to you? And surely you don't still think I have anything to do with the secret police?'

'You lied about Berlin,' I said.

He sighed. 'Yes, I lied. As soon as I entered your house tonight I saw you were hiding something. It was the opportunity I had been waiting for – to surprise it out of you. The little lie simply came to me in a flash and I used it.'

'But *what* did you want to surprise out of me? What is this thing you've been expecting from me all these months?'

'I wanted you to tell me what you knew about your past. About your parents.'

We had arrived at the point at last. '*Which* parents?' I asked quietly.

He nodded. 'That's what I needed to find out: whether you knew.'

I leaned back and closed my eyes. All around me I could feel the presence of Edmund and Eleanor. I wished Dmitri would go. I wanted to talk to them. This was a private matter, family only. He had no right to be here. I opened my eyes and looked steadily at him. 'Well. Now you know. Is there any other information you want from me?'

'You're angry with me.'

'Yes.'

'You have every right. And I have no right to ask your forgiveness yet. I've behaved badly. Will you allow me to explain?'

I raised one hand in agreement.

'It comes as a shock to most people,' he began, 'especially if they discover only in middle age that they were adopted. I wanted to spare you that. My father did, too. He was very firm on that point: that you must be left in peace if you knew nothing. That's why I had to be so devious.' He smiled bitterly. 'I have little practice in being devious, whatever you may think. My reputation is quite the opposite: as a cantankerous academic who says what he thinks and doesn't suffer fools gladly. So you see, I was a poor choice as messenger for something so delicate. My father knew that too, but there was no choice. There are now only two people alive who know the truth about your birth, and they are both sitting in this room.'

One. I knew almost nothing.

'Would you like to talk about it, Anna? Or are you too angry with me?'

I looked at the man sitting across from me. So many men he had been to me already: member of the secret police, amusing companion for a party, exotic foreigner come to liven up our town and my life. Lover. And now? His father's messenger, a well-meaning stranger charged with telling me something I didn't want to know.

'And did your father tell you to make love to me?' I asked coldly.

'Anna!'

'Well? Or was that just an amusing episode, something to liven up your stay in dreary old Sedleigh, to while away the time until the old girl decided to talk?'

'Anna, my darling –'

It was too late to push back the tears or care about the spectacle I was making of myself. 'Dmitri, how could you? I *loved* you. I gave myself to you in a way I've never done before, for that single night you were the centre of my universe, I held nothing back from you, I told you the truth with my body and soul and I trusted you completely and utterly, and to you I was only –'

'Anna, Anna, my darling –'

His arms were around me and I was sobbing uncontrollably and I didn't care about anything at all, only the sense of release from the hell he had put me through since that night. Now at last I could hate him as wholeheartedly as I had loved him. I shoved him away from me and stood up. 'Get out of here!' I shouted. 'Get out of this house!'

The words echoed in the room. For a long time he remained crouched by the chair where I had been, his face turned away from me. Then, slowly, he rose to his feet and began to walk towards the door. I don't know what I felt, watching him leave. I was no longer coherent, nothing but an explosive mass of raw emotion. By the open doorway was the suitcase he had brought with him. I gave no thought as to where he would go when he left. He reached for the case ... laid it on the floor ... and opened it. From it he extracted several sheets of paper. He straightened up again and, holding the papers, came back to where I was standing.

'Will you do just one thing for me? Will you read these letters? And then, if you wish, I'll leave.'

'I don't think you have the right to ask anything more of me.'

'I don't. But I hope you'll read them anyway. Please.' He held them out to me.

'Who are they from – your father?'

'No. From me. To you.'

I stared.

'There are only three – they wouldn't take long to read. The first was written in your library, when I discovered you were not the drab little librarian I expected. The second was written after the party when I made you weep for your past. And the third' – he paused a little – 'was written while the most glorious woman I've ever known was lying asleep in my bed.'

The rage was draining from me. In its place a kind of numbness. This wasn't me standing here, it was someone else, a robot drained of all feeling.

'Please, Anna. Please read them. Then I'll go.'

I looked at the letters this stranger was holding out to me, another stranger.

'Please, Anna. It matters a great deal – to you as well as to me.'

I nodded mechanically and took the letters.

A lifetime had passed when finally I put the letters back on the table. Phrases of love were swirling through my brain. Gypsy temptress. Queen of the plain and the forest. Splendid Juliet. Wicked little volcano. A jewel of a human being, priceless and heartbreakingly cherishable. I looked up at the man who had written them.

He was sitting in the chair opposite me again. While I had read he had moved about the room quietly, turning on the reading light by my chair, refilling my glass and his. There was a calmness and dignity in his posture now that belied the passionate words. Did he regret them? He smiled as if reading my thoughts, and there was no regret in his smile.

'Do you understand now?' he said softly. 'It's very simple: the messenger fell in love with the messagee.'

'And is he in love with her still?'

He nodded.

'Dmitri . . .'

'Not yet, Anna. There is business to attend to before I can cast off my messenger's sandals. Do you feel you can talk to me now?'

'I think so.'

'And do you trust me now?'

'I think so.'

'Only "think"?'

I smiled. 'I spent too long in the east.'

He nodded. 'Tell me what you can.'

'I don't know where to begin.'

'The day you learned you were adopted?'

November 1989. The television in Edmund's sickroom. Jubilant crowds at the Brandenburg Gate. Edmund's sunken eyes watching the teeming square with the same voraciousness with which he had so often viewed a new painting. The picture in the square changing to the BBC news desk and a man talking about the latest unemployment figures. Edmund turning his head towards me. 'Enough television.' Myself switching the television off, looking back to my dying father with a smile. No smile in return. 'Anna, there's something I must tell you.'

'Yes?' I said, to both Edmund and Dmitri. Then I began.

'It was a month or so before my father died. We'd been watching the news – the opening of the Wall in Berlin. I suppose it was a symbolic moment for Edmund as well as for everyone else, a signal that it was time to open up our own past. The fact that it was Berlin rather than any of the other revolutions was significant, too. As you probably know.

'Edmund knew he was dying. We both knew – neither of us could bear the indignity of pretence. It must have been a torment for him, pretending all those years that he was my father. Though of course he was my father in the ways that mattered most.

'I'd never had the slightest suspicion. Odd, isn't it, when you consider my appearance. Other people must have wondered from time to time how a daughter could look so wholly unlike either of her parents. Still, it happens.

'There was nothing in writing, Edmund said. For ... well ... for safety. There were other people involved and the secrecy had been necessary to protect them. That's why they hadn't told me when I was a child. No child can be trusted with a secret like that, not when other people's lives could be at risk. Later, when I grew up and began travelling in eastern Europe, the secrecy was needed to protect me too. They felt that if I genuinely didn't know anything, there was no way I could accidentally say something I shouldn't. Even so, they'd been worried every time I left for another trip. They'd hidden it well. They'd always been so encouraging about my crazy travels. They were the best parents anyone could have, Dmitri, they really were.'

Dmitri nodded. A sense of peace had settled over the room. How much of its source was Dmitri and how much Edmund's and Eleanor's spirits I didn't know.

'Did he say why he was finally telling you?' Dmitri asked.

'Now that the east was opening up there was less need for secrecy. Also, I'd settled down in Sedleigh, I was unlikely to do much more travelling. But mainly the lack of anything in writing. There was always a possibility, however remote, that someone from the past might approach me. As someone now has.'

Dmitri smiled.

'Edmund felt I should know the truth from him rather than from a stranger. Also, I might not believe it if I heard it from someone else. With Eleanor dead and himself dying, it was now or never.

'Do you know what upset me most? Knowing that for all those years they'd had to be silent about what they'd done for me. No parents could have loved their own child more than Edmund and Eleanor loved me. It was a generosity that took my breath away when I learned the truth. I wished I'd known before so I could have appreciated them more. As it was, it was a very emotional scene. As you can imagine.'

Dmitri nodded. 'And did he tell you how it came about?'

'As much as he knew, which wasn't a lot. They were both in Berlin on business – living there for several months that time. West Berlin, of course. One night an acquaintance of theirs called them to his house. It was fairly late at night. Berlin was going through a period of turmoil just then. My parents were uneasy. Strange things were happening in those days, people had learned to expect the unexpected. Even so, they were utterly unprepared for what did happen.

'When their acquaintance opened the door he was obviously in quite a state. He led them straight into a back room. There, in an improvised cot, was a baby squawling its head off. My parents were rather taken aback – children weren't their scene and they'd had no idea this man had an infant. He didn't. "I need someone to look after this child," he said. "Someone who is not German. Someone who is leaving Germany soon and can take the child with them." He looked at Edmund and Eleanor.

'Eleanor said she would ask around among the British community. "No!" the man said. "Nobody must know about this except us!" Eleanor calmed him down and explained gently that she couldn't possibly look for a courier without telling that person what the object was that he or she would be carrying. Especially if it was an infant.

'The man became more agitated. "No, *you* must take the baby!" he said. Eleanor was horrified. She had no experience whatsoever of babies, no interest in them at all. Surely there must be someone more suitable? No, he insisted, it must be her. Eleanor was trying hard not to become angry. She might be willing to act as courier but only as a last resort, if no one better could be found. But who was to take delivery of the child in London? And why couldn't that person come to Berlin to fetch the child in person? The man was now frantic. "No, you don't understand! *You* must take the child! It must become yours!"

'It was probably the first time in her life that Eleanor was speechless. So was Edmund. When finally they recovered they were adamant. Absolutely not. If they'd wanted a child they would have had one of their own. They had no intention whatsoever of adopting someone else's child, let alone in such bizarre circumstances. And then the man broke down and told them what had happened.

'Someone he knew – he refused to name him or her – had smuggled the baby over from East Berlin that night. There was no Wall then, it hadn't been all that difficult. The circumstances of the birth were fraught, there were political implications. Not only the baby's life but that of its mother was at risk. It was essential to find a couple willing to pass it off as their own and take it out of the country – for ever. It was also essential that no one else know. There was no alternative. He had tried to think of someone more suitable but there was no one. Edmund and Eleanor had been in Berlin for some months – long enough to cover a fictitious pregnancy and fictitious birth. They could return to London with no one suspecting the child wasn't their own.

'God only knows what went through my parents' minds in those few hours. Both of them were dedicated to their work. They didn't dislike children but there was no room for a child in their lives. Further, they both travelled a great deal and when they were at home they worked. Eleanor's work in particular demanded great concentration. What on earth would she do with a screaming infant? They weren't selfish – far from it. They simply knew that there were other people better suited to parenthood. What's more, they were both in their forties, far too old to adapt to the strain of bringing up a child. Nor could they bring me back to London as "their" child and then nonchalantly put me up for adoption. That would arouse the most intense suspicions, especially in their circumstances.

'I'll never know what made them relent. Edmund himself didn't know. As for the rest, it was fairly straightforward. The man made out a false birth certificate proclaiming Edmund and Eleanor Atwill the proud parents of a daughter called Anna. Then my "parents" and I moved into a hotel where no one knew us – I suppose that's where you and I first met? – until it was time for us to leave for London.

'And so began the life of the wholly fictitious Anna Atwill. Neither natural nor adopted. A freak whose only existence was in a false birth certificate ... and perhaps in a second birth certificate which wasn't false? My parents knew almost nothing about me, but when Edmund finally revealed what he did know it was 1989. It was only a matter of time before all the files in East Berlin would be opened. And in them there might be a genuine birth certificate. Edmund had no idea what sort of status someone like me would have if the truth came out. After all, every bit of documentation I possess depends on that false birth certificate. Britain isn't known for its kindness to illegal aliens.'

I smiled at my gentle interrogator who had kept silent throughout. 'Do you understand now why I was so resistant to your prodding? How could I reveal anything without revealing everything? And do you understand why I was so terrified that you knew so much about me? And why the spectre of the Stasi files made me break my favourite glass?'

It had grown quite dark outside. The only light was the pool shed by the reading lamp beside me. Dmitri was in the shadows. I couldn't see his face very well but his voice was full of sadness.

'My poor Anna. You shame me. I didn't give a thought to any of this. My only fear was of startling you with the news of your adoption. I didn't realise how many other implications it had for you. Will you forgive me? And believe that I was only a clumsy fool badly carrying out an unwelcome mission?'

'Of course.'

'And will it make you feel a little better if I say again that you and I are now the only people in the world who know your secret?'

'Yes, it does make me feel better.'

'And will you let me ask you one more question?'

'All right.'

Dmitri leaned over the bookcase beside him and switched on the lamp. There were now two pools of light in the room. That made me feel better, too.

'When Edmund told you all this,' he began, 'presumably he didn't tell you that during the fraught scene in which your parents were persuaded to "adopt" a child they didn't want, a second child entered the room?'

'No.'

'His presence went unnoticed for a little while; the principals in the drama were too agitated to have much attention left over for a ten-year-old boy hovering in the shadows. That boy was me, Anna. And the man who falsified the birth certificate – the doctor – was my father.'

TWENTY-TWO

The room was very still. The only sound was of moths beating their wings against the windows, trying to reach the light. It had been kind of Dmitri to turn on his lamp, to let me see his face as he made his own revelation. I realised now that everything he'd said and done this night had been kind – apart from the lie about his trip to Berlin.

'I'm beginning to understand,' I said. 'You know more about this than I do.'

'A great deal more.'

'Are you going to tell me?'

'As much as you want to know.'

'How much did the ten-year-old boy know?'

'Not much, but enough to be the weakest link. My father was horrified when he discovered me lurking in the shadows. He questioned me closely, and when he realised how much I knew he swore me to secrecy.'

'Did you keep the secret?'

'I did. In truth, I wasn't very interested in the ugly baby – and you were ugly – who was to play such a significant role in my later life. For my father, however, this was the final element in his decision to leave Berlin. My mother also wished to leave.'

'Was she there that night?'

'Not in that room, but she knew all about it. She was very angry with my father for concocting a completely false birth certificate. It was a very serious offence indeed. If the truth had come out my father would have been obliged to cease practising as a doctor – at the very least. But there were worse implications even than that. The girl who smuggled you to my father's house now had a hold over him. Perhaps she used it or perhaps she was found out. In any case, it wasn't long before a different girl came, with a "request" for a false birth certificate ... but no baby ...' He reached for his glass and sipped his whisky, never taking his eyes from me.

'I see,' I said.

Dmitri nodded. 'He had no choice. He created the false certificate. A week later we left Berlin.'

'How your father must have hated me.'

'He wasn't so unreasonable as to blame a new-born baby. But he did see where all of this was leading – had already led.'

'Did this new girl try to blackmail him into staying?'

'He made his arrangements quickly. There was no time for her to seek him out. She seems to have dropped from the story after that. And he was quite sure that she had no idea what had happened to you. So your secret remains safe.'

'Your poor father.'

'It was probably time to leave anyway. Especially with a young son who couldn't be trusted to keep quiet. London was large, anonymous and relatively far removed from the turmoil of continental Europe. We settled into our new lives fairly well. There was no sign of my father's deeds following him across the Channel. It was a new start and my father grasped it eagerly. There was only one complication. Anatoly.'

'Ah. I was wondering where he came into it.'

'Anatoly had been your father's client for some years – that's how your parents and mine met in the first place; Anatoly insisted that Edmund look up my parents in Berlin. He could hardly have expected it would have such consequences. But Anatoly had lived in London for several years, and when your parents returned with their new-born baby, Anatoly – like everyone else – had no reason to believe you weren't their natural daughter. People were surprised, of course. As you said, your parents were not known to have any interest in children. But nobody guessed that you were adopted, let alone in such extraordinary circumstances, least of all Anatoly. He was, like most painters, totally self-centred, too immersed in his own world to notice much about other people. None the less, he remained a threat, a link between the two families. Even more so when my family moved to London. That was the main reason your parents moved to Sedleigh to live permanently in what had previously been their holiday home.'

'The timing. Yes, it fits.'

'The less our families had to do with each other, the better. The distance between London and Sedleigh was useful. Until the day when Anatoly, on his way to Scotland to meet a prospective patron, insisted on stopping overnight at Sedleigh on his way. Why my father agreed to come with him and bring me is a mystery he never explained. Perhaps he couldn't resist seeing you just once more. He couldn't help taking an interest in you. I think it was a comfort to him to know that this insane "adoption" which had begun so badly was turning out so well, against all expectations.'

And Anatoly had captured the moment with his paintbrush. 'No wonder you were so surprised to see the painting above the fridge.'

Dmitri smiled. 'I hoped that would be the moment. I hoped you knew more about the painting – about the people in it.'

'And no wonder Eleanor said so little about it. There we all were – my parents, your father, you, me – brought together again for the first time since that back room in Berlin. But how extraordinary that she should hang it in our house.'

'Is it?'

'Anyone could have seen it and asked questions.'

'And she would have answered them with the truth: that Edmund's client had stopped in with his brother-in-law and nephew on their way to Scotland and painted a charming picture of the occasion. What better subterfuge than the truth? But I think there was another reason for hanging it where she could see it daily.'

'This is getting too complicated for me.'

'On the contrary, it's very simple. A tribute to you.'

'To *me*?'

'A reminder of the day, two years before, when you had entered their lives. How it must have delighted your parents to see that painting. To compare that fraught night with the happiness that had followed. Think how close they had come to not having you. How many times they must have blessed that crazy intuition which had led them to accept you despite everything. Just a little yes or no. And there you were, the result of their yes, bringing them a happiness they'd never anticipated.'

I bowed my head before my messenger. More than kind. So many acts of generosity had gone into making my life. And so many tiny quirks of fate had led me from that night in Berlin to where I was. Even this house, which had formed the backdrop of my childhood, even that was the result of that night. The need for secrecy had driven my parents to bring me to a place where it was impossible to be unhappy. I looked up at Dmitri. 'I wish I'd known all this before. To thank your father for what he did.'

Dmitri smiled. 'Seeing you on the day of the painting was his thanks. And all the news that filtered through to him from Anatoly. For years he was able to follow your progress indirectly. It was only when he was dying that his pleasure became shadowed by the knowledge. You see, after Anatoly died, he lost his only viable connection with your family. He had no idea if your parents had ever told you. If they hadn't, it meant that he was the only person alive who knew the truth. He couldn't let that knowledge die with him, just in case it would make a difference to your life.'

'I begin to see why your "mission" was so difficult.'

'And why I carried it out so clumsily. Have you forgiven me for my clumsiness?'

'Of course I have.'

He hesitated. 'And will you forgive me for any clumsiness yet to come?'

I was instantly alert – the old reflexes from my years of travel. Even now Dmitri could never be just a friend, even just a lover. These were strange and twisted threads connecting us. 'What do you mean?'

'I mean the rest of the story, Anna.'

My hand was shaking just a little as I picked up my glass and sipped the soothing whisky. I smiled uncertainly. 'The rest of the story is sitting here. Oh, of course – your sister. I'd almost forgotten – you did say you had a sister? Where did she fit into all this?'

'She knew nothing. She was younger than me and never knew about the baby who came to our house that night. She isn't what I meant, Anna. There are other people involved.'

'Only the two of us,' I said quickly. 'You said we were the only two who knew.'

'Now, perhaps. But in the past.'

My heart had begun its horrible drumbeat again.

'Your parents, Anna.'

The fear pushed into my throat, nearly choking me. 'You know all about my parents,' said a strangled little voice. 'Edmund and Eleanor. They're my only parents as far as I'm concerned.' I looked into the dead fireplace, at the table, at the bookcases full of Eleanor's books, the walls full of the paintings of Edmund's clients. Everywhere except at Dmitri.

'Your other parents, Anna. Please. Don't make this more difficult than it needs to be. I need to know how much Edmund told you about –'

'Nothing. He didn't know anything.'

'That's not true. He did know one thing. And he told you.'

I shook my head.

'The morning you left my house,' Dmitri continued. 'When I handed you your violin. "A fine fiddle," I said to you. "It's nothing special," you said. "Not a Stradivari or anything like that. But I like it. I've had it all my life – *my father gave it to me when I was born*," you said.'

'I told you what I meant,' I said quickly. 'That Edmund often accepted objects in lieu of payment. Look around this room, it's full of –'

'Yes, you told me. But I knew it wasn't the entire truth. That was the moment I'd been waiting for. You had let slip the first hint that you might –'

'I was distraught that morning, I didn't know what I was saying.'

'You're distraught now, Anna. I understand why. But we can't pretend any more. *What did Edmund tell you?*'

'Only that,' I said dully. 'That the violin had belonged to . . . my other father. The person – a girl, you say – who brought me to your father's house had brought the violin as well. It was the only . . . remnant . . . of my other parents. That's all Edmund knew.' I took a deep breath. 'And it's all I want to know.'

'Are you sure, Anna?'

I looked into my whisky glass. I'd drunk surprisingly little. Dmitri's glass was empty. I leaned forward and grasped the bottle, intending to refill his glass. Anything normal would do. But he leaned forward too and put his hand over mine. Not normal. Nothing to do with Dmitri was normal or ordinary. Can't we just forget about all this? my eyes pleaded. No, his answered. 'I suppose you know about them?' I said heavily. Please, the touch of your hand just now, it's more than I can bear.

He nodded.

'And this is also part of your "mission"?'

'To tell you as much as you want to know. My father didn't want to force anything on you.'

He took his hand from mine. I filled his glass. 'Then that's that,' I said briskly. 'I don't want to know anything.' Please can we turn the clock back? Return to that night when an impetuous and ignorant woman serenaded you beneath your window? Can we rewrite the sequel? Cross out the following morning? Let me wake up in your bed again, Dmitri, only this time *be there*.

'I'll respect your wishes,' he said at last. 'But there are two things I have to say. The first is this. I am the only person who knows about your original parents. If I die, this dies with me. Please think about that. Be sure you know what you're doing.'

I nodded. 'I'll think about it. But I don't think I'll change my mind.'

'And the second is this. Bernard knew what lay beneath Robert Vesey's land. Vesey refused to listen. Look where it got him. I know what lies beneath your life, Anna. Will you dare listen?'

I smiled. 'There was nothing beneath Robert's land. Except a tiny pocket of water that served the spring and your house, and now that's gone. That's why you're here tonight,' I reminded him.

It was a cheap attempt at evasion and he knew it. 'There were two people beneath your life, Anna. They gave you your life. Don't you think you owe it to them to listen?'

'Why? They gave me away. I owe them nothing. Some wrong-side-of-the-blankets romance. A one-night stand.'

'That isn't true. They were real people, Anna. And they loved each other.'

'Good. Then I'm a love-child. End of story.'

'You know it isn't –'

'I don't like love stories, Dmitri. They always have happy endings and I never believe them.'

A touch of hardness edged his voice when he replied. 'No east European "love story" in the 1950s could have a happy ending. You must know that.'

Yes, I knew that. And that was part of the reason I didn't want to know. My guardian angel had been formidably efficient, had given me an unusually happy life. I didn't want to know if that happiness had been built on other people's misery. I wanted nothing to mar my memories. Yes, I was being selfish, but – I rationalised – those two people who had produced me were dead; it could make no difference to them. Unless –

'Just one thing,' I said cautiously. 'Are they . . . dead?'

'Your father, certainly. Your mother, probably.'

And then a strange thing happened. For the first time, an image began to form in my mind. Those two people. They had been real. It wasn't something I'd ever imagined before. Now the image was there – no faces, not even distinctly outlined forms, just shapes struggling to come clearer. I pushed the image away. 'Then that really is the end of it.'

Dmitri said nothing. Again I had that sense of him waiting for me to do something, say something. This time I knew what it was. 'I don't want to know any more, Dmitri. Please.'

'As you wish.'

The image began to recede. In its place came another: myself fiddling my heart out beneath Dmitri's windows. Throughout the whole of this fraught evening, that scene had always been waiting just beneath consciousness. I wanted to return to that night. It was Dmitri I wanted, not his message. Everything that had happened since his unexpected appearance at the drilling site (was that really just this afternoon?) had been so confused I hadn't had a chance to think of the implications. Now I was thinking again. He had come back. Surely not just to deliver his message? No, he'd *said* he had fallen in love with me and said he loved me still. Then why was he still sitting in that chair so far away?'

'You're disappointed in me, aren't you?' I said.

'I had hoped you would want to know the whole story,' he admitted. 'But disappointed? No, not entirely. I expected too much.'

'But you think less of me now, don't you?'

'I could never think anything but good of you, Anna Atwill.'

'Dmitri . . .'

'What do I think now? I think: Thank God this business is over and done with. I have delivered my message, done my duty, put my father's soul at rest. My task has weighed heavily on me from the moment I first saw you. I knew then that you would turn my life upside down in some way, that you were not a woman who could be encountered and left again without a great piece of myself being left behind with you. I think: Now that this business is over, we can wipe the slate clean and begin our own lives.'

'Dmitri . . .'

'I think: Anna has read my three letters. She knows how I feel about her. Everything is known that needs to be known. My love is plainly declared in those letters. I cannot be accused of concealment. Of pomposity, yes. I have lived a dry life of books and they have left their trace. But however badly I express my love, I express it without reservation.'

'They're beautiful letters, Dmitri.'

'Are they? Do they find favour with my mistress?'

'They do.'

'There is a fourth letter, Anna.'

'Is there? Where?'

'Part of it is here.' He withdrew a slightly crumpled sheet of paper from his pocket. 'And part of it is in my head. Would you like me to read it to you?'

I laughed – 'All of it? The part in your head, too?' – and realised that it was the first laughter to be heard in my house all evening. The house had been used to laughter before – my parents had been the least solemn of people. Now I could feel the house relaxing again, anticipating a return of the good times.

'Yes, all of it. Are you ready, Anna?'

'I am ready.'

'Good. We begin:

'My dearest Anna, Anya, Anushka. Whatever name I call you (and in moments of exasperation I have called you things less pretty than those names listed above), you have become the infuriatingly adorable centre of my life. But I must tell you that I am extremely angry with you. On that morning when you exchanged my body for that wretched horse as a suitable object around which to wrap your delectable thighs, I thought: Now the time has come. Her stubborn reserve is about to break and give me the chance to fulfil my hateful mission, after which I can abandon this burdensome pretence and get on with my real task, which is to love my sublime girl as voraciously as she loves me. But no. There you sat, dishevelled after our night of passion, but proud and unyielding.

'Your silence, Ännchen, drove me away and sentenced me to weeks of boredom in the British Library instead of your bed. For I could not stay. Even you, dim-witted as I sometimes think you are, must see that after that night, when I abandoned my mission and my body and my soul and lost myself entirely in our delirium, I could not risk your presence any longer for fear of blurting out what I needed to hear from you first. It hurt me more than I can ever say to hurt you as I did that morning by pretending that our night together had been no more than a lovely interlude. But did your stormy little mind ever stop to wonder if the hurt might be mutual?

'Anna, you monster! Your stubbornness cost me dear. Thanks to you I frittered away several weeks of my diminishing lifespan in the wrong place with the wrong people. Picture me, your Russian bear, sitting day after day in that damnable library snapping at each passing librarian because she failed to be *you*. Picture me bowing my grizzled head over those books and roaring with fury because instead of the lines of print I saw the bruised mouth of my mistress and could not kiss it. Picture me storming among the desks filled with scholars and myself filled with rage because they could sit there so calmly when my whole existence was in question, depending on the whim of a whimsical fiddler.

'And then picture, Anna, one day. For several minutes, several whole blessed minutes, I had forgotten your maddening existence. The lines of print had remained lines of print and given me a scrap of information I badly needed. When, for no good reason, I looked up ... and saw a head of flaming hair. I shot out of my chair as fast as my confusion would allow. She has come! She has understood and come to rescue me from this exile! And then picture the face beneath the hair twisting into the features of some pale insipid girl. Not Anna. Not Anna? How dare she not be Anna?' He looked up from his reading and continued.

'And how do you, the real Anna, dare to sit in that chair a thousand miles away from me this minute, the lovely little lines around your eyes crinkled with amusement as you listen to this tale of torment from your lover? Why are you not here, beside me, wrapping your sturdy arms around me and saying, "There, there, Dmitri, it's all over, I'm here now, your very own Anna"? How can you – Ah, that's better. Much better. How soft and warm you are, my love, so much, much better than those horrible old books. Ah, yes, Anna, this is how we were meant to be. You see? You are exactly the size and shape that you are precisely because you were meant to fit into my arms like ... so. My stern old nose was fashioned in this way precisely so that you could run your charming finger down its length and end ... like that ... on my lips. You wish to silence me? Not yet, Anna. I have not yet finished upbraiding you for those lost weeks. What? Tears? Those weeks were your weeks, too? So they were, my darling. Come, let me kiss away the tears. We are not sad souls, you and I. We were made to rejoice in each other. Just another little one . . . here, before it drips off the end of your soft little chin. There. What? A tear on my face, too? That will never do, Anna. Kiss it away quickly. Ah yes, good. Only one, yes; I am stingy with my tears. But no, I mistake: here is a second tear. Where? On my mouth, Anna. Quickly, kiss it before . . .'

TWENTY-THREE

And that, quite properly, is where this story should have ended. But life has a habit of not respecting such niceties. It goes its own sweet way, carrying us with it through sex and scrambled eggs without differentiating much between them.

But one thing life did do for us that night was to grant my most fervent wish: to turn the clock back. The weeks of frustration and mutual recrimination vanished. Once again our bodies and minds and souls met in an explosion of joy. Was it different from that first night, now that we had come together with the gnawing mysteries resolved, no longer holding back even that tiny bit of ourselves? If so, the only difference was the addition of laughter. We were free at last to weep at our misunderstandings and laugh at our foolishness.

And then the blissful moment. Morning. The sun streaming in and lighting up my lover's sleeping face. How long I watched him I don't know, memorising every bit of that beloved person who was now wholly and utterly my own. What would awaken him at last? That strange intuition we have even while we sleep that we are being watched? The slam of a neighbour's door? The deep-throated hoot of a ship coming in to harbour?

Ahab. Loud and clear came his neighing from the paddock. Our morning run across the sands quite forgotten. No, Ahab. Even you take second place on this of all mornings.

The first stirring. The large, voluptuous body (made for love, my Dmitri) shifted slightly beneath the crumpled sheet. The powerful head turned on the pillow to face its observer. One eye opened a fraction. The mouth which I had quelled with a hundred kisses turned up slightly at the corners and my lover smiled his first morning smile at his mistress. For a long time we remained motionless, savouring the tenderness of the moment. This was the moment we had been born for, the culmination of our two lives. That exquisite moment when two lovers gaze in wonder at each other knowing that all that came before was worth it just for this.

Ahab whinnied again, impatient now.

Dmitri's hand reached out from under the sheet and gently grasped the back of my head. 'Damn the horse,' he whispered. And drew my head down to his.

I brought the steaming plateful of bacon and eggs to my lodger. 'Will that be all, sir?'

'Yes, miss. Thank you.'

I sat down across from him and tucked into my own breakfast. We were famished. Somehow, food had been forgotten the night before. I didn't know when Dmitri had last eaten but I had had nothing since lunch the previous day before setting off to the drilling site with –

'Maxine!' And Bernard. I'd quite forgotten them, too.

'My name is Dmitri Mikhailovich,' my lodger corrected politely.

During that night when Dmitri and I had exploded in love, Maxine and Bernard had been adding their own shock waves to Sedleigh's crust. At least I hoped they had. You never could tell with virgins. 'Maxine,' I explained. 'This was her first night with Bernard.'

'Ah. And you have a motherly concern over this event?'

'Don't mock. Maxine has no mother and her father's a swine. I feel responsible for her.'

His eyes glinted wickedly. 'You overestimate the girl's innocence. She played her role of procurer with panache.

Or is it my Anna who is the innocent, thinking Maxine no more than an accommodation officer arranging homely lodgings for the poor stray foreigner?'

'So she did,' I laughed. How annoyed I'd been, and how grateful now. Darling Maxine. I longed to see her. I also longed to stay here on the patio with Dmitri for ever. If only this morning would never end. I savoured it. The morning fresh and bright, before the inevitable heat and dust would reclaim it. Ahab munching peacefully in his paddock, keeping an eye on his errant chum. My lover, strong and handsome and happy across the little table from his doting mistress. I gazed at him with adoration. The months of anxiety and suspicion were over. We had nothing to hide from each other now. The cat-and-mouse game – so different from the one I'd anticipated – had ended. We were free to love each other openly and without reserve. Six months, I'd told myself. No, not this time. It was inconceivable that we would ever be apart.

'Oh hell!' I exclaimed. We would be apart – today. I dashed into the kitchen to check the clock. Still half an hour before the hated separation. 'I have to work today,' I explained on my return. 'How infuriating!'

'Most inconsiderate of time not to stand still,' he agreed. 'I shall miss my little volcano.'

'I'm terrified of leaving you, Dmitri. Afraid that you'll vanish and it'll all have been just a lovely lovely dream.'

He laughed. 'I am far too substantial to dematerialise, dear Anna.'

'What will you do today?'

'I shall drive back to my waterless mansion, collect my books and papers and return to my new lodgings, there to await my sweet landlady. Would she like me to cook lunch for us?'

'You cook?'

'My talents are boundless.'

'How blissful: to come home to a lover *and* food. Will you find time to pop into the library and reassure me that you do still exist?'

'My dear child, do you really think I could "pop into" that wretched place and see you chained behind the desk and pretend to be nothing more than a casual borrower? I shall not "pop into" your library. I shall remain here and curse every minute we're apart. Do you want me to do anything with that nag of yours?'

'Poor Ahab. No, he's all right. Unless riding is another of your talents?'

'It is. But I hardly think Ahab will take kindly to the villain who is usurping so much of your time.'

'He's bribeable. Give him an apple, scratch him under the chin and he'll forgive you.'

'I may just do that, and take him out for a spin. We have things in common, Ahab and I.'

And so the lovely half hour passed, in the foolish talk of lovers who abandon intelligence along with everything else and revert to the mindless babble of delighted children. When the dread moment arrived, Dmitri gave me a chaste kiss on my forehead.

'And please, give my thanks to Miss Maxine,' he called out as I sped down the path.

I'd never noticed just how colourful Sedleigh was. This morning it was vibrant, the red roofs tumbling down the hillside in a bright mosaic to vie with the accent points of green trees poking up among them. The pastel façades of the houses seemed deeper than before, the black-painted stones around the windows sharper, the occasional white cottage dazzling. Even the cars were lovely, a child's collection of shiny new metal toys. I must be mad, I told myself cheerfully. A vivid ginger cat grinned at me before leaping from a windowsill. I blinked as a snowy white gull whizzed past. The mud in the estuary – it was low tide – gleamed a creamy chocolate brown. The discarded aluminium cans sticking up from it failed to offend.

Sedleigh. My town. Now it really was mine, with the threat of exposure and statelessness no longer hanging over me. That too was a gift from Dmitri.

As I passed the town hall I remembered the conversation with Kate on its steps. Even that had had a happy ending. Robert's development would be abandoned, the trees saved.

Yes, it was indeed the best of all possible worlds.

The clock struck three-quarters as I poked the key into the lock and opened the library door. The familiar aroma wafted out to greet me: floor polish, old paper, air cooked by the sunlight streaming through the windows. I flung a few open to freshen the place up. It seemed years since I'd last been here. So much had happened since then. How bright the varnish was, and what a lovely pattern all the book spines made. Some of those books were Dmitri's. I would read them all. I would get to know everything that went on inside his head. We would talk and talk and in the pauses we would make love and eat wonderful little meals and linger over our wine. What had I done with my free time before Dmitri?

I uncovered the trays of issue cards. Borrowings were down a little. The good weather. Not much incentive to sulk indoors with a book. I checked through the request cards. As vague as usual, no one seeming to remember where they'd found out about the book. Here and there one was meticulously filled out, ISBN and all. I switched on the microfiche reader and flicked open *Whitaker's*.

The tick of the clock was soothing. It was an old-fashioned clock, like everything in the library, but its face seemed a little brighter than usual. I watched contentedly as the hands edged towards nine. Would Maxine remember something so mundane as work? Never mind. She was answerable only to me and I was hardly going to make a fuss on this of all mornings.

The library clock and the town hall clock struck nine together. I heard the rapid click of small shoes. They drew nearer. The door opened. I wouldn't look at her; she would feel a little shy. I would be terribly normal.

I plucked a fiche from its pocket and fed it into the machine. The glass snapped down on it. Frowning slightly, I manoeuvred it towards the required line of print. I glanced up at my friend. 'Morning, Maxine.' Then I turned back to the machine and fiddled with the focus.

A whoosh of fresh air and cedar – Eleanor's clothes had been packed in a cedarwood chest – and Maxine's arms were around me. 'Attila, how *can* you be so blasé?'

I abandoned the machine and returned her hug. Then I held her at arms' length and looked at my protégée. My mother's dress – a fresh floral print dating from the late fifties – had come back into fashion. On Maxine it was stunning, but if she'd been wearing a potato sack she still would have been stunning. Yes, her face was radiant. There's no other word to describe it.

'Happy?'

She sank on to a library stool in a charming flurry of skirt and confusion. 'Attila, how could I have been so stupid for so long?'

'You're barely eighteen,' I reminded her. 'You've hardly had any time at all to be stupid or otherwise.'

'He always seemed so serious and stern. So down to earth. I never dreamed.'

'Ah, yes. Well, that's the kind to watch out for. Still waters, you know. Where is he?'

The door opened. Bernard did not enter. A small boy entered instead, clutching a grubby card. I scowled at him but he was used to being scowled at and just grinned. He came sturdily to the desk and handed over the card.

'Mum says can I pick it up for her.'

Trust Trevor's mum to choose this of all mornings to send her son first thing to collect a book. I checked it out for him and waited impatiently as he dawdled his way out. Then I turned back to Maxine.

'At the site,' she said. 'To start clearing up. And Dmitri?'

'Who? Oh, that lodger you foisted on me? Done a flit – gone without paying.'

A slightly worried look. Poor Maxine, so delirious in her own happiness that she couldn't bear a cloud over anyone else's.

'Joke?' I said. 'He's gone to collect his books and papers. Oh, and he sends a message: "Thank Miss Maxine for me."'

Maxine laughed. Then we looked at each other in silence for a while, no longer Older Woman and Protégée but two equals. There wasn't a great deal we could say. Last night had changed everything. We had secrets now, even if they were open secrets. Part of us now belonged to our men in a way that precluded the old closeness we had felt for each other. I realised with a pang that this was how mothers must feel when their children flew the nest. It was inevitable and good, but still a little sad.

'Everything's different now, isn't it, Attila?'

'Yes.' A retired trawlerman came in and shuffled his way towards the maritime section as he'd been doing for years. He would stay there for hours, rereading every book he could find about the sea. I lowered my voice. 'What about your clothes and things? You'll have to go back some time and collect them. And your father. Max, I hate to play the heavy, but there's only a month to go before you go to Cambridge. You've got to sort out the finances soon.'

'Well, actually –'

'Good morning!' Mrs Johnson bore down on us, beaming, asking as she did several times a week if the latest royal biography she'd ordered had come in yet. I reminded her, as I did several times a week, that we'd send her a postcard when it came. She stayed to gossip a few minutes and slowly drifted out.

I turned back to Maxine. 'Have you done your figures?'

'Uh, sort of, a few days ago, but –'

'How do they add up?'

'Well, you know. The tuition and all that is paid directly. I've only got to pay for my living expenses. There's the money I've saved from my work, but the point is – '

'Right. What's the shortfall?'

She told me. I winced. Robert would do more than wince.

A middle-aged couple came in. Tourists, wanting a temporary registration. It was a simple enough procedure but still took a little time. Worse, the 9.32 bus was due, sweeping up the people from all the outlying villages for their day's shopping. A large chunk of them were elderly women who would make a beeline for the library, ruining any chance of serious talk. I scribbled out the temporary cards and recited my spiel to the tourists at breakneck speed. When finally they wandered towards the shelves I returned to Maxine. She was chewing her bottom lip, not something she did very often.

'Attila, please, I have to say this.' She paused. 'Everything's different now, don't you see? I mean, there's Bernard.'

'I know, and I feel for you. But you'll have a whole month together, and then there are the vacs and maybe you can manage the odd weekend.'

The wheezy sigh of the bus's pneumatic brakes. Only a few more minutes before the invasion.

The lower lip, released, was trembling. 'You don't understand. I can't bear to be away from him.'

I sighed. 'Life's like that, Maxine. People never seem to be in the same place long enough. How do you think I feel? Counting the weeks before Dmitri goes back to London.'

This was not something I'd faced up to myself, but I had to now in order to show solidarity. 'Somehow we'll manage – lovers always do,' I finished uncertainly.

The lip stopped trembling and joined her jaw in the ominous set I'd come to dread. 'Then I don't think you can love him very much,' she said.

'Maxine!'

Several heads turned towards me reprovingly – people had been drifting into the library during this conversation, though none of them had stopped at the desk.

I lowered my voice. 'I'll forgive you that horrid little remark because I understand how you feel. But believe me, you'll survive it – people always do. And if the thing with Bernard is for real, it'll last.'

Thud thud thud. The sensible shoes had begun their march, zeroing in on the library.

'It's for real,' she said quietly. 'Bernard always knew that and now I know it too.'

The shoes were louder, above them the descant of elderly voices chirping. Not much longer now. 'Maxine, I do understand, truly I do but –'

I stopped, suddenly seeing what this conversation was leading to. 'Oh my God.'

Maxine nodded. 'I can't possibly leave Bernard now. I'm sorry, Attila, and please don't be too angry. But I just can't go to Cambridge.'

The door burst open. The ladies entered. I groaned and sank on to my chair.

It was later than usual when I returned home. It had been a gruesome day. Sometimes, for no reason at all, everybody and their uncle decides to descend on the library on one particular day. This had been it. Worst of all, Dmitri had phoned from the old Holroyd house: exercising Ahab had taken longer than expected and so had his packing, and now he had an 'appointment' to see Robert Vesey.

No possibility of lunch but he would cook us something delightful for dinner instead. I'd clung to the phone for some time after, savouring the echo of that deep voice. It did things to me, Dmitri's voice, weakened my knees like Pavarotti in full flood.

Now I was rushing up the path to the front door. It was open. A good sign. He had to be there. He wouldn't leave it open if he'd gone. I still couldn't believe my luck, couldn't believe that this achingly desirable man was really here, in my house, in my life.

He was. He was sitting at the desk beneath the big windows. It was the first time I'd seen him wearing his reading glasses. He hadn't used them in my library – too vain? They made him look even more distinguished.

As I entered he took off his glasses, put them on the desk and came towards me with arms opened wide. I fell blissfully into them. The world shrank to the two of us. He was real, he was here, he was mine.

When finally he released me he scowled. 'My dear girl, you look as if you've spent the day fighting off a shipload of pirates.'

'I have. They're called borrowers.' I sank into a chair by the fireplace. 'I never knew a day could be so long. You've screwed up my sense of time. There are Dmitri hours – short. And non-Dmitri hours – endless.'

He laughed. The light glanced off the hint of a gold tooth. I adored his gold tooth. All the best foreigners had a gold tooth.

'To revive?' he said.

'A very large Cinzano, please. Ice. Lime peel.'

I fretted in his absence as he went into the kitchen to pour us a drink. Several non-Dmitri minutes. In them, I listened to the sound of Dmitri making himself at home. Nice sounds. Perhaps there were semi-Dmitri minutes? He returned, handed me my drink and sat down opposite.

He raised his glass to mine. No toast. There was no need. To us.

He waved a hand towards the desk behind him. 'I hope you don't mind. It was empty.'

'It was my fa – It was Edmund's desk. It's been empty far too long. It's lovely to see your clutter on it. But if you need more room, there's Eleanor's upstairs. She used the spare room as her study – she needed the space, with all her books and papers.'

'I'm quite contented here.'

'Good. Then I can keep an eye on you and make sure you don't vanish. I feel terribly possessive about you, Dmitri. Can you bear it?'

'You possess me with a light touch. I want to be possessed by you.'

I could feel my eyes filling. All my emotions were acute today. Like the princess with her pea, each tiny kindness bruised. 'It feels like a miracle, coming home to you. I never dreamed.'

He was watching me with gentle curiosity. 'What a strange woman you are, Anna. After all those years in the east, you have no guile.'

'Not with you. I feel like a child again. Wide open and vulnerable and too stupid to hide it.'

'You do trust me now?'

'Completely.'

'Except for the one thing?'

My parents. There it was, lurking in the background like some dangerous shadow, the one area of taboo I'd created for us. 'I'm not ready, Dmitri. Maybe some day.'

'As you wish. I won't press you. We'll talk of other things. Such as the supper I have prepared for us. I am very proud of my *okroshka* and will be deeply offended if it fails to delight.'

'I'm sure it won't. What is it?'

'A cold soup for the Russian summer. My mother was ridiculously sentimental about such things and made our households in Berlin and London more Russian than Russia. I spent much time in the kitchen because Cook was better company than my mother.'

'I know so little about you,' I smiled. 'You're like a big delectable novel I've only just begun to read. I'm longing to find out everything about you.'

'And so you shall, Miss Book. Beginning with my *okroshka*. Unfortunately I have never mastered the art of preparing *kvas* and so have learned to make do with some English ale with a dash of mustard and yoghurt to add to the soup instead. With it we shall have the Russian black bread I brought up from London yesterday, some cherry juice and some vodka. And when you are thoroughly cured of your Dmitri-less day I will ask a favour of you in return.' He raised an eyebrow.

I raised mine.

'I will ask you to transform yourself once more into that passionate gypsy girl and serenade me with your fiddle.'

Supper was over. Dmitri's *okroshka* had been delicious and I'd praised it lavishly. He'd been childishly pleased at my approval. Beneath his urbane façade there was a touch of insecurity I'd never suspected. Perhaps his childhood, more disrupted than my own. Yes, there was a lot I had yet to learn about Dmitri.

We were on the patio again. My kitchen was scarcely used these days except for cooking and washing up. All over Sedleigh kitchens were abandoned as the balmy weather continued, as endless as the horizon to the east. Tonight the sea was providing the main element in our scented garden. A lovely salty tang floated over us, as fresh as a glass of mineral water to a jaded palate. Ahab had come right up to the hedge and was peering over it at us with unabashed curiosity.

'I think you've made a friend,' I said. 'How was he today?'

'Deeply suspicious at first but far too well-mannered to say so. I took him on to the beach in a vain attempt to recapture that moment when you and Ahab whirled past me – do you remember, Anna?'

Old lovers already, recollecting our small shared past.

'Of course I didn't emulate your breakneck speed.' He smiled. 'But even so, the tourists were a little startled. One of them even photographed us. Ahab, I regret to report, is deplorably vain. He posed with relish.'

'You can hardly blame him. He is rather gorgeous. Your appointment with Robert – how did it go?'

'Not well. Mr Vesey and I are not the best of friends.'

'That was bound to happen. You're tarnished by association – with me, with Bernard, with Maxine.'

'He didn't fail to bring you in as evidence of my perfidious nature. None the less, I steered him back to the subject, namely, a refund of the money I paid in advance for a house now uninhabitable. He took a legalistic view: that he had accepted six months' rental and if I chose now to lodge elsewhere, that was my choice.'

'*Choice?*'

'He claims there is nothing in the contract stipulating that the house must have water.'

'*What?*'

'Calm down, my little Vesuvius. He may or may not be right; I was too busy concocting the *okroshka* to read it closely when I returned home – I may call your house my home?'

'Dmitri . . .' I melted.

'But I did point out that a small claims court would take a dim view of his attitude, regardless of contract. And that that court would be a local one, further diminishing his reputation should it rule against him. I have discovered one thing about our friend: he is a proud man, and vain. His reputation means more to him than one might suspect, and he cannot bear the prospect of failure.'

'But he has failed – his whole development plan's been ruined by not finding water. I suppose that's it: you're getting the brunt of his aggro over that.'

'I think so. And, as you've pointed out, he's mean. Further, he has my money, which puts him in a stronger position. Possession is nine-tenths of the law.'

'You're not letting him get away with it?'

'I could afford to lose the money, but it grates,' he admitted. 'None the less, it is politic for a stranger to abide by the rules of the locals. What is the opinion of my favourite local?'

'Unprintable,' I muttered. 'First he tries to destroy the wood – and succeeds in destroying the spring. Then he steals your money and if that's not enough he refuses to use it to help out with his daughter's education. Honestly, I could strangle that man.'

'Please – I would rather visit you in your charming home than in a prison.'

'You wouldn't be so sanguine if you knew how he's treated her. And how he treated his wife, too, before she had the sense to up stakes and go. Ah, what's the use,' I sighed. 'He's won anyway. And it's all my fault.'

'My sphinx speaks in riddles.'

'Maxine's decided not to go to Cambridge. She can't bear to leave Bernard and it's all my fault. I threw them together.'

Dmitri was frowning. 'I see. Your matchmaking was too successful. But surely Bernard wouldn't wish to destroy her chances?'

'In his right mind, no. But lovers aren't in their right minds, are they?' I smiled feebly. 'If you asked me to take a running leap over that retaining wall and smash myself on the rocks below to prove my love, I might just be insane enough to do it.'

The joke was backfiring. Dmitri studied my face for a long time before replying, and there was no humour in his voice when he said, 'I may ask much more of you than that, Anna. But for the moment we have other work to do. Have you spoken to Bernard?'

'No, but I will.'

'And have you pointed out to Maxine that by giving up university she would greatly please the father she loathes?'

I shot up in my chair. 'Dmitri! You're brilliant!'

'No. Merely a little more detached from the situation than you are. Though I'm not so sure even about that. To hold back a fine mind is abhorrent to me. And however flippant I may sometimes be about your young friend, I do see her potential.' He smiled. 'How could I not care? After all, Anna, it is more than your beautiful experience-etched face and sexy body that I love in you. I love the hard work which made you at home in so many languages. I love the way your painstakingly taught fingers coax such fire from your violin. I love your quick understanding of the ethnic music you studied. I love your ability to make your way through the countries of eastern Europe when it was Eastern Europe and negotiate all the monstrous obstacles to find out what's precious in those countries. I love the tact and skill you must have used to protect your friends there. I love the richness of your experience – yes, even your former lovers – and the generosity of mind it's given you. I love you, Anna Atwill, and I forbid you to jump off that cliff. Instead, I demand that you come inside and tune your fiddle while I light a small fire – the evening is growing chill. Then I will prepare us some coffee while you rack your splendid brain to think of a piece of music which will most delight me. Then I will settle into the chair by the fireplace and while the flames throw lively shadows across the room your violin will throw even lovelier sounds over your lover. And then, when we have sated our ears with music we will retire upstairs to sate our bodies with love. That is my agenda, Anna Atwill, and I will brook no argument.'

TWENTY-FOUR

The next morning Dmitri and I walked together up the paddock. Ahab was waiting, his glossy flanks quivering with excitement at the prospect of an outing. He watched expectantly, no doubt wondering which of us it was to be. Dmitri had brought him another apple to further their friendship.

As Ahab munched the offering, dripping juice all over Dmitri's hand, I fetched the saddle. Today was a business day, no time for a mad bareback gallop over the sands. Ahab gave one reproachful glance at the saddle (saddle equals transport; he prefers not to be viewed in this way) and then submitted. I slipped the bit into his mouth and the rest of the bridle over his head. As I did up the buckle Dmitri and I discussed last-minute details.

'If you sense that I might in any way be useful, don't hesitate to phone,' he said. 'I'll be at home all day. It's only a trifling thing to drive over.'

I kissed his nose (a business day, I didn't dare more). 'I will. And I appreciate your solidarity.' I swung myself up into the saddle and turned Ahab around. We walked up to the gate, Dmitri at our side. He opened the gate for us.

As he closed it and leaned his arms on the top bar, he suddenly laughed. 'You remind me of a knight going off to battle. Take care, my darling, that the dragon doesn't singe you.'

I blew him a kiss. Ahab, impatient at all this nonsense, set off down the path at a brisk trot. Several times I looked behind to see Dmitri still by the gate, still smiling encouragement and love. Then a bend in the path cut him off from view.

For several minutes I mused abstractedly on Dmitri. I still hated leaving him, severing myself from his life-giving presence. Away from him I felt diminished, not quite real. The whole is more than the sum of its parts.

But slowly the wood began to insinuate its magic into my inattentive mind. This was the first time I'd seen it since the dramatic day of its rescue. So much had happened all at once that I hadn't quite absorbed all the good news. The wood was saved. All the trees would continue to grow, innocent of the chainsaw. The paths, ancient rights of way, would continue to carry the people of Sedleigh into this haven of peace and sanity where the trees could work their gentle therapy. Countless times I had come into the wood for healing, for a quiet think to sort out a problem. Always the superfluous bits of the problem fell away to leave the core exposed. Always the soothing resinous scent of a pine or a fir cleared my mind. What did desert people do? I couldn't imagine life without this refuge.

Neither, apparently, could the robin who was singing furiously to keep his competitors at bay. Silly old thing; why can't you share? Plenty of room for everyone. But reason isn't a robin's strong point. He warbled away, filling the air with his claim. From far away came the answering song of a rival.

September. Autumn was really beginning at last. Beneath the trees, dozens of square cobwebs were spread lightly over the tops of the grasses like lacy grey handkerchiefs laid out to dry. A tall hogweed thrust its stem up and presented a flowerhead – its own pinkish-grey lace. An old-fashioned effect with an old-fashioned smell, the typical fresh sweet scent of all umbellifera. A clump of tansy with bright green leaves and even brighter buttons of yellow flowers was vivid beside it. Nearby, in a spray of straplike leaves, the first stems of a montbretia were adding their touch of flame. How clever Sydney Holroyd's gardener had been to boobytrap the wood with these little delights. And all of it saved, thanks to Bernard and Kate.

Only when we reached the central clearing did my pleasure diminish. I had dismounted without thinking and gone to the spring. The stone spout was dry, a sad reminder of the price the wood had paid for its rescue. There was still some water in the pool but already it had taken on the stagnant smell of neglect. Ahab snuffled the surface, tried an experimental slurp and turned his head away.

Beside the pool was a clump of hosta, another relic of the Holroyd days. A transparent sphere of water sat in a hollow on one leaf. As I moved the leaf, the crystal ball whizzed around like quicksilver without wetting the leaf. I looked more closely and saw bits of dirt and vegetation caught up and suspended inside it. The tips of some ferns had gone brown. The old larch that had persuaded Bernard to risk his reputation was still sporting its summer green, but nearby a single prematurely turned branch of a beech spread a yellow and russet swathe across the rest of its own greenery. Some unseen hand had scattered a sprinkling of golden leaves among the green of a few birches, giving a polka-dot effect. Slowly, quietly, the wood was moving through yet another transition in yet another year, as it had done so often and now would continue to do. Yes, there was life here. The death of the spring, however sad, had been a reasonable price.

We rode on.

We reached the rickety gate in the south boundary just in time. Bernard and Tim were about to drive their massive waggons away from the site. I waved frantically to Bernard and trotted up to his open window. 'Sorry to interrupt, but can I have a word? It's urgent.'

He smiled. The wood wasn't the only thing undergoing a transformation. I'd never seen him looking so happy. 'Business? Or other?' he said.

'Other.'

He got out of the cab and went over to Tim. After a

brief consultation, Tim began to manoeuvre the compressor waggon down the farm track. Bernard came back to where I'd dismounted. We led Ahab to where the digging of the trackside ditch had thrown up a big boulder. We sat down on it. I held Ahab's reins loosely so he could nibble what grass he could find.

Not much. The site was an ugly blotch of mud and grass trampled into a dried grey paste intersected by the ruts and gouges made by the waggons. The failed well itself had been capped to prevent birds and small animals from falling into it. Given the preposterous depth it would be a long fall. The trees on the other side of the wall still bore their gruesome weight of caked mud – no rain had come to wash it off. It would have to be a real deluge to shift that quantity of stuff.

Bernard followed my eyes. 'Awful, isn't it?'

'It'll heal. Next spring you won't even know a well's been drilled here, except for the cap. Where's your next job?'

He named a village ten miles inland and briefly described the circumstances. They were a good deal less fraught than the ones witnessed by this site. 'But this isn't why you've come,' he finished.

'No. I couldn't phone or ask you to come round.'

'Maxine?'

'Yes. I hate going behind her back, but it's necessary.'

'Cambridge.'

'Right in one. This is delicate territory, Bernard. Where do we begin?'

His soft grey faraway gaze moved eastward to where a scrawny belt of windblown hawthorns marked the edge of the cliff. Beyond them lay the sea and the sky, all those lovely open spaces that were his territory. With some reluctance he turned his head and looked at me. 'We talked about it last night,' he said slowly. 'I'm trying to persuade her to go.'

I said nothing. I could feel his pain too acutely. He'd finally captured his beloved girl and now he had to let her go, against his own desire and hers. Sometimes life has a brutal sense of timing.

I suppose some people somewhere manage their love lives efficiently, but Bernard and I weren't among them.

'I told her that if she stayed here with me now she would always have the gnawing What If? What if she had gone to Cambridge? What might have happened to her then? As soon as our first row came up the regrets would begin. I would become the monster who had made her give up her education. The time would come when she'd see me as a poor exchange for Cambridge. And she would be right. She protested, of course, but I did at least ask her to think seriously about what I said. I'm hoping she's doing that in the library today.'

'I don't suppose there's any chance of you and Tim transferring business to Cambridge?'

'Not really. Anyway, it wouldn't be the same. Maxine wouldn't be free. She needs these years of freedom to be sure. I know I'm not going to change my mind. As for her, who knows?'

Brave Bernard. The risks were enormous. All those exotic young Cambridge men, the glitter of its social life, the exciting nearness of London, the sense of release after a lifetime imprisoned on a Yorkshire farm. Even I, who probably knew her more than anyone, couldn't predict what would happen.

'I told her that if we really were meant to be together we would survive the separation and how much happier we would be then, knowing that we were sure. And it wouldn't be a total separation. Cambridge terms are short, there are long vacations, some weekends. We would still spend a lot of time together. And the month before she leaves. I asked her to imagine herself twenty years from now, her hair just taking on a few grey threads, still in Sedleigh, still working at the library – part-time, perhaps – still coming home to cook dinner or maybe we would cook it together when I came back all covered in grime to our narrow little life. It's not on, Anna. We all know it. She knows it, too. She just needs time to think it through.'

'And time is something we're short of,' I said. 'We still haven't sorted out the finances. I was planning to beard Robert this morning – depending on what you said. Obviously if you were going to leap into marriage or something there wouldn't be much point.'

'No leap. I'm not the leaping type. Nor, deep down, is Maxine. She'll come round.' He smiled. 'So your interview is on. I don't envy you. Robert's not in the best of moods. I went to see him yesterday about payment for the drilling. He's refusing, of course.'

'He can't. There's a contract.'

'I know. He knows, too, and in the end he'll pay – just at the point when we're about to bring in the solicitors.'

'He's doing the same to Dmitri – refusing to refund the balance for the waterless wonder he rented.'

'Of course – I'd forgotten. In fact, I'd forgotten all about your own domestic changes.' He raised an eyebrow.

'The new lodger seems to find the accommodation satisfactory and the landlady reasonable.'

'And you?'

'Passing fair. But if it's any consolation, there's more than one separation in the air. He does live in London, you know. Ah, Bernard, why is life so bloody messy? It's not as if true love's a common commodity. As soon as you have it in your grasp, some damn thing comes along to snatch it away again.'

'The gods hate any happiness other than their own.'

'Mean buggers. Speaking of whom, I must go to Robert's. As a matter of curiosity, have you *ever* met anyone as mean as Robert?'

'No. But then I don't know many farmers.'

I heaved myself off the stone. 'Come on, Ahab. Time to continue our social calls.'

He raised his head from an unsatisfactory piece of grass and looked hopefully at me. When I was back in the saddle, he pricked his ears forward and tossed his head, showing off yet again.

'Can you picture Ahab on Rotten Row?' I said.

'Actually, I can.'

I shrugged. 'Maybe it'll come to that. Otherwise I'll be thumbing a lift south with you.'

Bernard smiled up at me. 'God knows why, but you've cheered me up, Attila. Things *could* work out, couldn't they?'

'We'll make them work out. We're survivors, Bernard, all of us. And doers.' The sight of his hope was too much. I leaned down and kissed the top of my friend's head. 'Do you know, Bernard, I think you're the finest human being I've ever known.'

'Not Dmitri?'

'He's a rogue. Like me. That's why I love him. Bye!'

The sight of Robert Vesey's farm filled me, as always, with dismay. So much money, and all of it used with fine contempt for the land which had produced it. The hedges had long ago been ripped out and the post and wire fences that replaced them were overdue for renewal, the posts rotten and leaning at odd angles, the wire sagging and broken. The only trees left were the odd windblown hawthorn in a corner inaccessible to the tractor. Too many sheep and cows trying to shelter beneath them had trampled the grass to death.

The farmyard itself was a parody of an inner city slum but through indifference rather than lack of money. The farmhouse was the only building to retain its original stone. The rest were concrete monstrosities with corrugated asbestos roofs. Even when new they'd been ugly. Now the roofs sagged and the big wooden doors hung askew from what hinges remained. One building which had been heaped with silage oozed an evil greenish liquid all over the yard.

It was the only green. The tiny garden which Margaret Vesey and then Maxine had tried to maintain had finally fallen into neglect. I couldn't blame Maxine. Bad enough having to balance the needs of her schoolwork with the farmwork her father imposed on her. The house and garden had been the losers. It was a wonder that she hadn't followed her mother's example and done a flit years ago, but of course she'd had nowhere to go. Now she did – two places: Bernard's flat and Cambridge.

At least the farmyard gate had long ago fallen from its hinges and so I didn't have to dismount. I rode through the opening and found Robert leaning over the innards of a tractor in the yard.

'Morning, Robert.'

He looked up, grunted, and returned to his tinkering. He loved machines. It was the only aspect of farming that he did love. Machines, not animals, not plants. Anything with a bit of life in it threatened his control.

'Having trouble?' I tried again.

'Farming's nothing but trouble,' he muttered. After some more fiddling about, just to keep me waiting, he added, 'I suppose that crook sent you to screw some money out of me.'

I did a quick calculation and decided the crook in question was Bernard, not Dmitri. Bernard's bill was higher and hence of more concern. 'I thought Bernard was the apple of your eye.'

'That was before he cheated me.'

'Robert, why don't we drop this pretence? You know as well as I do that Bernard did exactly what your contract with him stated: drilled you a well. The fact that there was no water isn't Bernard's fault. He warned you quite clearly – and in front of a lot of people – that there was unlikely to be water. You made the decision. Both morally and in law you're responsible.'

'We'll see about that.'

'Do you want to add a solicitor's bill on top of it?'

'Steals my money and then my daughter.' He straightened himself up and faced me squarely. 'You tell Maxine that she comes back to the farm or I don't pay. You tell her that for me.'

'She's not coming back for at least three years. She's going to university.'

'Thought she was shacked up with that crook.'

'She's shacked up with Bernard because he's a damn sight better company than you are. Robert, I'd like to be civilised about this. Could we go in the house and talk about it over a coffee?'

'Can't afford luxuries like coffee with all these crooks waving phoney bills at me.'

I sighed. Conversations with farmers were so boringly predictable. 'All right, we'll talk here.' Before he could find another excuse I launched in. 'I'm not sure you realise what an exceptional person Maxine is. Despite slaving away for you on the farm and in the house, she's managed to get the most spectacular A-levels and an offer from a Cambridge college. Believe me, they don't offer a place to just any chit of a girl. She's done you proud, Robert. And in the future she'll do you prouder still. That girl's going to amount to something. Isn't it time you admitted it and started to help her?'

'Thought we'd get around to that. More money, hey?' He was leaning against the dusty side of the tractor, arms crossed belligerently across his chest, his red face radiating malice. I tried to conceal my gut reaction towards this unnatural man.

'Robert,' I said gently, 'any other father would be over the moon with a daughter like that. Anyone else would be bragging all over the place about my-brilliant-daughter-a-chip-off-the-old-block. Anyone else would be boasting about the help he'd given her, taking some of the credit, saying she wouldn't have got where she is without him. You can't say that, Robert . . . yet. The time will come when you'll want to take some of the credit . . . and you won't be able to.'

I stopped to allow a little space for this to sink in. It was Dmitri who'd provided the cue. *He is a proud man, and vain. His reputation means more to him than one might suspect.* Up until now that reputation had rested solely on his ability to make money. The extravagant development project was to have been the culmination of his financial wizardry. Now that it had failed he might just be open to a success in some other direction. I hoped against hope that Maxine might be it.

'There's no doubt at all that Maxine is going to become a very important person indeed,' I continued. 'What direction she'll take nobody knows yet, but whatever she chooses to do she'll make a raving success of it. She could even become famous, a household name. That name could be yours, Robert. It's almost too late, but not quite.'

He was staring at his derelict barn but not, I think, seeing it. He was simply avoiding looking at me. That, plus his silence, I took as a good sign.

'It's no secret in Sedleigh that you haven't exactly done a lot for Maxine so far,' I continued. 'People are beginning to talk and the talk isn't good. People like Maxine. They respect the hard work that's gone into her success. They're not going to think much of a rich father' – I held up my hand as he began to protest – 'who doesn't do a thing to help her.'

'What do I care what people think?' he snarled.

Quite a lot, I hoped. I shrugged. 'Well, it's up to you. But just remember: you've already had a sample of her independence. She had the guts to defy you and move in with Bernard. She'll also have the guts to deny you, once she's rich and famous.' I wasn't at all sure about the rich-and-famous bit but knew the power of such phrases on the Robert Veseys of this world. 'She'll have a different name by then – Bernard's maybe, or a pseudonym. Wait till Terry Wogan's interviewing her.' The scenario was becoming more ludicrous by the minute but I could see it was having an effect on Robert. 'Wogan asks her about her parents, about their role in her success. What do you think she's going to say?' I couldn't imagine and so didn't elaborate. 'And everyone in Sedleigh glued to the box, ears flapping. Is this really what you want, Robert?'

His face was inscrutable. Years of sharp bargaining with other farmers and grant-giving organisations had gone into that closed surface. The delaying tactics were part of it. He would make me wait for a response. This time I had to be patient, let the silence stretch until he had to break it. Eastern Europe again, my own training ground.

While I was waiting I counted the sounds that filled in for Robert's silence. A pack of sheepdogs were yapping inside one of the outbuildings. Some calves, recently separated from their mothers, fretted in a dusty pen. A plane droned high overhead, writing its childish scrawl across a cloudless blue sky. The tractor, ignored, chugged away unevenly to itself. Probably the unevenness was the reason for Robert's ministrations. Then it stopped.

As if it were a signal Robert spoke. Slowly he turned his attention from the derelict barn to my face. His own was still inscrutable but – unusually for Robert – he was looking straight into my eyes. 'She's not going to get there, is she?' he said. 'On the box. Not if she doesn't go to university.'

A new sound: my ears buzzing. I wasn't hearing this. It wasn't possible, those words, not even from Robert. I couldn't have misjudged so badly the depths he would sink to. Mean, yes. Uncaring, yes. But the viciousness of those few words was something I hadn't anticipated, couldn't quite believe despite the fact that they were echoing around and around my stunned head. Control yourself, Attila. This isn't the time for dramatics. Tactics. Think tactics. Keep your head clear and your voice calm.

'I don't think you mean that, Robert.'

'Don't I?'

I was making an effort to breathe evenly. None the less, the tension was transmitting itself to Ahab. He swung his head around to sniff my knee, as if fearing some stranger had suddenly replaced his old friend.

'If you do, Robert,' I said slowly, 'if you really withhold financial support deliberately in order to smash her future, I think there's something you should know: if you don't pay, I will.'

At last a spark of expression in his face. Incredulity. Suspicion.

'I had hoped you'd be reasonable,' I continued. 'I hoped you had some tiny shred of affection for your daughter despite appearances. But just in case you didn't I've been raising the money myself. She's going to Cambridge, Robert, regardless. She's going to make a success of herself, regardless of what you do to thwart her.'

'You're lying.'

'Try me.' Here goes, the trump card I had hoped I wouldn't have to use. 'My father was an art dealer. Some of the paintings he collected have gone up in value. My uncle came up last month and took some back to London with him. They're on the market now, Robert, and one of them's already sold. Already I've got enough to finance her first year. The rest will come in time.'

And it was true. All summer I'd hoped for a reconciliation between Maxine and her father, but her education was too important to risk on such a gamble. It had hurt, parting with the paintings, but not for long. It was wrong anyway that they should be concealed in my house, seen only by me and a few friends. Edmund thought so, too. We'd had one of our silent conversations before I'd made the decision. Afterwards I'd understood that Maxine's future mattered more. Indeed, it felt as if the paintings had just been waiting to play this role.

'I don't believe you,' said Robert.

I shrugged. 'Wait another month and find out.'

The bland mask was giving way. Anger flickered across Robert's face. 'You bitch,' he said. 'First Carr, then you. You're in this together, aren't you?' His voice was rising. 'Taking my daughter away from me. You've been plotting against me for years.'

'Not "taking", Robert. Giving. Giving her love and support. Giving her what you're too bloody selfish to give her yourself. Still, you're right: I won't mind taking some of the credit when Maxine makes it. Quite a nice little story for the media. Fairy godmother and all. People like that kind of thing. Gives them back their faith in human nature.' I smiled down on him – it took some effort. 'You misunderstood my reason for coming today, Robert. I didn't come to get money out of you. I came to give you a chance to reclaim your daughter's respect and affection. You've left it pretty late and it won't be easy for you. But it's your last chance, Robert. Once she's gone, she's gone for good. Nothing on God's earth will make her forgive you then.' A slight flick of the reins and Ahab's head went up, alert for departure. 'We've got about a week before we have to start making arrangements. Think about it and phone me when you decide – I'm in most evenings. Good morning, Robert.'

I wheeled round and cantered out of the yard. I didn't look back.

TWENTY-FIVE

I leaned back in my chair behind the issue desk and surveyed the library. It had never looked so festive. But then, it had never been called upon to provide a celebration like this.

Strings of tiny fairy lights were looped through the pine branches decorating the picture rail. The harsh overhead lights were off, replaced by a collection of softer lamps gleaned from our various houses. Some wag had pinned a laurel wreath above the portrait of Sydney Holroyd which looked down on the main hall. The issue desk was transformed into a bar, the drab paraphernalia of work replaced by a keg of local beer, a forest of wine bottles, fruit juice bottles, glasses.

In one of the alcoves Kate and Max were putting the finishing touches to the feast spread out on a long reading table. We'd all contributed to that. Dmitri had made a huge Zakusochny salad. I'd put together some Westphalian potato pies. Kate and Ian had produced trays of dolmádes (Kate was vegetarian), while Maxine and Bernard had stuffed endless eggs with endless local herrings. For desserts we'd come up with a Tuscan sweet cheese pudding, a Russian honey cake and a Hungarian chocolate mousse called Rigó Jancsi, as well as a fruit salad for the faint of heart (or heavy of stomach).

At the entrance to another alcove Lewis and Josh and I would be scraping away at our fiddles to provide the dance music. I'd queried this with Maxine. 'Are you sure you wouldn't like a pop group? I mean, this is pretty weird stuff for a bunch of Yorkshire teenagers.'

A touch of the old Maxine had returned. 'We are not "Yorkshire" teenagers,' she'd replied loftily. 'We are from Sedleigh.'

'What's with this sudden local pride?'

'When one reaches my august age,' she'd said from the heights of eighteen, 'one begins to appreciate one's background. Our background has been Attila and Her Huns.'

I hadn't thought about it but supposed it was true. I'd been churning out this crazy music for whomever I could recruit for nearly a decade, i.e. for as long as most of these kids could remember. It occurred to me to be worried. Had I warped their musical minds, turned them into freaks? 'Well, if you insist. But let's have some tapes of pop music ready in case there's a mutiny.'

But right now Josh and Lewis weren't here, nor any of the guests. Right now there were only the six of us, which is how I wanted it to be. Because I had a little surprise in store.

I came out from behind the desk and did a final survey of our preparations. It hadn't been easy turning the library into a party room in the short space after closing time. Mrs Johnson had been horrified at the whole idea. 'A library?' she'd said in her Edith Evans voice. 'For a party?'

'What better?' I'd parried. 'If it hadn't been for our library some of these kids would never be going to university.'

'But what would Sydney Holroyd think?'

'I'm sure he'd be delighted. Thanks to our revered benefactor, generations of schoolchildren have had somewhere quiet to flee to from their book-hostile homes.'

She hadn't been convinced but, as always, had no choice but to acquiesce. I could – and sometimes did – threaten resignation when crossed. Yes, there were certainly perks to being a dictator.

I went the rounds to check up on my press gang. Kate and Maxine had finished setting out the food and were now easing little bowls of autumn flowers into every bit of space left. Michaelmas daisies, of course, and clever arrangements of coloured leaves, berried branches, bright green twigs of fir. For a radical teacher and a bolshy schoolgirl (ex-schoolgirl – I must remember) they looked awfully domestic. 'Are the men doing something manly?' I asked.

Kate nodded. 'In the courtyard. Lights.'

I went to the courtyard. The only thing that wasn't perfect about this evening was the weather. After months of clear blue skies, our dear east coast had chosen today of all days to resume its brisk and bracing grey. There'd even been a dash of good old traditional drizzle and the forecast promised more. We'd hoped to have most of the party in the courtyard. Now its role was reduced to handling the overflow and providing a whiff of fresh air for the dance-and-drink weary. Near the door, Ian and Bernard were installing some temporary lighting.

'Looks ominous up there,' I said to the sky.

'It's all waterproof,' said Ian. 'There's not much anyway – just enough so people don't stumble around in the dark.'

They'd had to remove the draught excluder from the door to get the wires under. Bernard went inside to plug the cable into an outlet near the door.

'Where's my man?' I asked Ian.

'Looking for the tables and chairs.'

I glanced across the courtyard. At the far end, just emerging from the gloom of the shed, was a shadowy figure.

'Ready?' Bernard called.

'Yes,' Ian called back.

The courtyard leaped into light. Through the golden glow came Dmitri. My knees weakened and I had to lean against the wall. I was never quite prepared for these sudden sightings and tonight he looked more irresistible than ever.

Dmitri and I had driven Maxine to Cambridge to have a look around. We'd then gone on to London to spend the night at Dmitri's flat. I'd found the peasant smock crumpled up in a corner of his wardrobe. Even crumpled it was lovely: a wistful faded blue cotton covered with the most exquisite embroidery. Dmitri had made a face when I produced it. 'It's not a "peasant" smock,' he'd said. 'It's one of those glorified versions the estate owners wore when they played at being Tolstoy. A ferocious little egalitarian like you should disapprove.'

'A ferocious little aesthete like me has to approve. It's beautiful. Oh, *do* wear it to the party!'

'A Russian peasant in Sedleigh? What strange ideas you have, my Anna.'

'You should know by now that beneath my gruff exterior beats an incurably romantic heart. Anyway, you must have worn it before – why not to our knees-up?'

'I haven't. It was Anatoly's. He wore it to smart London parties to wow the natives.'

'Well, wear it to ours and wow us.'

So here I stood, being wowed. Even in the drabbest clothes Dmitri had never managed to look at all English. Now, in his Cossack trousers and the soft and sensuous shirt with its proud display of peasant craft, he filled the courtyard with an overwhelming sense of the exotic. Had the blue cotton been less faded or the material less worn, the effect would have been muted. But the shirt breathed a heritage which was strange and a little threatening to a place like Sedleigh. On it was written not only the skill of some peasant embroiderer but the history of Dmitri's family.

He came over and put his hands on my shoulders. His dark eyes, framed by the high Slav cheekbones and thick black brows, looked down on me with a mixture of danger and amusement. Volatile, the Russians. You never knew what they'd do next.

This one smiled, kissed the tip of my insignificant nose (his own had so much more presence) and said, 'You have come to help me set out your foolish tables and chairs?'

Together we crossed the courtyard and set out the tables and chairs. When we finished, we went behind the issue desk and lifted the champagne bottles from the bucket of ice we'd concealed there. Putting on my best librarian's scowl, I rapped for attention. The press gang converged. Dmitri popped the corks and poured.

'Champagne *again*?' said Maxine.

'Will you listen to this one?' I said drily to the assembled company. 'Hasn't even got to Cambridge yet and already she's tired of the stuff.'

A flush of peach joined the cream of Maxine's face. 'Attila, I didn't mean – I only meant – you know, that morning when my A-level results came.'

'I know. Just pulling your leg.' I was having to wear my gruffest manner to keep sentimentality at bay. Bernard wasn't the only one grieving at the prospect of Maxine's departure. Where would I be without my punchy little friend to liven up the tedium of library life? We raised our glasses to Maxine. 'To Sedleigh's contribution to Cambridge,' I toasted. 'May she knock 'em dead.'

We clinked glasses and drank.

'To *all* of us going out from Sedleigh next week,' Maxine countertoasted, 'and to the teachers who made it possible.'

We raised our glasses to Ian and Kate and drank.

'To Anna,' said Kate, 'for providing a decent library and a dash of subversion.'

We raised our glasses. And drank.

'To Bernard and Kate,' I offered, 'for saving the wood.'

We raised our glasses. And drank.

'To Dmitri,' said Bernard, 'for sacrificing his water supply for ditto.'

Laughter.

We drank.

There was a knock at the door.

The party began.

* * *

I was lurking in 947, Russian History. In my hands a book: *The Icon in Modern Russian History*, by Dmitri Mikhailovich Komarovsky. By my side its author.

'Strange party behaviour,' Dr Komarovsky observed.

'Not for a librarian. Actually, I've been meaning to read this for ages.' I looked at the date: 1988. 'I must have catalogued it. Funny to think. I suppose I dealt with it like any other book, had no idea that its author knew my parents, let alone that he would sneak into my life.'

'I did not sneak, Anna.'

'You did. You tried to enter my life by stealth. I remember that first day so clearly. Trying to blend into the oak panelling. Casual and unassuming like any other tourist.'

He took the book from my hands and replaced it on the shelf. I took it out again and put it back in the right place. A librarian's instinct. Order. Then he leaned his hands against the bookcase, one on either side of me, trapping me in the cage of his arms.

'This is a scene from a bad film,' I commented. 'Now you have to kiss me. The shot switches to the camera behind you and shows my hands slowly, reluctantly creeping up your back. Then the impassioned clinch – pan to close-up of faces, side on, slightly fuzzy focus if it's a really old Hollywood film.'

We duly carried out the directions.

'Honestly!'

We sprang apart. Maxine was standing at the entrance to the alcove, hands on hips like a parody of myself parodying a librarian. 'If you two are setting the tone for this party, heaven help us.'

I attempted a blush. Dmitri didn't even try. We were supposed, all six of us, to be providing a discreet presence to make sure the party didn't get out of hand and confirm Mrs Johnson's worst suspicions (passion in Politics, drugs in Deep Sea Diving, arson in Ancient History).

'If you two can bear to be apart,' said my stern assistant, 'how about some music?'

'Are you sure?'

'I think the party's at that stage.'

She was probably right. The party had been going about an hour, long enough to lubricate but just before hunger would set in. A babble of happy voices was oozing through the spaces between the books. Happy equals music equals dance. 'How about those nice tapes?' I tried.

'Attila, you promised.'

I sighed. 'All right then, but I'll just ease into it step by step – test the water, so to speak.'

'How about a Cossack dance?' she said to Dmitri. 'You know – all those amazing leaps?'

Dmitri's laughter boomed through the chatter.

'Really, Maxine. Leave the man some dignity.' I looked at the distinguished scholar with new interest. 'Can you?'

'Alas, no. The only Cossack skill I have is riding.'

Racing across the steppe on a sturdy horse, teeth gleaming against the darkness of his swarthy face as he bends low over the horse's neck. Not slackening his pace one iota, he leans dangerously to one side and scoops up by the waist a peasant girl sauntering along the riverbank. Scoops her up and with one powerful sweep of his arm plonks her in front of the saddle. She shrieks with fear and delight. They race to his hut.

My knees weaken.

'Attila . . .'

'What? Oh, yes. The music.'

I slipped across to the issue-desk-cum-bar and surveyed the scene. Who would have thought Sydney Holroyd's library would ever look so colourful? Autumn had brought out the most vivid dresses and shirts as if in defiance of the coming winter. Set against the sombre oak panelling was a palette Anatoly would have envied. Was it time to set it in motion? I leaned down and opened the fiddle case I'd stashed away on a shelf. As I withdrew my violin I thought again of its history, no doubt as far-reaching as Dmitri's shirt but unknown to me. I always felt a little diffident now playing it in front of Dmitri. It had become a symbol of what I didn't know and what he wished me to know.

Still, a promise is a promise. I located Josh and Lewis and gave a little nod. They nodded back but stayed where they were, drinking wine (not too much; we needed clearish heads) and talking. I moved to the furthest corner of the desk and settled myself into my chair. I tightened my bow and, with my ear close to the strings, plinked them quietly to tune up. Then, not facing the audience but sideways on, I began, *mezzo piano*, an Irish jig. It was one of those lovely lilting tunes that bounces along with the softness of the Irish hills themselves, inviting – but not insisting on – a little gentle movement from the listeners' feet. If people weren't ready to dance, a few aficionados would drift over to the desk and tap their fingers and their feet without disturbing anyone else, leaving the others to chatter away with just a little musak in the background. But if they were ready –

A cheer broke out. A few people carried on talking but everyone else turned towards the desk, their feet tapping the wooden floor, their bodies beginning to emulate the rhythm. I sighed. We were in business.

Still playing (*mezzo forte* now), I left the desk and walked across to the alcove furthest from Sydney's portrait. At least here we would be out of the way. Josh put down his glass, fetched his viola from behind the desk and came over to join me. He began a perky countermelody to set off the tune. *Forte*. More cheers. Then Lewis, lugging his double bass across the floor on which dancers were now bobbing like corks on a sea. As soon as he was settled he launched in with a deep strong bass to underpin the lot. *Fortissimo*.

A wild shout of joy and the room whirled into action.

* * *

A slap of cold air hit my face as I entered the courtyard. Bliss. We'd been fiddling away for hours it seemed, the dancers reluctant to let us go. Only when we mimed three souls crawling through the desert towards an oasis did they release us. I'd gulped down a glass of wine too fast and then fled outside to cool off. In a few minutes I'd be fleeing back inside covered in goosebumps but right now I was enjoying the icy air blowing in across the North Sea. No doubt about it, the weather was set for change. Even the voluptuaries among us, we who had luxuriated in the sensuous heat of the summer, were hoping for a downpour. Bernard had given some awesome figures of the amount needed to fill the underground aquafers we'd depleted during the summer. It didn't bear thinking about.

I wasn't the only one seeking the cool air. Dancers were drifting into the courtyard and sinking into the chairs Dmitri and I had set out. 'Great stuff, Attila,' some of them said as they passed me. It always amazed me that they liked my music, so utterly foreign, so blatantly out of step with fashion.

A fork of lightning illuminated Kate's entrance. She bowed in acknowledgment and came over to join me. 'We'll be lucky to get away without a power cut,' she said as she sat down.

'Heaven forbid. Remind me to look for some candles.'

'It's going well, isn't it?' she observed.

I nodded. 'Quite a send-off.'

Through the open door I could see Maxine and Bernard laughing with some friends. Maxine was looking more beautiful than ever in a plain blue dress that cost almost nothing. She never spent much on clothes. She didn't have to; even the cheapest stuff looked fantastic on her. None the less, her lack of vanity was surprising. She didn't seem to mind wearing the same old clothes while hoarding her wages for university. Any other father would have noticed, been touched by the seriousness that lay beneath the pretty façade. Any other father would have been eager to do his bit to help.

'You still haven't told me how you twisted Robert's arm,' said Kate.

'You're reading my mind. I was just thinking that any other father wouldn't need his arm twisted.'

'Well? Or is it a trade secret?'

'Blackmail.'

Kate's eyebrows shot up. 'Something nasty in the woodshed?'

'Would that there had been. No, I just painted a lurid picture of a rich and famous Maxine denouncing her tight-fisted father on the Terry Wogan show.'

Kate laughed. 'And he swallowed it?'

'You'd be surprised how vain he is. Dmitri was the one who tipped me off. Robert's worried about losing face – especially after the borehole fiasco.'

'When I think how that kid struggled.'

'I know. Talk about a pearl in a dungheap. Literally. How many Cambridge students memorise their French vocabulary while shovelling shit? It's not as if Robert couldn't afford to hire help – in the house as well as on the farm. Never mind, it's all over. Virtue rewarded. Next week she's on her way.'

We looked to where our protégée was still framed in the doorway. Bernard's hand rested lightly on her shoulder. Next week he would drive her to Cambridge. I didn't envy them the leave-taking that would follow. Still, if anyone could handle it, it was Bernard.

The scene shifted and I saw Maxine at another party, somewhere in Cambridge. Instead of her old schoolfriends, the cream of this generation's bright young things. Instead of Kate and Ian and Dmitri and myself, a dazzling array of brilliant dons. Maxine had no idea such people existed. She would be devastated for the first few months. The big fish in the little pond of Sedleigh would become a minnow at Cambridge. She would be confused and a little frightened.

Then, gradually, she would adjust, find her own niche, begin to regain confidence. Slowly, imperceptibly, her worldview would change. At Christmas she would come home, excited as hell, eager to share her experiences with us ... only to find that we had changed. Radical Kate would be just that little bit tamer than she remembered. Dmitri (Would he be here? Would I?) would be a little less exotic. And I, the middle-aged *enfant terrible* of Sedleigh, another big fish in a little pond, would be just a provincial librarian scraping away at her fiddle to pass the time. She would be tactful, of course, and loyal. She wouldn't forget her old friends or slight us in any way. But deep down she would know us for what we were: facilitators. Good, solid, well-meaning mediocrities whose main function in life is to recognise the rare spark of real talent and help it along.

And Bernard? Would some other man's hand be on her shoulder at that other party? Perhaps not for the first few months. She would continue to see Bernard through a haze of new love, longing for him through the lonely nights of her confusion, greeting him ecstatically when he came down to see her. She would show him off proudly to her tentative new friends and they would be impressed by his quiet intelligence, his maturity, his manner – so like that of the best of the aristocracy: modesty veiling class. Impressed, but for how long? And for how long would she impose Bernard's face on that of every man she met and find them wanting? How long before she began to see them as they were: brilliant, exciting, talented, the makers of the future?

Another fork of lightning split the sky and a crack of thunder jolted me to the present.

'We're losing her, aren't we?' said Kate.

'Yes.' I no longer marvelled at her mind-reading. The scenario I was imagining had happened so often in reality that its course needed no crystal ball.

'There's just one thing I don't understand,' she continued. 'If Robert had refused to pay, she probably wouldn't be able to go to university. That splendid cock and bull you gave him about Maxine denouncing him on the box – it wouldn't happen.'

Ah. 'Well, Robert's not the brightest. I guess he didn't think that one through.'

I hadn't told anyone except Dmitri about the paintings. I didn't want Maxine to know I was selling them to raise the money her father might withhold. I didn't want her to know that all along I'd been prepared to play the surrogate parent to its logical conclusion. I didn't want her to be grateful.

A few drops of rain suddenly came down, big fat ones hitting the paving stones with an audible thud. We got up along with the other fresh-air fiends and made our way to the door.

'It still doesn't quite add up,' said Kate as we entered. 'I feel there's something missing.'

There was, but it was my secret. Truth's a great thing, but there's no point in overdoing it.

Maxine closed the door behind the last of the guests. She leaned against it a moment before wearily making her way to the issue-desk-cum-bar where the rest of us were assembled.

The party was over but in my head it continued, chattering and throbbing away to the pop music which had adorned its last hour. I was no fan of pop but was glad the tapes had been used after all – clearly I hadn't warped the youth of Sedleigh too much. Still, it did pound most awfully.

Clear-headed Kate had done the sensible thing: gone into the staff room and brewed the six of us some coffee.

Clutching our mugs of sanity and leaning against the desk while the soft fairy lights glowed down on us, we surveyed the wreckage.

Actually, it looked worse than it was. No structural damage, though I'd feared for the floorboards more than once while the dancers jumped about. A couple of broken glasses and some wine stains on the floor, but they blended in with the other stains that had accumulated over the decades. Our library was here to be used, not preserved in aspic. A bit of litter but not much. The two or three people who'd had to be sick had thoughtfully gone outside and found a gutter. The smell of stale perfume and sweat wasn't overpowering, nothing that a few open windows tomorrow wouldn't cure. Tomorrow we would return to the library and clean it up. For tonight, we would sip our coffee and gather up the remains of the food which would form improvised lunches tomorrow. Or today. It was two o'clock in the morning. A reasonable hour. Any less and the party would have been a flop; any more, unbearable.

'Not a bad send-off,' Ian mused.

'A fantastic send-off,' said Maxine. 'I just don't know how to thank you all.'

Danger. Gratitude threatening. 'You did a lot of the work,' I said. 'Not to mention providing the excuse for a good old knees-up. Not enough of those in Sedleigh. Hard to realise that winter's nearly here. In a month or two we'll all be holed up in our little houses again, hibernating.' I sighed and looked up at the big windows facing the quay. A streetlight illuminated the rain pouring down the windows. Now and again a flash of lightning and clap of thunder reasserted itself, just in case we hadn't got the message.

'A few weeks of this and we'll all be cursing it again,' said Kate. 'All the weeping and wailing over hosepipe bans and standpipes will be forgotten. What fickle things we are.'

'No one's even had a holiday,' said Maxine. 'I'm the only one who's going away and that's to work.'

It was true. Ian and Kate were groaning beneath the bank loan needed to pay for their borehole – no hols for them for some years. Bernard and Tim always worked straight through the summer – the best time for drilling – saving their holidays for the winter. Numerous trips to Cambridge would be Bernard's holidays for some years. I never went anywhere; after years of roaming I was content to stay put. As for Dmitri –

'*I* am having a holiday,' he announced.

'You've been writing frantically every hour I wasn't pestering you,' I said. 'Some holiday.'

One of Maxine's friends, standing on the shoulders of another, had plucked the laurel wreath from Sydney Holroyd's portrait and put it on Dmitri's head. It suited him. One flick of the eye and Dmitri became Demetrius. With his dark colouring and the archaic smocked shirt he looked like some minor Greek god, one of those earthbound deities – Dionysus, Bacchus – who preside over boozy festivals and wreak havoc among their peasant subjects. Just to emphasise the point, the wreath was askew. It made him look rakish, unpredictable, just a trifle dangerous.

'A proper holiday,' he said. 'In a fortnight I am off to Hamelin.'

I stared. This was the first I'd heard of any departure.

'How exciting!' said Kate. 'As in Pied Piper?'

'Just so,' said Dmitri. 'The rats to be gathered together on this occasion are historians. We convene for a conference.'

'A conference is hardly a holiday,' I said lightly. And then, even more lightly, 'How long do you plan to be away?'

He turned his dark (dangerous?) eyes on me. 'The conference is only a few days, but I contemplate going to the Harz Mountains afterwards for a few more days.'

If anyone noticed the tension rising between us they gave no sign. 'A walking holiday?' said Kate. 'With *Lederhosen* and *Alpenstock*?'

He laughed. '*Lederhosen, nein. Alpenstock, vielleicht.*'

'Extraordinary,' I said blandly. 'I didn't think you were the walking type. Not after the fuss you made about walking to Kate and Ian's party.'

He spread his hands in one of those big continental gestures of mock helplessness. 'Even an old academic like me is capable of reform. You have given me a taste for walking, my dear Anna.' A pause. 'Indeed, I had even thought to ask if you would care to accompany me on this jaunt.' Another pause. 'However, I gathered that your loyalty to Sedleigh is absolute and thought better of the idea.'

'What exactly do you mean by that?'

'I mean, Anna, that for nearly a decade you have scarcely set foot outside Sedleigh, let alone England. There are even rumours of xenophobia setting in.'

'What nonsense. I'm the last person to be accused of xenophobia. After all those years.'

'Well then?'

'Moping around with a bunch of historians isn't my idea of a holiday,' I said grumpily.

'The conference is to be held in a spectacular *Schloss* just outside the town. There is a regular train service to nearby Hannover. You have been to Hannover?'

'No, but –'

'A beautiful city. And a beautiful *Schloss* to use as a hotel. And of course the Harz Mountains are world-famous. You have been to the Harz?'

'No, but –'

'Oh, Anna,' cried Kate. 'You must go!' She turned to Dmitri. 'If Anna doesn't, will you take me instead?'

A roar of outrage from Ian. It disguised the electricity that was beginning to spark between Dmitri and me.

Outside, an answering jag of lightning slashed across the windowpanes.

'But *why* won't you go?' said Maxine. 'I would. I mean, it's not as if you're stuck with the library any more. With *two* assistants now, you can come and go as you please.'

'That isn't why I took them on.'

'No, but now's your chance for a break.'

Bit by bit I was being cornered. Like a rat.

And then the kill. 'I am thinking of returning straight to London after my holiday,' said Dmitri.

This was private stuff, he shouldn't be doing this to me in public. 'I see,' I said evenly.

'I have been offered a series of lectures, unexpectedly, which I would hate to turn down. But it does mean leaving Sedleigh sooner than I thought.'

And now the sparks between us were all but visible. I looked at the faces of my friends. Uncertainty ... and a hint of reproach.

'It would be a shame,' said Bernard cautiously, 'not to have a holiday together. Before the winter.'

Before the separation.

Amazing, the power of pressure from one's peers.

'Yes, of course I'll go,' I said crossly. 'I don't know why everyone's making such a fuss about it. Unless the offer's been withdrawn,' I said to Dmitri.

He was smiling, and now there was no mistaking the danger in his eyes. 'The offer stands.'

'Very well. I'll go.'

The die was cast. In a few flippant words I'd committed myself to a return to the Europe I had hoped never to see again.

A little cheer rose among my friends.

'Was there a real Pied Piper?' Bernard asked.

'Indeed there was,' said Dmitri. 'The story is documented, even down to the date: 1284. Only the interpretation varies. In the most pragmatic version, the Pied Piper is merely the means by which the local authorities solved a problem of overpopulation.'

'*What?*' Kate, incredulous.

'It was not unknown, in the Middle Ages, for troops of children to be sent off to "colonise" the east to relieve pressure on the town. Whether they survived or not is unknown, but none returned.'

'How gruesome,' said Kate. 'And the piper himself?'

'Nothing is known except that a mysterious man from an unknown land arrived one day and demonstrated a remarkable talent for wooing creatures out of dark places. Beyond that –'

A clap of thunder, louder than any before, cut him short. A moment later the lights went out.

TWENTY-SIX

I arrived at Victoria before Dmitri. In a way I was glad. It would give me time to adjust to the idea of travelling again. How had I got myself into this? For years I'd resisted and then, in the space of a few minutes after Maxine's farewell party, I'd found myself agreeing as if it were a minor matter.

In the days that followed I'd tried to get out of it. I never flew, I told Dmitri. Flying was cheating; it whizzed you from A to B as if there were nothing in between. There was, and it should be experienced for B to be appreciated properly. Fine, said Dmitri; we will go by train. It had been years since he'd travelled by train, he would enjoy the novelty.

I tried again. I didn't like ferries either. Ferries were full of drunken louts.

Quite, said Dmitri. We shall cross by Jetfoil.

It was autumn, the Channel would be too rough for a Jetfoil. It wouldn't be able to get out of the harbour.

At this my lover shrugged and smiled. We are in the hands of the gods, he said. Let us be bold and risk it. Then he told me he had to return to London for a week or so before departure; he had to prepare his paper for the conference and needed the British Library again. Would I care to come to London with him?

Love to, but no. I had to clear my desk. There were some things the assistants couldn't do, like catalogue a pile of new books that had accumulated during the chaos before Maxine's departure. Like send off a batch of Old Favourites for rebinding. Like arrange for the glazier to replace the leaded light that had blown out during the gale after the party. Like –

He had raised a sceptical eyebrow at my list, but 'Very well,' he'd said. 'We will meet at Victoria.'

So here I was, standing beneath the departure board and watching the world go by. How many hours had I spent in the past, whiling away the time at international railway stations by trying to guess the nationality of the passengers? I suspect I had a pretty fair success rate. (One of the few I got wrong was my own.)

I scanned the crowd, surprised it should be so big in mid-October. Quite a few people appeared to be students, weighed down by backpacks that had become larger and more elaborate since the days when I had used them, and there were even more of those mysterious families who made you wonder why their children weren't in school. I'd become so accustomed to my own nine-to-five that I'd forgotten all the people who lived irregular lives, as I had done. A pair of nuns walked past in modern dress. The awesome black-clad figures who'd been such a feature of the continent had started to thin out even in my time. Now they were probably extinct. Not so the eccentrics, or those who wished to be thought eccentric. There were more of them than ever, their appearance either scruffy or bizarre. Their books hadn't changed either; obscure provocative titles protruded from pockets. On the train the books would be read with fierce concentration meant to be interrupted. I never interrupted. The real eccentrics, I'd early discovered, were the ones disguised as boring businessmen or solitary women respectably dressed.

I looked down ruefully at my own trouser suit. Soft green. Loose and comfortable for travel. Respectable. Attila the Librarian disguised as an academic's mistress disguised as his secretary. I sighed so audibly that a swarthy little woman as broad as she was tall looked up in surprise. In one hand was a small bunch of flowers, in the other a large piece of cardboard with a name printed on it in large black letters. 'Good morning,' I said to her in

Serbo-Croat, though it was strictly speaking no longer morning. She scuttled away in alarm.

I strolled round to the platform. Our train was in. Dmitri was not. A flash of hope: he's been held up, he'll arrive too late. Trip cancelled. Could I fake disappointment? Put off the dread day when he would lure me back to the continent that was no longer mine? A few days in London with Dmitri, an opera, one or two art galleries, a slap-up meal in a Thai restaurant before returning to Sedleigh with my peace of mind intact.

Cheered, I strolled back towards the departure board. Standing beneath it was the most scrumptious man I'd ever seen: a big tall solidly built don't-mess-around-with-me man with steely grey-black hair and a strong face which threatened and tantalised at the same time. The kind of man you should leave alone if you want an easy life. The kind of man who draws you after him like the Pied Piper a rat. The kind of man I always fall for. Smiling his irresistible smile, he came towards me. I stood still, transfixed. When he arrived, he twirled me round with his free arm and marched me to the train.

As we chugged past the green and pleasant land of a Brixton scrapyard, I turned to my lover. 'How does it feel to be travelling with us plebs?'

He gave my knee a patronising pat. 'I have suffered worse indignities in my life than travelling by train.'

All my attempts to ruffle his composure were failing. The train, which I'd hoped would be crowded and filthy, was clean, comfortable and roomy. Even the one-and-only eccentric, whom I'd insisted on sitting across from, had failed me. Overwashed black jeans; a black shirt stitched to death with beads and mirrors peeping from beneath the worn leather jacket; a black felt hat with a purple felt dove flying across its crown; blond beard and long blond hair pulled into a pony tail. I waited hopefully for the book: New Age? A slim volume of Tibetan poetry? Derrida? Martin Amis? At last the hand reached into the jacket pocket, the book came out.

Jeffrey Archer.

It began to rain, suddenly and hard. The boy glanced at the grey suburban scene outside, then turned a shy smile on us.

'Lousy weather for travelling,' he said. 'You going far?'

'Just to Hamelin,' said Dmitri, 'in Germany.'

'That's far,' said the boy. A pause. 'I'm only going to Calais – that's where my in-laws live. My wife's there with them now.' Another pause. 'With our son.' The shy smile broadened. 'We've just had our first baby, you see.'

We produced our congratulations and listened attentively as the boy told us about his son, his wife, their little flat in Enfield, his job – he was a computer programmer – and how great his in-laws were.

Some eccentric. I stared glumly at the toy trees of the Kent orchards. Only when we approached Dover did I cheer up a little, picturing the tatty docks, the dismal customs shed, the mad scrum of bodies shoving to be first in the long queue, propelled by the conviction that the boat was poised to leave without them.

No such luck. They'd spruced up the place in my absence, taught the staff some manners. The queue was short, the travellers amiable, the officials at Passport Control almost jolly. Without thinking, I smiled in return as I handed over my passport. It was stiff with newness, unused since I'd renewed it several years ago. I'd had no intention of using it. Renewing one's passport was one of those automatic gestures, as if without a passport one didn't exist.

Suddenly I remembered. I didn't. This was the first time I was leaving the country since learning the truth. Panic flooded my sweat glands. I sneaked a look at the controller's face. Did he guess? Was there some mystical way he would know it was based on a false birth certificate?

Was this the moment the truth would out? Worse still, would he let me go and save up the blow for my return? Would I be allowed to return?

He barely glanced at the passport before returning it with a smile.

My knees were still weak as I sank into my seat by the window. Dmitri sat down beside me. I looked out of the window, afraid to show my ashen face. It must be ashen. I felt as if I'd just seen a ghost. I could feel my heart doing a nasty little dance. Breathe deeply. Calm down.

A hand on my shoulder. I turned a little too quickly towards its source.

'Anna?'

I shut my eyes and leaned back against the seat. 'Why are you doing this to me?'

A startled silence. Then, 'Anna, look at me.'

I looked at him. There was no malice in his face, only concern. Did he really not understand?

'Please tell me what's wrong.'

The seats nearest us were unoccupied, the Jetfoil half empty. The thrum of the motors would hide my words from anyone but him. 'Passport Control,' I said quietly.

'Yes? They were civilised enough, were they not?'

I shook my head impatiently. 'This is the first time I've left the country since, you know, learning the truth.'

'Surely you don't think –'

'I don't know what to think. It didn't matter, as long as I stayed put. You've changed all that.'

'Anna. Please. For once, just listen to me. Imagine the worst possible scenario. Imagine that your lover, who adores you to distraction, is a villain in disguise. Imagine that I go to the appropriate officials and announce that my dear Anna Atwill is no such person, that a completely false birth certificate was created for her by my wicked father. Now, please, imagine what they would do.'

I said nothing. I couldn't imagine what they would do. I had no experience of such things.

'Most probably,' said Dmitri, 'they would laugh at me and tell me to go away and stop trying to make trouble for that nice Anna Atwill. At worst, they would ask me for proof. What proof does your villainous lover have? You and I are the only people who know. Nothing about that extraordinary little transaction in Berlin all those years ago was ever written down. Nothing. That is precisely why Edmund felt he had to tell you before the truth died with him. And that is why my father, not knowing whether Edmund had told you, sent me on my mission: *because* there was no written evidence which could inform you once Edmund and my father were dead. Am I being clear, Anna?'

'I'm not sure.'

'Then let me put it more plainly still. It would be my word against yours. My word against a perfectly respectable birth certificate. Why on earth should they believe me? And what could they do if they did?'

'Go to Berlin,' I said dully.

Dmitri smiled. 'And what would they find if they did? At worst, a birth certificate for some Anna X who happened to be born in the same week as Anna Atwill. Is that so strange? That two babies born in the same week in the very large city of Berlin should both have the good fortune to be given the charming name of Anna? And now, my Anna, you will please go through the ludicrous ritual of fastening your seat-belt while our stewardess shows us what to do with these toy life-jackets beneath our seats. Then, while our boat pretends to be a plane and flies across the Channel, I will buy us both a nice big whisky and with them we will drink a toast to the holiday your lover has arranged. And after that, you will promise me never again to withhold from me your fears. For though I chide you a little for the foolishness of this particular fear, I chide you much more seriously for not telling me sooner. Because

I love you, Anna Atwill, and if I have one purpose in life it is to make you happy.'

I looked down at the silly seat-belt, confused by the jumble of emotions his words had called forth. 'I am happy,' I said.

'Maybe yes, maybe no. We shall see. Meanwhile, please give me one tiny little kiss – there's no one looking and if there is it will amuse them to see the besotted roué and his delightful secretary-cum-mistress – as a penalty for your lack of faith. You do trust me now, do you not?'

I looked at my enigmatic lover. 'I'm not sure. Sometimes I think I don't know you at all.'

'You will, my Anna. You will. Now, please: that kiss.'

It was still raining when we reached Ostende, and cold. The weather provided diversions. As we fiddled with the umbrella I could ignore the multilingual announcements and pretend we were still in England. As we sloshed our way to the platform I could ignore the foreignness of the Deutsche Bundesbahn trains – so utterly different, so evocative of my past – in the struggle to keep my feet out of puddles. I didn't even look at the carriages. I left it to Dmitri to find our reservation.

But when he opened the door and – umbrella in one hand, case in the other – nodded me to board, I couldn't fail to notice the big white 1.

I shook my head and moved away.

He persevered. 'Quickly, please; it's cold out here.'

Reluctantly I climbed the steps and waited as Dmitri shook the umbrella, closed it and then joined me in the small space. I was slightly annoyed. It was so much more cumbersome to walk through carriage after carriage looking for ours. Despite the damp cold, I would rather have stayed outside until we found it.

But Dmitri was unperturbed. He opened the door separating off the service area and started down the corridor.

I hesitated, then followed him. He was scrutinising the reservation boards by each compartment.

'Dmitri, it's no good looking here – this is First Class.'

'Of course it is. Ah, here we are.' He reached for the door handle.

I intercepted his hand, picturing an irate German businessman inside. 'Are you mad?'

He raised my hand and kissed it. 'Mad with love.' Then he disengaged my hand, opened the door and motioned me inside.

I stood where I was, still not understanding the obvious. A well-dressed couple speaking French were coming down the corridor towards us. It was probably their compartment. 'Dmitri, please.'

'My dear, we are blocking the corridor.' He went inside the compartment and drew me after him, luggage and all. The well-dressed couple smiled and nodded their thanks as they passed. I smiled back uncertainly.

Then it dawned. 'You don't mean we're travelling First?'

'How else?'

'You never told me.'

'You never asked. Come, let us settle in. We have a long journey ahead of us.'

'But –'

'Come now, Anna. The role of country bumpkin does not suit you. My sleeping beauty has grown up during her years of slumber in Sedleigh. This is where you belong.'

I remembered the crowded compartments full of other disreputables like me, arranging our limbs as best we could to survive a night of snatched naps before tumbling out, bleary-eyed and unwashed, at our destination. Even a Second-Class couchette was a luxury I'd rarely indulged in, squashed inevitably in the top bunk sweating like a pig through the stuffy night listening to the snores of five strangers also playing at sardines. I searched Dmitri's face, looking for clues as to his motive. Indulgent lover giving his woman a treat? Or stern custodian of the hourglass, forcing me to face my maturity? I thought I had done just that in Sedleigh, relinquishing my wild youth and turning myself into a staid librarian and town councillor. Then Dmitri had come along and turned that life upside down. What did he want from me?

'Sometimes,' I said again, 'I think I don't know you at all.'

'You will, my Anna, you will.'

The motion of the train was rocking me to sleep. That and the champagne which had accompanied the picnic hamper.

'Alas, this train has no restaurant car,' Dmitri explained.

'So they provide this instead?'

'These things can be arranged.'

Clearly he had connections. I tried to imagine what sort of person you had to know in order to ensure a champagne picnic awaiting your arrival and gave up. It wasn't my world.

Neither was the extreme politeness of the Schlafwagen attendant when he came to make up our beds. Germans were always polite but usually non-committal. This one was smoothly anxious to make our journey as pleasant as possible. He had taken our passports and tickets so we wouldn't be interrupted by border officials in the night, then assured us that he would wake us in good time in the morning. With that he had disappeared, leaving behind the aura of a grand hotel writ small.

Just once had I been able to assert something of my old life into the new. I'd insisted on taking the upper berth. Dmitri had protested. Only when I'd pointed out that the lower berth was more vulnerable to intruders did he acquiesce. 'As you wish. I shall be your bodyguard and protect you from that wicked French couple in the next compartment.'

A real bed with real bedding, not the skimpy sheet sleeping-bag of a couchette. I should have been contented but wasn't. Dmitri was step by step taking over my life. With each kilometre into the continent he was growing larger and I smaller. By Hamelin I would have disappeared, absorbed entirely into his care. The *Schloss* where the conference was to be held would be opulent: his world, not mine. The other wives/mistresses/secretaries would click about on their high heels: his kind of woman, not mine. There would be huge formal meals full of the pretentious kind of food I hated, not a dumpling in sight. I sighed.

The deep voice rumbled up from below. 'You are awake?'

'Of course I'm awake,' I said crossly. 'I'm wondering what on earth I'm doing going with you to this silly conference.'

'It is not a silly conference.'

'It's silly for me to be there. What's it about anyway?'

'History.'

'I'd rather assumed that,' I said drily. 'What kind of history?'

'Recent history. Twentieth century.'

'Russian?'

A pause. 'In part. Go to sleep, Anna. We have a long day ahead of us.'

'Are you sleepy?'

'No. There's a chatterbox above me keeping me awake.'

I smiled. He always managed to sabotage my anger. 'Are you giving a paper?'

'Yes.'

'On?'

'History.'

I opened my mouth for a retort and then closed it again. The sound of the wheels changed slightly. Light squeezed through the edges of the blind to throw patterns across the curved ceiling of the compartment. We must be passing some small station not thought worthy of a stop. 'Will you let me come to your paper?' I asked.

'Are you interested?' he countered.

I shifted uneasily in my berth. Despite my good intentions, I hadn't read his books. Nor had I ever asked him about his life, his past, despite my desire to know him better. Dmitri's past was too bound up with my own and with things I didn't want to know. 'Is it on Russian history? Your paper?'

'In part.'

'I suppose you have a lot more contact with other Russians – colleagues – now that the Soviet Union's gone.'

'Other? I am no more Russian than you are. I was born in Berlin. As you were.'

I was learning how to avoid these unwelcome references to my past. 'How old were your parents when they came to Berlin?'

'Children. I don't know precisely how old, though I could work it out if you wish to know.'

'It doesn't matter. Idle curiosity.' The train was going round a curve, bringing the rain back on to the window. It made a noisy descant to the rhythm of the wheels. 'What part of Russia did they come from?'

'St Petersburg.'

'No country estate?'

'That too, on my mother's side at least.'

I remembered my first crazy image of him as a Russian prince turning my library into a glittering ballroom and said without thinking, 'Don't tell me she was a princess?'

'I'm afraid so. A very minor one. It's not something I admit to everyone but you probably know how insignificant it was. Not that my mother thought it insignificant. She always complained that if she'd married someone else I might have been a prince.'

Prince Dmitri in the ballroom, his white dress uniform laden with medals. God knows why, after all these months of resisting, but I wanted to know more. 'And the estate?'

'As insignificant as my mother's title.'

'Where was it?'

'Kazan.'

'Birch trees green-hazed in the spring, troika rides through the snow, wolves howling at the moon?'

He laughed. 'You obviously know my mother's type: charming at first but the stories wore thin after a while. She was so young when she left that she couldn't possibly have remembered most of what she said she did.'

The rhythm of the train was so regular, so soothing, lulling me out of my caution. 'What about your father?'

'He came from a long line of doctors. Distinguished doctors, but not of the aristocracy. If the Revolution hadn't happened and the two families had stayed in Russia, it's unlikely that their children would have married each other. As it was, there was some opposition from my mother's family. Or so my mother said.'

'What did your father say?'

'Not much. He never talked about the past. It was best to keep quiet about some things.'

'What things?' It was out before I could stop myself.

'My mother's Nazi sympathies.'

His voice was so matter-of-fact that it took some moments before I heard the words. How many moments I didn't know, but enough for Dmitri to ask, 'You are shocked, Anna? You think less of me, knowing this?'

'Of course not. You and your mother are two separate people. Anyway, it was common for –'

'– for White Russians to be ferociously anti-communist? Is this what you are going to tell me, Anna? Let me say it for you. "My enemy's enemies are my friends" – that was my mother's attitude. She was delighted when the Germans invaded Russia. She thought it would make the Russian people revolt against the communists and form a new nationalist Russia like the old one, which would then defeat the Germans. In one neat and tidy war, both the communists and the Germans would be vanquished. Then those nice Russian peasants would give her back the family estate. My mother was a fool, and a selfish one at that.'

We were getting into deeper waters than I'd anticipated, but before I could stop him Dmitri continued. 'My father was less keen on the Nazis. But then his origins were humbler and – as my mother often pointed out – he was only a body mechanic who had to earn his living. What she didn't understand is that it was my father's profession which kept us all alive – during the war and after. Doctors were too useful to be questioned closely about their political correctness.'

How politically correct had my own first parents been? I didn't want to hear any of this. 'What about you?' I said quickly before he could continue. 'Do you remember anything about the war?'

'Nothing at all. I was born during the bombing of Berlin. If I had any memory it would probably be of continuing darkness and noise: first the womb and the sound of my mother's panicky heart, then the cellar and the noise of the bombs. Quite possibly I never noticed the transition.'

'And after the war?'

'Silence. I was born into a dead city. There were only a few isolated sounds: wooden-soled shoes, handcarts – "post-war Volkswagens" the Berliners called them. An occasional wood-fuelled bus chugging in the distance. The sound of army lorries. I've often wondered how my family survived those first two months after the Russians arrived. *Frau komm* – you know the phrase?'

The Soviet victors' summons to the thousands of women they raped. I knew little about the post-war years except that the Russian troops' brutality had matched that of the Nazis and turned the city against Moscow for ever.

'Whether my mother was one of the victims I don't know. She was much more eager to talk about her mythical childhood than what came after. Understandably. The real terror, though, must have been that they would discover we were Russian. You can imagine how White Russians were treated. But my parents had been raised in Berlin and could speak German with the local accent. Perhaps that saved them, or perhaps they spent those two months hiding in cellars until the western allies arrived. My first memory is of standing with my mother at a standpipe, bucket in hand. That must have been after.'

Until now he had spoken in the same matter-of-fact tone as when he'd announced his mother's Nazi sympathies. Now his voice grew lighter. 'So you can imagine how displeased I was to be in the same situation after our good friend Robert Vesey removed the water supply from my house and I had to be rescued by my nice landlady in the berth above me.'

'It's hardly comparable.'

'No? My whole life has been one of great good fortune. Adversity turned sweet. Even after the war we were lucky. Our house had escaped bombing – only the windows were blown out – and because other relatives were homeless we were able to fill our flat with relatives rather than strangers. The Russians had stripped it, of course, and there was no fuel or food, but at least we had a roof and walls and the company of our kind. That was luxury. Even better, our house happened to be in what became the British sector. The British were surprisingly decent to their former enemies. Very probably that's why my father chose to move to London rather than Paris or New York when the time to move came. And as there were no physical boundaries between the western sectors, I was free to rootle about in the dustbins behind the American canteens. Pickings were better there than in the British dustbins.'

I didn't want to hear this, to witness my lover reliving his degradation, but there was no way to stop him any more.

'My mother accompanied me on these forays. My mother, the Russian princess. She tried to keep her children with her at all times because sometimes the Russians came over from their sector and kidnapped anyone who spoke out against the Soviets – usually adults and usually public figures but occasionally their children as well. Our parents shut up and taught all of us to shut up, too.'

'All of us?'

'My sister and our cousins.'

'I didn't know you had cousins.'

'You didn't ask. You have been careful not to enquire about my past.'

Because I didn't want to think about my own. Lying warm and comfortable on the train taking me back into Europe, I realised for the first time how selfish I'd been. I turned on to my stomach and looked over the edge. Dmitri was lying on his back with his arms behind his head. I couldn't see his face. I reached my hand down. 'I'm sorry, Dmitri. I'm not a very nice person.'

One arm disengaged itself and reached up to grasp my hand. 'We are neither of us very nice people, Anna. I was born during the worst bombing Berlin had ever known, you were born during the worst anti-communist uprising East Berlin had ever known. We are children of violence, Anna. Our pasts do not bear up well to close scrutiny. None the less, I have scrutinised mine closely, if for no better reason than my liking for a good night's sleep. I don't take kindly to nightmares produced by a hastily buried past. Those ugly parts of our past are like corpses dumped into the deep waters of the sea; far too often they bob up again, and in a state which – well, I will say no more. But I have no doubt that my dislike of concealing the past was one reason I became a historian.

'There were real corpses, too. One of my earliest memories is the smell of rotting flesh. Then the corpses stopped smelling because in the winter of 1946–7 they froze while awaiting burial in the frozen ground. Nearly 60,000 people died that winter of cold and hunger. Again we were lucky; only one of my cousins died. What little fuel there was was diverted from domestic use and industry to heat public buildings where Berliners could huddle together for warmth. Otherwise even more would have died. The shortage of food was translated into rickets, anaemia, tuberculosis and retarded growth in children. I was not among the victims. Many adults were so weakened by near-starvation that they couldn't work. The men rebuilding the city literally fainted from hunger and fell off the scaffolding. My parents were not among them. Sometimes I feel the guilt of the survivor, like those Jews who survived the camps. Why me? Why us? Your hand is cold, Anna. Come here.'

I scrambled down the ladder, into Dmitri's berth and into his arms.

'That's better. Though I could wish for a more generous bed – we were not made for such austerity. Still, if you squeeze up very closely, we may just thwart the unromantic provisions of the Deutsche Bundesbahn. What, tears?'

'I can't bear to picture you then, when you were a child.'

'Then I have failed as a historian. I tell you of my past not to conjure up your pity or even your compassion but because this is what I was and therefore what I am. You do not dislike what I am?'

'Dmitri . . .'

'Good. Then let me once again kiss away your tears. We have had enough history for one night. It is time to return to the present.'

I was in a motorboat. It was small and crowded and chugging with effort across the sea. There was no land in sight. The only object marring the seamless expanse of sea and sky was the cartoon bow of a ship sinking. We had been on it. Now we were in the little boat which was also sinking. There were too many people, it couldn't take our weight. Someone would have to go –

I awoke, but still the boat chugged and rocked. Slowly I realised that the boat was a train and I was somewhere in the heart of Europe, far from any sea. I reached for Dmitri, craving comfort. He wasn't there. I opened my eyes fast in the panic of the deserted.

He was standing by the washbasin, both splendid and absurd in his nakedness. Shaving. I smiled. His lathered face smiled back from the mirror. '*Guten Morgen, Fräulein Anna.*'

'*Guten Morgan,* you. What's with this Schlafwagen attendant who was supposed to wake us?'

'He did. That is to say, he woke me. My better half was snoring too loudly to hear him, so I decided to leave her alone for a few more minutes of sleep.'

'I do not snore.'

'You do. Magnificently. Even Herr Schlafwagen was impressed. Though he declined to remark on it. Or on the fact that you had spurned his domestic craftsmanship in the upper berth to share mine.'

'You could have pulled the sheet over my face like in a decent French farce.'

'And spoil the effect?'

'Where are we?'

'In Germany, I believe.'

I reached for the blind.

Dmitri's voice stayed my hand. 'Anna, please. I would prefer to display my naked body to you and you alone. The German populace has no role in this scene.'

'Sorry.'

It still seemed strange, the smell of shaving soap in my life. After one last expert stroke, he rinsed the razor and then his face. He towelled it dry with vigour, but there were still a few spikes of damp hair at the edges when he finished. I liked these little touches of imperfection, signs of carelessness in his authoritative life.

He sloshed on some aftershave and deodorant and started to dress. 'Make haste, my love; we're nearly there.'

I washed quickly and quickly gathered up my things and put them in my suitcase. The train stopped just as I finished. Already a line of luggage-laden people was moving cumbersomely down the corridor. I stood by the door of our compartment, Dmitri right behind, and looked one last time at the tiny room which had witnessed his revelations and our love. I felt a twinge of premature nostalgia. So small and all-enfolding, the room, like a Wendy House or a womb. In our haste, we hadn't raised the blind. I took a step towards it but Dmitri was in the way.

'What are servants for?' he said, and nudged me into the corridor.

The Schlafwagen attendant was near the exit, smiling pleasantly and helping with luggage when needed. Nothing in his face betrayed that he had heard my snoring or seen my dishevelled form in Dmitri's berth. We needed no help with our luggage – there wasn't much for such a short trip.

Alighting passengers blocked the exit. I noticed that somewhere between Ostende and Hamelin it had stopped raining, that I felt unusually fresh after the journey compared to all those nights of youthful travel and that the prospect of being in Germany again no longer made me quite so nervous. I almost but not quite noticed that there were surprisingly many people getting off at this small and rather insignificant station.

Not until I had descended the metal steps and stood on the platform did I see the sign announcing the name of the station.

ZOO BAHNHOF BERLIN

TWENTY-SEVEN

I froze. There was no movement in my body, no thought in my mind. Like a statue I stood on the platform just beneath the train's steps while passengers behind squeezed around me. If I was jostled I didn't feel it. If there was a Tannoy I didn't hear it. I was alone in a vast dark space, a limbo in which no feeling at all intruded.

When finally sensation returned it was with the violence of a vacuum suddenly filled. I wheeled round. The emotions pouring into me poured out again in an incoherent jumble.

'Oh God! – the attendant! – mistake! – overslept!'

My mind raced, organising itself into how to deal with the disaster. Dmitri's hand was on my arm. He was trying to manoeuvre me away from the train. I lunged for the steps, pulling him with me. 'Quick! Before it leaves!' As if the train would obediently turn round and take us back to Hamelin.

Dmitri's grip tightened. His voice was calm. 'It's no mistake. Come over here, Anna; we are in the way.'

'But we have to get back!'

'No, Anna. We are here, at our destination.'

'But the conference!'

'Come with me. I'll explain when we get out of this crowd.'

Trancelike I followed him across the platform and into the building. I didn't recognise it. The dark dirty station I had known so well was a bright, light hall made of glass. The smell of toilets and disinfectant had vanished, though the dealers and prostitutes and drunken tramps hadn't. My brain reached for an easy answer: this wasn't Berlin. I had misread the sign. This was Hamelin after all. I turned to Dmitri for confirmation.

He shook his head. 'They did a lot of rebuilding some years ago for the anniversary, don't you remember?'

Mechanically I replied. 'I wasn't here.' Here. Already some small part of me must have started to accept the impossible: that I was back in Berlin.

'Of course. But you must have read about it. The city's 750th anniversary.'

I said nothing, still too dazed.

Outside, Dmitri hailed a taxi. I got in meekly. What was the point of objecting? I was in his hands now. Dmitri got in beside me. He spoke an address to the driver, then put his arm across my shoulders. 'There was a great deal of smartening up for the anniversary. There is much you won't recognise.' He spoke casually, as if I were a tourist and he a tour guide.

'Where is the conference?' My own voice was dull, without emotion. I looked straight ahead. I didn't want to see him.

'In Hamelin.'

'Why aren't we there?'

'We are going to another conference, a different one.' The taxi started up, eased itself into the traffic.

'You lied to me.'

'Not entirely. I did plan to go to the conference in Hamelin. I changed my mind when you agreed to come with me.'

'Why didn't you tell me?' There was more traffic than I remembered, much more. We squeezed into Joachimstaler Strasse just ahead of a Trabant whose horn honked angrily. 'Why didn't you tell me?'

'It seemed better not to. And there was no need. You left the travel plans entirely to me.'

'Because I trusted you.'

'Then trust me now.'

'How can I? When you deceived me.'

'I regret that, and I apologise. But now the time for deceit is over.'

The taxi turned right, into the Kurfürstendamm. I looked away from the waxworks museum and into Dmitri's eyes. Hard. 'So where are we going now? Or will you lie about that, too?'

He returned my gaze calmly. 'To a very nice hotel in Wilmersdorf.'

We came to a standstill, encased in a motionless sea of cars, buses, motorcycles. Clearly we weren't going anywhere. The conference would be over before we reached the suburbs. 'And this other conference is in the hotel we're going to?'

'In part.'

'When does it begin?'

Slowly the traffic edged into motion again. 'It has begun,' he replied.

A solid block of vehicles spurted ahead, bearing us with it all the way to the Uhland Strasse junction before giving up the ghost once more. The crowds of tourists at the Möhring Café were missing, as if all of them had been swept from their tables and deposited in this hell of idling cars for the sin of gluttony. I looked at my watch. Too early for cafés. Suddenly my mind clicked into the obvious. 'This early? When did it begin?'

'Last night,' said Dmitri.

I didn't bother to ask him why we hadn't taken an earlier train. I didn't care. If he wished to miss the beginning of his conference, fine.

I nurtured my resentment all the way down the Ku'damm. We passed the art galleries my father had known so well. Clusters of early morning strollers were gawping through the windows. I hated them. A modern sculpture had sprouted in the central reservation. I hated it. At the corner of Leibniz Strasse, beneath the exquisite Iduna-Haus where once I'd had a profitable day busking, a derelict woman with a baby was begging. I hated the building, the woman, her baby, myself. I hated the cute little old-new lamps that had been installed along the Ku'damm to tweak the nerve labelled 'nostalgia'. Above all I hated Dmitri. Of all the dirty tricks he'd played on me, this one was the worst.

At Lehniner Platz we stalled again, right by the Schaubühne. I'd been to the legendary radical productions of the old Schaubühne in Kreutzberg and then to the not-quite-so-radical productions when it moved to Lehniner Platz. I'd been to the first night of the first play in its new premises. These had been proud memories. Dmitri was despoiling them. I had placed my memories in the file labelled Past, catalogued and classified them as lovingly as my library's books. I looked away from the Schaubühne and at Dmitri. A vandal. One of those yobs who broke into people's homes and messed up their possessions without even the dignity of a theft. 'Why are you doing this to me?'

'Trust me. Please.'

At Rathenau Platz was yet another modern sculpture: two Cadillacs embedded in concrete.

'This was all done for the anniversary celebrations,' my tour guide explained. 'The "sculpture boulevard".'

'I'm not interested.'

We turned left on to Hubertus Allee. We were going south now, down into the Grunewald district, the most expensive part of Wilmersdorf. That, too. At every stage of our journey Dmitri was wiping out the crazy hand-to-mouth existence I'd been so proud of and replacing it with the slick veneer of wealth. I looked at the huge turn-of-the-century villas lining the streets, each in its luxurious tree-secretive grounds. Here and there a modern building had replaced a bombed-out villa, but even these were carefully designed not to interrupt the aura of privilege.

'Do you know this area?' Dmitri was asking.

'I lived in Kreutzberg,' I said shortly.

Sometimes two or three of us had borrowed bikes and cycled across town to the Grunewald, the forest that had given the district its name. We'd passed through these streets on our way, mocking the opulence, laughing at the pompous brass plates on the gateways which announced the names and professions of those within. Most of the villas were divided into half a dozen or more units: flats, clinics, offices, nursery schools. A few of the largest had been turned into hotels.

Like the one at which the taxi stopped. It was even more grandiose than most, in the style of the Italian Renaissance. Very probably it had been a minor palace before its transformation into a doss house for the rich. Was Dmitri rich? I'd never asked, never cared. He was rich in love, that's all that had mattered. How could he demean not only me but himself by this awful ostentation? The First Class sleeper I could just about accept, but hotels were different. Hotels were nothing but places to sleep out of the rain. I'd never understood the need to pay for being unconscious.

The doorman took our luggage. Or porter or bellhop or whatever. I didn't even know the terminology of a place like this. With effort I gave him a smile. It wasn't his fault I was here. He was just earning a living. I was saving my anger for the real villain. Dmitri. Waiting for the moment when no taxi driver or doorman would impede my indignation.

At last the door closed behind our grateful servant. Our room was large, light, beautifully furnished in the best of all possible taste. I barely glanced at it. I zeroed in on Dmitri. He had gone straight to the window. I went to the window. We were on the top floor. Only a few streets away the first trees of the Grunewald set down their green-gold carpet, then spread it out as far as the eye could see. A stunning view. An expensive view.

'Look,' said Dmitri.

'I have. It's time for talk.'

'No, not over there. Here.' He pointed across the street.

I looked down. Across the street was yet another villa in yet another garden. 'Very nice. Now tell me about this conference.'

Dmitri said nothing.

'Tell me about the paper you're giving.'

Silence.

'There is no conference and you're giving no paper,' I said. 'You lied, Dmitri. I want to know why. I want to know what you think you're doing, dragging me back to this city.'

Finally he spoke. Still gazing down at the villa he said, 'There is a conference. I am giving a paper.'

'When? What on?'

'Now.' He turned to me. 'It's a small conference, Anna. Just you and me. My paper is a long one. You've already heard the first part of it. It began last night, on the train. Do you see the villa down there?'

What was he talking about? Confused but obedient, I looked again at the building.

'That's where I was born,' said Dmitri.

I closed my eyes in shame. When I opened them, the green-gold-and-white of the villa and its grounds had gone. In the sepia-coloured picture that replaced it, a door opened and a woman came out. She had the high Slav cheekbones of the country she had left behind, the same cheekbones as the baby she was carrying. I watched her tuck the blanket round him against the October chill. She glanced up at our window once and then vanished. My rage vanished with her. It was his past we were revisiting, not mine.

'Why didn't you tell me?' I said softly.

'Would you have come with me if I had?'

Would I? I thought back on the things he had told me on the train. All along I'd been so concerned about my own past that I'd failed to notice his. How much more selfishness had to come out before I got the message?

No more. Twice was enough. I smiled uncertainly at this man I barely knew. 'Do you want to tell me about it?'

He searched my face. Vulnerable. Who would have guessed? 'Do you want to know?'

'Yes.'

He looked down at the villa again. 'There's not a great deal to tell. We had a flat on the ground floor along with my father's consulting room. I don't remember what it was like before the Russians stripped it, of course. My main memory is of thinking that the building across the street must be the biggest building in the world. It seemed immense to such a small child. The first time I came back to Berlin – some time in the 1960s – I was shocked at how it had shrunk. Even so, I still had a crazy desire some day to stay in this hotel and see how our house looked from here. Childish, isn't it?'

Not much of the villa was visible through the thick stand of trees surrounding it. The Germans were on more intimate terms with their trees, didn't mind them crowding right up to the door. Only the front door, a few windows and the occasional flash of white stucco could be seen. An image superimposed itself – charred stumps of trees, a lurid red background – and then vanished.

'Do you know who lives there now?' I asked.

'Only the name on the plate. I did try to summon up courage to ring the bell once – it must have been some time in the 1970s – but I couldn't. I didn't want to frighten whoever lived there. So many of them lived in dread of someone coming back to reclaim their property – usually the child or even grandchild of a Jew who'd been thrown out.'

'Would you like to try again? With me?'

'I don't think so. It's only a house. Stone and stucco and timber. It no longer seems to matter.' He hesitated. 'Perhaps because you're here with me this time.'

A journey into the past. But it was his past, not mine. I looked round the luxurious room, no longer resenting it. I was seeing it through the eyes of a small child, cold and hungry, staring through the glassless windows of a plundered flat at the fairytale palace beyond. Longing. Hoping for a future that could contain such magic.

'Have you forgiven me?'

His voice brought me back to the present. I looked into the big strong face of the boy some fifty years on. 'Can you doubt?'

Morning in the Grunewald. Racing through the forest with the wind whipping through my hair, the mare's mane stinging my face as I bent low over her neck. Up ahead Dmitri's horse was thundering down the bridleway as if all the demons of hell were in pursuit.

We were. 'Come on, Gräfin!' I yelled. 'Don't let that fleabitten nag beat us!'

Gräfin bunched her powerful muscles and sprang forward. Her hooves pounded the hard earth, eating up the stretch of it between herself and her rival. I could almost see her eyes narrowed in determination. Berlin females are tough – even the horses.

'That's my girl!' I shouted gleefully.

She snorted her reply. Her neck was stretched as far as it would go, her nose nearly level now with the other horse's tail. Dmitri glanced behind, startled to see how quickly we'd narrowed the gap. He urged his horse on. I urged mine on. Slowly but steadily we were gaining. To my left the blur of greenery was peeled away, in its place the sweating flanks of Dmitri's horse. Then Dmitri's thigh. Then his horse's shoulder, pumping away in a futile attempt to gain speed. Then the lathered neck and at last the head.

I gave a whoop of victory and reined my horse in. She was tired but still fresh enough to prance about a bit in a little victory dance. 'Well done, Gräfin!' I cried, patting her sweat-darkened neck. A blob of foam from the mouth of one of the horses had landed on my arm. I flicked it away and then wiped my hands on my jeans.

'Put on your jeans,' he'd said. 'We're off for a morning in the Grunewald.'

I'd packed them on his instructions for walking in the Harz Mountains. Instead we'd walked only a short way into the Grunewald forest before coming to a junction with a bridleway. There, framed picturesquely beneath an archway formed by overhanging pines, had been a stablegirl holding the reins of two horses.

'Herr Komarovsky?' she'd said. And handed over the horses.

An hour earlier I would have been furious. I'd seen riders in the Grunewald once or twice before but they'd been Rich People, creatures who inhabited a different world from the one I shared with my Kreutzberg friends. So distant this world had been that I'd never even queried where the stables were, who owned the horses, whether they were for hire. Even now I was pretty sure they weren't. These were big sleek hunters of the sort photographed during the St Hubert's Day meet in the Grunewald and I didn't think their owners would hand them over for Deutschmarks to just anyone. No doubt about it, Dmitri had connections, was as familiar with the city as I had been. Only the Berlin he knew was on a different planet than mine.

An hour ago, furious, but now? How could I begrudge the dreaming child in the burnt-out nightmare that had been Berlin 1945? It was impossible to be anything but happy, riding side by side with my lover through the glory of the autumn forest.

I looked back at him. He had dismounted to adjust a stirrup. 'Is that your excuse?' I said, still flushed with victory.

He smiled. 'Would I be so mean? You won fair and square. You're a tough lady, Anna Atwill, and if I had a hat I'd take it off to you.' He swung ponderously back into the saddle and rode up to me. Then he leaned over and kissed the tip of my nose. 'What prize do you claim?'

'This.' I leaned over further and kissed him full on the mouth. Two other lovers, entwined, came walking round a bend in the path ahead. Smiles of complicity as they passed us. We rode on.

The sun was trying to break through a thin haze. Every so often it succeeded for a moment and the forest leaped to life in a rich palette of green, gold, red. Beneath our horses' hooves a matching display of fallen leaves swished with every step, *basso ostinato* to the treble descant of a pair of warring robins.

'Is this where you learned to ride?'

He shook his head. 'In London, believe it or not. The Grunewald I knew was no fit place for riding. And even by the early 1950s we had no money for such luxuries.'

'Of course. I'd forgotten.'

The thick silvery trunks of the beech trees gleamed dully against the bright green of the pines. The oak trees, branching lower, spread a sculptural pattern of lines across the perpendicular painting.

'These would have been only saplings then,' he said. 'I probably wouldn't have noticed them. All I remember is coming into the forest with my mother and sister scrounging for fallen branches from what older trees remained – many of them had been felled for fuel after the war.' He looked round at the stately forest that enfolded us. 'It's hard to believe this is all so new – at least in the time measured by trees. Then again, not so new. It's also hard to believe so much time has passed since then.'

It hadn't. Past and present were with us together, the picture of the felled forest superimposed on the grandeur we were riding through, just as the sepia picture of his childhood had spread itself over the view of his former home. In between were my own memories of the forest. During the years I'd lived intermittently in the city, the ferocious love affair between Berliners and their trees had been understandable. The forests had been the only countryside they'd had in their walled island, their one escape valve, the place they fled to on weekends to feel human. There'd been good reason for Berlin being one of the greenest cities in the world. 'Do you remember anything of the blockade?' I asked.

'Not much. Mainly the constant noise. Planes were landing or taking off about every three minutes. It was the most beautiful sound in the world. It meant supplies were still coming in, we might survive, they hadn't abandoned us to the Soviets. Sometimes the planes were grounded by bad weather. You could feel the panic rising in the people then. It was almost tangible. There was a stink of fear in the air during the bad weather. Even I felt it, though I can't have known all that much about what was happening.'

The path widened and a moment later we were at the edge of a lake. A middle-aged couple were swimming. There were a few people like that in Sedleigh, too, people who gritted their teeth and plunged into the sea throughout the winter to prove something or other to themselves. Dmitri was watching them with obvious amusement. I could imagine what he was thinking. Several families with the inevitable Alsatian dogs were picnicking on the sandy banks. I'd never once seen any of the Grunewald lakes deserted, whatever the time of year, however late at night.

'Do you remember the raisin bombers?' I asked.

He smiled, partly at me but also, I suspected, at the memory of that young boy. 'You've seen those photographs of children waiting on hills or piles of rubble for the *Rosinenbomber* to come? I'm in one of them. It was taken over there, on the Teufelsberg.'

I looked in the direction he was pointing. The radar station, with its curious onion domes so like those of Russian Orthodox churches, floated above the trees. It was the highest hill in this flat city and even it wasn't 'natural'; it had been created after the war from millions of tons of rubble. I'd once gone tobogganing down it.

'I had my first taste of chocolate during the blockade,' he went on. 'That Christmas, and again at Easter. Not much, but still it was unimaginable luxury. Though we ate better during the blockade than at any time before. We still weren't getting whatever the minimum daily requirement is, but we didn't starve. There was even fresh bread for a while – really fresh, still warm from the ovens.'

'You're joking.'

'It was too bulky to fly loaves in and also too heavy – the water content. It was more efficient to fly in the flour and the coal and bake it fresh.'

The hardy couple rushed out of the water and into thick red towels. They looked awfully grim, as if they'd done their duty. Gräfin shook her head but it was only to dislodge a fly.

'At home?'

'No, that would have been a waste of electricity. It was only on for four hours a day and you never knew when you'd get one of your two-hour blocks. My mother used to have everything ready and then she or my aunt would cook a whole day's-worth of food for everyone in the flat. But not bread; that was done centrally.'

'Where was your father?'

'In the hospital, working. You know the old peasant trick of putting a hot meal in a box packed with cotton wool and then wrapping it in blankets? My mother's politics were pretty damned stupid but at least she turned herself into a decent housewife when she had to. My father appreciated those warm meals when he came home. Again we were lucky – we had enough blankets to spare for this luxury. We even had a Thermos. God only knows how my mother got hold of it.'

I looked closely into his face. 'You make it sound like a jolly Boy Scout outing.'

Dmitri shrugged. 'It was all I knew. I had no idea what normal life was like.'

We gazed out across the lake. Flashes of artificial colour turned themselves into a line of joggers. From this distance we couldn't hear their rasping breath or see their reddened faces.

'And then the blockade ended and for the first time in my life I encountered an orange,' said Dmitri. 'It seemed an extraordinary object, after all the dried food. I could hardly believe it was real.'

The joggers looked like multicoloured banners fluttering among the trees, set out for a woodland festival, a celebration.

Dmitri turned to me. His black eyes gleamed with the freshness of the cool October air and perhaps with pleasure, too. He looked so much at home on the big bay hunter it was hard to believe he hadn't been born to a life of casual wealth in which riding through the Grunewald was taken for granted.

'I wish it were possible to recapture the excitement of that first orange,' he said. 'We grow so complacent with the years, become so difficult to surprise and delight.' He smiled suddenly. 'You surprise and delight me, Anna. You brought into my life the same fresh amazement as that orange.'

I peered into his eyes with mock severity. 'This is hardly conventional love-talk, Herr Komarovsky. If you won't compare me to a summer day you might at least try a pomegranate.'

'Shall we settle for a *Bratwurst* instead? There's a nice little restaurant not far from here. Let's shake up the diners, gallop up to the door in a cloud of dust and tether our horses to a tree – like someone I know did not long ago. I trust you have your violin with you?'

'Alas, my tour guide forgot to list it in his requirements.'

'Then we will make do with the wind singing in our ears. Come!' He wheeled his horse round and together we raced through the confetti of falling leaves.

TWENTY-EIGHT

It was evening, the evening of a long day. The taxi dropped us at the edge of the Tiergarten and sped away in a halo of exhaust fumes. A few seconds into the park the smell disappeared, soaked up by the hard-working trees. I wondered how long they would last before dropping dead of the fumes. 'Do we have to take all these taxis?' I said irritably.

'As you wish,' said Dmitri. 'But you'll have to teach me. I'm never here long enough to learn the public transport.'

The mildness of his reply shamed me. After the exhilaration of our ride in the Grunewald the day had gradually become more fraught. Each time he talked about his own past he seemed imperceptibly to slide the conversation towards my own. We had nearly had a row when he'd taken me to a small Turkish restaurant in Kreutzberg for dinner. The restaurant had been fine, the food excellent, but did it have to be Kreutzberg?

'I'm sorry,' I said now. 'It's just that I never had a car here – hardly any of us did, what with being into Things Green.'

'Of course. I'm just a lazy old man in need of reform. You will reform me?' He crooked his arm invitingly.

I put my arm through his and we walked together in reconciled silence. Slowly my own silence refilled with scenes from the restaurant. Kreutzberg had changed a lot since the Wall had come down. When I had lived there it had been an anarchic brew of young radicals, artists, Turkish immigrants and genuine working-class

Berlin. Now, overcrowding and high rents were eroding the famous Kreutzberg tolerance. GIVE US BACK OUR WALL was displayed on one diner's teeshirt. TURKS OUT was sprayed on a building across the street. I'd used a spray can too, in the old days, but not for messages like that. That had been the extent of my own radical activities. I'd had to keep my nose clean for my work. I couldn't afford to be arrested, get a police record; it would have made my travels in eastern countries too difficult. In any case, I'd never lived here long enough to be involved in serious politics – I'd only camped out for a few weeks or months between jobs. Nor had I been interested in the heavy end of the 'scene' – drugs, sleazy bars, smuggling from the Friedrichstrasse duty-free. I hadn't even been keen on the pop music – too loud – and had tried to avoid the illegal concerts in East Berlin cemeteries.

Dmitri's voice snapped me back to the present. 'What do you remember of the Tiergarten from your time in Berlin?'

'Not a lot,' I said cautiously. 'An occasional day lolling about on the grass in the sunshine. Having an ice-cream. Walking through it the first time I came to Berlin, just to suss it out.'

'I remember a moonscape. Not a single tree was standing when I first saw it. It looked like the Somme.'

I looked at his face, softly illuminated by the streetlights along the path. Older than mine and with a touch of melancholy. I hadn't thought before about how big a difference the war had made. Like a thick black line drawn between one lifetime and another. We were two different races of people: those who remembered the war, those who didn't. The thick black line was between Dmitri's lifetime and mine.

'There were piles of rubble in the part of the Tiergarten where all the government offices and embassies had been,' he continued. 'My mother was one of the *Trummerfrauen*

– rubble women. She used to sort through the rubble and chip the old mortar off any bricks that were reuseable. The pay was low – piecework – but every little bit helped. Her reclaimed bricks must have gone into buildings all over Berlin. Perhaps even some of the flats you lived in.'

The Russian princess-turned-*Trummerfrau*, providing me first with housing and then with a lover.

'After the rubble was cleared there were allotments here,' he continued. 'The park was ruined anyway; allotments were the best thing to do with it at that time.'

On either side of the path the trees were rustling in the breeze, talking to each other in the way trees do. 'Did your family have one?'

'No, we had a garden. As soon as we could get hold of some seeds we planted it. Cabbages mainly.'

We were passing one of the little lakes. The long graceful fronds of the willows swept down into the water and tickled it into patterns at the edge. Further out, the moon floated serenely on a smooth silver surface. In the glare of the city I hadn't even noticed there was a moon. Here, with nothing but a few streetlights for competition, it reasserted its supremacy.

'I remember when the first new tree was planted in the Tiergarten,' Dmitri mused. 'A linden, in 1949. It was almost as if that was the moment the city was waiting for. A signal that life was indeed still possible here. From then everything was different.'

Some smooth dark stones at the edge of the path stirred at our approach and quacked. One of them stood up, stretched her wings and waddled a few steps away from us before settling down again. The streetlight showed a beady eye fixed on us in mild resentment. Then she tucked her beak into her back feathers and went back to sleep. The whole scene radiated peace. Moonscape. Rubble. Allotments. It was unimaginable. Yes, there was a line drawn between us. I was a post-war baby, spoiled rotten.

'You talk about your mother,' I said, 'but never your father.'

'I barely knew him then. He was always at the hospital working or at home sleeping. He worked very long hours. There was a shortage of doctors; they had to get the most out of the ones they had.'

A plane droned far above. Planes must sound different to him than to me. To me they carried neither bombs nor raisins. 'And later? After you moved to London?'

'He was working hard to build up a practice. When I did see him he seemed rather austere. It took me many years to see what lay beneath his manner. Not until after my mother died. She was the bigger-than-life character always filling the canvas. He was the ghostly figure at the edge.'

'Not a very happy marriage?'

'It's hard to say. I think they respected each other though they had little in common. He missed her when she died, but he started to come into his own. He was gentler than I'd thought. He didn't say much, but when he spoke he was worth listening to. He was a thinker, a brooder. He was very pleased when I became a historian.'

Three skinheads came noisily down the path towards us. Automatically I avoided their eyes but they left us alone. 'Did he talk to you about the war?'

'In general terms, yes. But nothing personal. It wasn't until he was dying that he began to talk about his own life. In fact, it was you who brought us together.'

'Me?' I exclaimed without thinking.

'When he told me your history. He could hardly do that without telling me his role in it.'

My nerves, lulled by the peace of the park, resumed their dance of apprehension. We stepped into the bright lights of a main road crossing the park. On the other side we quickened our step until we were swallowed up in the half-light of the path again. I must have had a vague idea where we were but I was too preoccupied to think about it.

Dmitri continued. 'It was a relief for him to talk about it. I wish he had done so sooner. For years I'd been prodding him as gently as I could but neither he nor my mother wanted to talk about their past. It was understandable.'

'Quite. They'd lived through some terrible times.'

'My mother in particular had good reason to keep quiet. She had a lot to hide.'

'Don't we all. Anyway, the present is more important.'

'It didn't do either of them any good, repressing the past,' he said.

It doesn't do you any good either, was what he meant.

'It doesn't do any good digging it up either,' I said.

'It did my father a great deal of good,' he said.

It would be good for you, too, he meant.

'I'm glad,' I said.

'It made me wish I'd pressed him more, earlier,' said Dmitri. 'And my mother, too.'

'It's no good brooding on these things, Dmitri. We all miss chances in life. Aren't we near the Wall?' I said suddenly. 'I seem to remember it's somewhere near here, somewhere over –'

'The Wall's gone. It's been gone a long time.'

'Yes, of course. How stupid of me. Habit, you know. Actually, I hardly ever saw the Wall except glimpses in Kreutzberg. It lost its fascination very quickly. We lived here, they lived there, and that was that. Oh hell, it's starting to rain.' The trees were thinning out, withdrawing their umbrellas. It had probably been drizzling for a while. Up ahead the sky was lighter with the artificial light of a main road. My coat had a hood. With my free arm, I pulled it up and peered out from it as from the entrance of a dark cave. 'Well, there's not much point in walking further,' I said. 'There must be an S-Bahn somewhere up there, there usually is, at the very least a bus, though I don't know this bit of the city very well, never had any reason to come here.' The light was growing stronger. 'I was usually too busy writing up notes from my last trip and thinking about how to organise the next. That and busking or whatever and the Ku'damm was the best place for that, what with the tourists being in a spending mood they might as well pop a few coins in my hat. Oh God.'

There it was, right in front of us. The Brandenburg Gate. The most beautiful and most terrible of all the images of this beautiful and terrible city. Napoleon had entered the city through it. Two Kaiser Wilhelms had made their exits and entrances through it. Torchlight processions of stormtroopers had marched through it. The East Germans had built a wall around it and tourists had ogled it and photographed it from the safe distance of the viewing platform. Television cameras had whirred themselves dizzy recording the East Berliners flooding through its arches and whirred again on New Year's Eve as acrobats pranced on it and fireworks flared above it and champagne corks flew.

The Wall was gone, the viewing platform was gone, the Vopos were gone. There were no television cameras or champagne corks and if there were tourists they merged with the little groups of Berliners to-ing and fro-ing beneath the arches as if this were just any old street.

I looked in the other direction, down the bright expanse of the Strasse des 17 Juni. 'There must be a bus stop somewhere, probably over –'

'Later, Anna. It's not raining much. You don't mind, do you?' He steered me gently towards the arches.

'Well, actually I do, rather. I know it sounds silly, but it gives me the creeps, all this open space and no nice little Vopo keeping us all in order.'

He laughed that big deep Russian laugh. Several people turned round and stared. 'Then I will keep you in order instead.' He pressed his arm closer to his side and with it my own. I was clamped.

'Dmitri, I'd really rather not, if you don't mind. Habit, you know. If we absolutely must go over there can we at least take the U-Bahn or something, you can't just *walk* across like –'

'Of course we can.'

'Well I know that, but it just doesn't feel right and anyway there's nothing to see over there, just a lot of boring old buildings and people and things. Why don't we go back to the hotel, that looked a nice little bar they had downstairs and I could do with a drink after all that spicy food.'

'We can get a drink on the other side,' he said cheerfully, and walked on, bearing me with him.

The place looked naked without the Wall and I felt naked walking towards where it should have been. 'Goodness, look over there, are they still selling pieces of the Wall? There can't be any of it left, it must be like Christ's cross, if you put together all the pieces you could build the Great Wall of China ten times over. I never hated the Wall as much as a lot of people did, I always had this sneaking suspicion that it was the Wall that stood between us and nuclear disaster, what with people on both sides having to have daily chit-chats about where to dump the rubbish. I mean as long as the Wall was there they *had* to talk and that had to be a good thing, right?'

My own talk stopped abruptly as we entered the archway. I waited for the stones to crash down on us or a thunderbolt to nip in and strike us dead. Even after all these years the sense of the Brandenburg Gate as the ultimate no-man's-land was deeply ingrained.

As we emerged on the other side I looked balefully at its transformation, at all the street vendors selling *Bockwurst, Currywurst*, plastic souvenirs, military oddments and yet more chunks of the inexhaustible Wall. There were even models of the wreath to the 'unknown refugee'. The original had been a moving site in its unobtrusive position near the Wall, memorial to all those who'd died trying to escape. Here it was tat. The whole of Pariser Platz was tat, a cheap fairground where once there had been a raw statement of the clash of two ideologies.

'What a bunch of sleaze,' I said. 'You see? There really isn't anything to see here. Let's go back, it's raining harder and I'm cold, there must be a bus and if there isn't I'll even let you demote me to a taxi.'

'Then you need a nice hot drink to warm you up,' he said.

We had been wending our way slowly among the nasty little stalls. Now he set off at a brisk pace, making a straight line towards Unter den Linden, straight towards the heart of East Berlin.

'Oh, look, there's a stall here selling drinks,' I tried. 'There's no need to go all the way into town.'

'It's raining. We will find somewhere warm, out of the rain.'

'Who cares about a little rain? I really could fancy some of that –'

My words were drowned out by an amplified guitar and voice wailing one of those dismal songs about the Wall. Beside the culprit was a stack of cassettes. We strode past him, no sale, straight as a bee towards Unter den Linden. People were stepping aside to make way for us. Berliners are a stroppy lot, they don't make way for people. Dmitri's face was giving out signals that brooked no argument. Like a military motorcycle with me playing the role of sidecar, we ploughed through the throng and on to the avenue.

Behind us the sound of the fair slowly subsided, beside us rose the stately buildings of the old east European embassies, their stern façades softened by rows of lindens. 'You see? There's nowhere at all to have a drink, this is the really boring end of town, nobody comes here.'

That wasn't entirely true. Despite the rain, people were strolling beneath the trees just as they had in the bad old days when tourists on a day visa made a quick foray from the Friedrichstrasse station to sample the east. East Berliners had resented them and shown their surliest side. I'd once been nearly knocked over – accidentally, of course – by a woman on an otherwise deserted pavement. I couldn't really blame her.

'Then we will just have to carry on until we find somewhere more promising,' said my guide, unruffled. And at the next intersection, he turned left.

Friedrichstrasse. Just down the street was the most notorious station in the east.

'Look, I hate to be a wet blanket but I really do dislike being here,' I said. 'Always did. It's the one part of the eastern bloc that always gave me the creeps.'

His face conceded only a small scrap of sympathy. 'I can understand how strange it must feel. But it's really not worth making a fuss about. Nobody else does.' He indicated the people walking towards the station, away from the station.

'Sure. They live here, or most of them do. We don't. We're tourists for a few days, that's all. Why do we have to waste our time here?'

'Humour me, Anna. Just this once.' He put his arm across my shoulders and propelled me forward. The station was looming, was there. Meekly I followed him into it.

No trace remained of the cavernous border wasteland designed to scare the hell out of transients like me. It looked just like any other station now. I brightened. And it *was* a station, a major junction for both U-Bahn and S-Bahn. There must be heaps of trains back to the west. There were crowds of people milling about. I scanned the walls above their heads, looking for a schedule. Finally I found one. I tried to steer Dmitri towards it. He steered me in the opposite direction.

A minute later we were on a train. There'd been no time to get my bearings. I had no idea where it was heading.

Dmitri had made his way to the platform as confidently as if it were the London tube.

'I thought you said you didn't know the public transport.'

'Only a few obvious routes,' he conceded.

'This is obvious?'

The train clattered along, the steady beat of wheels on track making conversation difficult. Few people were trying. People hadn't talked much in the old days either, or looked at their fellow passengers. Averting one's eyes was ingrained. I had to hope Dmitri did know where we were going and that where we were going was west. I barely knew the east of the city, had only gone across a few times when pressed by friends. I'd always resisted. I came to Berlin for relief from the difficulties of my east European assignments. The last thing I wanted was more complications, more tensions, and it was impossible not to feel tense here.

We stopped – and my heart sank. We were at Alexanderplatz. We got out and almost immediately got into another train. Again I hadn't seen its destination, but it no longer mattered. I was well and truly in unknown territory now. I sighed, resigning myself to Dmitri's care.

It was a long journey, way out into the eastern suburbs. The train was emptying bit by bit at each stop, leaving exposed the wooden seats polished by decades of bottoms. Few people were getting on. By the time we got off it was nearly deserted.

So was the station.

The wind hit us as soon as we stepped outside. It had risen considerably while we'd been cocooned in the train. In it was enough rain to make me raise my hood again. There was no point asking where we were. 'Are we going far?' I asked instead.

'Not very. I'm sorry about the rain.'

Not sorry enough to call off this expedition. 'I hope you know when there's a train back,' I said. 'I'd hate to be stranded here all night.'

He nodded. 'There's plenty of time.'

'To do what? Dmitri, I'd really appreciate it if you'd drop this Man of Mystery thing. It's not funny. We've had a long day. I'm tired and thirsty and I really don't want to be here, wherever "here" is.'

'There's something I want you to see.'

What was the point of arguing? I was in his hands now. An image of Sedleigh – the view from my patio – flashed through my mind and with it a pang of longing. So far away.

Just beyond the station entrance we turned into a street. The wind was more or less behind us now. The street was fairly narrow. On either side were neat little houses, each in its own little garden. I didn't know the sociology of the east, couldn't tell if this was a desirable neighbourhood or not. The concrete was rough and there were one or two potholes. Perhaps not so desirable. There was also no pavement, though there were a few streetlights. There were lights on in most of the houses too, and here and there the blueish flicker of a black-and-white television. Clearly not a neighbourhood with a lot of money. At one house closer to the street than the others, a dog rushed to the window and barked at our tapping feet. Its owner pulled it away roughly. His face looked as sullen as I felt.

Not a lot of cafés, or bars. In fact, approximately none.

The houses petered away into rough land with a scattering of wooden sheds. The street was rougher too and the streetlights were sparser. Near the last one was a rusty metal fence with a gate in it. Dmitri stopped and opened the gate. Inside I glimpsed the crooked white teeth of tombstones.

'A cemetery? What kind of a joke is this?'

Dmitri's face was illuminated by the streetlight. He wasn't laughing but neither did he look unduly solemn. His face looked... ordinary. That in itself was odd. This was hardly an ordinary place for us to be. It crossed my mind that he had composed his features deliberately in an effort to reassure me.

'You're not superstitious?' he said.

'Not at all.' I thought of all the conversations I'd had with Edmund and Eleanor after they died. Ghosts didn't worry me. My ghosts were friendly.

'Come inside,' he said. 'I want to show you something.'

I went inside. Dmitri closed the gate behind us. There was nothing ominous about that; not only in the east but everywhere in Germany you closed gates behind you. It just wasn't worth risking the ire of some pedantic official.

'Over here,' he said, taking my hand.

We walked a little way into the cemetery. It wasn't very well tended. The grass was long, soaking my legs after a few steps. Some of the tombstones were askew. I couldn't see the inscriptions but guessed that there had been no new burials for some years. There were no flowers on any of the graves. The silence was oppressive.

'Surely not a rock concert?' I said to break it. In the past there'd been concerts in those churchyards that had sympathetic clergy. Churchyards were off-limits to the police.

'You've been to them?' Dmitri asked, his tone more casually conversational than my weak joke warranted.

'Once. A friend wanted to go and didn't have anyone else to go with. I didn't enjoy it.'

'Not your kind of event.'

'Neither is this.'

'We're nearly there. Bear with me.'

'I haven't got much choice.'

With his free hand he reached into a pocket, drew out a small torch and switched it on. I was glad. Despite my lack of superstition the place was beginning to spook me. The wind and the rain didn't help.

Dmitri flashed the torch briefly on to the nearest stones. I didn't try to read them. This was his trip, not mine. I looked instead up into the sky, narrowing my eyes against the rain. The wind was throwing big fat blobs of cloud over the moon. The moon kept peering out for a few seconds only to be engulfed again. The flickering light was irritating, like a child playing with a switch.

I looked back to earth. Dmitri's torch had come to rest on a small tombstone nearly lost in the grass. He released my hand and bent down to pull the grass away. When he took my hand again his own was wet. He shone the torch full on the stone but he wasn't reading the inscription. He was looking at me.

'This is the one,' he said. 'Will you read it?'

His voice was now unmistakably nervous, and his face too. Reluctantly I looked at the tombstone and read:

KOLOMPÁR CSABA

'Does the name suggest anything to you?' asked my guide.

This was surreal. Had he really dragged me right across Berlin to play guessing games with a tombstone? 'I'm not an etymologist.'

'But you have some familiarity with east European names. Surely this one tells you something.'

'Only the obvious: he was Hungarian. Is this a Hungarian cemetery?'

'No.'

'Then what's he doing here?' I looked at Dmitri. 'More to the point, what are we doing here?'

'Please, Anna. This is important. I want you to tell me everything that this name suggests to you.'

It must be important. I'd never seen Dmitri so serious – or so nervous. Whatever he was doing, this was no time for flippancy or childish displays of pique. I turned back to the tombstone and summoned up my long-disused store of knowledge.

'Well, for a start he was a gypsy. Is that what you wanted to know? Most Hungarian names are interchangeable. Kolompár is one of the few which only gypsies have. Kolompár was his surname,' I added foolishly. 'I suppose you know that – Hungarians always put the surname first.'

Dmitri nodded. 'Anything else? What about his other name?'

I felt like a child in a schoolroom being drawn out by a patient teacher. 'Well, now that you mention it, that is odd. Csaba is a very patriotic name. You wouldn't expect a pair of gypsies to give their kid such a nationalistic name. I could be wrong, of course. I don't know a lot about Hungarian gypsies – I never worked with them. Gypsies are a closed community. I didn't have the right kind of contacts to get access. Did you know this man?'

'No. That's why I want you to help me. I'd like you to try and build up a picture of this person.'

I looked at my lover. 'What a strange person you are,' I said softly. Then I turned back to the task in hand. 'Well, for a start we need to know his dates.' I leaned down and pushed aside the rest of the grass. The numbers told a poignant story. 'He died young – in his twenties.' I stood up again, slightly uneasy. He had died in the year of my birth. But then, so had a lot of people; it was the year of the workers' uprising.

'What do we have so far?' said Dmitri.

I thought about the bare data on the stone. Then I tried to conjure up a picture. 'Well, we have gypsy parents who felt unusually patriotic towards their country. Probably they thought of themselves as more Hungarian than gypsy. And presumably they were ambitious for their son, expected him to leave the narrow world of the gypsy community and make something of himself outside. And very likely he did just that – or started to. Otherwise he wouldn't have died so far from home.'

'Can you make a guess as to what he was doing in Germany?'

'You're expecting a lot from just two words,' I smiled. 'Fortune tellers usually have a crystal ball or some lines on a hand.'

'Try.'

'Well, there's really only one route to success for a gypsy and that's music. Usually they go to Budapest and get a job in some gypsy orchestra in a restaurant. This one went further, all the way to Berlin. I don't suppose there were a lot of Hungarian restaurants in Berlin, so perhaps he was trained in classical music and somehow made his way up to an orchestra in Berlin.' The unease was growing. Resolutely I pushed it away. I didn't want to think about this dead man any more. 'But we're getting into fantasy land now – this is all wild speculation. I'm sorry, but I really can't tell you any more.'

Dmitri relented. 'All right. Just one more thing: is this a person you would have liked to meet?'

'What an odd question. Yes, I suppose so. He would have been a bit unusual, another person who didn't fit into an obvious mode of life, perhaps a bit of a wanderer like me.'

'You would have compared notes?'

'I suppose so. Dmitri –'

'What instrument do you suppose he played?'

'There are a lot of instruments in an orchestra. Dmitri –'

'But a gypsy?'

'Well, all right: a violin. Almost certainly a violin. Dmitri, I'm cold, I'd really like to leave now.'

'Soon. Anna, you must have some idea where all this is leading. I've tried to find a way of telling you as gently as I could –'

'Dmitri, please –'

'Csaba Kolompár was your father.'

'NO!'

The word shot into the air, smashing the peace of the cemetery. The wind blew it back into my face along with a fistful of rain. I turned and began running but the rain blurred my vision and I stumbled over a tussock of grass. Dmitri caught me before I fell. His hand gripped my arm like a vice. 'Don't deny your father, Anna.' His voice was hard, too. If I'd hoped for a little comfort I was wrong. The big bearlike man who had so often wrapped me in the protection of his arms was gone. In his place was a cold, hard adversary.

And suddenly I was glad. There was no need any more for careful negotiation across the minefield on which our relationship was built. It was out in the open now, a fight for survival. I jerked my arm but he held it fast.

'Anna, at least do him the honour of acknowledging him!'

With my free hand I slapped his face, hard. 'Don't you tell me what I should do or what I should feel,' I spat. 'What business is it of yours? I was perfectly happy with my life till you came along and wrecked it. Let me go!'

He grabbed my other arm. His voice was as cold and hard as mine. 'What business is it of mine? How can you be so stupid? My father told me what he knew. Now I'm the only person in the world who knows your story, and it's a story you need to know, whether you like it or not. The weight of this thing is crushing me, Anna. Every time I cross a road I wonder if this is the bus that's going to extinguish it. Look at me, Anna. I'm over fifty. I could die any time now and your history would die with me. How much longer do you expect me to bear this responsibility just so you can pretend you came into the world by immaculate conception? You were *born*, Anna. You had other parents and if they couldn't live to see you grow up at least you could listen to –'

'All right! Put it in a letter!'

'For you to burn? Anna, I'm human, too! I have needs, too! Do you really care so little for me that you won't let me share this burden with you?'

I closed my eyes in pain but not because of the pressure of his hands. I'd tried so hard to turn against him and harden myself against him, but it hadn't worked. I did love him. I cared about him all too much. Already my jaw was trembling in the infant's wail that was coming.

And then his arms were around me and he was whispering words of comfort, nonsense words that meant everything to the child I'd become. 'It's all right, Anna, cry as much as you like, it's only natural, that's right, Anna, the worst is over now, take your time, it's all right, it's going to be all right,' rocking me gently in his arms all the while. It was warm and dark in his arms. His coat was rough against my cheek. It smelled faintly of petrol fumes, aftershave, Dmitri. Warm and dark and safe. Words of comfort lulling my fears, his lips against the hood of my coat. 'It's all right, there's nothing to be afraid of.' Slowly my whimpering subsided and stopped. I wanted to stand there for ever but I knew I had to leave the safe refuge of his arms and give something to him in return.

At last I pulled away from him and looked into his face. My own was wet with tears and rain and I felt weak but I was ready. I nodded.

'Would you rather go somewhere out of the rain?' he asked.

'No. Here.'

He led me to a flat tombstone and we sat down. From here I couldn't see the writing on my father's stone or the telltale dates. My father. There, it was out. The acceptance had begun. 'The picture I painted of him.' My voice was still rusty from tears. I cleared my throat. 'Was he – is that how it was?'

'Yes. He was very talented. Probably nothing would have come of his talents if the communists hadn't given opportunities to people like him – people who hadn't had a chance in the past. He went to music school and then straight into an orchestra. Then, during a tour, he defected. The orchestra had been playing in East Berlin. He simply left one morning and crossed into West Berlin. It wasn't too difficult at that time. There was no Wall.'

The rain was easing a little, the intervals of moonlight were becoming longer. The light picked out the tombstones but not the lettering.

'From there he went into the Berlin Philharmonic. That was easy, too. There was a shortage of good musicians after the war, and your father was good.'

My father was good. A picture began to form. Bending his head towards his violin, a half-smile on his face . . .

Dmitri continued. 'In those days the different sectors used to put on social events for their counterparts on the other side. One of those occasions was a concert in which your father played. He met your mother at a reception afterwards. It was probably a pretty modest reception by today's standards but I doubt if your parents noticed. Love at first sight.'

He would have been a fairly small man. Gypsies usually were. Small and dark with bright black eyes and beautiful smiles usually reserved for their own kind. A handsome man, exotic. And my – It was hard to say the word, even to myself. 'And my . . . mother?'

'Your mother was the daughter of an East German official – that was how she came to be at the event.'

I shifted uneasily. 'What sort of official?'

Dmitri hesitated. And in that moment I knew why I'd been resisting this knowledge for so long. 'My father didn't know his title or his name. But from what happened later, he deduced that your . . . grandfather . . . was quite high up in the party.'

'I see.' I pulled my coat closer around me. 'I don't suppose he was pleased for his daughter to fall in love with a gypsy?'

'These prejudices didn't die with the war,' said Dmitri softly. 'Especially in Germany.'

Slavs, Jews ... and gypsies. All those people it was easier to label 'alien' than risk acknowledging their humanness. People who threatened the brave new Germany of the 1930s and after. 'This story you're telling me,' I said. 'It has an unhappy ending.'

'I can't change history, Anna. I wish neither of us knew this story, but I can't change that either.'

'Then get it over with. Please.'

'There's not much more to tell. Your parents kept their relationship a secret for some time. Then your mother became pregnant. There was no question of an abortion. She loved your father and wanted to marry him. Then her father found out.' He hesitated. 'Whatever his position, he had police forces at his command. He instructed a small group to go over to West Berlin and seek out the man who had "violated" his daughter. Anna, I would like to spare you this but I can't. They found him, and they broke his fingers. He never played the violin again.'

I doubled over as if I'd been hit in the stomach. Spasms of dry futile retching came over me in waves and the taste of bile was in my mouth. Dmitri was silent beside me. He made no effort to comfort me and I was glad. There had been no comfort for my father either. My hands were bunched up against my stomach, the fingers curled tightly in self-defence. Not the pain, I thought, thinking through my father's mind; the pain could be borne but not the empty life that lay ahead. 'Why didn't they just kill him and get it over with?' I whispered through clenched teeth.

'You know why. That would have been too humane. Your grandfather wasn't a humane man.'

My temples were throbbing and I felt the hot blood coursing through my body, blood poisoned by the monster whose genes were my own. I wanted to drain it out of me, every evil drop. I wanted to be dead.

The disembodied voice above me was carefully controlled as Dmitri finished his narration. 'He was no more humane to his own daughter. He sent her to a maternity home and forced her to have the baby. Your father found out where she was and came over to the east. Nobody knows what his intentions were, but a few days after you were born the workers' uprising erupted and the city was in chaos. Russian tanks and troops were called in to quell it. The official story is that your father was caught up in the fighting and killed along with all the other people who were killed in the uprising. The truth is that your grandfather had had him followed right from the border by the same men who'd broken his fingers. Their instructions were to kill him as near the maternity home as possible, which they did.'

The wind was moaning through the cemetery. Dmitri had to raise his voice to be heard above it.

'Your mother's best friend saw what happened as she was coming to see your mother and broke the news to her. Something snapped. Perhaps it had snapped a long time ago, when she learned that your grandfather intended to have you adopted by a staunch communist couple and observe whether careful control could erase the gypsy taint.'

The moaning stopped and I realised it had been me. Taint.

'In any case,' Dmitri continued, 'he never had the chance. Your mother begged her friend to take you to the west. How the girl got you out of the maternity home unnoticed is something we'll probably never know, but the city was in upheaval, there was heavy fighting in the area. Perhaps in the confusion it wasn't too difficult to slip away.'

I was barely listening. One word only was repeating itself over and over in my brain. Taint. I stood up abruptly and went to my father's grave. Dmitri didn't try to stop me. He must have known I was far past running away from the truth. I crouched down and read the inscription. The moonlight was now clear and strong, picking out the letters. Taint. I said my father's name aloud. 'Kolompár Csaba.' It sounded strange. I said it again. 'Kolompár Csaba.' The emphasis on the first syllable, always in Hungarian. A little of the strangeness faded. A third time I said his name. 'Kolompár Csaba.' Rolling the r in the strong proud way that Hungarians did. Then, 'Kolompár ... Anna.' The cemetery was utterly silent. Perhaps the wind had dropped or perhaps I had entered a different world, my father and I speaking quietly to each other in the silence of the dead. Tears pricked behind my eyes but not for myself. They were for the young couple who had conceived me and borne me at a time and in a place where a love like theirs could only end in tragedy.

Footsteps swishing through the long grass. Dmitri beside me. 'And my mother?' I said at last.

'Nobody knows. I hoped to find out more before we came to Berlin, but there wasn't time. She seems to have disappeared soon after you were born.'

The pieces were falling into place. 'All those times you left Sedleigh. You weren't in London. You were in Berlin.'

'Only last week. Before that I used archival contacts. I wanted to give you the whole story. Your mother's friend mentioned no names – of course. My father only learned who your father was from a small obituary in a West Berlin newspaper. He put together the information in that with the information he'd been given. It fit perfectly. There's no doubt that Csaba Kolompár was your father but it's difficult to find out anything about your mother. It's possible, of course, that she's still alive – she would only be in her sixties.'

He said the words so casually that he couldn't have anticipated the impact. Up until then he'd spoken like a historian of a past long dead. Now, in a terrible rush, past and present fused. 'And my "grandfather"?' I said with contempt.

Dmitri seemed taken by surprise. 'It's virtually impossible that he could still be alive.'

'That's not what I meant. He would be alive in her mind, and now he's alive in mine.' A spark of the anger that must have flamed up in my mother – strong enough to steel her against the pain of giving away her baby – rose in me. 'Taint,' I said. I looked into Dmitri's eyes. 'No communist would use that word.'

He looked down at the tall grass so quickly that I knew he understood. 'There were a lot of them in both governments, Anna. People concealing their past. I can't rewrite history for you,' he said softly. 'It's because of him that I hesitated about telling you. All I can say is that my mother was no better. We're all of us "tainted", Anna, though not in the sense that these people meant. We're tainted by history.'

'Evil.'

'Yes,' he said simply, and now he looked up and into my eyes. 'I won't try to deny it or excuse it. Your grandfather was an evil man. But some good came out of that evil despite him. Your mother was her father's daughter, she had the same blood. And yet she had the courage to defy him by taking you out of his control. Who knows what the consequences were for her when he discovered what she'd done? Her friend had courage, too, taking you across the border. And didn't my father show some courage? He could have refused to take you. He could have sent that girl back with you and saved himself and our whole family a great deal of anguish. Your other parents, Edmund and Eleanor – they could have refused to accept you, too.'

He took my hands in his – my hands that hadn't been smashed. 'And didn't some good come of that?' he said. 'And when because of all that had happened before, I walked into your library more than forty years later and fell in love with you just as your father must have fallen in love with your mother? I like to think that some good has come of that. Or, if not good, at least some happiness. Or do you want to deny that, too?'

'You know I don't.'

'Then please don't deny what lies behind it. You and I are children of violence, Anna, and not just us but the whole of this continent. The good and evil are too strong and too mixed together to make for a comfortable life here. I think that's the real reason you never came back. It was easier to push the muddle into a place called the Past and live out the rest of your life in a peaceful seaside town. I don't blame you. I tried to do the same thing in London. Probably we both would have succeeded if my father hadn't sent me on that unwanted mission. But over the last few months I've come to accept that a quiet life isn't possible for me. Or for you. You and I are as bound up with this messy continent as we are with each other. Can't you see that now?'

I looked round the quiet cemetery. The rain had stopped altogether and the wind had dropped to a breeze. It ruffled the leaves of the trees scattered among the tombstones. I hadn't even noticed the trees before. They didn't look planned. Probably they were self-sown seedlings which nobody had bothered to tear out. There were no trees near my father's grave. I looked down at the stone again. It answered Dmitri's question for me. 'Yes,' I said.

He pushed back the hood of my coat. The breeze felt good riffling through my hair. Had my mother's hair been red and wild? Then he put his hands on either side of my head. 'And do you see why I had to play the villain and trick you into coming here?'

I smiled. 'Yes, I see that, too.'

He ran his fingers across my face and stroked the high gypsy cheekbones which nobody had questioned in over forty years. 'And do you forgive me for all the lies and deceptions?'

'No,' I said. 'Because there's nothing to forgive.'

And suddenly, just when they were least called for, the tears were there, hot and sweet and warm with relief, spilling down my cheeks and on to Dmitri's hands until he took his hands away and gathered me into his arms.

'It's all over, Anna,' he said into my hair. 'There's nothing to be afraid of any more.'

TWENTY-NINE

Morning sunshine flooded over us as we stepped off the bus at Potsdamer Platz. Dmitri had been dubious but had given in gracefully. 'You asked me to teach you the public transport,' I'd reminded him. 'That includes the humble bus.'

The bus looked bright and shiny as it disgorged the last of its passengers and lumbered away. Even the grey concrete expanse of the square seemed inviting this morning.

'The Wall used to be just over there,' I said. 'Remember? That's where I wrote my bit of graffiti. I thought about it for ages – the graffiti was all so clever, I had to come up with something really good. I felt as nervous as if I were writing a book. Worse – more people would read it. Funny to think some total stranger's bought that bit of the Wall.'

'No more Wall, Anna,' he said firmly.

He put his arm round my shoulders and together we strode across the concrete. Sweet sixteen and freshly in love, or so it felt, despite the grey hair I'd found among the red this morning. 'Don't you dare pull it out,' my lover had said. 'Leave it to attract a few friends. You'll look good with a sprinkling of grey.'

'You know the old cliché, "Today is the first day of your new life"?' I said now. 'It feels like that.'

He fixed on me a stern look. 'My wild gypsy girl spouting clichés? If this is what love does to you I shall fall straight out of it again.'

'You do that and I'll climb down and fetch you back,' I said with matching sternness. 'You're not getting away from me that easily, Dmitri Mikhailovich.'

'My dear Anna, don't you think the time has come to move on to more intimate terms? You may call me Mitya.'

I tried out the new word to see how it fit in my mouth. 'Mitya. Mitya. Yes, I like it. It makes you less august. The distinguished historian becomes a small boy. Yes. Whenever you're too pompous and overbearing I shall fetch you back with a diminutive.'

'Hostage to fortune,' he sighed, and kissed me, right there on Potsdamer Platz.

An elderly woman on her way to the concert stared, as well she might. Our appearance was far too respectable for such displays: Dmitri in a suit, me in a neat blue dress and coat with my unruly hair swept up and tamed by pins. The kind of people who manage to get tickets for the coveted Sunday morning concerts at the Phil.

And there it was, the Philharmonie, the real symbol of Berlin for me, a monument far more lovable than the Brandenburg Gate, the golden curves of its roof sweeping up to meet a clear blue sky. Bold and beautiful, shunning ornamentation, built single-mindedly for one purpose alone: to capture the most elusive of all the elements – air – and give it back to us as music. No politician had fouled its spaces with his rantings, no troops had used it for displays of power. The only violence it knew was the passion of musical creation – and the fight to be among the subscribers.

'How *did* you get tickets?' I asked suddenly.

'My nefarious contacts again. Allow me to retain a few shreds of mystery.'

We entered the foyer. It was a huge space, high and light and airy, with great lozenges of coloured light thrown across its sleek surfaces by the long windows. The open stairs and walkways teemed with people who in their constant motion turned the space into a mobile. All the surfaces were in pale neutral shades, waiting for the people and the sunshine through the windows to give it colour and life. It was like being inside a modern sculpture and we were the artists creating it. The building hadn't changed a bit in all the years since I'd been here. It was as wonderful as ever.

'Do you have any idea how beautiful you are when you're happy, Anna?' asked my lover.

'Are you teaching a course on gallantry this autumn, Dmitri?' asked his consort.

'Still keeping your nose clean, Attila?' asked a voice in German behind me.

I wheeled round and stared at the soft middle-aged face and neatly waved light brown hair of a standard bourgeois Berliner. The smirk was a little less standard. And slightly familiar. And hadn't the hair once been blonde . . . and cut in a bob so easy to duplicate with a wig . . .?

'Leni!'

'None other. And don't look so surprised: it took me ages to recognise you, too. What the hell are you up to in that posh disguise?'

'And who let you out of the pit?'

'Old age. It gets us all. Motherhood, you know. Kids' guts and cat gut don't mix. Hey, how long are you back for this time? And who's this gorgeous man you've got in tow, or don't I rate an introduction?'

'Oh hell. Sorry. Dmitri Komarovsky, Leni Fichtner –'

'Schuster, Frau.' She made a face and then grinned engagingly at Dmitri.

He took her hand and made a slight bow. 'Of course: the lady who tricked Karajan.'

Leni shrieked with laughter. 'She's told you that? She's the one who tricked him – I did a flit to Hamburg. Or was it Frankfurt? Oh well. You know the story's still doing the rounds?' she said to me. 'Some of the versions are pretty wild. Hey, you: I've got a bone to pick. You never answered my last letter. Or was it a postcard? So where the hell have you been all these years?'

'Sedleigh.'

'I'm supposed to know where that is?'

'If you sent a postcard to it.'

'Oh yes – by the sea.' She stared. 'You're *still* there?'

'It's a very nice town.'

'What about your work?'

'I'm a librarian now.'

'A what?' Then she laughed. 'Oh well, if I can wipe up kid spew I guess you can stamp books. Sad, though, isn't it? Remember when we used to get drunk in Kreutzberg and swear we'd never turn out like this? Look, how long are you in town for? Give me your number and I'll see if I can scrape together some of the old crowd for a party. You're invited too, if you can stand it,' she said to Dmitri.

'I'd be delighted.'

'Great! Gotta go now and rescue my own man – I left him in the clutches of Dietmar Schultz. Remember Dietmar? Or was that after your time? See you in the interval? Bye!'

She sped away into the crowd.

'My past is catching up with a vengeance,' I said. 'Would you go to this party?'

'If you'll come to mine in London. I think it's time for our two worlds to meet, don't you?'

Yes. It was time for a coming together of a great many things that had been separated far too long. Something strange had happened in the cemetery the night before. When Edmund had told me of my adoption I'd thought only of how generous he and Eleanor had been to this unexpected child. I'd never given a thought to the generosity of those shadowy figures who had preceded them. I'd been afraid to know, and with good reason. But now I realised that ever since Edmund's revelation there'd been a hole in my life containing the mystery I was so determined to ignore. No one had seen it, not even myself, until Dmitri had come along. What uncanny intuition he had used was a new mystery but one I could live with. I could live with anything now, now that I was whole again. Who could have guessed, a mere five months ago, that the exotic stranger who entered my library and my life would be a healer as well as a lover? I had been happy with Dmitri before, but never so much as last night. And this morning, waking up to greet the new person I was.

I smiled at my magician. 'It's also time for us to find our seats.'

We made our way into the auditorium. A pre-concert was already in progress: the buzzing of 2,000 voices, feet tapping and shuffling along the aisles, the rustle of clothes and of programmes. The auditorium was as revolutionary in layout as the external architecture: music-in-the-round, with the audience seated in terraces rising from the central space occupied by the orchestra. Just as in a theatre, it gave a sense of intimacy and involvement special to Berlin. It was this that had made me long to try it out from a musician's point of view that crazy night when Leni and I had hatched our plot.

The big central space was coming to life, musicians strolling in with their instruments and joking with each other, exchanging gossip.

Our seats were good ones: right at the front of the lowest terrace overlooking one side of the string section. I peered down directly on to the bald pate of a double bass player, then leaned over further to squint at the score on his stand. He turned his head and gave me a quizzical look. I feigned embarrassment as he held up the score for me to see better. Then he gestured me to come and take his place.

'Sorry – I'm only a violinist,' I mouthed, and mimed a few notes on an invisible fiddle.

He drew his face into a portrait of mock disdain and, dismissing my inferior status, went back to tuning his instrument.

'Do you think he remembers you?' Dmitri said.

I shook my head, still smiling at the mute exchange. 'I was disguised as Leni. But he may well have been there that day.'

The trickle of musicians taking their place was increasing. I'd always loved watching them come in. They were a tough lot, the Berlin Phil, the first orchestra in the world to organise themselves and elect their own conductors. They knew they didn't need the musician whose only instrument was a baton; they merely tolerated him for appearances. Any guest conductor rash enough to tell them how to play was annihilated.

I glanced at the programme. There was a guest conductor.

I studied the faces of the players but it was too early to tell; not until the conductor arrived would I be able to read whether this was a man they would tolerate or not. My eye travelled round the untidy arrangement of chairs and stands and stopped at the last desk of the second violins. I had once sat there. It had been the pinnacle of my erratic musical career, scraping away at my fiddle in the anonymity of the blonde wig and the obscurity of the back desk. I had been young and rash, on the edges of radical Berlin. Now I was middle-aged, respectable and in the audience. Did I feel a twinge of regret for that impetuous ghost of myself? No. Last night had changed that, too. Some mysterious rite of passage in the cemetery had brought me at last to a maturity reconciled with the past.

I was leaning back in my seat, idly watching the sandy-haired young man occupying the place where Leni and I had both sat. He bent down to pick up something he'd dropped on the floor. When he sat up again he was smaller, dark-haired and dark of face, bright black eyes eagerly looking round at his colleagues. Somewhere in the audience was a red-haired German girl ... A moment later he vanished, his place resumed by the sandy-haired fiddler.

My father had sat at that desk.

A moment later that thought vanished, too. The building I loved so much hadn't existed then. My father had probably been too talented to sit at the back desk. None the less, something of the vision persisted. There was a connection, some nagging memory ...

Karajan.

I sat up abruptly, the movement shaking the programme from my lap. Dmitri leaned down to retrieve it. He raised an eyebrow.

'Dmitri, who was it after the war – conducting here?'

He frowned in concentration. 'I'm not sure. I'm not even sure there was a regular conductor. Furtwängler's past was being investigated by the allies – he'd had some connections with the old regime. I think Karajan might have taken his place some of the time, though I'm not sure when they elected him their principal conductor.' He smiled. 'That's your department, not mine.'

'Dmitri, just think – my father and I – we played for Karajan, both of us – I'm sure of it – just think – and with the same violin!' I was so excited I could hardly speak. 'Oh, if only my father could know! Do you think he would be pleased? Do you think it would be some small consolation for the terrible things that happened to him?'

'Who knows? Why don't you tell him? After all, you still talk to your other parents.'

'I know it sounds childish, but I'd like to go to the cemetery again and try. Just in case.'

'Why not? Tomorrow morning?'

I opened my programme and tried to make the letters change. I wanted them to spell out Beethoven's Fifth to complete the strange comings-together of this morning. Karajan, my father and I, our violin – even Leni was a connection and there she was, somewhere in the sea of faces waiting for the conductor.

Sibelius: Finlandia, said the programme.
Bartók: Konzert für Klavier und Orchester Nr. 2.
Sibelius: Sinfonie Nr. 2 in D-Dur, op. 43.

Oh well, nothing's perfect. It didn't matter anyway. Tomorrow we would go to my father's grave. This time I had nothing to fear. I would pull aside the grass and read again the brief poignant statement of his life. I would speak to him. It would be a little awkward at first – after all, I didn't know him like I knew my other parents. I would have to be very careful, no trace of sentimentality. His life had been hard and short with a brutal end. 'Kolompár Csaba,' I would say, 'my name is Anna Atwill. You never knew me, but if things had been different, I would have been called Kolompár Anna. I would have been proud to carry that name. I hope you would have been proud of the daughter I became. Do you remember your violin? They destroyed your hands and for a long time no one played your violin. But the girl who took me to my adoptive parents brought the violin with her. I have it now. It's a good fiddle. I probably don't play it nearly as well as you did, but from now on I'll think about you when I do and try to play better.'

What then? It was so difficult, so one-sided. I knew almost nothing about him.

I pictured the cemetery, wishing it wasn't such a sad and neglected place. If one of the self-sown trees were nearby, even that would help. There would be growth, action, something happening every day, a sense of life.

Very well: I would plant a tree. Mid-October. Just about late enough for the roots to be dormant and safe for transplanting. Tomorrow was Monday. There must be a nursery open somewhere in Berlin. Dmitri and I would find it, find someone to borrow a spade from – Leni, perhaps, or one of her friends.

The leader of the orchestra appeared. The oboe sounded its A. The muddle of the tuning-up zeroed in on it in a long drone.

Then I would tidy up around the stone, pull out all that tangled grass. On second thought, maybe not. Why not leave it? It softened the sadness of that stark stone.

The conductor appeared. Mechanically I applauded like everyone else. Vaguely I scanned the musicians' faces.

Difficult to tell. Berliners didn't give much away, but they didn't look too antagonistic. Probably they would tolerate him, perhaps they even liked him.

The applause was dying down, we were approaching that breathless moment of silence when everything was potential.

Stone.

The breath went out of me in a whoosh of astonishment.

Who had put the stone on the grave? Not his parents, far away in Hungary. Not his colleagues in the orchestra either – no one would be fool enough to risk career and even life to put up a memorial to a colleague shot in the wrong part of the city. He couldn't have been in Berlin very long, he probably had no friends close enough to risk it and anyway they would be western friends. It had to be someone from the east.

It could only be one person.

The auditorium had gone silent. In the stillness my mind raced.

Not then – her father would have been watching her. Not to mention the police. But she had known the place where he was. She must have bided her time, waiting for the moment when she could do that one small thing for her lover. Had she run away and come back years later for this task? Or had she feigned the dutiful daughter while waiting? Two things were almost certain: she hadn't died during those terrible months after the tragedy, and it had been a long wait until it was safe enough to do so public a thing as order a memorial stone for the man her father had murdered.

Perhaps a very long wait, decades of waiting until the Wall came down and she could enter that cemetery again free of everything except her memories.

And then the silence was shattered as the first forceful chords of *Finlandia* filled the auditorium, no surface display imposed from above by mere instruments but a powerful welling-up from the depths as only this building and this orchestra could produce, this orchestra for which first my father and then I had played. And in that moment I knew with absolute certainty that my mother was still alive.

EPILOGUE

A veil of pale grey mist hung over the wood. Through it the trunks of the trees loomed a darker shade of grey as we approached, and then, when we walked on, faded again into ghosts of their fair-weather selves. The wood was insubstantial, breathless and unutterably beautiful.

We stepped into the clearing. Beside us was the grand old larch who had persuaded Bernard to risk his reputation and save the wood. Its soft needles had turned tawny in our absence, their colour muted to sepia in this faded old photograph we were walking through. Soon the needles would drop, along with the remaining leaves of its companions, and the wood would settle down for its long winter's sleep. A wistful time of year.

'Maxine seems to be getting on quite nicely without us,' I said to Dmitri. 'Three weeks and only one crummy little postcard of King's College Chapel.'

'Would you want it any other way?'

'Not really. I knew I'd have to let her go some day.'

'Good girl.'

'Who? Me or Maxine?'

'Both. But I meant you. You have your own life to lead. You can't spend the rest of it clucking over young hopefuls.'

The future was hanging over us as soft and grey and insubstantial as the mist. Tomorrow Dmitri was leaving.

'Where to now?' he asked.

'Let's go to the cliff for a change.'

We turned and left the clearing, heading east. The path was narrow and more overgrown than most. Rowans and elders had colonised the edges, their black and red berries punctuating the grey. Some of the trees were so small they must have sown themselves within the last few years.

I thought of the self-sown trees in the cemetery far away in East Berlin. There was another tree there now, not self-sown. We'd given a lot of thought to it. Oak had been the obvious choice. After all, it was the national tree of both Britain and Germany and prized in Hungary. But it was too obvious. My father had not been an obvious man. I wanted something different, special, a link between us that no one else would think of.

In the end the decision had also been obvious, though in a different way. Pine. The common pine. Violins were made of pine. From this humble tree came the fiddles that brought beauty and joy into the lives of those who heard them. My father's origins had been pretty humble too, but his life had brought some joy to other people.

Up ahead the trees were thinning and the light was becoming a more luminous grey. We were approaching the junction with the path that ran along the top of the cliff.

What a quaint domestic scene we'd made, Dmitri and I, planting that tree. Neither of us had done it before and the nurseryman had been a typical pedantic German, his instructions too detailed to remember. We'd been rather clumsy but we'd laughed at our ineptitude and managed it in the end. We'd laughed quite a lot. Gypsies did. My father must have, too, before everything went so horribly wrong. It felt good to provide a bit of the laughter that would have been his if he hadn't been in the wrong place at the wrong time.

We came out on to the cliff top. Along the path was a thick hawthorn hedge bent inward by the wind. It was reinforced by a strong metal fence to deter children from trying to squeeze through the hedge.

'I'm still not sure it's the right thing – trying to track down my mother. It must have been terrible for her, coming to terms with what happened and making a new life for herself out of all that horror. She probably wouldn't want to remember.'

'Like you?'

'There was nothing for me to remember. I didn't know anything.'

'And are you sorry now that you do?'

'No. Not knowing is worse.'

Over the hedge the world vanished altogether, sea and sky stitched together into the soft grey curtain of mist. Beyond it was the continent I'd turned my back on for so long. Beneath it was the sea which had so conveniently separated me from my past.

And beneath that was the sea floor, solid land connecting Sedleigh with the continent. Bernard had shown it to me on his geological map. The map didn't differentiate between dry land and land covered by water. As far as the rocks were concerned there was no difference. The water between us wasn't even very deep.

'I suppose if I do find her I'll have to pretend I don't know who she is, try to put out feelers and sense whether she wants to know or not.' I sighed. 'I'm not sure I'm very good at that sort of thing.'

'Then you'll have to call in your friendly local expert. I wasn't very good at it either but I've learned from the experience.'

I laughed. 'Poor Mitya. I really did give you a hard time.'

'My darling Anna, anyone who wants an easy life would do well to steer clear of you. Attila the Librarian is not for the faint-hearted.'

I put my arm round his waist, thickened by the warm jacket. He put his arm round mine. I thought about Anatoly's watercolour, still hanging above my fridge. In it the two of us as children were linked and drifting serenely out to sea beyond Eleanor's garden. It was the one picture I would never sell.

And now the link was to be broken.

'When you first came into my library I thought, "Oh yes, definitely my type. A nice little cat-and-mouse game: two months for teasing and four for the affair. Six months." And now you're leaving after five. I feel cheated.'

Dmitri laughed. 'The cat was too impetuous; she caught her mouse sooner than anticipated.'

'And now you're turning into a rat. Do you really have to go back for a bunch of lectures?'

'Do you really have to stay here for a bunch of books?' Stalemate.

'Bernard's driving down to Cambridge in a fortnight. Maybe I can cadge a lift, nip over to London and complete the six months.' I smiled up at him mischievously.

He wasn't smiling at all. He turned to me and put his hands on my shoulders. 'Anna, let's drop this nonsense. It's time for some decisions.'

I smiled uncertainly. 'Are you offering to renew the contract? I could do with another six months I must admit. Much to my surprise. I've never . . . it was never like this before. You've changed the rules.'

'Don't be so irritating. It's not a matter of six months or six years and you know it. If you must play this silly game, then let me state my rules: a contract for life. Till death us do part. Is that clear?'

'Good heavens,' I said faintly. 'Is this a proposal?'

'Yes, damn it. With or without the ring. I'll give you that much choice.'

'No bended knee?'

'Anna, the ground is wet and I'm cold and I want to go home now and make love to you. Stop dithering.'

'What about Ahab?'

'There are stables in London.'

'What about me?'

'You may live in my flat. No stable would have you.'

'You know what I mean. What would I do?'

'Catalogue my books. Issue them to my students if it amuses you. Cook wicked little dinners with me. Come to parties and outrage my colleagues. Put on your harem trousers and fiddle the traffic to a halt in Leicester Square. Do whatever you please, Anna, but *with me*.'

'Goodness, I never realised you were such a male chauvinist pig.'

'And I didn't realise you were such a stubborn little beast. Very well: we'll live six months in London and six months in Sedleigh if that pleases you. If you insist, we'll buy a battered old bus and turn ourselves into gypsies. We'll do anything you wish, but *together*.'

'What about over there?' I said, motioning towards the invisible continent which was once again a part of my life.

'All right. Four months in London, four in Sedleigh and four "over there". We can start with a nice big honeymoon in Hungary.'

'Dmitri, please don't be angry but I really don't think I could ever be married. Not after Edmund and Eleanor. They had as near-perfect a marriage as any two humans could. Not an act I'd like to follow.'

'Then we'll dispense with the bit of paper. These are trivial details, Anna. What matters is that both of us are going to rage against any chunk of time that separates us now. Raging is a tedious activity. Let us dispense with that too. Agreed? Good. Now give me a kiss and then we can go home.'

I kissed him. Standing there in the swirling mist I felt as insubstantial as the sea and the land and the trees behind us. Kissing Dmitri made me weak at the knees after five months. I had a feeling it would go on doing so for a very long time.

'I can see you're not going to allow me a peaceful old age,' said my lover when I released him at last.

'Not on your life.'